SANCTUARY LOST

WITSEC Town Series Book 1

Lisa Phillips

First Edition 2014
Published by Lisa Phillips

Copyright © 2014 Lisa Phillips
All rights reserved

This book is a work of fiction. All characters and events are products of the author's imagination. Any resemblance to actual persons, living or deceased, is entirely coincidental. Any references to real people, historical events, or locales, are used fictitiously.
No part of this book may be reproduced or used in any form without written permission from the author, except for review purposes.

Paperback ISBN-13:978-1499638981
ISBN-10:1499638981

Edited by Kristen Ventress

Cover art by Kristine McCord, Blue Azalea Designs
Images from Shutterstock

Also By Lisa Phillips

DENVER FBI SERIES

Target (A Prequel Story)
Bait

HARLEQUIN Love Inspired Suspense

Double Agent
Star Witness
Manhunt

WITSEC TOWN SERIES

Sanctuary Lost
Sanctuary Buried

Chapter 1

John Mason looked beyond the gun to the eyes of the man about to kill him. Only a coward shot someone unarmed and duct-taped to a chair. John couldn't even twitch the tape was so tight around his chest, pinning his arms to his sides so he could grasp only air in his fists.

His breath puffed out like smoke and the sweat on his forehead was a layer of permafrost. How long until he sank into hypothermia? Probably not faster than it would take to be on his back in a pool of his own brain matter...still tied to this chair.

Two heavies stood behind him, one at seven o'clock and one at four. The mouth-breather was starting to get on his nerves and John had more important things to think about. Like last requests, and not crapping his pants.

The gun being aimed at his front shifted with the gunman's movement. John bit the inside of his lip in a concerted effort not to flinch.

"Think you're a big man, don't you? Mr. U.S. Marshal John Mason." The gunman's lip curled. "That's right. I know all about you, the big shot who takes all the hard cases. Trackin' down guys like me who just want to get on with their lives. I took the trouble to escape from Allenwood. You'd think that might tell ya'll somethin'. You think you gonna take me back?"

John dropped the blank mask and lifted his chin. "At this juncture, I'm thinking that option might be off the table."

The gunman raised the weapon and slammed it against John's temple. Pain struck with the strength of a three-hundred-pound enforcer. John kept his eyes closed, swallowing the nausea.

"Too right..." The words he said next washed over John. He'd been living in this world too long if the double-barreled insult didn't even make him blink. He was going to die here, drowned in the ocean of filth that had penetrated his pores for the last twelve months and become part of him.

So why wasn't he dead yet?

The gunman shifted his stance. John dipped his head to the side and wiped the blood from his cheek onto the shoulder of his formerly white t-shirt.

The ceiling was two stories high with bird nests where the metal beams crossed each other. Pallets were strewn on the floor, like someone just tossed them and walked out...fifteen years ago. The air was thick with dust and a cat had possibly died in the corner to his left, sometime in the past decade.

The mouth-breather was at it again, until a car pulled up outside. "Boss is here."

The gunman's spine snapped straight. "Good. I'm done dealin' with this guy."

Or he'd done enough to warrant an extended sentence and didn't want the wrap for murdering a federal agent. Apparently, the gunman was happy to pass the privilege on up the chain.

John kept his eyes on the door while two car doors slammed... a third.

Four men strode in. Tailored suits, the two at the back had automatic weapons. How many bullets were they planning on putting in him?

The front man of the pack was more myth than bona fide human. He never came out in daylight, never met with anyone. Did all his business through his lieutenants and had never in his life been convicted of anything. Why he needed an army of federal fugitives on his payroll was open for estimation, but no one had a clue. Least of all John.

The man's hair was dark and slicked with grease, his forehead completely smooth, which meant he either got Botox or he'd had a stress-free life. John wasn't convinced enough to put money down on either. His suit was brown and he had an honest-to-goodness gold tooth to brighten his smile.

"I'd shake your hand, but..." John shrugged with his head as much as was possible.

"I see that. It's unfortunate, I'm not a fan of killing a man when he's restrained."

"Untie me then."

"I didn't say I wouldn't do it. I just said I'm not a fan." He motioned to the gunman with his fingertips and the gun was placed in his hand.

Everyone shifted.

It was now or never.

John said, "So, you're the great Alphonz. Honestly, you look more like a Charlie."

"Is any of us really what we seem? Take you for example. On paper John Mason is a two-strike car thief with no assets and poor taste in shoes."

What was wrong with his sneakers?

"However, when one digs beyond the smoke screen, John Mason is in fact the fourth son of a deceased Kansas plumber whose widow currently resides in Richmond, Virginia. Dropped dead in his truck, didn't he?"

How did Alphonz know this?

"The brother of the Dolphins newest quarterback."

Nate made the team?

"And one currently unemployed, former U.S. Army logistics specialist."

Ben might appear unemployed on paper but he did have a job. It was just none of them knew what it was and he wouldn't talk about it when they asked.

"And last but not least, the oldest son. Grant Mason, the director of the U.S. Marshals."

John bit down on his lip.

"In addition to this salt-of-the-earth pedigree, John Mason also has an ex-wife who has since remarried and an eight year old son who barely knows he exists."

John tasted blood.

"It would be a shame for any of them to meet an untimely demise. No?"

"What do you want?"

Alphonz lifted the gun. "It appears I already have it. But I'm not a bad man. Do you have any last words? Some pithy sentiment I can personally pass to your boy?"

John struggled against the tape but he was bound too tight to move. "You don't touch my son."

"What do you care? It's not like you ever see the boy. He's perfectly happy with his mother and step-father. I should know, since I personally looked into it."

A guttural noise emerged from his throat. John tried to swallow it down but he couldn't. His eyes filled with tears.

"Goodbye, John Mason."

John squeezed his eyes shut. His last breath was a shuddered inhale.

The gun fired, followed by another—a rat-tat.

John felt nothing. The rear right leg of the chair gave out and he crashed to the floor. Lights flashed on and a wave of booted federal agents ran into the room.

Everyone scattered.

Automatic gunfire rang out and someone returned fire. The gunman hit the floor in front of him. John tried to shift with the chair but only got an inch. The blood from his temple shifted to run into his eyes. John jerked harder against the tape but he was still bound.

"Drop your weapons!"

He knew that voice and the others who yelled, "Freeze! Federal Marshals, you're under arrest!"

John's chest got tight. Someone knelt by his face and he was being jostled. He moaned at the pain in his shoulder. The tape loosened and he was pulled to his back. A sleeve closed in, wiping off his forehead and then he saw who it was.

"Grant?"

"Sorry, man. Your brother couldn't make it. He was tied up in something but he said he'd call you later." Marshal Banks' bushy gray eyebrows folded together. He flashed a tiny light in one of John's eyes and then the other. "Anything hurt other than your head?"

"Shoulder."

"We'll get you checked out." Banks leaned back to sit on his heels. "It's been a long year. How are you doing?"

"Is it over?"

"Thanks to you, yes."

John turned his head. Alphonz was on his face with a knee in his back as the marshal cuffed him. Alphonz's dark gaze settled on John. "You're a dead man."

"Pretty sure I'm alive, actually."

Marshal Banks squeezed the wrong shoulder. John blacked out for a second. *Dislocated.* "Don't worry about him."

John blinked a few times and found the older man's face. "How's Pat?"

"I'll get you a phone. You can find out for yourself."

"No, he'll be in bed."

"Better off if you get a shower and a good night's rest and go see him in the morning." Banks' eyes shifted. "Medics are here."

John took a shower at the hospital. After they admitted him and did an MRI to check for cranial bleeding. Good for him, his luck wasn't that bad. They kept him for observation and he barely slept since every marshal on the east coast traipsed through his room to shake his hand and congratulate him on their largest take down in years.

"Good job, man. Well done."

"Glad no one else was hurt. You did good."

"Congrats, Mason. Your brother must be proud."

"Keeping all the glory in the family, eh?"

Except John had been sent in to find out why Alphonz was recruiting federal fugitives, something he still didn't have an answer to.

He lay awake in the hospital room, the light in the bathroom on and the door cracked like the nurse thought he needed a nightlight so he could sleep. John stared at the ceiling tiles.

Why had the team breached tonight of all nights?

The whole point of going undercover was being out of contact. So how did they know Alphonz was going to show up and try to kill John? There must have been someone else in Alphonz's operation. Or they'd gotten a tip from a fugitive with an attack of morals who knew John's real identity and didn't want to see him killed.

The whole thing was beyond bizarre. Not that he wasn't thankful to be alive. Even if his shoulder being put back into place hurt more than any other injury in his life. Pain meant you were still breathing.

Grant had to know where he was, so why hadn't his brother called? What could be more important to the director of the marshals tonight than their biggest take-down in years?

John would have asked him, but Grant never called and John didn't remember the number.

**

The key stuck in the lock. John muscled open the front door of his apartment and dumped his duffel bag on the entryway floor. The place smelled like bleach bathroom cleaner and the surfaces were free of dust. John found the patio door key and opened it, trying to air out the place. His mom must have come by or hired someone to clean.

Everything was just as he'd left it twelve months and three days ago—when his son had been seven. Now Pat was eight but it wasn't long enough he'd have forgotten who his father was. Given time, they could reconnect. If Ellen let him.

John sank onto the couch and kicked away his boots. He gritted his teeth and stripped off the scrubs top the hospital had given him after they cut his shirt away.

Dawn crept across the dining area between the vertical blinds, but he didn't sleep. Alphonz might be in custody but John didn't feel any of the satisfaction which should've been there.

The satisfaction he'd felt with other undercover assignments.

By the TV he hadn't watched in a year was a framed picture of him and Pat when his son was about four. Pat was on his hip and they were smiling at each other, his tiny hands touching John's face.

John fell asleep with the feel of Pat's hands on his cheeks.

**

Pounding on the door woke him. It was dark and his watch said six-thirty p.m., same day. He yanked the door open, still blinking away the blur of sleep. "What?"

"Charming as always, Jonathan." Ellen cocked the hip of her tiny skirt, not an ounce of fat on her. If he hugged her she'd probably feel like a tree branch. But that would mean she let him touch her, which hadn't happened for a lot longer than the four years they'd been divorced.

"It's been a long week."

"Your mother told me you were home and I didn't want to wait any longer to speak with you."

Uh-oh, she was using her city-girl lawyer voice. That was never good.

John shifted and looked around her. "Where's Pat?"

"That's what I wanted to speak with you about."

Something heavy settled in John's stomach. "Come inside."

"Perhaps you could put a shirt on."

It wasn't a question. John turned and flipped on the light switch. Ellen gasped. He ignored her and trailed to his bedroom closet where he grabbed the first t-shirt he laid eyes on. A bruise stretched across the back of his shoulder. He could see it in the mirror even with the dim light of his bedroom.

John strode back out. "You want some coffee?"

"There's no need. This won't take long." She set her purse down on the couch—if she put it on the floor the bottom would get dirty—and opened the latches of her lawyer-bag to pull out a manila envelope, which she set on the breakfast bar.

"We already got a divorce."

She didn't smile. "Those are custody papers. I had them drawn up."

All the fatigue in him dissipated. "If you think for one second I'm going to give up my right to—"

"Perhaps you could make that claim if you ever actually saw your son." Ellen's already tiny lips thinned into a pressed line. "But be that as it may, you're home now. I'm not waiting any longer. Stefan was offered a position in Boston and he has taken it. I'm to join him as soon as possible and I'm afraid this move is not conducive to bringing a small child."

"Our boy is cramping your high-falutin' lifestyle?"

"Can you, for one second, not be the hick-town boy so we can have a civilized discussion?" Her body tightened so much she looked like a popsicle stick. "I have been the lone parent of our child for long enough, John Mason. It's time for you to quit being so selfish and be the parent now."

"Fine." John folded his arms across his chest. "Where is Pat?"

"I dropped Patrick at your mother's this morning."

"If I take him, I want full custody for good. No changing your mind."

Her lips pulled back to reveal unnaturally white teeth. "I am not the bad guy here. You're the one who hasn't seen his son in a year."

"I was on assignment."

"You didn't have a phone?"

"You know it doesn't work like that. You of all people know what this job entails."

"The job of being a marshal, or the job of doing everything possible to make your brother proud of you?"

Neither of them needed to go there. "Ellen—"

"I signed the papers. All I need now is your signature and I will file them with my attorney. I want two weeks in the summer and alternating Christmases."

"Fine."

John would have his son with him permanently? He had no idea what position he'd be in next. Surely Grant would make sure John got home for dinner regularly.

He almost said, "Whatever you want" but that was never a good idea with Ellen. He'd worry about how this was going to work with his job later. She was right, even if he didn't like the fact she was essentially dumping Pat on him.

It was his turn to be the parent.

John strode to the counter, signed the forms and then handed them to her. "If we're done here, I'd like to get to Pat."

Ellen took the papers and collected up her purse and leather briefcase. "I almost feel as if I should say something. Mark this occasion somehow. After all, it's been a whole fifteen minutes and we've managed to not shout at each other."

John felt his lips twitch. "Let's not get carried away."

"Take care of him, John." Sadness edged into her gaze, darkening her face despite the light blond shade of her hair and the peach color that flashed every time she blinked. "I knew Stefan didn't want children of his own. I thought that meant he was content to be a step-father to Patrick. But this move will be good for us. The time alone means we can...re-connect."

Was she going to stop talking sometime soon? John wanted to know if his son was okay. Now. He swiped up his keys.

Ellen sighed. "I don't expect you to understand."

"Good because I don't. You're giving up your son for your marriage?"

She looked down her nose, despite being two inches shorter than his five-foot-eleven. "You gave him up for your job."

"I'm not arguing with you." He clenched and unclenched the hold on his truck keys. Was she going to leave already? Ellen stared back at him.

John sighed. "Take care, darlin'."

Her stern face melted. "We did have some good times, didn't we?"

Yeah, and currently the good part of their marriage was at his mom's house in who knew what state. "I guess we did."

Right up until John started working undercover. It had been a step in the right direction for his career, but ended up costing him his marriage when his wife of five years decided she didn't want to be a single parent. Then she divorced him so she could become one anyway, with the added bonus of child support.

"You'll call me if Pat needs anything?"

"Sure." But he wouldn't.

John was done with undercover and he was going to make sure Pat didn't need anything ever again.

**

He didn't knock on his mom's door. John grabbed the hide-a-key from the crack in the siding and let himself in. "Mom, it's me."

It was Grant who strode from the living room, his hair still more brown than gray even though he was pushing forty-seven. "She's at bingo."

"She left?" John ran a hand through his already disheveled hair. He needed to get it cut.

"Pat promised her he was fine. He's stubborn, like someone else I know."

"Where is Pat?"

The little man stepped into the hall, which was lined with cardboard boxes. Pat's stuff? John zeroed in on his son's face—a mini version of his own but with Ellen's nose before she had it fixed. Pat looked at his feet, rubbing one shoe against the toe of the other.

"Pat?"

His son looked up.

John bit his lip. "Hey, kid."

Grant frowned. John's brother and his wife had three girls—now teenagers—so he might think he was the expert on parenting, but

Grant had never understood the bond between father and son. At least, John hoped they still had one. Maybe he'd killed it.

He rubbed his chest, right above his heart. Pat's eyes were wide but he didn't look angry or upset. That was good, right? John sank to his knees in the foyer, ignoring the pain in his shoulder. He rubbed his forehead, his fingers scratching at the bandage. Right. His head. He'd forgotten about that.

"Dad?" Pat's voice shook.

John lowered his hand. "I'm okay."

He tilted his head and motioned Pat over. *Okay, that hurt.* Thankfully Pat didn't hesitate, so John didn't have to suffer Grant watching him fail as a father for the seven-billionth time. It was bad enough without an audience.

Pat's steps gathered speed as he crossed the foyer. John opened his arms and Pat hit him at a full tackle, knocking John onto his backside. He wrapped his arms around his eight-year-old son and held him for the first time in a year. The assignment wasn't supposed to have taken this much time, but he'd known going in it would be as long as it took to complete the job.

"I'm sorry."

Pat's body jerked. "You don't want me to live with you?"

"Buddy—"

"I can stay here with Grandma. It'll be fine."

John touched his cheeks, the same way Pat had done with him in the picture. "Listen to me now. I'm not going anywhere, not anymore."

He hoped Grant heard him, just as much as Pat. Because John didn't want any more assignments.

And if his brother didn't like it, he was going to quit.

Chapter 2

"I can't believe you're not mad at her. I would be furious."

John flashed his badge to the lone security guard at the rear entrance and followed his brother Grant into the back of the Congressional building, re-holstering his weapon. "I am mad. Why do you think I'm not? But it's not like I can be angry at Ellen for leaving Pat—"

"Abandoning him." Grant clipped down the strap holding his gun in place.

"Not when I essentially did the same thing a year ago."

Grant stopped, the clip of his dress shoes echoing in the abandoned hall. "That wasn't your fault."

Why weren't there more people around? "I took the assignment."

"I was the one who gave it to you."

John cracked a smile. "So we're both to blame then. But neither of us are hypocrites."

Grant smiled back a bigger-and-better-at-everything version of John. Ellen's words had hit a little too close to home. But who didn't have someone in their life whose opinion mattered more than anything?

"How's your head?"

John could feel the bandage but other than that… "I guess I have a hard head."

Grant clapped him on his shoulder. "Knew that already."

John backed away, wincing. "My shoulder is sore, though."

"Sorry. You could probably use some down-time, huh?"

"That was the plan. Now mom is taking Pat to a movie and for some reason I'm here with you."

"Because I'm your boss."

John sighed. "So what are we doing here?"

"In this hallway?"

"In D.C. In this building." John shrugged. "I've got better things to do than watch you politicking."

Grant folded his arms. "Not if you want to keep your job."

"Fine, Mr. High-and-Mighty Director. What's the deal? Why are we here?"

Something crept into Grant's eyes. A satisfaction borne of cunning John hadn't realized his brother possessed.

"Okay, spill. What is this?"

"You want time with your son, you get a new assignment." Grant turned and continued down the hall. "Maybe."

Seriously, why was this place so desolate? It was like the grocery store during the Super-Bowl. "What is this maybe?"

Grant opened the door at the end a cavernous room with plenty of chairs, all empty. Four people—one woman and three men—sat at a high table at the front. Evidently Grant had an appointment at a congressional hearing and no-one else had been invited. The panel all wore suits in shades of drab. The woman was smiling, glancing from the men beside her to Grant and back with a light in her eyes.

A stout, older man left of center looked up. "Director Mason, nice of you to join us."

Grant stopped behind the table but didn't sit. "This hearing is scheduled for five-thirty, is it not?"

John stopped at the first row of chairs and checked his watch. Five-twenty. He sat on the opposite side of the aisle.

"We moved up the timetable. Your secretary was informed."

"She was. The amendment was forwarded to me, but I'm a busy man. Last minute changes designed only to disrupt my schedule and throw me off my game aren't something I intend to acquiesce to."

The stout man picked up a pair of spectacles and focused on the page in front of him. "The rest of us have things to do, so let's get on with this."

Grant didn't react and he hadn't brought any papers with him. Still, there was no way he was unprepared. John had rarely seen him lose his cool over anything.

The stout man, who John decided to refer to as *pompous windbag*, cleared his throat. "The town of Sanctuary has been in operation for thirty-eight years. There are currently one hundred eighty-two residents—"

"It's actually one hundred eighty-three. There was a birth recorded two weeks ago."

"Be that as it may, the federal witness protection program has chosen to seclude each of these high-profile targets for a reason." He lowered the paper and looked over his glasses. "And you wish to close the town?"

Grant rested only his fingertips on the desk, his eyes on the panel. "Sanctuary started out as an experiment. It was never designed to continue on a permanent basis. Yes, several of the witnesses are recognizable household names. But we've relocated famous people before. There's a strategy in place. Sending them to Sanctuary to see if they could survive as a community in their own right is a gigantic security breach waiting to happen."

John wasn't looking at his brother any longer; he was looking at the director of the U.S. Marshals. A man he didn't see too often outside of the occasional briefing they were both present at.

"I'm honestly surprised we've managed to keep the lid on an entire town for this long. But the potential threat is something which cannot be ignored. If anyone discovered Sanctuary exists, the result would be catastrophic. Everyone in the town would need to be relocated immediately and not without great expense to the tax payer."

Pompous windbag's eyes widened. "And I suppose you think we're going to overlook the astronomical expense of relocating each of these families now, providing them with a stipend until they can find employment and arranging for housing. Not to mention the personnel required to transport each of them to their new homes, should the town be closed."

"It would be a lot. But—"

"And all because you feel that the potential security risk is too high."

John glanced at the Thane, recognizing him now he was able to put the name with the face. The guy was never happy about anything, constantly on news programs complaining about one thing or another.

Grant's shoulders stiffened, but John figured only he noticed it. "Congressman Thane, with all due respect, my job is to understand the risks and take the necessary steps to protect these people."

The congressman to Thane's left huffed. "And our job is to sign the checks."

"Which is why we're all here." Grant sighed. "I suppose you have made your decision then?"

The female, Congresswoman Stefanie Shafer, nodded like the teacher's pet, sure she knew the answer. "The town will remain open."

Congressman Thane didn't look at her. "Sanctuary will indeed remain as is. If you wish to keep these people safe, then do so. But not at further cost to taxpayers. You want to avoid a security breach? That's your job. We're not spending more on this. Granted, some of these people are likely innocents. But the vast majority of them turned state's evidence to escape a sentence of their own. That cannot be ignored."

Grant's head shook. The movement was so small John wondered if he'd even seen it. "The United States Attorney seemed to feel the conviction gained by the testimony of each of these witnesses was valuable enough to warrant the expense of enrolling them in WITSEC in the first place. If you feel differently, perhaps he should be here instead of me." He paused. "Be that as it may, we do not pander to our witnesses. Each of them has provided a valuable service to the justice department and in return has been given the chance to start a new life."

"A clean slate, just like that?"

Grant sighed. "We are not here to discuss the merits of the witness protection program. We're here to ensure the safety of all the citizens of this country, whoever they may be. Sanctuary was never designed to exist in the long term. The town's infrastructure is woefully outdated and in order to remain open, Sanctuary requires an influx of federal funding simply to be brought up to code."

Congressman Thane's mouth opened and shut, causing his jowls to wobble. "Well, I never..."

"If your intention is simply to save the government money, I assure you closing the town will be far more cost effective in the long term. Sanctuary will continue to grow. If the justice department continues to enroll protectees into the witness protection program, I will have no other choice than to send some of them to Sanctuary."

John waited, his mind spinning around the idea of a town established entirely for the sake of housing high-profile witnesses. If it was true, it was such a secret he'd never even heard a rumor of it. In the community of law enforcement that was next to unreal. And what on earth did it have to do with his—maybe—next assignment?

The woman leaned toward her microphone, not that it was needed when it was just the six of them in the room. "We will need some time to further deliberate."

John glanced between Grant and the panel. He wanted them to spend more money and keep the town open? There was no way they were going to go for that.

"We most certainly will not deliberate further." Congressman Thane shoved the woman's mic away from her and spoke into his own. "Despite what you have said, the town of Sanctuary will remain open. A reasonable budget will be provided for necessary renovations. That is the final decision of this panel."

The woman's lips pressed together. John stared at Thane. Why did he want the town to stay open if it was going to cost more money? In claiming the town had to be closed, Grant had strategically maneuvered more money for the town to remain open. Had that been his plan all along?

"Very well." Grant nodded. "Thank you all for your time."

John got up and followed him out, trailing behind his brother like always. The minute the door shut, John said, "A WITSEC town?"

Grant stopped. "This goes no further than that room."

"What's the assignment?"

"The sheriff of Sanctuary has cancer. Terminal. He's being transferred out this afternoon so there's an opening."

John stared at his brother. "You want me to take my son to a town full of federal witnesses?"

"The job isn't much more than light duty as the sheriff and security drills. It's mostly keeping your finger on the pulse of those people and then letting them live their lives." Grant ran a hand through his hair, his "Director" persona evaporating. "I need someone I can trust there, someone I know who needs a fresh start himself. A change of pace for his family."

"Except my family is here."

"I mean Pat."

"I know what you mean."

Grant's eyebrows lifted.

"So you want me to do what Ellen did? Go spend quality time with my son in this secret town and never see the rest of you ever again."

"We'll have to work out the details." Grant grinned. "Maybe Sanctuary can host the Mason family Christmas this year."

"Despite the security risk?"

"Potential risk."

"You realize this is nepotism, right?"

"Not if everything about it has been redacted."

John started walking. "You need someone to take this job and I'm the only one you can force into it. Because I'm your brother and you know I won't say no. Not to mention I just sat through the meeting wherein I found out this secret. So either I sign away my free speech or I take the job." He sighed. "I'm guessing, wherever this town is, there are mountains on either side called a rock and a hard place."

"Quit being so dramatic. This will be good for you, somewhere you and Pat can spend time together. A slower pace of life, away from all the risk inherent in your usual assignments."

"If it's that great, why don't you take the job?"

Grant ignored the question. "Family oriented, small town. Nestled in the mountains, surrounded by trees and blue skies."

"Read the brochure much?"

"I wrote it, actually."

"I believe you." John folded his arms, even though it hurt. "But this all seems just a little too convenient. My assignment ended hours ago, the result of a breach that captured Alphonz and, look at that, just in time to get out of town and hide away."

The muscle in Grant's jaw flexed.

"What aren't you telling me?"

Grant blew out a breath. "Fine. Alphonz is blowing whistles left and right, making sure everyone he's ever met goes down with him. The U.S. attorney is talking deal." He hesitated. "When Alphonz's business associates discover a marshal was undercover, when Alphonz has been taken care of, who do you think they're going to come after next?"

"So will I be the sheriff of Sanctuary, or are you actually putting me in witness protection?"

Grant's head jerked in a shake, like he didn't believe John had figured it out. "Honestly? A little of both."

"Were you planning on telling me this?" John paced away two steps and turned back. "You know, you didn't have to twist everything for your sake. You could just explain for once."

"I'm not doing this for me. I'm doing it for Pat."

"So you're the grand puppet-master, manipulating everything to be what you think is best for everyone else." John folded his arms. Had his brother always been like this, or was he just now noticing it?

"I'm helping you keep my nephew safe."

"Because you don't think I can do it on my own, but you think I can sheriff a town? That makes no sense."

"It's a good assignment." Grant nodded. "A promotion. You should be proud I think you can do it."

"But you don't think I can be a father. Is that why you gave me all those undercover assignments?"

"If I did, then it didn't work now, did it? Ellen quit. So I guess you're going to have to step up. Your son needs you."

John studied his oldest brother. "What happened to you while I was away?"

"Genevieve left me."

"What? When?"

"Two months ago. Now I get the girls one weekend a month. I have eighteen months until Bev and Helen leave for college and then I'll as good as lose them forever."

"So you're taking your issues out on me, is that it?" John glanced at the ceiling. "You can't fix your family problems by forcing me to figure out my life. Ellen and I are divorced, we're not going back there and I'm going to take this time to give Pat what he needs."

"Yeah, since yesterday."

John shifted. "Don't lash out at me just because your family is in the toilet."

Grant lifted both hands. He let them fall, like they weighed too much to hold up. "I just want things to go back to normal."

"Uh...newsflash, dude. Women do not want that. They want stuff to be changing all the time, growing and improving. Tell me Genevieve never said anything to you about counseling."

"I'm not interested in a bandage."

John slung his arm around his brother's neck. "Do you want her to divorce you?"

"Of course not."

"Then listen up."

**

John's mom was in the kitchen, pulling a dish from the oven. "Hey."

She glanced over her shoulder. "Hey, honey." Her white-blond hair swayed with the movement as she danced to the tune of a song only she could hear. "Did you know a billion and a half pens are made every year but only a hundred million pencils?"

"Uh...no."

Her heels clacked on the tile floor as she moved to the counter and the makings of a salad. "Pat and I had a lot of fun today. After the movie we went to the library and he found one of those weird fact books."

John smiled. "I'm glad."

He'd spent the whole ride back from D.C. reading the file on Sanctuary. It was insane how someone's idea of witnesses forming their own community had spiraled into this actual thing, in existence now only slightly longer than John had been alive.

After Grant dropped him off at his condo, he'd packed a bag and called a shipping company to get the rest of the things he wanted to keep. The bulk of it was going in storage until his mom could organize a garage sale. Or, that was the plan at least.

"Where's Pat now?"

"He's in his room, reading." The corners of her lips turned down. "I think he tried to call his mom. I heard him leave a message but he didn't want to talk about it."

John got a water from the fridge. On the door was a whiteboard calendar with every available space filled in. "Busy."

She grinned. "I was nominated the community's social coordinator."

"Of course you were." His mom lived in a community of retirees who golfed and hung out at the complex's centers and clubs. After half a lifetime on a Kansas farm, his mom had morphed into a social butterfly. He was also pretty sure she currently had a boyfriend.

She'd toned up, lost weight and dressed stylishly now. But not like she was trying to look fifty instead of seventy. "You look good, Mom."

She danced to the opposite counter and opened a high cupboard. "Thanks, darlin'. But I'm thinking that's not why you don't look happy."

"I'm happy."

She stopped her near-constant movement and focused on him. "I'm not buying it. What did Grant say? Did he tell you about Genevieve?"

John nodded. "He wants me to take a job out of town. A sheriff's job."

"And Pat?"

"He'll be going with me."

She was quiet for a minute. "You walk the path the good Lord puts in front of you. There's nothing else. Not if you want to be really, truly happy."

"You're not mad you won't get to see Pat too much?"

"That's what Skype is for, darlin'." She picked up the knife and grabbed the lettuce again. "Besides, your momma's a busy woman."

John drained the bottle of water.

"Did you think I'd be mad?"

"That seems to be going around lately."

"Tell me about it. Your brother, last night." She shook her head. "That boy needs help."

"He's forty-eight, Mom. That's not the definition of a boy."

His mom nodded once, fast. "Ellen showed up at Grant's place last night with Pat, before she brought him here. Genevieve answered the door. One of the girls called him and he rushed over. Wouldn't accept all the boxes the delivery men were trying to leave, yelling about how kids should be with their fathers." She sniffed. "I don't think it was about Pat. Not totally."

"No kidding." John sighed. "Did anything else go to crap while I was gone? I heard Nate made the Dolphins' team."

The ghost of a smile flashed on her face. "He's happy. I think."

"And Ben?"

Her nose wrinkled. "Who knows with that boy? He's too much like your father, keeps everything to himself."

Like high blood pressure.

She didn't have to say it; John heard it in the silence. She was worried Ben would die the same way their father had. John wrapped his palm around the back of his mom's neck and kissed her forehead. "You're not going to lose us. I promise."

She waved him away. "Tell your son dinner is ready."

That was two promises in two days. Unless you counted the promise to Grant that he'd give him an answer soon.

John trailed through the modern house to find Pat. If this was his mom's taste, how had she ever survived being a plumber's wife? She'd either done what was necessary to fit herself into his dad's life, or she'd since discovered something she hadn't known before.

The light was on in the guest room where all the grandkids slept when they visited. "Hey, Pat." John sat on the side of the bed and squeezed his son's white socked foot. "You doin' okay?"

Pat lowered the book. "What's this word?"

John looked where he was pointing. "Liege. What are you reading?"

"It's about knights." Pat chewed his lip. "Are we really moving?"

"If that's okay with you. It's a mountain town, kind of remote."

Seriously remote. As in, no roads, no cell reception, very limited internet and more stipulations than tax law.

"I'm going to be the sheriff. The school has five kids so they only do class in the morning and then you'll get to spend the rest of the day hanging out in town or with me at the sheriff's office."

"Can we go hiking?"

"Sure."

"Fishing?"

"Maybe."

"Camping?"

John laughed. "Whatever you want."

"Okay." Pat smiled but he wasn't fully happy. "I tried to call mom. I think she was out."

John did the same thing he'd done with his mom, he held the back of his son's neck and kissed his forehead.

"Gross, Dad." Pat broke away and wiped his sleeve over his face. "You slobbered on me."

"Get used to it, kid." John pulled his son to his feet and put his arm around Pat's shoulders as they headed back to the kitchen.

"Are we going to have a house, or an apartment like you have now?"

"A house, I guess. We'll have to see."

"With a yard?"

"Probably."

"Can I bring my rat?"

Just before five the next morning, someone moved through the darkened living room. John was about to sit up when his son crawled onto the couch and snuggled against him.

Chapter 3

John sat in the back of the black, unmarked car. Beside him, Pat gripped the small cage housing his rat. They pulled up to the Air Force base and the driver gave a set of papers to the guard. When they were handed back, the guard moved to John's window. He rolled it down and handed back his badge and ID.

"Good morning, sir."

John accepted his stuff back. "Good morning, Sergeant." He looked at his son. "Pat, you want to say hi to the sergeant?"

"Hi."

The sergeant grinned. "What's up, little man?"

John smiled and beside him on the leather seat, Pat giggled.

"You guys are good to go."

"Thank you, Sergeant."

"Y'all have a good trip.

The car pulled forward through the barricade. John left the window down and Pat leaned over his lap to get a look at their surroundings. They drove through residential areas and military buildings to an airstrip on which sat a huge plane that would take them across country to Mountain Home Air Force Base in Idaho. From there a helicopter would take them to Sanctuary.

By air was the only way in or out. Sanctuary was inaccessible by road, since the closest dirt track lay fifty miles away. The surrounding area was a stadium of virtually impassable mountains it would take two days to hike over. John had searched for it online, but the satellite image of the general area showed only the ring of mountains with a bunch of grass in the middle.

Sanctuary had its own water treatment plant, waste management, medical center, a small school, a farm which grew the bulk of their produce and a cattle ranch. Anything else they needed was flown in by plane, which was also how the mail and medical supplies were delivered. A dentist—which the town currently did not have—was flown in once every six months.

Everyone in the town was required to perform a service that kept the town running, for which they were paid. That job was either their former career or their choice of a new job.

Internet activity was contained to the library and every resident was given half an hour a day to go online, although their usage and activity was logged and monitored by the NSA. Anyone who broke their WITSEC contract was taken away by helicopter where they were either kicked out of the witness protection program, or put in jail. The "Memorandum of Understanding" each witness signed was a binding contract.

No one ever just left, or went on vacation, as far as John could tell from the files. Any child born in town who wished to leave when they came of age had to opt out of the program and could never return—including going to school. If a Sanctuary resident left to go to college they could never return.

John held the door while Pat scooted from the car. Their two suitcases were loaded onto the plane along with the lockbox holding John's weapons. He led Pat to where Grant stood at the bottom of the steps.

"Ready?"

John looked at Pat, trying to figure out if the boy was happy about this or not. He hadn't said a word about leaving his friends. What was John supposed to make of that? Pat gripped the cage and gave John a small smile, apparently content to let his dad lead. John ruffled his son's hair. "We're all set."

"Call me when you get there?" Grant held out his hand and they shook.

John pulled his brother to him and slapped his back. "Sure."

"I want weekly reports. Let me know if you need anything or if you have any questions. When the month is up, I want your final decision in writing."

"Got it."

John was eager to get the lay of the land and figure out how this was going to work. The file had confirmed what he'd suspected—there was little recorded crime in Sanctuary. But who knew what went on beyond what was recorded on paper? It depended on the people. And how the previous sheriff had chosen to do his job.

Hours later, the military helicopter flew over mountains separated by a snaking river. Civilization dropped off to miles of trees and peaks topped with snow. When they rose over the highest peak, John heard Pat gasp and they dropped into a huge circular valley. It really existed.

Faced with the evidence of a secret town hidden away in the Idaho mountains, he realized he'd doubted the story. John stared at the place he might live the rest of his life. The place his son would grow up—until he came of age and was able to make the choice to stay or leave forever.

If they were to stay in Sanctuary, all the conditions of residency would apply to Pat. When he grew up and chose his own path, John might rarely see him. It was a high price to pay for a job he wasn't even sure he wanted.

The helicopter flew over fields of crops, a barn and a farmhouse. They passed two strips of residential streets. Three rows on the north and three on the south with a wide street between that was likely Main Street—enough housing for two hundred people. The town was a mile long with the ranch at one end and the farm at the other.

To the north was all green—pathways and play equipment at the town's park. Beyond that was more trees, followed by fields of cows.

The helicopter flew overhead to the ranch, where a square of concrete had been turned into a landing pad with a giant H painted on it. They circled once and the pilot set them down. The radio in John's headphones clicked. "Welcome to Sanctuary."

"Thanks for the ride."

John climbed out, pulling out the suitcases and his lockbox before he lifted Pat down. The rotors whipped up his collar. Together, he and Pat dragged their belongings a safe distance from the chopper before it lifted off, leaving them standing on the asphalt.

A rusty, red pickup truck topped the rise, driving toward them from the fields. A Hispanic man in his late twenties jumped out. "Boss man says I'm to drive you into town."

His jeans and chambray shirt were worn. He clearly didn't see shaving or getting his hair cut as a priority, since his dark hair curled from under his tan cowboy hat. "I'm Matthias." He pulled off his glove, sticking his hand out.

"Sheriff John Mason." He might as well get used to saying it.

"Yeah, I heard that. News travels fast around here. How about you, little dude?"

"Patrick Garrett Mason." He puffed out his chest. "I'm eight and a half."

"That half is very important." Matthias grinned. "You wanna ride in the back? It isn't far to town, just a mile."

Pat looked at John, fear mixed with little-boy excitement.

John smiled. "I'll ride back there with you, if you want."

"Yeah!"

They loaded the suitcases and John lifted Pat up before he climbed in himself. Once they'd settled, Matthias climbed in the driver's seat and slid open the back window. "Ready for the grand tour?"

"Yeah!" Pat's excitement was infectious and John actually laughed along with his son as they bumped across the field onto the gravel road.

Main Street was flanked by storefronts with wooden walkways, a café, a diner. In the center was a meeting hall that looked big enough to hold every resident at once. People walked up and down the street, waving at the truck before they stopped to chat with someone. John half expected to see a horse tied up outside the hardware store, the whole place had such an "old west" feel to it.

Aside from the ranch truck, John didn't see another vehicle. Not even in the parking spaces, or around the island of grass and the tree dead-center in town. A golf cart came around the corner, driven down the center of the street until the man parked it nose-to-nose with the now crawling truck.

MAYOR was painted on the hood.

The driver hopped out. He had fully silver hair and a trimmed silver beard. A woman climbed from the opposite side of the golf cart, a purse on the shoulder of her pink skirt-suit. She wore pearl earrings and a pearl necklace and she'd done that thing women did to their nails, making them big with white tips.

The man strode in his gray suit to the back of the truck and shot them what could only be described as a million-dollar smile. "You must be the new sheriff. I'm Mayor Samuel Collins."

Matthias gave the couple a wide berth and lowered the back hatch of the truck bed. John caught the grin Matthias shot Pat as he took the rat cage and then helped Pat down.

John climbed out and shook the mayor's hand. "John Mason."

The woman smiled. "I'm Betty Collins."

The mayor squeezed her shoulder hard enough she winced. "The old ball and chain." He chuckled, but by the look on her face his wife didn't find it funny.

"We're the welcoming committee." Betty smiled. "We'll show you to your office, where you can meet Deputy Palmer. Then there's an eensy amount of paperwork and we'll be out of your hair. Lots of things to organize before the welcoming dinner tonight."

Pat shuffled closer to his side and John gave his shoulder a squeeze. "This is Patrick."

"Aren't you darling?" Betty squeezed Pat's cheek and looked back at John, her face set like she didn't know what else to do when faced with a small child. She squared her shoulders. "Ready to get started?"

The mayor chuckled and they followed Betty across to the storefront with SHERIFF above the door. "Keeps me in line, that one."

"I'll bet." John smiled.

Matthias passed them, carrying John's bags. When he turned again to the truck, John followed. They dumped all the belongings inside.

Betty said, "The sheriff's office has an apartment upstairs, which you're welcome to utilize unless you'd rather have a separate house. It's a one bedroom apartment, so not conducive to a family. We'll let you decide. There's an open house but you may wish to be closer to the office."

Betty glanced down at her clipboard. "The sheriff's vehicle is parked out back. It's maintained by Max, who takes care of all our vehicles. Deputy Palmer has a vehicle, the ranch has two trucks. The farm has one plus his tractor and all that stuff for harvesting and whatnot. There are also four ATV's, two with snow plow attachments and three snow mobiles. One is currently broken. Gas is delivered on Monday mornings."

John sucked in a breath at the flood of information and looked at Pat, who had wandered to the open jail cell at the back of the office and was looking around in awe, touching the bars.

There was a door to the right of the room marked PRIVATE, which he figured went up to the apartment. Three desks, two of which were clean, filled the room along with a set of floor to ceiling cupboards, a coffee pot and small fridge. Pat was sitting on the bed in the jail cell, listening to Matthias, who had crouched to speak to him. His son grinned and nodded. Matthias ruffled his hair and strode out, giving John a nod.

"See you around, Sheriff."

"Thanks."

Betty Collins cleared her throat. "As I was saying, keys for everything are on your desk and the paperwork needs to be mailed off at the next pickup, which leaves Monday morning. That's once a week anything arrives in or leaves town. Due to the nature of your position here there is a radio on your desk which doubles as a satellite phone. You can also send texts and basic emails from it.

"The unit is encrypted. It's a DOD prototype, so you can use it indoors or if there's a lot of tree coverage. Your computer, as well as Deputy Palmer's, connects to the internet. That's something new. The rest of the town uses the library. Your log-in and the code for the safe are on your desk. You have twenty-four hours to change the passwords and set up a new combination to the safe."

She checked her clipboard. "Friday night is movie night at the meeting hall. Town members are requested to attend dinner before the movie, but it's not mandatory. Since it's tonight, we'll be having a welcome dinner for you and Patrick."

"You can just call me Pat." He hopped onto the chair at the desk that said SHERIFF and toed off his sneakers. "That's what my dad calls me."

John grinned at his boots.

Betty Collins started up again, but the mayor slung an arm around her shoulders. "We'll let you boys get settled. If there's anything else, we'll let you know. And if you have any questions ask us at dinner. It's at six. Four doors down other side of the street."

"Got it." John shook their hands again, even though it made his shoulder throb. "I appreciate your being here to welcome us."

"You're welcome." Betty shot him a beauty-queen smile.

The mayor and his wife wandered out. The bell above the door clanged and then it shut. John turned to his son and lifted his arms. "So...what do you think?"

"Pretty cool."

"What did Matthias say to you before he left?"

"He said he came here when he was six. He was really scared. But not for long." Pat smiled. "He said if it's okay with you, I can come out to the ranch sometime and he'll show me how to rope a steer."

"Awesome."

"Yeah." Pat paused. "What's a steer?"

"It's a...uh...girl cow." John cleared his throat. "Want to check out the apartment?"

Pat hopped off the chair. "Can I leave my shoes down here?"

John took the bags and suitcases up the narrow staircase and unlocked the door at the top. He wasn't too sure about living this close to the sheriff's office. What if he had to arrest someone dangerous? He didn't want to detain them so close to where his son would be sleeping at night. A house might be a good idea.

The main room was a small living room/kitchen area with a round table and two chairs. The TV was the size of John's old microwave. The curtains were mustard colored, the walls were covered in wainscoting and the kitchen was yellow.

"It smells like old man in here."

John smiled. "Guess we should crack a window."

The bedroom was small but the bed was big enough Pat hopefully wouldn't kick him in the middle of the night. Still, they'd need new sheets and a new comforter. The bathroom was decorated in puke green tile, complete with a green toilet.

"Eew, Dad."

"You're not wrong, kid." They shared a smile. "It's only for a month. If we want to stay then we can look at moving into one of the houses, okay?"

"I'm hungry." Pat pulled open the fridge. "There's a ton of stuff in here. Can I have a PB and J?"

"Sure, bud. I'll make us both one."

"I can do it."

"Yeah?" John wandered over and leaned against the counter while Pat got out the stuff and a butter knife.

John pulled two plates from the cupboards and found glasses. He got the milk from the fridge and broke the seal. "We'll have to find out who stocked the fridge and say thank you."

"Hello, hello...anybody up here?" Footsteps ascended the stairs and a tall red-headed man in a tan sheriff's uniform emerged. "There you are."

The man wasn't more than thirty years old. Red stubble on his chin clashed with his bright green eyes. He stuck out his hand. "Deputy Arnold Palmer at your service." He shook with Pat. "Nice to meet you."

John introduced them. "We just got in."

"Yeah, sorry I wasn't here. Had a call out uptown and it took longer than I thought."

"Anything interesting?"

"Nah." He waved off John's question. "Just some kids being kids, messing up old lady Tanner's garbage cans."

John leaned his hip on the counter, one eye on the job Pat was doing with the sandwiches. "Have you been a deputy long?"

"Born and raised in Sanctuary. It's been maybe eight years since Sheriff Chandler—the marshal who was here before you—hired me. He'd been here since the town was founded. The one and only Sheriff, for thirty-eight years."

"Wow, cool." Jam dripped from the knife Pat held onto the counter.

John had read the file. Arnold Palmer applied for the sheriff's job but had been turned down in favor of a U.S. marshal taking the position. It was essentially the job of a WITSEC Inspector, not a regular citizen who'd never been a marshal. Just the deputy sheriff of a town which didn't exist.

John sized him up and saw Palmer doing the same to him. He folded his arms. "Far as I'm concerned, respect is earned. And it goes both ways. We don't know each other but I hope we can form a good working relationship. I might be the sheriff but I'm also the new guy here. I'll need help navigating my way around."

Something sparked in Palmer's eyes. "I can do that."

"So run it down for me. What's the job like?"

Palmer shifted, scratching under the brim of his tan hat. "Well, office is open nine-to-five weekdays unless it's a holiday. We have a dispatcher who mans the phones during that time. Dotty. Her husband was a Fed and she was his assistant. Outside of those hours we switch off who gets the phones forwarded to them. It comes straight to your radio but mine isn't a sat phone. We don't get calls too often. There isn't a lot going on around here, mostly it's keeping an eye on things."

John nodded.

"I can take this weekend, if you want. You and Pat can get settled and we'll work out the schedule starting Monday."

"Good idea." John put the lid on the jam and set it back in the fridge. "Anything else I should know?"

"I dunno." Palmer shook his head. "I've never lived anywhere else, so I don't know if it's not what you're used to. You'll have to tell me."

John laughed. "Okay."

"I'll let you boys eat your lunch. Later."

Deputy Palmer shut the door and John heard him trot back down the stairs. He didn't mind the fact his deputy had essentially led a sheltered life, growing up in Sanctuary. A lot of people lived in closed communities. John just needed to learn the culture, the rules. This could to turn out to be a lot like being undercover. The people he'd infiltrated had particular ways of doing things and their own lingo.

This job might be more suited to him than he'd realized. So long as he could get past the separation he'd always kept between him and the people he was trying to get close to. Should he and Pat decide to stay here long term—and it was partly Pat's decision too—they would have to become part of the community and not live separate lives.

This trial would only work if they made friends, lived in town, had fun and joined in with what was going on. Their quality time together was going to be spent navigating this new culture, this WITSEC town.

"I hope they do fun stuff here."

John smiled around his bite of sandwich.

"And Uncle Nate's game is tomorrow. I don't want to miss it. You think that thing gets ESPN?" He motioned to the TV.

John swallowed a mouthful of milk. "I'd like to see him play."

"He's awesome." Pat launched into a story of Nate winning a game for the Chargers John had actually seen. Nate's one-in-a-million catch during a blizzard in Chicago, slipping on the field, spraining his ankle and still scoring the touchdown. The way Pat told it was like hearing the story for the first time.

John laughed. "We'll have to Skype him soon. I'll give him a call and find out when he's going to be free."

"Maybe he can come visit us in the off season."

"Maybe." John took his plate to the sink. "We'll find out from Uncle Grant how we can work that out. But I'd like it." He sat back down across from his son. "Do you want to try calling your mom again?"

Pat looked to the side. "I dunno. Maybe later. Can we walk around town and see what all there is?"

"Sure bud. Whatever you wanna do. I don't have to work until Monday so we've got the whole weekend to meet everyone and explore the town."

"I wonder what movie they're going to play after dinner." Pat trailed to the sink and set his plate inside. "I hope it's a good one."

The kid was acting like this was summer camp.

"You know, if we decide to stay in Sanctuary then we'll be living here until you're an adult. So we've got to think really long and hard about this decision. Can you do that for me, Pat?"

"Yeah, I know, Dad." He wrapped his little boy arms around John's middle and gave him a hug, then went his bag. "If I find my football, can we play catch in the street?"

John smiled. "Sure, bud."

"When do you think Uncle Grant will have my bike delivered?"

"I don't know." John's smile broke into laughter. Did the kid ever get nervous about anything? He was taking this whole move in stride, like he was on some grand adventure. John should be feeling the same, shouldn't he? New beginnings and all that.

But there was a note of caution somewhere inside him that wouldn't let the newness of it penetrate. He chalked it up to being an adult, a parent and on a new assignment. There weren't many people in town. The ones who'd been criminals previously were supposed to be turning over a new life. Crime was low.

What could go wrong?

Chapter 4

By five forty-five, Main Street had filled with groups of people all walking over to the meeting house. John locked up the sheriff's office, flipped the sign to closed and led Pat out the backdoor instead. It was the wrong way out but he wanted to get a look at his "vehicle". That was the one thing he didn't like about moving here—having to leave his truck behind. There wasn't anything special about it. But he'd had the Chevy for years and keeping it running had become a point of honor. Now it was in storage with his couch, his bed and all the other furniture he'd scrounged up after the divorce. If they decided to stay in Sanctuary it would be sold.

The air outside was chilled but not thin like he'd thought it would be considering they were up in the mountains. Maybe something about the circle of peaks surrounding them meant air got trapped in the valley.

Two vehicles were parked out back in the marked spaces, both nineties model Jeeps the same color as the uniform Grant had given him. The rear of the building had their two spaces, plus two more. Another road ran the length of the back of the stores and across from that was a row of houses.

With Main Street as the center of the town, someone had simply run the residential streets parallel to it on both the north and south sides. It wasn't particularly imaginative, but it worked.

Pat tugged on his hand. "Is that your Sheriff's car?"

"Looks like it."

"Cool!"

"You think so?"

"Yeah." Pat grinned. "You're gonna be the sheriff!"

"That I am." They went through the alley separating the sheriff's office from the laundry next door and crossed to the bowling alley sized building with MEETING HOUSE in big letters across the siding above the double doors.

Inside, a crowd of people stood around a sea of circular tables all set for dinner. The far end was lit up like a stage, complete with a podium and microphone. To the side of the stage was a set of swinging doors with circular windows which looked to lead to a kitchen. Buffet tables were set up along one wall, stretching front to back of the room. They were covered with dishes of all shapes and sizes heaped with food.

Pat gripped John's hand as people turned to get a look at the new sheriff. John gave them all a wave. Two-thirds of the people were over fifty. There were a couple of small children but not as many as John expected, given families were gathering.

"Sheriff!" The mayor strode over. "I'll introduce you when everyone is here. For now let me show you to your seat."

John only followed since it seemed to be what the mayor expected. Collins led them to a table on one side of the podium just as a rotund woman strode out with a giant pot that smelled like chili. She hefted it onto the table, her smile wide and her long earrings swinging. She wiped her hands on the apron tied around her waist over her muumuu. "Well, is this our new sheriff?"

The mayor motioned to John. "Olympia, this is John Mason."

She bent down in front of Pat and stuck her hand out. "It's very nice to meet you, Sheriff." Her accent had a Mediterranean lilt which made her sound elegant.

Pat giggled. "I'm not the sheriff! My dad is."

"Oh, I'm sorry. You're just so tall. My mistake." She winked and straightened, turning to John. "Olympia Hernandez."

"John Mason. This is my son, Pat."

"As in, Patrick?"

Pat bounced, yanking on John's hand. "As in Patrick Garrett, the marshal who killed Billy the Kid!"

"Well, now." Olympia grinned at him. "Those are some pretty big boots to fill. You think you can do it?"

Pat nodded.

Olympia turned to the room. "Dinner's ready!" Her voice boomed even in the large room. John flinched, while the mayor shot Olympia a scowl.

John and Pat joined the line grabbing paper plates and bowls. The room buzzed with noise, even though a portion of the town seemed not to have arrived yet.

A diesel engine roared outside and headlights flashed across the front of the room. The mayor huffed, his attention on the front door. The engine shut off and seconds later a group of men strode in. All dressed in jeans and work shirts, dirty boots and cowboy hats, the last man carried his black hat in his hand. He was a good six inches taller than the others, with dark features. Matthias was among the group. Pat ran with his plate to greet him. Matthias swung him up onto his hip, plate and all, while the tall man glared.

The man in front of John said, "That's Bolton Farrera."

John looked at the guy in line ahead of him. Early thirties but he was nearly bald, his glasses drooped on his nose and he gripped his plate of mostly bread and green beans. "I'm Terrence Evangeline." He pointed at an older couple by the salads. "That's my mom, Shelby and my dad, Aaron. They run the town's community arts programs."

The couple wore stylish clothes that said they'd dressed up for this occasion in their Sunday best.

"Once a month they put on a show after dinner. You know, like a dinner theater. Anyway, the man with the truck is Bolton. He's the boss over at the ranch. The only one that actually likes him is Matthias."

That told John enough, given how Matthias had been with Pat since they arrived. Currently the twenty-something man held two plates and Pat rode on his shoulders while he weaved about like he was going to fall. Pat squealed with laughter and gripped Matthias's hair like he was on a rollercoaster.

"Nice to meet you, Terrence." John gave him a polite smile and grabbed the spoon for the mashed potatoes. "So what do you do in town?"

"I'm the trash guy." His chest puffed up. "Trash gets sent with the outgoing transport. I take care of what's left, supervise the recycling and all that. My compost is impressive, if I do say so myself."

"I'll have to come by and check it out."

Terrence's eyes glowed. "I'd like that. I'll give you the tour all the way from lumber to paper goods."

"Sounds exciting." John let the grin open into a full smile and made his way to the table. Half the people were already seated and eating. By the time he was done the rest had filled up the remaining seats. Matthias bounced over, jiggling Pat on his shoulders. He set the plates down and bent so Pat slowly tipped until John caught him. Matthias held out his hand and got a high-five. "Later, little dude."

He grabbed his plate and strode to the table occupied by ranch guys at the back. John's table had two couples, the mayor and his wife and an older, refined gentleman who looked how John imagined all plastic surgeons did. Sixty, but with the skin of a forty-five year old, and silver streaks in his hair so precise they could have been dyed that way. His wife had blond curls, perfect nails, and her nose looked like it was out of a magazine.

John gave the guy a chin lift, evidently surprising him enough he had to clear his throat with a drink of water.

The mayor waved again. "Sheriff, this is our doctor, Stephen Fenton and his lovely wife, Harriet."

"Nice to meet you."

"They also serve as our emergency personnel, doing the job of paramedics when someone isn't able to make it to the medical center."

The doctor smiled like it was an Olympic sport. The wife quit her hushed conversation with the mayor's wife to do the same.

The doctor squeezed his wife's hand. "Harriet is my nurse."

"That's right." She smiled. "We love working together. It's been great for our relationship."

John smiled. Perhaps that's what he and Ellen had needed at the time their marriage was in crisis—for both of them to get put in WITSEC, thereby forcing them to co-exist civilly. Not that there weren't couples in the program who'd gotten divorced under their new identities and been placed separately. Maybe they had a lawyer or a judge in Sanctuary, even if there was no court to uphold the law. But if neither party could leave town unless they left the program, did they simply move to opposite ends of the street? There had to be some discord, if people were forever running into their exes at community dinners.

"Well, I'm up." The mayor pushed his chair back and approached the podium, leaning down to the microphone. "Check, check. Is this thing on?"

The microphone hummed to a screech and everyone in the room winced. Olympia emerged from the kitchen and stood with her hands in the pockets of her apron.

The mayor cleared his throat. "Thank you all for coming. We're here tonight to welcome our newest resident. Sheriff John Mason will be taking over from Sheriff Chandler. We should have an update on the latest on Chandler's condition after he has surgery on Monday. John Mason has brought his son, Patrick, who goes by Pat." He shot John's son a smile and Pat swung his feet back and forth under the table. "Please join me in welcoming them."

The room swelled with applause. John looked around, seeing tables of similar faces—families—alongside tables of co-workers like the ranch guys. There was even a table of what looked like aging bikers. A small amount of young people and kids were spread around the room. All of them seemed to co-exist in a place John felt for the first time maybe he could be at home in.

"Next up on our agenda—"

The door opened. A slender, dark haired woman in jeans and a brown jacket stepped inside. She looked around, saw everyone's attention was on her and ducked to the side of the door.

"As I was saying," the mayor continued. "Tonight's movie will begin in one hour after cleanup. Those of you on the schedule will need to stay behind to help pull down the tables and set up chairs."

John kept his eyes on the woman. Something about her made him want to stare. He couldn't make out her features from this distance. The mayor's reaction had been interesting—disapproving. But of the disruption or the woman herself?

The safe in the sheriff's office contained the WITSEC file for every person in this room. It would take John forever to read through them all. But he supposed he needed to that if he was going to know these people, what they were capable of and what they'd endured. Several of the faces were familiar, in a general sort of way. There was a guy across the room with a table of men in military haircuts who John thought might be the former chief of staff of the army.

Given what the town was established for, he'd expected to see more household names. But maybe the government had them change their looks when they went into the program. He'd have to find out who still needed to testify and learn how that worked. Find out who had been here longest, so he could pick their brain for how to do this job in a way which made everyone in town's lives as safe as they could be.

The previous sheriff might have upheld the law with a light touch, mostly leaving people to get on with their lives. On the other hand, he might not have tolerated even the slightest infraction. He'd have to ask Palmer. His deputy was sitting with a table of people who all had his red coloring—an older couple and two younger boys. John didn't want to interrupt his family time.

"Battle Night will commence at eight p.m. on Saturday. If you're not part of the proceedings you are advised to stay in your homes after dark in order to avoid becoming a casualty."

The mayor was frowning at his paper. "Guns can be collected from the radio station after noon tomorrow and are to be returned after the operation is concluded. If you are under eighteen, you must have a signed permission slip on your person at all times and wear the appropriate colors."

John leaned in the Betty's direction. "What's this?"

Her lip curled. "Paintball. But the Major General organizes everyone into teams and claims it's all about strategy and mounting assault versus defense." She shook her head. "It's just an excuse to run around like hooligans if you ask me."

Judging by the looks on the faces of more than a few people, "Battle Night" was something to look forward to. Being cooped up like this probably got old. The chance to blow off steam, even with paintball of all things, could be seriously fun.

The mayor continued, "Safe zones are the barn at the ranch and the marked area at the farm. But Dan says if you mess with the crops you're disqualified and banned from participating for a whole year. Teams will meet at their respective zones at seventeen-thirty." He moved the paper to the back of his stack, displaying precisely how he felt about "Battle Night."

Pat pulled on John's sleeve. "Can I go to that?"

"Let me find out more, first. Okay?"

Pat nodded but slumped lower in his seat. John looked around again. The woman was still there, leaning against the back wall with her hands in the pockets of her coat. Her hair was swept over one shoulder, covering the side of her face.

The mayor continued to make announcements about a raccoon getting into someone's trash, and a church that met Sundays in the Meeting House. Probably that was a good way for John to meet people and be sociable outside of the times he was around town in uniform. People needed to get to know him as a man and a father as well as their new sheriff.

"Father Wilson, would you like to come and pray over us?"

A grizzled man stood. He had a minister's collar on his black shirt and walked with soft steps to the podium, even though his craggy face said *gangster*. He held the sides of the podium with both hands. The ranch guys all removed their hats and all around the room people bowed their heads.

The minister bowed his head and spoke in a voice that sounded like he had laryngitis. He thanked the Good Lord for food and fellowship and asked Him to watch over the town and keep each one of them safe. He prayed for Sheriff Chandler's health and that John and Pat would feel welcome. At the end he tacked on an addendum that the B team would be victorious.

The room erupted into cheers on one side and a chorus of "boo" on the other. Everyone laughed. The minister looked up a gap-toothed grin on his face. "Amen!"

Most of the people in the room yelled back, "Amen!" But there was a lot of, "No way!" and "Not gonna happen!"

People got up, dispersing with their plates to where Olympia stood beside a trash can and a cart of basins, one full of soapy water and one empty.

Matthias clapped him on the back. "Did you meet my Momma?"

"Olympia?"

He nodded and motioned to the three Hispanic women behind him. Two were tall and slender and one was younger and plump. But all of them were beautiful. "These are my sisters, Maria who is married to Tom. They have two kids. And this is Antonia and Sofia. They run the nursery and organize all the landscaping in town."

John shook their hands.

"That's my brother, Diego."

The young man Matthias pointed to stood with the table of ranch guys but waved at him. Diego's features differed from Matthias, his coloring darker whereas Matthias seemed to favor his mother.

Matthias must have seen John's frown since he added, "Takes after the Puerto Rican side of the family. Mama is Greek."

Olympia wandered over.

John included her in his smile. "You have a beautiful family."

"They're a handful, every one of them."

"Mama!" Plump Sofia's hands shot to her hips.

John laughed at the gleam in Olympia's eyes. They might drive her crazy but she loved each one. He looked around, searching for Pat. He was at the back of the room in conversation with the lone woman who'd entered late. She'd crouched to Pat's level and nodded at something he said.

"Excuse me." John made his way over and put his hand on Pat's shoulder. "Hello."

The woman looked up and his breath caught. Her eyes were dark almost black and the same shade as her long, straight hair. "Sheriff. I'm Andra."

"Andra?"

"Yeah, Dad. Like Alexandra, but without the Alex part."

She shot Pat a smile. "I should be going."

"Somewhere to be?"

Her smile dimmed. "Yeah, home. And it's a decent walk so I should head out before it gets too dark."

John nodded. He didn't make a point to argue with a woman if he could help it and she seemed pretty determined to leave. Though, run away was probably a more accurate description.

"It was nice to meet you." She kept her eyes on Pat and then turned to the door.

John looked at his son. "How'd you get all the way over here?"

Pat shrugged. "She didn't have anyone to talk to, so I came over to say hi."

"That was nice of you." John squeezed his shoulder. "What's she like?"

"I think she's lonely. Don't you think so?"

"Could be. We'll have to find out."

"There's no need to worry about Ms. Caleri, Sheriff."

He turned back and saw the doctor, one arm around his wife.

"Caleri?"

Harriet swallowed like there was a bad taste in her mouth. "Andra Caleri. She keeps to herself and in return no one bothers her. Except when she shows up at the medical center and yells at me for no reason whatsoever."

"Is there something about her I should know?" John could look it up in Andra's file but it was better to get people's opinions. That said more about someone than a report did.

"Just give her a wide berth as much as you can. That's what we do."

The doctor nodded. "It's best that way. I've heard she's not very sociable. People who show up at her house on accident don't have anything good to say about the experience."

How did you show up at someone's house by accident?

The question must have shown up on John's face because the doctor said, "She lives outside of town, up in the mountains some but no one knows precisely where."

Harriet nodded. "Some people think she's lived by herself for so long it's affected her mental state. If you know what I mean."

Right. She seemed sane enough to John, but how did you tell? "Well, I appreciate the heads-up."

"Goodnight, Sheriff." They swept out the door as a single unit.

"Why were they mean about Andra? She's nice."

John looked down at Pat. "I'm not really sure. Maybe Andra doesn't get on well with some of the people in town. Or maybe she just likes her privacy."

"Like when you go in a stall because you don't want to stand by everyone else at the urinal?"

John laughed. "That is exactly what privacy means."

"But Andra's a girl."

"Girl privacy is probably different, but she could still want that." John ruffled Pat's hair until the kid shifted his head from under his hand. "Let's go see about the sleeping arrangements, yeah? It's been a long day."

"Can't we stay for the movie?"

"Not tonight. It's late and we still need to unpack."

They stepped outside, waving to those who called goodnight to them. John took Pat's hand and they walked across the street. To the right of the Meeting House the doctor and his wife stood together, both looking up the street. A quarter mile up where the street ended, Andra walked along with a flashlight in one hand lighting her way as she stepped off the road toward the trees.

A second later, she was gone.

Chapter 5

Just after nine the next morning John stood in the sheriff's office with his second cup of coffee. He stared at the map of the town tacked to the wall. Sanctuary was shaped like a wrapped piece of candy. The buildings and houses in the middle were an oval and the sides fanned out—the ranch on one side and the farm on the other.

He stepped closer and looked in the direction he'd seen Andra walk last night. The map showed nothing but trees, although a broken line delineated a path running from that corner of the town up into the foothills. It was possible a structure had been built but never added to the map. The previous sheriff must have known something, but John couldn't exactly call him and ask.

The bell over the door rang and Deputy Palmer strode in. "You're up. I figured you'd be getting settled."

"Just getting a feel for the place." He didn't intend on working his first day. But there was a lot to this job he felt didn't have much to do with office hours or procedure. Too much of it was human interaction and dealing with people co-existing alongside one another. He needed to do that in a way it would last.

With Pat still sleeping, John had pulled on jeans and a t-shirt and dug up some clean socks before he slipped his sneakers on and came down for a look around. The apartment door was open, in case Pat called out. Especially since in the middle of the night he'd burrowed into John's side. Again.

Deputy Palmer sat at his desk and fired up his computer. "Questions?"

John sat at his desk. The chair was huge and the stuffing had been squished into submission buy someone whose frame was considerably larger than his. "Sure. Was most everyone at the dinner last night?"

"Far as I could tell. I think old man Jenkins is still at the medical center but he might have been sent home before the dinner. He has the flu but he's like ninety." Palmer grinned.

There was a lot about him that reminded John more of a little boy playing dress-up than a man in uniform protecting his town.

"You're probably sick to death of shaking hands. I know I'd never remember all their names if I learned them in one night." Palmer clicked his mouse and typed, his eyes scanned the screen and then he logged it off again.

"The files are all back here?" John motioned to the wall of cupboards behind him. Each was locked with a padlock, the keys for which were in John's safe. "For everyone in town?"

"Families are grouped together, so you can find out who testified and who they brought into the program with them. They're more like case files than personnel files and there are one hundred thirty-two which cover all the residents' cases. Families are in one file, so there are more than that many people. Still, it'll probably take a year to get through all of them."

John glanced at the cupboard doors. If he started with Andra's, would it be obvious why? "And the reports filed by the sheriff's office?"

"All that's computerized now, so you'll find it on your desktop although Chandler liked paper so mostly he had Dotty type up his reports even though that's not part of her job. She'll be in on Monday."

Palmer filled a hot cup from the pot John had brewed and set his hat back on his head. Was John going to have to wear one of those? It was clearly part of his uniform but Grant hadn't included one. Was that because he figured John wouldn't wear it anyway?

"I'm off to walk around a bit, stretch my legs." Palmer zipped up the jacket over his uniform. "I don't take the car unless it's an emergency. Mostly I can get anywhere in town in ten minutes if needed, but it's still quicker to run here from wherever I am and then grab the car." His face fell. "Still, it's been two years at least since anything remotely interesting happened."

"I see."

"The worst thing that happened recently was a bunch of people's lawn gnomes got stolen before thanksgiving. But then they showed up in Hal's Christmas display over at the radio station all dressed up as little elves, so everyone got a good laugh about it."

"There's a radio station?"

"Sure." Palmer indicated the small radio over by the coffee pot. "Broadcasts most of the day and into the night. All old school classic rock and nothing else. Absolutely no girl music, he says." Palmer chuckled and it sounded like a mouse squeaking. "Hal's a hoot and the best source for the weather. He just knows when it's gonna turn. And if you need to get an announcement out people will hear, most everyone listens in just after dinner. Other than that we've got a weekly paper and we get limited channels from the satellite. That's why Betty started movie night."

"And this Battle Night they were talking about last night?"

"The Major General started that up. He decided if there was an invasion then we should probably be ready. He runs training three days a week, running and push-ups and all that." Palmer blew out a breath. "I tried it for a while. I thought it would be fun but it wasn't."

Given the obvious paunch in Palmer's middle, John figured being out of shape and not inclined to work out might have something to do with it. The guy needed to start working out instead of just sucking it in, or he was going to hit a downward slope when he reached forty and things wouldn't be pretty.

"Twice a year they have Battle Night and the teams are split into squads, some attacking and some defending. It's basically capture the flag, which the kids do. But with masks, and black clothes and paintball guns." He puffed out his chest. "It's all in fun."

"How many people do it?"

"Like thirty, maybe? Bolton heads up the A team and they usually win. But Dan Walden from the farm took over the B team, since Tom broke his foot. There's a rumor going around about some secret weapon but no one knows what it is. Or who." He headed for the door. "Should be fun. I'll see you there?"

"Maybe." John leaned back in his chair. "I might hang around, check it out."

While probably a whole lot of fun and the dream evening for practically every male in town, John couldn't help mentally listing all the things which could go wrong.

Palmer lifted his coffee cup in salute. "See you later, then."

"Sure. You need anything today?"

He shook his head. "Y'all just get settled in."

The man seemed content to run the show for as long as John needed to get unpacked. Sure, John needed to figure out getting Pat enrolled in the school and it would take a few weeks to settle in. But he didn't need Palmer to act as his crutch in the meantime.

When the door shut behind the deputy, John grabbed up the phone and dialed Grant's number.

"Hey brother."

"How's things?" John turned on his computer and logged on.

"How are things in town?"

Grant was going to brush off John's question? "The town is fine. I want to know what's going on with Genevieve and the girls. Did you call the therapist I recommended?"

"Yeah." Grant sighed. His steps echoed through the phone line and then a door shut. "Brenda's going to call Genevieve first thing Monday and ask her if she'd be amenable to sitting down with me and us talking. But she recommended I come in alone also."

"That's good."

Grant huffed. "The director of the marshals does not need to sit down in a...what did she call it? Oh, yeah. A safe place to talk about his feelings."

"Be that as it may—"

"No. I don't want to do it."

"Do you want your family back?"

Grant sighed but didn't answer.

Pat emerged from the apartment stairs and John waved him over. "I'll take that as a yes. Do this, Grant. Suck it up and get them back."

The kid stumbled over, his eyes unfocused. He climbed onto John's lap, burrowing in the same way he'd done during the night.

"Fine," Grant said. "But you know there's a therapist in town. It's customary for new residents to meet with her at least once so she can file a report on how they're acclimating."

"Good luck with that." John wrapped his arm around his son. "I'm way too busy. Maybe next month."

Grant laughed. "Door swings both ways, brother."

"Not here it doesn't. Didn't you know that?" John laughed. "Did you approve Battle Night? Apparently it's this thing they do here."

"Sure, what's the harm? The Major General wants to re-live his glory days commanding troops and the rest of them are just blowing off steam. It's mostly harmless."

That seemed to be the party line.

John clicked his mouse and pulled up the sheriff's office reports for the past month. There were less than twenty entries. "I'll check it out. If it's not in the best interest of the safety of the town, I'm pulling their authorization. I'm not condoning something that creates mobs of people racing around trying to injure each other, a mess of stuff to clean up the next day, or more than a minimum of five minor injuries logged at the medical center. They can get their jollies elsewhere."

"Your call."

"You're right. It is."

Grant chuckled. "I think you're going to do fine. Check in with me next week, yeah?"

"Sure." Pat lifted his head. Before he even asked, John said to Grant, "Pat wants to know when his bike will be here."

"Tell him it'll be in Monday's delivery along with some stuff mom sent."

John related that to his son, who said, "Awesome!"

Grant said bye and they hung up.

"So." He gave his boy a squeeze. "What do you want to do today?"

"Can we go exploring?" Pat's stomach rumbled. "Can we have pancakes first? I'm hungry."

John flipped on the radio in the apartment while he whipped up pancake batter. Two rock songs sung by men who were likely in their seventies by now aired back-to-back before the DJ came on.

"Better batten down your hatches, folks. Battle Night begins at eight tonight. If you're on the street, you will be shot. Both teams are reporting in, ten privates each and two sergeants per five-man squad. Lieutenants are Bolton Farrera for A team and Dan Walden for B team. Major General Halt has confirmed all slots are now full and the rosters are closed. Good luck to all. Stay safe. And remember; only losers get dead!"

**

"I want to come!"

John glanced aside at him. "I know you do, Pat. But it might be dangerous." He pulled on a jacket, his shoulder holster snug across his back and under his arms. The weight of it was familiar, like a pair of boots not worn since last winter. "You should stay here. Watch one of the movies you have on your iPad and call me from the phone at my desk if you need anything. I doubt I'll be out for long."

"I won't get in the way."

"Pat, I said no. I need to be able to trust you're gonna listen to me and do what I say." Pat looked at the floor. "Why don't you hang out downstairs? I don't want you answering the door to anyone, but maybe you can call Uncle Nate."

"It's too late tonight. He's in Florida and he has a game tomorrow."

"So call Uncle Ben or Grandma."

"Okay."

"Look." John crouched. "I'm not saying you can't go to Battle Night ever. But we don't know these people. Once we make friends, then when the next time rolls around we'll talk about it again. Does that sound okay?"

Pat bit his lip and tears filled his eyes. "Are you going to come back?"

"Nothing's going to happen to me. Haven't I come back every time?" John squeezed the back of his neck and touched his forehead to Pat's.

John kissed the top of his head and pulled his son to him. The kid put on a brave face but inside he was dead scared he was going to get dumped off by another parent. John hadn't done him any favors being gone so much. Still, that wasn't going to happen anymore. Part of the reason why they were here was so they could spend time together. To finally be a family, for real. And forever. It didn't matter what the town threw at them. It didn't matter who these people were. John was going to win at this—being sheriff being a parent, all of it.

He was going to make that happen.

**

The command center set up at the Meeting House was a bust. John couldn't very well observe people acting natural when they knew he was watching them. Conversations turned clipped the minute he entered.

The personnel stationed around the folding tables were mostly aging men who strode around with military bearing. The coffee flowed thick and fast, courtesy of Olympia who gave him a wave. The major general shook John's hand, but quickly turned his attention back to the map spread on a table in the center of the room.

Little flags on the map marked each of the team members, the safe zones and the location of each team's flag. Two team colonels were there—Father Mathews, who had given the prayer at dinner along with a stocky man who had a long beard and a leather vest and introduced himself as Hal, the radio DJ. Each of them used separate radio channels to communicate with their lieutenants.

John didn't know why either was qualified to command a team, but there it was.

What bothered John was the two black flags on the map. When he asked about it, the major general just glared. A woman in a pant suit who looked like she should have been on staff at the Pentagon, snapped straight and said, "Those are dark agents." As if that explained it perfectly.

John filled a paper cup of coffee and headed out. He strode by the front window of the sheriff's office. Pat was on the computer, probably online. That wasn't exactly what John had told him to occupy himself with but he wasn't going to argue the point right now. Pat was a good kid but John had been away from him for a long time. He needed to rebuild Pat's trust.

He strode down Main Street toward the farm, since he hadn't been over that part of town yet. Eventually he'd have to figure out a route to run in the mornings, get a better idea of the layout of the town and a good six mile course.

This end of town had a gym opposite the hardware store, but the glass windows out front showed a boxing ring and a series of punching bags around the place and that was it.

The last building on John's side looked like a café or diner, with tables and chairs outside wrapping around the corner. Both the front and side had windows, and the interior would seat fifty people easily between the booths and tables. Sunday's advertised special was going to be roast beef and mashed potatoes.

Two figures dressed in black strode from the opposite side of the street. John ducked against the side of the building and hid in the shadows of the diner's front door. Armed with paintball guns and wearing wool caps and goggles, they walked like it was Sunday at two and they were going out for ice cream. Both had the letter A drawn on their cheeks.

"...so Sheila told me she didn't want to see my sorry butt again. By the time I got over there she'd thrown all my stuff on the front lawn. It took me years to build up that collection of The Amazing Spiderman. I had nearly every single one except number three-hundred, you know, with the first appearance of Venom. Now I'm back at my mom's house."

"That's harsh, dude."

"You're telling me." The first guy sighed. "Issue number seven got mud on the corner."

The two guys couldn't have been older than early-twenties. John waited until they crossed in front of him at a right angle to Main Street and then he sprinted across.

The road to the farm was much like the road to the ranch. As wide as a two lane road it was blacktop all the way to the open gate. Air puffed from his lungs in clouds as John moved down the side of the road where the tree line was. He couldn't hear much, but past the gate there was movement and the low rumble of men talking.

John froze. He ducked against the nearest tree. Ten feet to his right something moved between the trees. The steps were silent but he heard the rustle of fallen leaves as someone made their way to the farm. John lifted his wrist and illuminated his watch.

8:47 p.m.

"Freeze!"

John pulled his gun surrounded by four men, all masked. They pointed paintball guns at his chest. Every one of them had the letter B drawn on their cheeks.

"Easy, man."

John waited until they lowered their guns and then re-holstered his weapon. "Sorry. Reflex."

The one in front grinned. "Looks like we caught ourselves a dark agent boys." The man took John by the arm and hauled him with the group to the yellow light of the barn. John figured he'd just go with it.

A tall, dark haired man wearing a black t-shirt and black cargo pants sat on a bale of hay. He was younger than John but had an air about him that was solid. Salt of the earth, his mom would have said. Even with a B on both his cheeks.

"Sheriff?"

John nodded.

The man cracked a smile and stuck out his hand. "Dan Walden. You'll have to excuse me for missing last night's welcome dinner. I was elbow deep in mare placenta."

John blinked.

"Thankfully it all came out okay." He motioned at a stall to their left, where a brown horse with a smattering of white hairs across its neck and back stared at them. "That's Bay."

The guys who'd walked him in gathered closer to the huddle. "He's the dark agent," one said. "He has to be."

Dan looked at John a question present in his eyes. It was hard to imagine the man ever getting flustered, even when he was "elbow deep in placenta". Whatever that meant, John didn't even want to know.

"I'm not the dark agent."

Dan's eyes narrowed. "Still, you'll remain here with us where we can keep an eye on—"

The lights went off. John stood completely still. The room smelled like hay and other less appealing farm odors. The men around him spun, bumping into each other. John pulled out his flashlight and flipped it on. Behind Dan, a slender figure darted through the room.

"Right there!"

The flagpole across from Dan tipped over. Someone fired several bursts of paint like the steady slam of a nail gun.

"Get her!"

Dan ran for the figure. Paint slammed into his back but he didn't stop. Animals whined and shifted about in their stalls. The guys ran after the farmer out the single door at the back, leaving John alone in the barn.

From a dark corner the slender figure emerged. A wool cap covered the woman's hair and a mask like Zorro covered her eyes. She wore all black and made no sound as she crossed the room with a red flag in her hand. Black C's were drawn on both of her cheeks. Another team? She tucked the flag into her back pocket, the bright red bait clearly visible to anyone in pursuit. She lifted one gloved finger to her lips and then sprinted out the wide front doors of the barn.

The men ran back in. "Where is she?"

"That was the dark agent!"

"Who was it? I've never seen her before. Have you?"

"No, never. She disappeared into nowhere."

They talked over each other until Dan came back in. "Tanner, radio the colonel. Tell him our flag has been taken." He glanced at all of them. "Saddle up boys, we're going after her."

Chapter 6

The boys jumped into a rush of movement, dragging out horses and loading them up with saddles. John lifted one finger.

Dan halted. "Make it quick."

"She had the letter C on her cheeks."

"What?" Dan shook his head. "That's not possible, there's no team C."

John shrugged. "Take it or leave it." He turned to the door.

"Hold up."

John turned back. Dan accepted the reins of a gigantic black horse. It took every ounce of will not to step back in an act of self-preservation. Dan smiled. "Here." He threw a set of keys and John caught them. "The truck's been on its last legs for five years but it runs. Or thereabouts. I don't have anything else with four wheels and I usually ride Indigo everywhere anyway." He patted the flank of his horse, while the animal stared at John.

"The ranch has more than one truck, don't they?"

Dan rolled his eyes. "Yeah, I'm aware of that." He swung up on the horse. "Truck's over by the house."

"Hey, thanks."

Dan shrugged and kicked the horse into gear. At least that's what it looked like to John. The farmer, and the four guys with him, took off in a cloud of dust kicked up by horse's hooves and a thunderous noise.

John looked around, half expecting the woman to emerge again. Had it been Andra?

On the surface she didn't seem the type to get involved in a game, even if the participants he'd observed so far seemed to take it seriously. Could she put aside the way the mayor and his wife—and the doctor and his wife—had dismissed her as being irrelevant? She probably wasn't the first person they'd snubbed and he didn't figure she'd be the last. No one else at the dinner had spoken to her. Did that mean everyone knew what the town's figureheads knew, or did they simply follow their lead? Most of the men he'd met so far didn't seem like the kind of guys who followed anyone's lead but their own.

John found the truck and drove back into town. Streets were deserted. The whole town looked like the fake towns he'd done training in, both in the military and with the marshals. He half expected to see a dressed-up mannequin on the sidewalk.

John parked outside the sheriff's office and took the stairs two at a time. Pat was asleep on the couch, all the lights were on and the iPad had died. John set it on the coffee table and put his son in bed but left both the lamp in the bedroom and the light above the oven on. He left the truck and walked to the Meeting House.

Deputy Palmer still wasn't there, though it was hard to tell when everyone buzzed between radios stationed around the room to the table. Pieces were shifted, knocked over and moved to opposite ends of the map. By the looks of it, Dan's team B had made it across town.

"Team A's flag has been taken." Hal strode over. "That's both teams who've had their flag taken by a member of this team C. What is going on?" He stared down the major general. "There isn't supposed to be a C team."

The major general stood perfectly still. "There is no C team."

John stopped at the other side of the table. "I saw one of them."

Both men turned to him. The noise in the room dissolved into silence. The major general's eyes narrowed. "Impossible. I would have been notified. That was not part of the battle plan."

"Did A team say it was a woman who took their flag?"

Hal said, "They did."

"Probably the same woman I saw. Probably decided to make her own team and show you all what she's made of." John liked the idea. He'd always admired women with cunning, which—it turned out—

was both the reason why he'd gotten married and also the reason why he was now divorced.

"Impossible."

"She took the B team flag at nine-seventeen. When was the A team flag taken?"

Hal grinned. "Nine thirty-five."

"There is no way..." The major general's rant dissolved into rambling.

John folded his arms, liking this woman even more. "So she made it from one end of town to the other in fifteen minutes and got herself two flags."

The major general's craggy face turned red. "I would have been notified!"

"Because things always go the way you planned in battle?" John shrugged. "Sometimes a new enemy crops up, one you weren't expecting. It would be a shame to let her get the jump on both teams and get away with it, wouldn't it?"

The major general rubbed the palm of his hand across his girth, which was covered with a wool vest. "Not under my command!" He turned to the pentagon woman. "Call all troops back to the command center. I want all intel before we mobilize the teams to retake the flags."

She snapped straight. "Yes, sir!"

Five minutes later both teams poured into the Meeting House. Dan and Bolton both strode over, but not without glancing sideways at each other. Bolton was the first to talk. "Whose idea was it to have a team C?"

John studied the man's dark features. He'd seen him somewhere before but couldn't place where. Likely it was a law enforcement connection; DEA by the look of the man. He seemed the type to infiltrate drug cartels and bring down their empires while simultaneously winning the heart of the cartel boss's virgin daughter.

John didn't trust him at all.

He was going to have to do a serious amount of reading in the next few weeks if he was going to get to the bottom of who each of these people were. And that was the short-hand route. It would take too long to meet each individual person and determine the threat level of them living in this town. He had to know what they were capable of if he was going to decide whether to trust them with the formative years of Pat's life. Because there was no way John could shelter the kid from a whole town.

Bolton chewed out the major general on his lack of sharing. It appeared Bolton didn't know the old man had no clue what was going on, either.

Dan glanced aside at John. "The truck start okay?"

"A little slow on the uptake but once it got warmed up it was happy."

Hal leaned toward them. "Sounds like my kind of woman."

John burst out laughing, as did Dan, but the farmer didn't seem to find it quite as funny. Bolton glared at them. "Do you mind?"

John stared at the man and tried to remember any big cases or busts but he'd been undercover for a year, which put him severely out of the loop on that stuff. He glanced at each of the men. "Any of you seen Deputy Palmer? He was supposed to be in here tonight, supervising."

The men glanced at each other.

"Care to share?"

Dan was the one who spoke. "Palmer's not a bad guy. He's just a little...exuberant. Probably wandered off to give someone a citation."

"He said he's lived here all his life. Does that happen often?"

"I'm a native, too." Dan shrugged. "Palmer and I went to school together. The guy never met a rule he couldn't follow."

John smiled. "Anyone else feel like weighing in?"

Bolton sniffed and turned away. Hal said, "He's fine enough. For a young un'."

"All right." John motioned to the map on the table top. "So what's the plan for team C?"

The major general lifted his chin. "Intelligence indicates it was the same woman who took both flags."

Dan said, "So who is she? You saw her, sheriff. Any idea who it is?"

John had a fair idea, but he wasn't going to give them everything. These were the kind of men who had to figure it out for themselves instead of having him take half the fun out of it for them. Besides, he could be wrong. "I've met maybe a dozen people in town. I couldn't say for sure who it was in your barn. Slender. Five-seven. Hair was covered, dressed in all black. Dark brown eyes. That's about it."

"Great." Bolton rolled his eyes. "I had one of those in my barn, too."

Was he questioning John's ability to sheriff, or just his observational skills? John studied him. "You got a problem?"

Bolton didn't even blink. "Marshal Mason whose older brother is the director, gets all the cushy assignments. Living life on the edge, undercover, reeling in the fugitives and walking away clean."

"Right." That was why there was a cut on his forehead and a bruise the size of a football on the back of his shoulder. Still, John wasn't sure this was totally about him and not also in part about Bolton's feelings over whatever it was that had happened to him.

He was going to have to read up on that later. "Have you considered talking to someone about your pent-up frustration for authority figures? I hear there's a shrink in town."

Bolton's chest shook, which in anyone else might have amounted to actual laughter. "Ah, so you're the hand-holding, hug-your-fellow-man type then?"

"Not hardly." John stuck his hands in his pockets. "I just have enough issues to know when I'm staring at them." The man wasn't going to respect John's sob story of Alphonz or his associates looking for revenge. "Just looking for somewhere quiet to raise my boy."

"Dude, you picked the wrong town if you're lookin' for a quiet life." Bolton's lips twitched and he almost smiled. Almost.

"Thanks for the heads up."

The door flung open. One of the two kids John had seen on the street rushed in, winded, with snot dripping onto his upper lip. "She's dead. We found her." He sucked in a breath. "She's dead."

**

The street behind the Meeting House on the south side of Main looked much like the street behind the sheriff's office. The rear of the buildings faced a row of residential houses. John half-expected the dead woman to be the same woman he'd seen in the barn. He checked his watch as they jogged to where the second of the pair he'd seen stood. The boy's hands shook and he made gagging sounds.

10:05 p.m.

"Okay, here's close enough." John held out his arm to stop the group who'd run with him from the Meeting House a ways back from the body.

None of them should be here with him. But did they listen? His repeated attempts to get them to remain at the meeting house were ignored. He hardly needed an audience for this.

John motioned to the kid. "Step this way, please."

The guy stumbled to them.

"Did you check to make sure she's dead?" John could see her, sprawled at the bottom of a wall. He could also see the blood. When the guy turned greener, John looked at the crowd who'd followed. "No one goes closer than this."

The major general shoved to the front. "I'll take care of her. This woman needs to be treated with respect."

"And with all due respect to you, this is my job."

"You only just arrived. That hardly makes you one of us."

"Perhaps that's a good thing. Since it makes me impartial." He waited but the Major General didn't say more. John turned to Bolton. "No one goes closer than this." He motioned to the two guys who discovered the body. "They don't leave and they don't talk to anyone either. Not even each other."

For a second Bolton looked like he was going to refuse, but he nodded. John looked around, scanning the area as his brain worked through everything that needed to be done.

"I need someone to find Deputy Palmer." Matthias' brother, Diego, broke away from the crowd and sprinted down the street. John turned to Bolton, who stood at the front of the crowd staring at the body. "I'll need the doctor, unless there's a medical examiner in town. I also need to know if there are any retired cops, a judge, a district attorney. Anyone like that." He took a breath. "I'm going to need all the resources available."

Bolton nodded and turned to one of his guys. "March, go get Simmons. Bring him to the sheriff's office. Oh, and start a pot of coffee." Bolton sighed. "It's going to be a long night."

"Simmons?"

"Former superior court judge."

"Justice Anthony Simmons?"

"That'd be him."

Great. That guy was pushing ninety years ago when an angry protestor bombed his office, killing five people and declaring war on the Supreme Court and Simmons in particular. John scratched the side of his head and the scab from Alphonz's guy's gun-butt.

He'd figured witness protection when Simmons disappeared, only showing up again to testify against the eco-terrorist. The rest of the group had tried to kill him. But no one had ever been killed while under the protection of WITSEC. At least not if they followed the rules.

John strode to the body. Her blonde hair was matted with dirt. Face down on the ground, she was tucked against the side of the building as though someone tried to make her as inconspicuous as possible. Her white pants and red blouse were smeared with dirt. She could be any number of the blonde women he'd met the past two days.

He made his way back to the group. "If I'm going to process this scene, I'll need to run by the sheriff's office." For supplies *and* coffee.

Bolton's eyes flicked to settle on John. "Get what you need. I'll maintain the scene."

He should just ask the man if he'd been a cop. No one else talked like that other than people in the business, wannabes and true crime fans. So which was Bolton Farrera?

John crossed the street to the back of the sheriff's office, trailed by another set of footsteps. He glanced back and saw Matthias behind him. "Need something?"

"Not me, but if you're going to be up all night working do you want me to hang out in case Pat wakes up?"

John stopped at the back door. "Actually that would be great." Too bad nice people always weirded him out. No one was that selfless. Because John had never met anyone who started out nice and stayed that way, instead of revealing an ulterior motive. Could he trust this guy with his son? Everything so far said yes. But was it enough to go on?

"I can take him to my mom's for breakfast, if you're still busy, or sleeping or whatever. He can meet my nephews and then Pat'll know kids his own age he can play with."

"Okay." John unlocked the door and they went in. He should have thought of that. But for some reason John assumed Pat being here with him would be enough. He must have had friends at school and in his neighborhood and he'd need that here, too. "There's a couch and TV upstairs and someone stocked the fridge."

"That'd be my mom. She likes to make everyone feel welcome when they get here."

And yet she wasn't on the "welcoming committee" as Betty Collins had called it. The unassuming way Olympia had made their first days better meant a whole lot more.

"Tell her I said thanks."

Matthias grinned. "Sure thing."

"Make yourself at home. If I'm not here, leave a note when you go to breakfast."

John pulled open cabinets in the office, searching for anything that looked like stuff he'd need to process a murder scene—tweezers, police tape, gloves, evidence bags. A body bag. He pulled a duffel bag from the shelf above a rail where someone had hung vests and winter coats and unzipped it. "Bingo."

Still, he needed his camera.

Matthias was still standing at the bottom of the apartment stairs.

"You need something else?"

"Well..." He ran a hand through his scruffy black hair. "I don't know where you're at with all this, but if it comes time tomorrow is it okay if Pat comes to church with my family?"

That was all? The young man looked nervous. John turned back to his bag. "That's fine. Just call me on the radio if you guys need anything."

"Okay, cool. I'm going to head up."

John followed him up and dug out the camera he'd packed just because he always used the thing to take pictures of Pat. That was years ago now, but it wasn't like he could've upgraded his ancient phone to one with a camera. It wouldn't even work here.

Pat was still sleeping soundly, so John wrote him a note about Matthias but not the dead body and left it on the other pillow.

Matthias barely glanced up from his shoot-em-up movie when John slung the bag over his shoulder and headed out again. If he was done with the scene by morning, he'd probably need a break. There wasn't much of a better way to contrast death than with church. He understood the fundamentals of religion. Although why God needed to die and come back to life didn't make much sense. Couldn't He just could poof whatever and do what He needed?

John blew out a breath as he walked. The night air wasn't too cool and when he got back to the scene, Bolton was holding the crowd back. John dumped the bag and cordoned off the area with police tape and the help of two street lamps and a rusted ladder on the corner of the building. The area was huge but he didn't have anything else to use to hold up the tape. And since this was his first murder investigation, he didn't want to make the area too small and miss something.

He looked at Bolton. "Is the doctor here yet?"

"On his way."

"Anyone else? Palmer?"

Bolton turned so his back was to the group all straining to see the body. "Not yet."

John moved closer and lowered his voice. "Any idea who it is?"

Bolton shook his head. "Can't tell from here. Not from the back of the head."

"I'll call you over when the doctor gets here and we flip her." John dug in the bag for his camera.

"What happened to her?" It was the woman from the command center who'd looked like she belonged at the Pentagon. "Who would cause an accident like this and then leave?"

"I want to know why she was out on Battle Night. She's wearing bright colors, so she wasn't part of it." Hal frowned in the direction of the woman. "Maybe she bumped into someone coming around a corner and hit her head."

The major general planted his feet, hip width apart. "Clearly she was up to something. Check for paint. If there isn't any on her then it'll be clear no one involved with Battle Night was the cause of this. She probably just had a heart attack or something. Terribly tragic, but nothing to get all fussed about."

"We'll have to wait to draw any conclusions." John gripped the camera in his hands. "There isn't much you all can do, unless you have some prior training processing a crime scene."

At least two of them gasped.

"You think its murder?" The woman covered her mouth.

"This was just a horrible tragedy. Like I said." The major general shook his head. "There's no need to get all riled up now. We've still got a team C to rustle up."

"Speaking of which, why don't you do that?" John didn't care what the reason was. He didn't need an audience for his first real case as a sheriff. Dan looked about as happy about all this as Bolton. John headed over to him. "Any way I can get some floodlights or such to light this place? It's pretty dark to work."

The farmer tore his eyes from the body. "I'll rouse Shelby and Aaron. See if the theater company has stage lights we can use."

"Thanks." He turned to Bolton and handed him a notebook and pen. "I want a list of their names and then a record of everyone who comes and goes. Then get them to go home." John motioned to the two who'd found the dead woman. "They don't leave."

"Right you are, boss." There was humor in Bolton's eyes.

John didn't think this was a man anyone had ever ordered to do anything, but now wasn't the time to mince words. Not when he was likely looking at a murder investigation in a close community of people fiercely protective of their privacy.

"You think its murder?"

"Not for sure until we get her turned and figure out what happened." John nodded. "But it could—"

A golf cart turned the corner travelling fast, followed by another immediately behind it. The doctor and his wife hopped off the first, the mayor from the second. The ranch hand who fetched the doctor jumped from his perch on the back of the mayor's cart and jogged over behind them. He opened his mouth, but the mayor started yelling.

"Betty!"

He started to run to the body but John grabbed him. The older man fell to his knees.

"Betty!"

Chapter 7

Harriet Fenton hung back with the mayor, looking shell-shocked at the death of her friend. Was it really Betty Collins lying there? John and the doctor went to the body. "So you're the medical examiner as well as the town's doctor."

The doctor nodded; his face somber. "I have authorization to perform the duties of coroner, medical examiner and town doctor. Complicated surgery has to be done at the air force hospital. I can stabilize trauma and they'll be airlifted out. We have a trained midwife, but I perform C-sections and I sign death certificates for everyone in town."

"Well, I appreciate you doing this. Especially given Mrs. Collins is a friend of yours." He gave the man a second and then said, "Are you going to be okay?"

The doctor stopped and faced him. "There's no one else in this town who even comes close to having the skills or the grace to deal with this."

"Very well."

They kept walking.

Dan had shown up with stage lights just after the mayor's outburst and set them up to illuminate the body and the surrounding area. John watched the ground as he walked, looking for anything that might be helpful. Either of them stepping on something in their paper booties wasn't going to be helpful. Never mind John had absolutely no clue how he was supposed to run the tests that should be run on whatever evidence he collected.

It was as good as being a wild west sheriff before there was any technology to test blood or collected materials, or even finger print analysis done with more than the human eye and a magnifying glass. How many of the old marshals from years ago wound up getting a wrong idea and sentencing an innocent man to death? John was going to have to be very careful, even given the fact he was impartial compared with the rest of the residents of this town. It would be easy to be swayed by the force of their opinion.

He glanced over at the huddled crowd growing larger by the minute. Who knew what secrets they protected? They didn't even seem to comprehend Betty could just as easily have been murdered, assuming instead it had been an accident.

John drew his sketch. He took pictures from all angles and then they turned her. The dead body was Betty Collins. He took more pictures, concentrating on the blood stained front of her shirt, while the doctor closed her eyes with the fingers of his gloves. John took more pictures of the area. There didn't appear to be anything here—just dirty concrete and the body. No murder weapon, despite the blood on her torso. It was just the rear of a building; street, walls and a collection of trash cans that would have to be sorted through. His nose couldn't tell if the raw smell was the scene or the garbage.

John glanced back at the mayor. Harriet Fenton clutched his arm as though trying to hold him up lest he dissolve into grief. Her face was perfectly set in a painful grimace so pronounced he could see it even from this distance.

John stepped back from the body and let the doctor get to work. Killing always turned his stomach, more than natural passing. It was like all the emotion spent at the time of death—from both the killer and the victim—was imprinted on what was left. What lay there was a shell which used to be a person, one who had been loved and full of life.

John walked up and down, scanning the road. When he passed the doctor, he said, "What can you tell me about her?"

The doctor kept his eyes on his task but spoke in a low voice that matched John's question. "Betty is the welcome coordinator, which you probably know. She's met everyone in town. Generally happy. Liked. She hangs out with my wife, Harriet." His eyes flicked aside to where she stood with the mayor. There was something there that looked a lot like disapproval. "Although apparently not as much as I'd previously thought. But that's women for you. Smiling sweetly, and when your back is turned they're off giving it to someone else."

John didn't nod, even despite the suspicions he'd had regarding his own marriage. The truth hadn't been necessary, not when what he had known was bad enough.

Doctor Fenton sighed. "We get a new resident maybe once every eighteen months, so Betty wasn't all that busy. Although she does like to stick her nose in social stuff and organize the crap out of things which didn't need overcomplicating in the first place."

"Anyone obvious you think might dislike her?"

"Just the usual tension with some people who don't like how she does things. But we try not to ruffle each other's feathers if you know what I mean. We all have to live here. But enough to murder her?" He shrugged.

"I have to interview the boys who found her, so I'll leave you to it."

The doctor gently pulled what looked like a meat thermometer out of Betty's stomach and made a notation on his clipboard. "Sounds good."

John went back to Bolton. "Any word on Palmer yet?"

"My guy isn't back." He motioned to the body with his chin. "What's the verdict?"

"That would require a trial."

Bolton huffed. "You know what I mean."

Maybe the guy wasn't former law enforcement. "I'm only at the beginning of my investigation. As soon as I have any answers I'm sure it will be all over town before you can say, 'damage control.'"

John strode to the two men who'd found the body. "Masks off boys. Tell me your names."

"I'm Sam. This is Bill." They were both spindly. Their revealed faces were dotted with acne and the smeared remnants of their team letter.

John indicated Bill with his finger. "Stay here while I talk with Sam."

The kid nodded, relieved. John walked with Sam until they were several feet away. "Talk me through what happened, how you found the body."

"We just came around the corner and there she was." He sucked in a breath. "We'd been around this way twenty minutes before and nothing. This time, there she was. Just lying there. You don't see stuff like that outside of the movies."

"Did you see anyone else in the area?"

"I dunno. It was dark."

John gave him a minute. "But?"

"Maybe I saw something."

"Care to share?"

"It might've been a woman. I'm not sure." He sniffed. "Small enough to be a girl. But she was in all black and her hair was in a cap or something or short, because it wasn't long that I could see."

John made a note in his book. "What was she doing?"

"Running."

He glanced up. "Where were you and where was she?"

"Over there." The kid pointed to the corner at the end of the street behind John. "She was up there but she ducked between Elmer's—that's the hardware store—and the mayor's office. She was bookin' it."

"In a hurry?"

"That's what I said."

"Did you touch the body at all or move anything?"

"Eew. No way!" The kid paled. "I just told Bill to stay here and I ran to the command center."

"Okay. If you think of anything else, you know where to find me."

The kid nodded and then scurried off up the street, leaving John to speak with Bill. Something made them seem younger and John feel old. Technically he was old enough to be their father. But only if you fudged the numbers a little.

When he was done with the second interview, the mayor rushed over. "Enough of this standing around. My wife is lying over there and what are you doing? Moseying around like the new sheriff in town and chatting."

"Mr. Collins, I'm very sorry for your loss." John paused. "This is not a process you want to rush. Investigating takes time. If you want answers to what happened to your wife, then I need you to let me do a thorough job, not a half-baked attempt that doesn't get to the bottom of it." He let that sink in. "I'm going to need you to walk me through your itinerary for the evening."

His mouth gaped. "I'm not some kind of criminal."

"I need to establish a timeline of your wife's whereabouts for this evening. When was the last time you saw her?"

"At dinner. I didn't stay long." He sucked in a choppy breath. "I was in my library by eight. I'm working on a proposal I'm establishing for town expansion as well as a way to generate revenue that will mean we'll be able to rely less on outside supplies."

John spoke, just to get the mayor to stop talking about his expansion project. "Did anyone come over, or did your wife go out at all? Did any calls come in?"

"I was on the phone between eight forty-five and nine oh-five." The way he said it indicated he wasn't going to share the subject of the call, or who in town it was with. At least not without a considerable amount of pressure. "I don't know what my wife was doing."

"Is there anyone who might've wanted to harm your wife?"

"What? No. Betty was loved."

Right. "This might be my second day here but I understand the responsibilities of this job. I'm going to find out what happened to your wife and if this truly was a murder, then the person who committed this crime will be brought to justice."

Beyond the mayor, Harriet stood with a balled up tissue pressed to her face. Her eyes were wide and she looked like she wanted to say something.

The doctor waved to get his attention. "Sheriff?"

He would have to find time to talk with her later.

John thanked the mayor and jogged back to where the doctor crouched beside Mrs. Collins. "Yes?"

Deputy Palmer sprinted up to them, red faced and breathing heavy like he'd run all the way across town. "Good-ness. Was this a hit and run? Who did it?"

"That's what we're going to find out."

Palmer swallowed, his eyes on the body. "I don't have to touch her, do I?"

John glanced down. The man's shirt was misaligned, buttoned in a hurry, and his hair was ruffled. "Why don't you go to the office and get us some coffee?"

"Right." Palmer blinked and looked at John, his face balmy. "Was it a hit and run?"

"Since she was stabbed six times, I'm going with no." Doctor Fenton turned to John. "And she's been dead less than an hour."

John looked at his watch. 10:30.p.m. That meant she was killed shortly after John saw the flag taken.

"No-o," Palmer sputtered. "She wasn't murdered."

John eyed him. "And you know this because..."

"There's no murder in Sanctuary."

"Since when?"

Palmer blinked. "No, I mean ever. Not once in the history of this town has there been a...*murder.*" His head shifted side to side fast enough John got dizzy just watching.

"Calm down, Deputy."

"Do marshals investigate...this type of thing?" Palmer motioned to the body. "Have you even done this before?"

"I've been involved with several, just never took the lead."

"I don't even...I can't..."

John crouched. The wounds were all located in the victim's abdomen. Palmer shifted behind him and wretched. John lifted his eyes to the heavens and beseeched whoever was up there that Palmer hadn't just destroyed perfectly good evidence.

It was going to be a long night.

**

Hours later, John hauled the duffel bag of evidence collecting equipment into the sheriff's office. An elderly man whose skin closely resembled a mummy sat in John's chair, arms folded across his chest. He might have been dead, except for the drool running from the corner of his white, handlebar moustache. The superior court justice looked smaller in real life, swallowed up by John's predecessor's chair. He still looked like a mouse, just an elderly one.

John locked the evidence in the safe, piling the paper bags and containers on the shelf above the guns he'd decided to store there. He had no idea where Palmer kept his. The coffee pot was half full but cold, so he nuked some in his kitchen. Matthias popped up on the couch but John waved him back down and he was snoring again within seconds.

John sat in Palmer's chair and got the initial paperwork done on his tablet. He emailed his brother a preliminary report that would be fun breakfast reading for him. Then he shook the old man awake.

"Ha...what?" The old man smacked his lips and blinked up at John. "The new sheriff, I presume."

"Yeah and you're in my chair." The old man's laughter sounded like a monkey screeching. John turned away to hide his grimace, dragged Palmer's chair over and sat facing him. "John Mason."

"Justice Anthony Simmons." The old man's gray bush eyebrows twitched. "Any relation of Grant Mason?"

"The director of the marshals is my brother." John linked his fingers on his stomach.

"Director Mason allowed me to maintain my authority, but only within city limits. I have the power to grant a warrant for arrest, contingent on the requisite evidence being in place. Among a few minor things, such as my vote on the city council, that is the bulk of the reach of my position here. With the exception of being able to perform weddings."

Simmons continued, "We do not hold hearings in town. You make the arrest and they're detained here, under guard, until they can be taken out of town in the custody of the marshals. They are then transferred to Boise where they will be remanded without bail until their hearing—that's part of the agreement each of us made. If the outcome of the hearing is a conviction, they are given a new WITSEC identity and serve their sentence in the federal prison of the director's choice. If they're acquitted, they come home or they can get transferred somewhere else. Depends on the circumstances."

John's brain spun. Since it was almost four in the morning he settled on the last thing that crossed his mind. "How do you do it?"

"Do what?"

"Live this life. Give up what you had for...this?"

The old man shifted in his chair. "All that power and position exchanged for what essentially amounts to impotence?" He huffed but there was no humor there. "I'm an old man, Sheriff. I'd achieved the highest position I could. You could say it was stolen from me but then there would be little left for me except bitterness. In this life, in this town, I have my wife, my granddaughter and my great granddaughter here. I see my family every day, all of them. We live a quiet life, closer than we ever would in Washington D.C. with cell phones and busy lives.

"If my great granddaughter grows up and wants to leave, go to college, that is her choice. I'll likely be dead by then, so I doubt I will care overly much." He grinned, a face-full of dentures.

John smiled. "No, I don't suppose you will."

"You have your boy with you?" He glanced around like it was brunch and they were having coffee, not the middle of the night. "I thought I heard that."

"You did. Patrick, he's eight. It's been a while since we saw each other. My last undercover assignment ran long, but I'm hoping we can build a life here. If we decide Sanctuary is where we want to live."

"Some of the locals call it death valley." The old man's wrinkled face shifted with the force of his expression. "Why not? We all come here to die."

He shifted and stood, rising to a full five feet in his shoes. "Well, the wife would be mad if I was remiss in telling you she wants you and Pat over for dinner some time. She'll try and set you up with our granddaughter Cassie, since she feels Gracie needs a father figure in her life. Like I'm chopped liver or something. Anyway, I'll expect to see you at dinner soon."

"Yes, sir." What else did you say when it was a Supreme Court Justice asking? "Soon as the case is wrapped up I'll be sure to take you up on the offer. I'm not much of a cook."

The old man's eyes narrowed. "My Cassie makes a delicious meatloaf."

"I'm sure she does, sir. I'll look forward to it." John opened the door for him.

"Thank you for calling for me." The old man grinned. "This is the most excitement I've had in months."

"Happy to oblige."

He disappeared, the monkey screech laugh echoing in his wake.

Palmer stuck his head in the back door. "Is he gone?" He glanced around, strode in and blew out a breath. "Phew, I though the old man would never leave."

"Is there a problem between you and Justice Simmons?"

Palmer shook his head. "He's hardly anything special anymore. Just an old man wishing for the good old days."

Yeah, that was exactly what John had gotten from him. He nearly rolled his eyes. "Where have you been anyway?"

Palmer took his coat off. "What are you, my mother?"

No, but I am your boss. John sat at his desk and gathered his papers. "Did you find the murder weapon?"

"No, and now I smell like trash since I had to search through every single bag."

"You know, in some places that job would be a rite of passage for a cop." John grinned, not the slightest bit remorseful. "You can take a shower later. Right now we have work to do."

"It won't keep until tomorrow?"

"Welcome to real police work. It doesn't respect the boundaries of the nine-to-five existence you've been living." John sighed. "Look, it's late. I'm tired, you're tired. Why not just write up what needs writing up and then head home. I'll work figuring out what needs doing with the evidence."

"What evidence?"

John counted to ten. *It's not his fault he's never done this before.* "I'm waiting for her clothes. That will be huge, if we can get DNA from the killer. A drop of blood or a hair sample isn't all that likely but it could give us his or her identity. We have her shoes. Once we find the murder weapon, we can check that for prints. We also need to find the location the murder took place. Since there was no blood on the wall and little blood had pooled around her, it's reasonable to surmise that wasn't where she was killed. In a town this size, we should be able to do that by process of elimination assuming she wasn't killed in someone's home. We can't just go barging in."

"Actually, we can. It's a stipulation of our positions and the fact residents are in the witness protection program, even the people born here. In the event of extenuating circumstances we can force entry."

"Did Sheriff Chandler ever have to do that?"

"Just once. That was when the Fuller kid committed suicide. I was in junior high but I heard all about it."

"What was he like? I mean, what kind of a sheriff was Chandler?"

Deputy Palmer leaned back in his chair. "He wasn't bad. Gruff sometimes, but his leg bothered him in the winter. He'd been here since the town opened, like I said. I don't know how he got the assignment or if he was in WITSEC too. He never told me. Anyway, Chandler made me learn all the rules and put me through all these tests and stuff he said I had to do, so I could become a deputy, you know? It wasn't all that fun, but I wanted this job so I did it."

"You should be proud. You've held the fort down since he got sick, right?"

The guy nodded. John wasn't convinced Palmer was even a halfway decent cop, except in a town like this where nothing much happened. But he'd still worn the uniform through the previous sheriff getting a terminal diagnosis. He might not be the biggest proponent for something like Battle Night, which John had actually thought was fun. But Chandler had clearly seen something worth something in the kid.

For the time being, John was willing to coach him along. These were evidently unprecedented circumstances if there'd never been a murder in Sanctuary's history. It was so far from John's experience of the world that a crime level this low was almost unreal. It would take some getting used to, for sure. In fact, this whole town was like a foreign country.

John's satellite phone rang.

"Sheriff—"

"A homicide? What are you doing to my town?"

"Grant—"

"No, I don't want to hear your excuses. Fix this, John. These people are supposed to feel safe. I promised them that."

John leaned back in his chair and grinned. "Did you give me this job so you can yell at the sheriff of Sanctuary without remorse because I'm your kid brother?"

"No, I gave you this job because Alphonz made bail. He lasted three seconds before he was blown up on the front step of the courthouse in Montgomery." Grant huffed. "Alabama, for goodness sake. No one was even supposed to know he was there. Now I wake up to murder in my town."

John pressed his lips together. "Were you going to tell me that, or just mention it in my Christmas card?"

"John—"

"Have you ever actually been here?"

"That's not the point."

John swallowed the laughter. "Dude, calm down or you'll need an aspirin. I can handle this if you can get my evidence tested for DNA."

"Get it on Monday's transport. Mark it up with the orange stickers in your safe. I'll get it sent to a lab. But the likelihood is it's gonna take weeks, at least. No one's gonna take a rush job, even if it is from me. Labs are way too territorial. They always give preference to the local guys they know and they're always backlogged."

"So I have to solve this myself."

"The old fashioned way." Grant said it like it was a terrible affliction.

The bell over the door jangled and Harriet Fenton pushed her way in.

"Gotta go." John hung up.

Her face was all blotched and puffy. John held back the grimace and stood. "How can I help you, Mrs. Fenton?"

She stood straight and lifted her chin. "I know who killed Betty."

Chapter 8

John managed four hours in bed but he barely slept. Harriet's declaration had left him sleepless.

Andra Caleri killed her.

When he got up, the words were still ringing in his head along with all the questions. Matthias had left him a note explaining what time church started, so John walked over to the Meeting House.

The air outside was clean and the sky a clear blue that made him wish he'd unearthed his sunglasses even though it was fall. Inside, folding chairs had been set out in rows. At the front of the room there was a podium and a guy tuning a guitar—the farmer, Dan Walden.

John searched the gathered crowd for Pat and found him with Olympia's family, one hand grasping Matthias's sleeve.

"Dad!" Pat ran for him and John crouched, receiving the now familiar tackle of a long absence.

John waited until Pat looked at him. "How'd you sleep?"

"Dad, Reuben has a Wii. He said I can come over and play whenever I want!"

Matthias strode over, hauling a boy on each of his shoulders. They were younger than Pat, four or five maybe. Twins, their features were similar but not identical. Both of them had dark hair, light blue eyes and a lighter skin tone than the bulk of Olympia's family had.

"This is Reuben and Simeon. They're twin hooligans who'll probably completely corrupt Pat's sweet nature and turn him into a troublemaker." Matthias laughed and the boys joined in but not because they got the joke. He swung them around, making the boys squeal.

"Thanks for the tip."

Matthias looked like he wanted to say more, but made his way back to the rest of his family instead.

"Want to sit with us, Dad?"

"Sure." John let Pat pull him all the way to the front of the room, where Olympia's family took up a whole row on the right side.

Father Wilson stepped up to the podium in his minister's shirt and collar. Black pants and dirty sneakers completed his outfit. "Welcome." He smiled wide, his attention settling on John for a moment since he was likely the only person everyone didn't know.

John nodded but his head was too full of what had happened to concentrate on announcements.

Andra killed her.

How Harriet had been so certain, John wasn't clear on. When he'd asked her about it, she'd just said, "She hated Betty." As though dislike was a good enough reason to stab someone six times. It wasn't outside the realm of possibility, but Andra did not seem like the type.

They stood to sing. John didn't know any of the songs and they weren't the hymns he'd heard as a kid. He'd have to see where the evidence led; interview anyone who might have been around at the time other than the two young guys who found Betty's body.

Palmer had been adamant Harriet wouldn't lie and they should go rouse Andra out of bed. The deputy was a little too exuberant—probably because he'd only wanted to finish the investigation and get home to bed. Like you could solve a homicide in four hours.

John figured he'd likely spend the bulk of the month he was in Sanctuary occupied with this case. Hopefully it would be solvable but without the knife and with him having no access to testing equipment, that wasn't looking good.

They sat and Father Wilson spoke. His gravelly voice smoothed out until the words sounded like poetry; praising God even when he was surrounded by the enemy. John had never felt the need to appeal to a higher power when he was in the thick of something—like being tied to that chair awaiting Alphonz. The idea was interesting, even if it wasn't something he'd tend to do. Who wanted to admit they were helpless?

They stood again, while Father Wilson prayed and then dismissed everyone for coffee and treats.

Pat yelled, "Awesome!" The crowd rippled with laughter as they stood and dissipated.

John's attention caught on the back of the room. Andra sat by herself in the back row. He knew the minute she saw him because she got up and left.

John turned to Pat. "Go with Matthias. I'll be back in a minute." He rushed out, but she was two buildings down already. He ran and was about to call out when she spun around. John pulled up. "Not staying for treats?"

She didn't cower or respond. She just lifted her chin. "I didn't expect you to be at church. I imagine you had a long night."

"You heard about Betty Collins?"

Andra's face didn't give away anything. "Word spreads. Even to my corner of town."

"Anything you'd like to tell me about that?"

"About my corner of town?"

John shook his head. "No, about Mrs. Collins."

"Why would I have anything to say? She stayed away from me and I returned the favor. I spoke to her the first day I arrived, ten years ago next month. We've never had a single conversation since. But there are a lot of people I never speak to. I don't come into town much."

"And yet I've seen you three times in as many days."

Her lips twitched. "Extenuating circumstances."

"So that was you, last night in the barn? Team C?"

"I'm sure I have no idea what you're talking about." But her eyes said different.

"It would be better if you just told me. That way I can account for your whereabouts for at least part of last night. And if you told me where you went after the barn and whether you met up with anyone else, I'll be able to get started working out who was where while the homicide took place."

"So I'm a suspect?" Something flashed in her eyes. It could have been guilt, but there was so much genuine surprise he couldn't be sure. Was it surprise he'd spoken with her so quickly, or surprise that he'd think it in the first place?

"If there's someone who can confirm where you were and what you were doing between nine-thirty and ten-thirty, I'll need to speak with them."

She frowned. "I didn't see anyone else after the barn. When I got to the rendezvous point for team C—which was actually just myself and Nadia Marie—she wasn't there. She didn't show up until a while after."

"I need to know where Nadia Marie lives so I can talk with her."

"Am I seriously a suspect?" Andra's attention drifted behind him.

John turned to see people exiting the Meeting House. Most had on jeans, and more than a few folks wore working clothes. Bikers. Families. None of them were dressed up. Apparently not feeling the need to impress—which had seemed to him as a kid more important than what was being learned at church. It hadn't mattered if John was listening or not, just that he was quiet. It didn't mean these people were more or less earnest in their beliefs, just that they didn't feel the need to put on airs.

"So? Am I?"

John looked at her face. What her molasses eyes hid wasn't discernible. But she didn't disguise the fact she was hiding something. It was obvious just looking at her. Andra wouldn't be the kind of person who gave easily. Whatever experience she'd had in the past meant she'd withdrawn from people. Whether it was for her sake or theirs, was a different question.

"I can't comment on an ongoing investigation." The words came out with little thought.

So much of what he knew about investigating was ingrained in him, but was it the real him? John didn't even know, outside of wearing a badge, what kind of a person he was. He'd lived and breathed cases and operations for so long he needed time to just be…himself. Too bad he wasn't likely to get that conducting a murder investigation.

"Where is your place?" He grinned. "You know, in case I have any follow up questions." She was a mystery. But he fully intended to solve it.

"You don't find me. I'll come to you."

"And you'll know when I need to speak to you?"

She backed up a step, slipping from the grasp of his attention. "Just mention it in town. It'll get around."

Right. "I don't play things that way."

"Too bad." She smiled. "Because they're my rules."

John shook his head as she walked away, but he was smiling.

Nothing about this was going to be easy but for the first time he felt the rush of a challenge that didn't require him to forfeit his life in the process. There were a handful of reasons why staying might prove more interesting. At least more interesting than leaving town at the end of the month and turning down the job. Andra was, without doubt, one of those interesting reasons.

"Dad!" Pat ran over.

John swung him up before the tackle and settled his son on his hip. "What's up bud?"

"Um..."

John walked back inside the Meeting House, where Olympia stood in the center of her family. She spread her arms wide. "What'll it be?"

"They want to know if we'll come for lunch!" Pat's eyes were wide, like he'd been offered a trip to Disneyland. The kid clearly didn't know what genuine cause for excitement was. Too bad John couldn't take him out of town for a weekend. Not for a while at least.

Olympia nodded, so John rubbed his stomach. "Lunch? I don't know. I was planning a feast of frog's legs and monkey poop."

"Eew!" Reuben and Simeon joined in with Pat and then dropped to roll on the floor, pretending to throw up.

"Real food for lunch sounds great."

They turned for the door as a group when the mayor flung it open, nearly hitting one of the boys. His face was flushed, like he'd run all the way there.

John set Pat down. "Let's go somewhere and talk."

"I don't need to talk. I want to know why my wife's—" He swallowed. "—body, has been locked away. I can't even see her!"

John took his elbow and led him to the side but the mayor shook off his grip. "I want to see my wife."

"I understand. But it's necessary for Doctor Fenton to make sure that where she is, her body is safe."

She had to be locked up, since there wasn't the personnel to provide security. The "morgue", such as it was, was located in the windowless basement of the medical center which had been designed for precisely that purpose. Doctor Fenton had secured the body behind a locked door but provided John with a copy of the new code.

"I can take you to see her, if that's what you wish."

The mayor sucked in a shaky breath, his red face contrasting the white of his hair and his usually pressed appearance was wrinkled like he'd slept in his suit. One of his shoes was untied. "I want to know when you're going to bring the killer in. I want to know when Andra Caleri will be arrested."

**

Andra took a step back. Anger rolled from the mayor in waves all the way across the room to the kitchen door.

Stupid. Why had she doubled back just for some of the cilantro Olympia grew on the Meeting House's kitchen window? Didn't she know by now she was better off up the mountain where no one came by?

The mayor's eyes narrowed and he launched at her. "You!"

She braced. There were at least eight people between them. The force of his emotion was so strong she stiffened anyway.

"You did this! You killed her!"

John grabbed him. "Easy."

The mayor fought against his hold. "I want her arrested! She killed my wife!"

John looked at her but Andra couldn't move. She hated that she couldn't move. Someone touched her sleeve and she flinched. Olympia. Andra wanted to grasp the woman back, but she'd never initiated physical contact and Olympia seemed to understand the distance was something Andra needed.

The mayor was still yelling. Olympia held out a hand toward the kitchen. "Let's step in there."

Andra followed her. The metal counters were clear and the room was quiet. On the rare occasions Andra came down for meetings, the kitchen was usually a bustle of noise since offering food inevitably drew more people in. It was an effective tactic.

"Are you okay?"

The Spanish language Olympia spoke was both a source of comfort and of pain. Andra pushed that aside along with everything else. Olympia didn't know better. After all, Andra was the one who'd initiated their conversations in the first place. "Sí."

"I think not." She gifted Andra with a warm smile. "I think you like to pretend you're strong but you do not have to do that with me. A broken heart knows a broken heart."

Andra folded her arms. *Defensive.* She unfolded them and stuck her hands in her back pockets. "Who says I have a broken heart?"

The older woman chuckled.

"I only came back because I forgot to ask for cilantro."

"Of course." Olympia moved to the window above the sink and returned with the herb in a small pot. "This is for you."

"No, that's not necessary. I only need a small amount." Andra tried to give it back but Olympia wouldn't accept.

"My gift to you, since you won't come to lunch."

Andra relented. "Gracias."

Olympia nodded a queen in an apron, bestowing riches on the populace with a grace that just wasn't found anymore. "The mayor is crazy in his grief."

"I know."

"He did not mean what he said. Lies may soothe his pain now but they will not heal his heart. Only the truth can do that."

Andra of all people knew truth was the only thing that let you move on. Especially when it wasn't just a heart that was broken, but an entire life.

Olympia gave her a measured stare. "You know who said this, don't you?"

"Yes." Andra clenched her hands into fists. "I do."

"The sheriff will find the truth and Harriet Fenton will be exposed for the liar she is."

Andra shook her head. "I know that's the best thing. I do. But—"

"No one believes you did it."

Which just showed exactly how badly she had them all fooled.

"Listen to me. Anger is a tempest. You surrender to it and there is no control. Innocents always get caught up in the damage." She sighed. "If you came to town more, maybe joined in—"

"No." Except she had. Even if Battle Night hadn't turned as planned, it had still been a great idea. They would just have to wait until next time to figure out what happened. "Nothing good ever comes of it."

"What about the sheriff?" Olympia's lips twitched. "I've seen him looking at you."

"Don't." Andra sniffed. "He has a son."

"And boys need a mother."

"That might be getting a little too far ahead of things, since I only met the man yesterday."

"So you see a future then?"

"Olympia." Andra sighed. "I have no future."

Only days and days and more days stretching out like a kind of prison sentence.

The older woman's smile fell. Andra's stomach churned, but it was better Olympia knew the extent of it now. She needed not to get her hopes up; even if she did keep telling Andra she needed to get out more. Meet a man.

"I'm sorry, child. I didn't know."

"It's for the best."

A throat cleared. The sheriff stood in the doorway, his eyes moving between Andra, who was still holding the potted herb, and Olympia.

Andra made for the back door and hit the safety bar. She didn't want to know what nice thing he was going to say to make her feel better. She needed to pretend he would turn out to be a jerk, instead of a nice guy who loved his son. Nothing good was ever going to come of it.

She made it to the end of Main Street and then headed left instead of right. Harriet Fenton's house was also half as big again as everyone else's, like the mayor's humble eyesore of an abode. Why those two couples alone in town needed the biggest, newest houses, was anyone's guess.

Andra knocked, but it was more like pounding. Lingering heat from her pace mixed with frustration in her blood to pump warmth through her body. Why couldn't they just leave her alone? She only wanted to live a quiet, solitary life and they all thought that was somehow wrong or that there was something wrong with her. And worst of all...it needed fixing.

Harriet pulled the door open and her smile died. Not who she'd been expecting.

"You're telling everyone I killed Betty Collins?"

Harriet sputtered but recovered fast. "Of course you did. Who else hated her as much as you? I could just tell, every time you looked at her, you were so jealous. Of everything about her!"

"Jealous?" Andra blinked. Was she crazy? "None of you ever bothered to learn the slightest thing about me. How could you possibly think I wanted to be anything like her?"

"Not like her, just...*her*. Her life, her job, her style, all of it! Admit it!"

This was unbelievable. Andra lifted her hands and then dropped them. *Shoot.* She needed to not lose the cilantro. "Why would I admit that? I'm not the crazy one. You are." She took a breath. "Look, I'm sorry your friend died. But that had nothing to do with me."

Harriet sneered. Her gaze flicked past Andra's shoulder and she screamed. Was the killer coming for her? Andra whipped around. John sprinted over, his jacket flapping to reveal the weapon under his arm.

Harriet shrieked. "She killed Betty. A-And now she's here to kill me, too!"

Andra flipped around. Harriet screamed again, like Andra was in the process of attacking her and then she stepped back. The woman was certifiable. Andra backed up more and John passed her. "Don't go anywhere."

He went straight to Harriet. "Mrs. Fenton, go in your home. I'll take care of this."

Harriet gripped his arm. "Thank you. Oh, thank you so much." Her voice even quivered. "I was afraid for my life, you know."

"Lock your door. Everything is fine."

Andra started walking.

"Hey." His footsteps caught up to her at a jog. "I said, don't go anywhere."

She didn't stop, forcing him to jog beside her.

"Maybe you should lay low. Try not to get folks all riled up." His eyes were sad, but he didn't look like a crazy person. Yet here he was, telling her to do what she'd been doing for the past decade up on her mountain. "I'll figure this whole mess out and then we'll see where we're at."

She rolled her eyes. "But not that I'll be in the clear."

"I can't comment on an open investigation."

She should probably count to ten. "So you do think I might have gone from the barn and side-tripped to kill a woman I don't like. A woman I can't say I've said two words to in ten years."

"I'm not ruling it out."

"This is unbelievable!"

"I'm not saying that's what happened, either. I can't. I have to be impartial, that's the whole point of coming from outside Sanctuary to be the sheriff. Look, if you're innocent then you have nothing to worry about."

Andra laughed. Even she wanted to wince at the sound. "You really haven't been in this town long, have you?"

He stopped. "Now what is that supposed to mean?"

She shook her head and walked away.

"Andra!"

"I'm going home."

Where else was there to go? Andra was going to do what she always did—retreat to her mountain. At least until the people of Sanctuary invaded her peace with more of their accusations. The minute Harriet had uttered those words it was only a matter of time before John arrested her. It didn't matter what evidence there was, her fate was set and their judgment would be swift.

Once the sheriff read her file it would be out. She wasn't going to kid herself that her past could be kept under wraps. There was no such thing as confidentiality, not in this town. Then everyone would know the person she had been and the things she'd done. No matter that it had all been in a life that seemed a million years ago.

But by the grace of God I am what I am and His grace toward me was not in vain. On the contrary, I worked harder than any of them, though it was not I but the grace of God that is with me.

And all of it would be for nothing.

Chapter 9

For years John's uniform had been a bullet-proof vest, a shotgun and a jacket with US MARSHALS on the back. Monday morning he pulled on the tan pants, shirt and the belt Grant had given him. The collar was stiff and the material felt like it needed a week's worth of wear before it would give enough he could sit down.

When he emerged from the bedroom, Pat looked up from his cereal. "Cool, Dad!"

John smiled. "Glad you like it."

Pat changed out of his pajamas into jeans with a hole in the knee and a blue t-shirt and they headed downstairs.

A dark shadow filled the glass of the front door. John waited a second while he booted up his computer. The guy didn't knock, so John strode over and unlocked it.

"Mail day. Special day." The young man's smile was infectious, his mouth a jumble of teeth. Stubble covered his jaw and his hair was a tangled mass shaved close on the sides. He looked barely twenty, though John couldn't be sure since the young man's gaze darted around the room and didn't stop long enough to focus on anyone.

The guy squeezed between the frame and where John held the door open. "Mail day."

"I'm Sheriff John Mason."

The young man shuffled to the rear of the room. "Aaron."

"Aaron what?" John shut the door.

"Aaron." He opened the closet and pulled out a rolling cart. "Mail day."

Pat kept his distance but said, "Are you the mailman?"

Aaron puffed out his chest. "Mailman."

"Awesome. Can I help?"

Aaron's head whipped around and he narrowed his eyes. John's body tensed, ready to get between them the minute Aaron made a move toward his son.

"Can't touch."

John moved closer and set his hand on Pat's shoulder. "You're in charge of the mail, Aaron?"

"Cataloguing, recording, delivering. Checks and balances. Ones and zeroes. All Aaron."

John motioned to Pat with his head and his son sat in the waiting area chairs. "I have some mail needs to go out today. Can you help me get it ready?"

Aaron yanked the file cabinet drawer open and pulled out a form, which he set on the desk in front of John. "Fill out all appropriate boxes, including your name and address and the recipient's. Contents must be printed, indicating which item is in which package. Envelopes must be clearly labeled. Prior authorization must be obtained for all mail containing matches, lighters aerosols or other hazardous materials, small arms ammunition battery-operated heat-producing equipment, wet spillable or non-spillable batteries, fuel cells, internal combustion or fuel cell engines, specimens in formaldehyde, liquid nitrogen or gas cylinders." He took a breath, not even looking at the paper which he was quoting verbatim.

"The transportation of weapons alcohol or body parts is strictly prohibited. All mail will be screened by authorized personnel and restricted items will be incinerated."

"Of course they will." John grinned. "Sounds like something the government came up with."

Aaron went on. "All mail must be catalogued with a registration number before it leaves Sanctuary and a record kept in the sheriff's office."

John took a look at the kid. "Tell me the record number of the last item Sheriff Chandler sent out."

Aaron didn't blink. "January fifth. Hand-written letter addressed to Elizabeth Chandler of Rhode Island. Registration number 0105-7552."

Thought so. John smiled at him. "Sounds like you're just the right man for the job."

Aaron puffed out his chest again. "Cataloguing, recording, delivering. Checks and balances. Ones and zeroes. All Aaron."

"All Aaron."

John got a smile out of the guy. He pulled the evidence bags from the safe and Aaron took a step back. John glanced between the young man and the paper bags containing Betty's bloody clothes and shoes. "Aaron, if I fill out the form will you make sure I did it right?"

Aaron pulled a spiral-bound notebook from the file cabinet and got a stubby pencil from his pocket. Two pieces of paper and a quarter fell to the floor. He bent and grasped them, shoving them back in. Aaron shuffled to the waiting area and sat right next to Pat, who was playing a game on his iPad. Aaron flipped the notebook open and started making notations while John filled out the form.

John understood the need for secrecy, but clearly someone in charge had decided putting every resident under permanent scrutiny was the way to achieve that. Other than the allowance each townsperson got for internet usage at the library, mail was their only form of contact with the outside world since their phones only dialed internally. John had heard several people—like Hal, who ran the radio station—sold their internet time to others since they didn't use it.

The door opened to a young woman holding a taped-up box. "Good morning."

Aaron scribbled on his paper.

"One package to go and I've got my form all filled out." The woman was beautiful and all curves. But young—probably mid-twenties, not much older than Aaron. She set the box down and handed Aaron the paper. He took it but didn't look at her.

John stood. "Sheriff John Mason."

She strode over with her hand out, her smile wide. "Francine Peters. Nice to meet you." Her blond hair was thick and fell past her shoulders, and her blue eyes eclipsed her face.

"I'm Pat."

She shook hands with him, too. "Frannie. I run the bakery on the west end of Main Street, two doors past the spa and salon. It's called Sweet Times. So if y'all need a cupcake later, you should come see me."

"Awesome!" Pat was clearly sold on the idea.

John laughed. "We might have to take you up on that."

She smiled. "You too, Aaron. I hope to see you later."

"Cataloguing, recording, delivering. Checks and balances. Ones and zeroes. All Aaron."

"Well, it can't take you all day. Can it? When your work is done you should come by for a break, okay?"

"Break okay." Aaron continued writing.

Francine shot John a smile. "Later, guys. Nice to meet you, Pat."

Aaron stood. "Mail pick-up."

Pat set his iPad aside. "There's a mailbox?"

"Main Street west and Main Street east."

Pat looked at John. "Can I go, Dad? Please."

"Sure bud. I'll see you in a bit. Hey, maybe Uncle Grant will send your bike today."

"That would be awesome!"

John watched them go. The sun was up and he'd had a good night's sleep where he wasn't woken up by Pat's shifting around every five seconds. So long as Andra continued to keep to herself while he found Betty's murderer, things would be fine. The clock ticked past eight forty-five. Where was Deputy Palmer?

The bell clanged and the door opened to admit a matron with a perm who dressed like a Sunday school teacher. And smiled like one too. "Good morning, good morning."

He'd seen her the day before at church but hadn't gotten a chance to introduce himself. "I take it you're Dotty."

Her eyes gleamed. "No doubt my reputation for being notorious has preceded me."

John laughed although she might not have been joking. He'd have to be careful with these people. Who knew what kind of person she'd been in her old life?

She grinned. "I'm Dotty Bennett...as in Elizabeth and Jane?"

"Uh, sure." He had no clue.

"Pride and Prejudice, dear." She settled at the tiny table in the corner and plugged headphones into the radio, keyed the mic and did a sound check. She came through loud and clear on John's radio. Then she pulled the stack of papers from her inbox and within a minute had her computer on and was typing so fast the click of the keys broke the sound barrier.

Time to work, then.

**

Pat looked up and down the street as they walked, turning in circles. He'd lived in D.C. his whole life. This place looked more like Main Street at Disneyland since all the buildings were mushed together.

Aaron didn't say much, but he was smiling. Pat thought it might be because he was there to help. They pushed the cart all the way to the mailbox at the end of the street where Aaron pulled a key from his pocket. The mail was mostly letters, but there were some big orangey-brown envelopes like he'd seen at his dad's house. Maybe some people here had gotten divorced, too.

That had to be weird when they lived in the same town still. Like two Christmases wasn't complicated enough.

Still, there wouldn't be two Christmases now. Not if they stayed here. But Pat didn't want to think about his mom if she wasn't even thinking about him. Would she know why he couldn't come and see her?

He missed his friends too, but he'd emailed Bobby. Too bad there were a bunch of rules about what he could and couldn't say about Sanctuary. It was pretty cool here and Bobby would be really jealous. Except Bobby's mom and dad were still married, so maybe he didn't have much to be jealous about.

When the mailbox was empty, Aaron said, "Main Street west!"

They walked all the way back, so Pat got to wave at his dad through the window and they did the same thing with the mailbox at that end. If Aaron had to catalog and record all this mail it was going to take forever.

They passed Sweet Times on the way back.

"Are Fannie's cupcakes good?"

"Double chocolate, fudge pieces. Sprinkles on top."

Pat's mouth watered. "Do you have a bike? I might get mine later, maybe we could bike ride."

"Cataloguing, recording, delivering. Break okay. Bike ride."

"How about cataloguing, recording, delivering. Lunch. Bike ride. Break okay."

"Okay." Aaron grinned.

He was an adult but he didn't talk like it. He sounded like Bobby after he got hit in the head by the ball from T-ball. The throwing up had been pretty bad, but Bobby got two weeks off school and he didn't have to do his homework.

Matthias's nephews were cool and all, but they were little kids. Pat figured he could be friends with Aaron. Maybe they played softball here. But football would be okay too; he liked playing catch with his dad. Sometimes Pat even pretended he was Uncle Nate.

"Good morning, Aaron." A nice lady smiled and then looked at Pat. "And who are you, young man?"

"Are you the teacher?"

She laughed. It was a nice sound. "As a matter of fact, I am. Mrs. Pepper."

"I'm Patrick Garrett Mason. I'm eight and I'm in third grade."

"Well, now. That's practically all grown up." She ruffled his hair. "My how tall you are." She glanced at Aaron and then back at Pat. "Looks like you're on important business. But it is Monday, Pat, so I'll expect you in school at three-thirty. I need to see where you're at. Your dad is busy with this...new case. So I doubt he needs you underfoot when he has work to do."

"Yeah because someone got—"

Her eyes went all big and she shook her head. Aaron was making a sort of whining noise, but with his mouth closed. "Three-thirty okay, Pat?"

"Yes, Mrs. Pepper."

"You and I are going to get along just fine." She strode away.

Pat glanced up at Aaron, who didn't look happy anymore. It was all Pat's fault. What was he supposed to do? What was it Aaron had said? "Checks and balances."

"Cataloguing, recording and delivering." Aaron burst forward, shoving the cart in front of him. "All Aaron."

Pat grinned and trotted after him.

Waiting while Aaron recorded all the mail in the notebook he called his "ledger" was pretty boring, but Pat went upstairs and made a stack of turkey and mayonnaise sandwiches. Dotty didn't want one. She had a salad and a white plastic fork. But everyone else had two sandwiches, except his dad who ate three and said they were the best sandwiches ever. He was probably lying—they didn't even have lettuce because Pat wasn't allowed to use a big knife to cut it—but Pat didn't care.

Then it was one o'clock and Pat heard the helicopter. The three of them loaded all the mail on the cart into the back of his dad's sheriff car and Pat got to ride up front.

"That helicopter is huge! It's even bigger than the one that brought us here." Pat couldn't stop staring at it. "My bike has *got* to be on there!"

Soldiers climbed out holding big guns, but Pat wasn't scared. "Awesome!"

His dad grinned. "Stay here for a second okay?" He glanced at the backseat. "Aaron, you with me?"

"All Aaron."

They climbed out and Pat watched them load the mail. What came off was one bulky bag probably full of more packages and letters...and Pat's bike. Soon enough they'd get to go have one of Frannie's cupcakes.

Aaron got back in the Jeep but his dad stayed by the helicopter. Pat saw Matthias driving the ranch truck with something in the back. He swallowed. It looked like one of those bags they put a dead person in on that TV show he wasn't supposed to watch. Was that Mrs. Collins?

Back at the sheriff's office Aaron had to enter all the incoming mail in his ledger. Pat got to read the numbers off each envelope, so they'd know they got every bit of it.

"This one's for Andra." Pat turned the white envelope over in his hands.

"Si, Senor."

Pat didn't get that, so he looked at his dad.

"Andra speaks Spanish."

"Like Matthias?"

His dad nodded. "And their whole family. I guess their dad was from Puerto Rico but Olympia is actually Greek."

Pat got to go with Aaron to deliver it all. They used a golf cart that said "Sanctuary Mail", but someone had written it in marker. Aaron drove all around town while Pat put the letters in people's mailboxes. Everyone waved and said hi to them. He'd even put his bike on the back, so everyone got to see that, too. His Grandma had given it to him for Christmas, even though she'd said it was from his dad. They didn't know his mom said he couldn't get a bike because his step-dad thought Pat was already outside too much and he should study more. But what did Stefan know about being a kid?

The golf cart jerked to the side, just past a huge house that didn't look like it belonged there. Aaron stopped at the base of a path which wound up between trees into the mountains. The trees wrapped around the whole town like a ring donut, stretching up so far he couldn't imagine going that high. Who lived up there?

Pat checked the bag. The last envelope was for Andra. "Ms. Andra lives up there?"

"Si, Senor."

**

Andra stirred the lemonade, though she didn't know for sure whether Aaron would have anything for her this week. It still felt nice to anticipate company, even if she wound up enjoying the drink on the rocker on her porch watching the sunset.

She set the pitcher in the ancient yellow refrigerator. The minute the door shut, the thing rumbled to life with the whirring sound it made when it was cooling. Eventually it was going to go caput, but for now she'd thank God every day it still worked. Heaven only knew how she'd get a new one all the way up here.

Andra crossed the wood planks of her kitchen and living room floor, both of which matched the color of the logs on the wall and the rafters bracing the roof up. From the front door to the rear wall of the bedroom and then the kitchen window to the fireplace, her home was precisely square and the size of a studio apartment.

Up here the only noise was the rustle of birds and the back and forth motion of tree branches when the wind blew. She'd lived in Barcelona for years, in London, Vienna and Moscow. Crowded, grimy places that liked to think they were great. But the constant press of people all trying to get whatever it was they wanted did not make her feel at home. Andra had left that life behind, getting out of the business she'd fallen into even after she was pressed into going legit. But all that was years ago.

This life was nothing like it; the analogy of being reborn wasn't lost on her. New creation and all that. It was true, but in the early hours when she woke up sweating and couldn't get back to sleep because of the crowd of faces in her head it was still hard to shake the past. She may have received all the mercy—for the price of her knowledge—that the government could grant, as well as the heights of mercy God chose to give her. But she still had to live with the memory of what she'd done.

Aaron stepped into the clearing along with Pat Mason. Andra opened the screen door she'd built out of wood scraps and tulle and installed herself, and smiled as they ambled over. "Hola."

Pat looked confused, so she said, "Hi, Pat."

His face lit up and he presented her with her letter. "We brought your mail!"

"I see that. You boys look thirsty. Lemonade?"

Aaron sat on the porch step, which she took as a yes. Andra poured two glasses and took them out to the boys. Well, Aaron was technically an adult, but there was nearly fifteen years between them so he seemed like a youth to her.

She waited for Aaron to take a sip, and then nod that he liked it before she said, "I'll go get my box."

More like a crate, it was full of things she grew behind her cabin. Corn, carrots and onions. Strawberries that were taking over the flowerbed and would have to be cut back soon. She got a lot of sun on her little hill, so she could plant three times a year and have as many harvests.

She'd coupled the cilantro from Olympia with tomatoes and made a batch of salsa. A jar was in the crate.

"It's a little heavy." She set it in front of Aaron. "I think you can manage. And Pat can help."

The boy smiled. Andra looked away.

"Check, no balance."

"That's right." She glanced at Pat then. "There's a family in town that isn't doing well. Their baby has been sick and the mom and dad are having a hard time."

"That happened to my mom and dad. Not the sick part. They got divorced and now my mom is in Boston with Stefan."

Okay, so that was more than Andra wanted to know about John's love life. But it did answer a few lingering questions about the new sheriff and his "single dad" status. Not that she needed to know.

"The crate is for them, to help them out."

"So we take it to them and they don't know where it came from?"

Andra nodded.

"Cool, like secret agents!"

Was there anything that didn't get this kid excited? There was so much life in him; too bad it cut her all the way through to the space where her heart was supposed to be. She didn't know if it was still there or not.

"So this is your house?"

She nodded. "This is home."

"It's like a cabin. That's cool. My dad took me camping once but it was freezing and it rained the whole time. We just played Uno and ate the marshmallows that we were going to use for s'mores."

"Sounds like you had fun anyway."

"Do you really speak Spanish?"

Andra said, "I certainly do," in the language she'd spoken from childhood all the way until she left the boarding school in Barcelona and got lost in the world.

Pat smiled. "Will you teach me?"

She switched back to English. "If you want."

Aaron picked up the crate. "All Aaron and Pat." His eyes settled beyond her, over her shoulder.

It was his way, and she'd never minded people who needed their world to be ordered and unchanging. She knew what it was like to suddenly find she was somewhere the rules made no sense. Even this life of peace that surpassed understanding probably made the least sense of all the versions of herself that she'd been. Metamorphosis. It was deep but she'd had plenty of time alone to think about it.

Boot-steps stomped up the hill and the man came into view as he trod across the grass to her cabin.

John. *Great.*

"Dad!" Pat hugged the sheriff around the hips. "We delivered the mail and Andra gave us lemonade."

Andra pressed her lips together while Aaron crossed the clearing to the sheriff.

"That's awesome, Pat. But don't you have an appointment at school?"

"Ah, man."

Aaron gripped the crate. "Checks, no balances. Break okay. School. All in good time."

It sounded like Aaron had it figured out.

John squeezed his son's shoulder. "You boys get going and keep an eye on the clock okay?" He watched them go and then strode to Andra's porch. The man was huge. At least a foot taller than her, with his hair shaved short on the sides and not much longer on top, revealing the square shape of his head. His shoulders were broad and his shirt and pants still had horizontal creases from being folded up in the packaging.

"I don't suppose you're here for lemonade?"

All trace of the pleasantness he showed his son was gone from his face. And why did that bother her? He thought she was a murderer.

"I don't put that much sugar in it but it's not poisoned."

John folded his arms. "I'll be speaking to Pat about coming to your cabin without checking with me first but that's not why I'm here. I knew they had mail for you."

Andra sat on her steps, pulled her knees up and stared at the trees. "My door is open. Feel free to check but I can tell you now none of the knives in my kitchen are missing."

"You see, here's the thing." He cocked his head to the side. "Now I'm wondering how you could possibly know Betty Collins was killed with a knife?"

Chapter 10

She didn't move. John stood still and watched for her to react. There was nothing about this woman that said, "Murderer." But then, some people were bad underneath that veneer of sweetness and light and it was hard to tell what was below the surface.

She held her gaze on the landscape. "Everyone was talking about it at church."

"You didn't have a conversation with anyone except me."

"I overheard at least two different sets of people talking about how they saw Betty Collins before her body was removed. I drew my own conclusions."

"The body is on the plane now. I sent it off this morning."

Andra stood and brushed off the seat of her jeans. The sun had gone behind the clouds, casting her into dim light that seemed to mute the world around them. She turned and ducked inside. Was he supposed to leave? He looked out at the trees surrounding her clearing. There was almost no noise up here. It was weird.

John grabbed the forgotten envelope from the porch step and followed her inside.

On the left two rustic armchairs faced a wood stove. Beside that was a crammed bookcase, against the wall. A stack of four books was on the floor beside one of the armchairs and none of the titles were in English.

The kitchen was to the right along with a small table and two chairs. In the center of the table sat a glass jar of dirt in which a plant with one big green leaf and not much else was growing. Beyond the living room was a single door he figured led to a bedroom and bathroom. In the far corner there was a fiddle on a stand beside a taller music stand with sheets of paper—music notes.

Andra pulled a container from the fridge and dumped the contents into a skillet on the stovetop. She pulled out a jar a tub of sour cream and a package of tortillas.

John set the envelope on the dining table. It was written to Andra Caleri with a USO address and the return address was Cartagena, España but didn't have a name. Andra strode over, swiped the envelope off the table and took it to the stove. She set it on the window ledge beside another tiny potted plant.

Guess that answers that question.

They couldn't talk about the case being as she was technically the lead suspect. And beyond her statement there wasn't much that could be said between them during the course of his investigation. Still, John wanted to know...her.

"So, what's with the Spanish thing?"

The ghost of a smile curled her lips. "I like it."

"I guess. I mean it's not just a method of communication, even if it's something you share with Olympia that creates a distance between you and everyone else. When you converse in Spanish you do it because you enjoy it as well as the privacy it gives you. It means something to you."

She shook her head, eyes on what looked like chicken that she stirred in the skillet. "How could you possibly know that?"

He glanced at the books. "Plus every book you have is written in Spanish."

"I dream in Spanish, too." Her voice was low, and he wasn't sure she meant to say that out loud. From the looks of it, her dreams probably weren't good.

She pulled out two plates and made up three burritos, which she brought to the table. Andra set the plate of two on his side and pulled out her chair.

Evidently, he was staying for lunch.

"How do you know I haven't eaten?"

"Have you?"

"No." He sat.

Her lips twitched and they ate. John could smell the dirt in the pot on the table and the burrito was a spicy blend of tomato and peppers. "This is delicious."

"I lived in Barcelona. I went to an all-girls Catholic boarding school where the nuns ruled with wooden rulers and the math problems made your eyes hurt."

He smiled.

"I left before the end of my final year, so technically I never graduated." She lifted her chin as though challenging him to think less of her.

"I'd guess your parents had something to say about that."

"I never really saw them but maybe three or four times after I was twelve. They travelled a lot. The Med. I think they had a place in New York." She stared at her plate. "After I left school I didn't see much of a reason to visit them. Not if they couldn't be bothered to see me."

"Do you know where they are now?"

She shrugged, neither confirming nor denying. "What's the point? It isn't like they want to know me."

He wanted to reach out but she was sitting back in her chair. He could offer his hand, but then there would be that awkward wait to see if she put hers in it.

"Where did you go after you left school?"

She lifted her gaze, her eyes dark with something he couldn't begin to decipher.

"I couldn't imagine being alone at that age."

"I wasn't."

"Why'd you leave?"

She didn't speak for a minute. "You really haven't read my file?"

John held her gaze. "I want to give everyone the benefit of the doubt. I'd planned to read all the files, but if I do that then I'm getting to know everyone through the lens of who they were and the things they've done. So maybe that wouldn't be fair."

"Everyone?"

"Eventually I'll probably look some people up, just to save time." He smiled. "It might be worth the benefit of the doubt in most cases. But I've been a little preoccupied, what with the dead body and all."

She froze.

"Sorry. I shouldn't have said that. But I did mean to do some research. Now I'll probably end up reading Betty Collins' file first."

Her brow flickered, like she questioned whose he would have read first had it not been for Betty Collins' death. The answer was hers, but she didn't need to know that. "Anything you want to tell me about her?"

She said nothing.

"Your relationship with her?"

Silence.

"Why someone would accuse you of Betty's murder?"

**

Andra pushed her plate away, her burrito half eaten. She'd shared more with John than anyone else since the U.S. attorney wanted to know what she knew—at least from her adult life. Why hadn't he checked her file?

At first she'd been sure he came to arrest her, waiting until the boys were gone so he didn't put her in handcuffs in front of his son. If he'd read her file he probably wouldn't even have made that consideration. She would already be in jail at the sheriff's office.

He was waiting for her to answer.

Andra should probably tell him. Instead, she settled for answering no more than the question he had asked. "No, I have no idea why Harriet would say that."

No one knew, because if they did they wouldn't leave her on her mountain, despite the stories of her running off visitors—which was ridiculous. It was only the one time and she'd been mostly nice to the skinny guy who bussed tables at the diner. She hadn't even threatened him.

"She mentioned an incident at the medical center. What happened there?"

"That was two years ago." Andra sighed. "She kept me waiting to see the doctor for two hours. I was mad."

"That's understandable, when you're sick and probably not feeling well."

"I'd broken my arm falling from one of the ridges up the hill. *Nurse* Harriet squeezed it, said she couldn't feel anything and sent me to sit down."

Andra took the plates to the sink. Why did she tell him that? Now he was going to think she was just telling him all this...her parents, her arm...just to make him feel sorry for her. He probably thought she let him stay so she could persuade him she was actually the victim in all this. Betty Collins might be dead, but some people would try to save their own skin. If they were guilty or if they figured—given their pasts—a jury of their peers would not be kind.

He moved from the edge of her vision until he was at the sink beside her. "I don't know what to say."

She didn't either. She wasn't any good at this. Her past proved that at least. Andra's life had been about dodging the law, while John brought justice. "La compasión triunfa en el juicio."

"What does that mean?"

She smiled to the sink. "Mercy triumphs over judgment."

"Since when?" He shifted and she turned to him. "That makes no sense. Judgment is the truth. It's the punishment appropriate to the crime. Mercy is only for the innocent. It can't beat out judgment, that wouldn't be right."

His face was incredulous.

It made her lips twitch. "The law man has spoken."

They were doomed.

"It just makes no sense, is all."

"I get that." She smiled and took a step back. "But sometimes mercy is a whole lot more powerful than judgment. Think about WITSEC. Judgment would be right. But sometimes granting mercy gains more than judgment ever could."

"That's a bargain."

"The best kind. Both sides win; both the one who grants mercy and the recipient."

John shook his head. "I get that. Mentally, I understand what you're talking about."

"Perhaps you have to receive it in order to fully understand the implications. It's not something I take lightly."

"You seem to have made peace with it."

"It's been a long time." She squeezed her fingers together in front of her. "Sometimes I think it's more that mercy has made peace with me. If I beat myself up about it, what good would that do? Accepting it releases me to move on."

"I'm glad."

John didn't seem like the kind of man who ever had to work through anything. He simply...was. Sure, there was likely some depth to him. Would he ever let her see it? And if he did, how could she resist wanting to know more?

He ran a hand through his hair, shifting so the light reflected off his badge. "I should get back to work. Thank you for your time."

She'd opened herself up and he was just going to say, "See ya?" Could she even ask for more, though? Likely not, when he was investigating a murder she may or may not have committed. Not considering when he was done, he would never speak to her again.

"One more thing."

Andra waited.

"What do you do for work?"

"Work?"

"Yes. Everyone in town has to earn a living." He glanced around. "Your lifestyle doesn't appear to require a significant amount of means, but you still probably work. I'm curious. Humor me."

Andra shrugged off the whole "trust fund" thing, since she got bored once in a while so she did actually have a job. Was she supposed to be offended her life didn't look like much of anything in the opinion of Sheriff John Mason? He didn't have to live up here. This was what she'd chosen, for her own reasons.

"I prepare taxes."

"For everyone in town?"

"Some of them at least. I'm busy from January to April, but the rest of the year I can kick back because I earned enough to sustain my insignificant lifestyle."

"Andra—"

"You're right. You should be getting back to work."

**

John leaned back in his chair and ran his hands down his face while the phone in the office rang. That hadn't gone well at all. Well, parts of it had been good. Like when Andra told him about her school and her family, and her accent had thickened. Despite the fact her parents essentially abandoned her, a smile still played on the edges of her lips when she spoke of them. Was there an old school friend she remembered? That could be who had written the letter to her.

He liked that idea more than thinking on the animosity Harriet and the mayor both had for her. Olympia and Andra appeared to have a close relationship, though he hadn't been able to understand what they were saying. The soft look on Andra's face that said she welcomed Olympia's mothering and the comfortable way they had with each other spoke loud enough.

The phone rang again, so he turned to Dotty. "Are you going to get that?"

One eyebrow rose. "That's your satellite phone. I'm not authorized."

John straightened in his seat. "Right. Sorry." She waved away his concern, and he pulled the satellite phone that was his radio off his belt. "Yeah, Mason."

There was a second of silence on the other end and then Grant huffed. "Nice to hear from you, too. I got your delivery."

"And the autopsy?"

"Should be completed within the week. Soon as I have the results, you'll be the first to know. I'll send you hard copies." Grant paused a beat. "Do you know how difficult it is to get the military to ignore a dead body? Let alone take my paperwork at face value without asking a million questions. Getting shot was more pleasurable than that experience."

John gritted his teeth. He had to let Grant get it out. There was no one else his brother could say something like that to. "I'm sure."

If he was base commander and the marshals wanted to transfer a body on his runway, they'd sure have to explain who it was and where it came from. Not to mention what they were doing with it.

Grant said, "How is the investigation coming?"

Palmer strode in a paper cup in one hand. John could have used a coffee.

"No solid suspects, nothing conclusive as far as evidence. No witnesses yet, just the two guys who found the body. I have more people to talk to but it's hard since I'm still learning how things are done around here."

The murder couldn't have come at a worse time. Well, for Betty Collins it probably would have been better if it hadn't happened at all. But John would've liked at least a week or so to get the rhythm of this place and the people who lived here. As it was, he was going on gut instinct trying to figure out who was honest and who was stringing him along.

He didn't like it. And if it put his son in danger then heads were going to roll. He didn't care the marshal's service had offered these people his protection.

"Murder weapon?"

John lowered the phone and looked at Palmer. "Do we have the murder weapon?"

The deputy shrugged and turned to his computer. "Nope."

Great. John's stomach clenched. "It hasn't been found, yet." The last word he tacked on more as a wish than anything else. It didn't matter how much he wanted it, that wasn't going to happen. Going out and scouring every inch of town would up the odds but they might still never get their hands on it.

"I want this wrapped up, Johnny." Grant had slipped into big brother mode. "The congressional committee is breathing down my neck about the amount of money the tests on this evidence is going to cost. I want to be able to report back that the killer has been found. Tell me you have an idea of who it was."

"You know I can't do that. I have nothing more than accusations and I won't have a witch hunt when there's no evidence to back it up. At least, nothing more than a grudge."

"Who is it? Who is the finger being pointed at?"

John squeezed his free hand into a fist. "Andra Caleri."

Palmer jerked. An interesting reaction but not one John could follow up on just that moment. Grant reacted also, his voice muffled but John heard a few choice words. "I don't believe that. Get to the bottom of this, Johnny."

"What don't I know?"

"Now I know you haven't read her file."

"I will." He would rather she told him.

Andra had steered clear of that part of her life at lunch but he needed her to be honest with him. Okay, more honest than she already had been. He wanted to rule her out and he needed her help to do that. There was no way she killed Betty Collins. He just couldn't see it, not with her beliefs dictating her actions now. Surely Christianity didn't advocate murder.

"You realize I barely know these people, right Grant?" If they'd been talking in person—and kids—they would have been rolling around on the floor punching each other by now. But that was a long time ago. They both had different ways to exorcize their frustrations now. "I need more than two days."

"Just read her file."

The bell over the door clanged. Two older ladies toddled in, spoke to Dotty and got waved to a seat.

John gripped the phone. "I'm going to figure this out. I get how important it is to you but don't worry. You didn't make a mistake in bringing me here, even if this is a trial period. I might not stay, but I will do my job."

"I know that. But you've been pretending for years now, undercover, playing the game, talking the talk. Are you sure you can do this? It's homicide."

Rolling his eyes wasn't going to look too professional. "I'm good. How are things with Genevieve?"

"Don't worry about my marriage, okay? Keep your head on task."

"Nate has a game tonight."

"I'll be watching."

They hung up.

John figured some kind of apology needed to be made, so he rounded his desk to Dotty's card table in the corner. He braced on hand on the desk and the other on the back of her chair and leaned in to speak quietly. "I'm sorry I was short. I should apologize for that." He smiled. "Just smack me upside the head next time, okay?"

Her eyebrow crept up again. "Perhaps."

"You're going to make me grovel aren't you?"

"Definitely." She laughed at her own humor. "These ladies are here to see you."

"Right." He straightened and smiled at the two older women in the waiting area. Clearly sisters, he couldn't tell which was older. "Of course."

A man opened the door. Suit. Forties maybe. He glanced at both ladies and frowned. "Mom, Auntie May, you were supposed to wait for me." He shot John a commiserating smile. "Sorry. They're not supposed to be in here bothering you when there are probably more important things you need to be doing."

The ladies looked at each other. One tutted and the other rolled her eyes as though both were perfectly accustomed to having him question their antics.

Someone else pushed in behind the man, a woman with a baby stroller and a toddler in tow. She was followed by another couple of men older than him.

John glanced at each of them and then let his attention settle on the ladies. "What can I help you with?"

They both stood. The one on the left spoke first. "We heard you have a suspect."

"We haven't slept since it happened."

"We're scared to go out after dark."

"We want to know when you're going to arrest the killer!"

People pressed in the door, which stuck open as more and more townspeople pushed their way in. Dotty's desk was surrounded. John stepped back. Palmer rounded his desk, hands raised. "Folks—"

They pushed him aside.

"What are you going to do about this, Sheriff?"

"Someone was murdered!"

"My children are having nightmares!"

"When are you going to arrest her?"

"Andra killed Betty! I want her out of town!"

"Yeah, get her out! She shouldn't be here."

John stepped on his chair and then climbed onto his desk. He stuck his fingers in his mouth and whistled. The sound pierced his ears, but they all shut up even if half of them were wincing and he made the baby cry.

"Listen up." He took a breath and then launched in. "This is a murder investigation. It's not about who thinks who did what. Coming in here and pressuring me to make an arrest with no evidence and no warrant does nothing but waste my time and yours. Let me do the job I came here for."

The crowd launched into a fresh round of shouting accusations.

"Quiet!"

They hushed.

John folded his arms. "If you wish to make a statement with regard to me as the new sheriff or my conduct or the marshals service in general, then Deputy Palmer will escort you to the Meeting House where you can sit down with him and have your say. I have a case to solve, so when you're all finally done and Palmer can join me in finding the murder weapon, then we'll do that. Unless you would care to use up more time yelling about us not making you safe when you're the ones stopping us from doing just that."

Palmer's face went from furious—apparently he hadn't liked the idea of taking thirty-five statements—to admiration. At least someone was on his side.

"Preach it."

John glanced over and Dotty winked.

"Does anyone want to make a statement?"

No one said anything.

"Thank you for stopping by. Please leave now."

Dotty cackled with laughter. Even Palmer chuckled as the crowd filed out.

John blew out a breath. "Are they always like that?"

Dotty thought for a minute. "Yes."

"Great."

"I think you handled them just fine, darlin'. If this was a democracy you'd have my vote. But, sadly, the powers that be installed you in this position and I had no say in it." She gave him a look. "Neither did those people. No one's ever been murdered here. This place is their sanctuary and all this probably brings up memories they'd rather forget. Too bad the past will always find you in Sanctuary."

John stood. "I'll try to be nicer next time."

"Oh, no, darlin'. You give it to 'em straight."

He laughed. "Come on, Palmer. Let's go find that murder weapon."

Chapter 11

John slumped into the booth across from Pat. The murder weapon was still nowhere to be found and the chances that they'd find a blood-stained knife lying around were growing smaller and smaller.

Then again, it could be anything; lots of things could make an inch wide deep cut that weren't necessarily knives. If it had been cleaned, John would have to rustle up some Luminol to test for blood. Did they even have any, or was he going to have to wait a week for another delivery? Then there was the question of whether it would actually have the killer's prints on it.

John didn't know how homicide detectives did it, considering they worked multiple cases at once.

Pat's face was hidden. John pulled down the plastic menu with his finger. "How was school?"

Pat's nose wrinkled. "She just made me do a bunch of worksheets and read a couple of chapters of this book about a magic tree. I did some math problems, and we talked for a while and she asked me about a whole bunch of stuff. She said she's going to get me set up with the computer. They do school first and then go to the library and work on the computers because the stuff they do is online. Then they're done after lunch." He shrugged his little shoulders. "It sounds okay."

"What time do you have to be there tomorrow?"

"Like, nine-fifteen or something."

Right. John would have to check on that. Still, "Nine-fifteen? When I was a kid we had to be at school at six-thirty and it was two miles away. We walked the whole the way. And in the winter there'd be snow and freezing rain."

Pat erupted into giggles. "You did not. Grandma told me you rode the bus."

"I can't get away with anything, Grandma always ruins it." John smiled. "This one time, Uncle Nate and Uncle Ben threw my backpack out the window and I had to get off the bus to get it. Then the bus drove away while I was standing there. They'd told the bus driver I was going home because I was sick. It was cold and I had to walk all the way to school. Uncle Grant got off and walked with me, though. He told the driver he was sick too. We got to school an hour late and we were frozen, but it was fun. We played a prank on Uncle Ben and Uncle Nate to get them back for it."

Pat sighed big and loud. "That sounds cool. I wish I had brothers."

"I know buddy."

It wasn't going to happen. Even though John's mom had pulled him aside before they left and told him to be "open" to relationships. Something about how Pat needed a complete family and not just one in pieces like he had. As if John didn't know that.

For now all his free time needed to be making up for the lost year with his son. And trying to figure out why someone had killed the mayor's wife.

"What'll it be?" Maria, Matthias's sister, smiled at them. Her waitress uniform was yellow and she had on a whole lot of make-up. Why did women do that?

John smiled. "Two cheeseburgers, fries and two chocolate shakes."

Pat nearly jumped from his seat. "Awesome!"

"Coming right up." She strode away, the awkward movements of someone in pain and trying to hide it.

A dark figure stepped up to their table and John looked up. And up. The man was over six-six. He looked like a bear. A familiar bear. "Sam Tura?"

The man laughed. "In another life, I believe."

John stood and introduced himself, got his hand crushed, and turned to Pat. "Sam's a boxer." He looked at the bear. "I saw that fight against Pecos. That was rough, man." It just wasn't the reason Sam was here.

"You fight?"

If John said yes, was he going to end up in the ring? Did he want that? "A little."

Sam pointed a beefy finger at the window. The name on the building across the street was *Sleight of Hand*, the gym John had seen on Battle Night. "The paint is peeling, but the bags are heavy."

The man was a bona-fide poet. Who knew? John smiled. "That's your gym?"

"For sure. You think I could survive in this cage without an outlet?" Sam grinned. "It's better than beating on the locals by a long shot."

"I'm gonna have to agree with you on that one." John pointed at his badge. "Sheriff and all."

"Come by sometime. I'll see what you've got."

John didn't particularly like losing—or being pounded on—but he'd pay money to be in the ring with Sam Tura. "That sounds great."

"Dinner's on the house."

"Seriously?"

Sam shrugged. "It's my place. I can do what I want and I don't take no lip."

The stenciled lettering on the front window said *Estelle's*. "This is your place?"

"Long story." He pulled the white dish towel from his shoulder. "Enjoy your dinner."

Maria came back over carrying a tray and set it on the table with a wince. "Here you go boys."

Beyond her, Sam narrowed his eyes but didn't say anything. John met his gaze and Sam nodded. John was content to let the man handle his own business. But he'd be sure to ask Sam about what was going on with Maria when they met up at the gym.

After dinner John walked his son back to the apartment so Pat could put on his Dolphins jersey and then they headed back to the Meeting House. A screen had been pulled down from the ceiling and groups of guys sat around the room, watching the pre-game chatter. John pulled up the case file on his tablet and read over his notes, making a list of people from the scene he'd need to interview. Talking to the mayor again also wasn't a bad idea. He needed to see how the man was doing with his grief and if he'd remembered anything else.

The lack of information was disturbing. Murder didn't happen for no reason and John wasn't willing to accept there might never be an explanation. Not at this point.

Pat whooped and John looked up. Nate ran down the field, turned and caught the ball. He ran two yards and threw it down.

"Touchdown!"

John grinned. The kid really needed a foam finger.

Twenty minutes later Nate stood on the side of the field. His forehead dripped with sweat. How hot was it in Florida? It was after dark there, so the stadium floodlights lit up the crowd of players. Nate looked at the camera and waved it closer. He signed P-A-T with his fingers then blew a kiss to the camera.

"He did it!" Pat jumped up. "Uncle Nate sent me love!"

John laughed, as did several people sitting around them. His son was going to win this town's hearts over for sure.

This was what John had missed for the past year. His focus had been solely on the assignment. Situations like that where you couldn't just play the role but you had to live it, there wasn't much headspace to be worrying about home. Still, in those quiet moments when he was alone, John's heart had hurt for his son.

Before long, Nate was helmeted up and back on the field. John lowered his tablet to watch the play.

His brother ran down the field, turned and was slammed by a Giant.

John winced. The guy climbed off Nate but Nate didn't move. Pat lowered his arms. John put his hand on Pat's shoulder but his son moved forward, parting two chairs so he could get closer to the screen.

The Meeting House was quiet. On the screen, medics ran across the field and crouched beside Nate.

John's phone rang. He pulled it from the clip on his belt and looked at the screen. It was Grant.

"Are you seeing this?"

John bit his lip. "Yeah, we're watching."

Pat glanced at him. "Is Uncle Nate okay?"

"I don't know buddy. He got hit pretty hard. But he's wearing a lot of pads. We have to wait and see."

"Gees, you suck at this." Grant groaned. "Tell him Nate's gonna be fine."

"That might work with your girls." John wasn't going to lie to his son, not again.

This wasn't telling him he'd be back soon and then being gone for a year, but it was still important. Nate could be seriously hurt. It could be something that would heal in time or he could be back on the field in ten minutes. Pat needed honesty, not truth so veiled it was basically just a disguised lie.

"Call me if you find out anything."

Nate was lifted on a stretcher and carried off the field. John crouched by his son.

He didn't know if this was going to work, but he had a hunch his son was enough like him it just might. "I'll call Grandma. I bet she's worried. If you talk to her, do you think you could cheer her up?" John smiled but he didn't feel it. How hard had Nate been hit? "I'll make a call too, and we'll find out if Uncle Nate is okay. All right?"

Pat tore his eyes from the screen, where the game continued. "That sounds okay. I bet Grandma is really worried."

His little fingers gripped John's as they walked back to the apartment. John slumped on the couch and Pat came to sit on the other end. His son's whole demeanor had darkened. Maybe Grant had been right. "I'm sure he'll be okay, buddy."

Pat sniffed and looked away. John had no idea what to say to make his son feel better. He was so out of practice it wasn't the least bit amusing how much he sucked at this. He didn't know what his son needed. "Pat—"

"Can we just call Grandma?"

"Sure." John dialed.

"H-Hello?"

"Hey Mom, it's John."

"Is Nate okay, do you know? Ben wants the number for his coach or someone with the team, so he can call and find out."

"I'll see what I can get while you talk to Pat, okay?"

John handed the phone over and ran down to his computer, which had internet access. He scoured the team website and then sent an email to Grant asking if he knew how they could find out.

Pat stood by the desk, holding the phone out. "Grandma had another call coming in. She thought it might be Uncle Nate."

"You okay, buddy?"

"Can I watch a movie in bed?"

John sighed. "That's fine."

What was he supposed to do? Solving a murder was logical once you broke it down into tasks. Eventually he would get to the end, and find out who did it. Navigating his son's emotions was so much harder. Pat didn't give anything up easily.

**

Pat sat in the back of the classroom. He wasn't really reading from the book, even if it was more interesting than what they were talking about. He still didn't know if Uncle Nate was going to be okay.

There were six kids in the class, but four of them were big kids and the other was a girl. Pat was the youngest because Matthias's nephews weren't in Kindergarten yet.

The school was only as big as one of the classrooms at his old school, plus some bathrooms. There was a playground outside but it didn't even have swings, so what was the point? They were out west of town almost at the road to the ranch. Maybe if Matthias came into town Pat would see him drive past. But he wouldn't be able to go out and talk to him.

Pat probably couldn't help Aaron with the mail on Mondays, either. He'd just end up sitting here for years and years until he was old and he could get a job doing…something. A professional at BMX tricks would be cool. Bobby's older brother designed computer games where you shot people's heads off and blood spurted out. But Pat wasn't allowed to play those, so he didn't figure his dad would let him do that.

"Okay." Mrs. Pepper looked at the clock. "That's enough debate for today. Let's all head over to the library and get our work done, shall we?"

Pat grabbed his backpack and swung it over his shoulder. The library was across the street, another building all by itself. It wasn't attached to the one next to it like the ones on Main Street were. If they had to walk by the sheriff's office, he could at least find out if his dad knew something about Uncle Nate.

The teenagers went out first. Pat followed them and the twelve year old girl whose name he couldn't remember.

"Hey bud." His dad was leaning against his Jeep.

"Dad!" Pat ran over and hugged him. "How's Uncle Nate?"

"Just another sprained ankle. He's gonna be fine."

Pat blew out a breath. "That's good."

"Your uncle said he'd call you later, when you're out of school."

"You talked to him?"

His dad smiled. "He sounded funny. The medicine they gave him made his voice slur and he kept laughing. But I made him give the phone to a nurse who promised she'd make sure he called you on my phone."

"Okay, good."

"Pat?" Mrs. Pepper stood at the edge of the street, ready for him to go with her to the library.

"I gotta go."

"Okay." His dad pulled him close for a hug. Pat squeezed him and then ran to Mrs. Pepper, who made him hold her hand while they crossed the street like he was a baby.

The library was cool, but it was small and they probably didn't have any comics. Mrs. Pepper typed in his log-in and password and had him tell her what he wanted it to be for next time. He did the assignments he was supposed to while she sat on a chair and read a book on her tablet-thing, only looking at the teenagers every now and then to tell them to be quiet and get on with their work.

One of his English assignments was to write a story about himself. Pat thought for a while and then typed the title.

Lost in Sanctuary

**

The mayor's house was on the east end of town, set aside from the rest of the residential streets to the north of the road which led out toward Dan Walden's farm. The house was also twice as big as the row houses everyone else lived in.

Both the outside and inside looked to have been repainted recently. The carpet was new, the fixtures were all modern and nothing looked anything like John's aging apartment.

John set the paper cup of coffee he'd gotten from Sam at the diner down on the coffee table. The mayor was in a suit, but it was creased like he'd been wearing it all night.

"How are you doing?"

The house was silent and John didn't imagine the little pillows would have been on the floor instead of the couch before Betty's death.

He'd read up on the two of them before he came over. The mayor had been involved in an extortion ring involving a consortium and high-end money laundering. He'd turned on his partner in exchange for a new identity and a fresh start. Coming to Sanctuary had been their choice, and he'd been voted in as mayor only months later. He'd been in the position ever since, although Dotty had told John it was because no one saw much point in running against him.

"Is there anything I can do to help?"

"Father Wilson asked that. Spouted all these platitudes about God's plan, like this was supposed to happen." The mayor's face morphed into disgust.

John knew plenty of people who believed that, even if it didn't always get expressed eloquently. It had only helped ease the pain after his dad passed after he'd finally accepted he couldn't have prevented the old man's heart attack. He'd been out of state at school at the time, living above Grant's garage.

"No one knows what it feels like." The mayor sat with his hands by his knees like a rag doll. "My wife is gone. Murdered by some heartless—" His voice dropped off into mumbled rambling.

"Have you thought any more about who might have wanted to do this?"

Collins snapped up straight. "I know exactly who did this!"

John kept his tone measured. "Did Betty keep files anywhere? Notes from her work welcoming people, papers or a journal maybe? Anything like that?"

The mayor hauled himself off the couch. John followed him upstairs to the end of the hall at the back of the house. The two doors at the other end were open, beyond which was an unmade king-size bed. "My office is on Main Street, but Betty worked from home." He stopped at the door. "I haven't been in here since—"

"You don't have to come in. You can wait in the hall."

John accepted the key, wondering why a wife would feel like she had to lock an office in her own home. What secrets had Betty Collins been trying to hide in here?

The window was open and there were papers everywhere on the floor and the surface of her dainty white desk. Too much mess for the wind.

"What on earth..." The mayor looked in behind him.

"Stay in the hall."

John crouched and looked below the desk where he could see under the window. The chair had rolled aside and there was a dirt print which looked like the toe of a shoe on the wall. The computer monitor, one of those with the tower built into the screen, was on its side on the floor.

John pulled the radio off his belt and called for Dotty to send Palmer over with their duffel bag of evidence collecting equipment.

When Palmer showed up, John grabbed a pair of gloves and took a look at some of the papers. Descriptions of people from town. Some physical, some relating to their personalities. None of which appeared to be flattering. The woman had amassed files on everyone. "We'll need to take all this back to the sheriff's office and go through it."

"Yes, of course. Take whatever you need." The mayor's shoulders slumped like the fight had seeped out of him. His gaze flicked around the room. "Who could have done this? It's unreal. I've been out of it, but still, someone broke into my home."

Now he wanted to claim ownership of the office? "Palmer, take Mr. Collins downstairs and get a statement on the break in."

"Let's go talk." Palmer motioned to the stairs and let the mayor go first.

John crouched over a pile of papers. Could Betty Collins have had information on someone that they didn't want to get out? This was certainly a community where secrets were kept. It was also a place where things could easily become common knowledge. Besides, the people he'd met so far had been way too pragmatic about their pasts. Even Andra had said she'd made peace with hers—not that she'd given him the details.

Now was the time to read her file.

Despite the scuff mark he'd have to photograph and the open window, this didn't feel like anything but making a mess just for the sake of making it. A distraction designed to throw him off his end goal of finding the killer, or maybe even to paint Betty Collins in a bad light. John picked up one of the papers. There wasn't much damage that *has a bad attitude* could do in a town like this. Unless there was something more incriminating here or on the woman's computer. But the computer hadn't been destroyed. Whatever was on there wasn't the focus of this.

John got to work photographing the scene. This case was turning up little-to-nothing of any use in catching the killer. Someone in town had stabbed Betty Collins repeatedly in the stomach and John was no closer to finding out who had done it.

When he was done with the scuff mark he looked out the window. A portion of roof jutted out over the kitchen window below, which could have been the entry point. The yard was open land merging into the trees, which curved up the mountain past where early snow speckled the grass in spots.

All green, except one spot where the grass had been spread apart. It almost looked like an arrow pointing at whatever was there. Anyone looking outside would have seen it.

John locked up the office and found the back door. He crossed the grass to where the object lay between two trees. It was a navy cloth, rolled up but long—as long as his forearm. John lifted it with his still-gloved hand and unrolled the cloth. The blade of the knife was covered with dark stains no longer blood red. He glanced around but saw nothing, save trees...and the path that led up to Andra's house.

Chapter 12

John sat back in his desk chair, his eyes on the blade. He couldn't help thinking he was meant to find the knife. Even as he took a picture of the latent partial fingerprint he'd found on the handle, the thought wouldn't leave him.

He stowed the blade in the container, then in its paper evidence bag and locked it in his safe. He downloaded the picture to the computer and emailed it off to Grant. His brother would be able to run it through IAFIS and see if he could match it anywhere else. Interpol wasn't out of the question, given some of the pasts Sanctuary residents likely had.

John cleaned up and pulled out the papers he'd found in Betty's office. The first one he looked for was Andra's, not that John was going to think overly long on it. He would read all of them in turn. He just happened to be starting with hers.

Short hair—apparently she'd grown it since she came here—surly, quiet. The description was of a younger woman who said next to nothing and seemed averse to physical touch, even something as innocuous as shaking hands. John tried to remember if they shook hands when they'd met. He didn't think so. She hadn't even touched Pat. Their fingers hadn't brushed when they'd eaten together, like they tended to when something was passed, person-to-person.

The comments section of Betty's welcome form on Andra said, *Loner. Did not answer any questions about past. Did not accept recommended accommodations. Ms. Caleri took her backpack and walked away. A copy of this report was given to Sheriff Chandler. Maybe he can find out where she disappeared to.*

John hadn't figured the cabin was her designated residence, since no one else had been provided one. It wasn't unheard of for WITSEC to grant certain concessions, as was probably done with the mayor's house. But the previous sheriff hadn't forced her to move into town and the cabin had gotten there somehow. Had she built it herself, or did she have help constructing the place? Most of Sanctuary's residents seemed content to leave her to her quiet life—which begged the question of who, aside from Harriet, wanted John to think Andra was a murderer?

John grabbed the key off his belt. The town's files were in the row of file cabinets, drawer after drawer of the dark secrets and terrifying events that brought them all here. It also contained a copy of the "Memorandum of Understanding" each one of them had signed.

He pulled out the first drawer and found the C's, files for Sheriff Chandler, Betty and Samuel Collins. Each one was packed with an inch-thick collection of papers. In the drawer below, the file for Bolton Farrera was one paper, a page of personal information he'd filled out and signed.

John went back to the first drawer. Andra's file was just as thick as Betty and Samuel's. John slid it out and set it on the desk. The first page was a file photo of a much younger Andra, her hair cropped close to her head but longer on one side, and her eyes dark with makeup.

The radio buzzed, signaling an incoming call. John keyed the unit and looked at the clock. 23:34. "Sheriff's office."

"Someone's behind my house." The man's voice was gruff. Shaky. "In the trees."

John shut the file cabinet door and grabbed his notepad. "Your name?"

"Peter Nelson."

"Address?"

"You don't know where I live?" The man sighed and rattled off the address.

John looked it up on the map. He scribbled a note to Pat and ran upstairs, shoving the collection of cups and books back from the edge of the kitchen counter so he could leave the note in a clear spot. They should probably clean up.

John sprinted out to his Jeep and drove to the north side of town. At some point he might even get to use his lights and sirens. Despite the dead body, there hadn't been an actual emergency yet. If it didn't happen before their month trial was out, he'd have to take his son for a drive before they left and have him turn it on. Pat would probably get a big kick out of that.

The house lights were on and it looked the same as every other house on both sides of the street.

The middle residences on every street were two stories, two bedrooms one bathroom and a square front yard the same size as the back yard. The houses on both sides of Peter Nelson's residence had flowerbeds either side of the door. Bigger houses were at the end of each street, those having four bedrooms and an extra bathroom. All of them had a minimal amount of space. He knew from Betty's welcome speech that there were only one or two open houses.

The older man had the door open before John got up the front walk. "Peter Nelson?" When the man nodded John said, "Sheriff John Mason. You said someone is behind your house?"

"I'll show you."

They crossed grimy carpet in the living room through the old seventies kitchen. It looked a lot like the counters and cabinets John had, although this guy had a newer fridge. He unlocked the back and John stepped onto a square slab of concrete with two fraying deck chairs. Beyond the square of grass was a six-foot chain-link fence and beyond that, nothing but trees. The kids' park was closer to the northeast end of town.

"Someone was out there."

"You see who it was?"

He shook his head, looking perturbed that he hadn't. "I know what I heard. There's a murderer running around town. What if I get stabbed next? I'm not dying here, no way."

Right. John nodded as though that was a perfectly understandable train of thought, even though there was little chance of a kill-happy stabber running around town looking for their next victim.

"I'll go take a look. You stay inside."

The guy shut his door.

"Okay, then."

John climbed the fence and jumped down on the other side. The ground was uneven, as though the town had just been set down in the middle of nowhere—which, in a sense, it had.

The trees were close together over dirt carpeted with pine needles. John swept his flashlight from side to side but didn't see anything. There was barely any noise aside from his footsteps and a house a few doors down blaring their TV. How had the old guy heard someone over that?

John checked for shoeprints by the fence and then walked a circle further out. Something rustled behind him. He pulled his gun and spun around, half expecting the killer to be standing there brandishing his knife even though the weapon was locked up in his office.

A twig snapped. John swiveled left and a deer stepped between two trees. The whites of its eyes reflected in the beam of the flashlight. He lowered it, but not all the way.

"Put your hands up."

The deer walked on.

John smiled to the dark. This was what he'd been called out for? Murder aside, was this what a career as the Sanctuary sheriff would entail?

Chasing deer and calming everyone's nerves wasn't a bad calling. Better than getting shot at every day, or going undercover and sticking his neck out. Even if it was the middle of the night and not yet the middle of what had already been a long week, John didn't have much to complain about. His son was safe and they had the space to spend time with each other.

He glanced around. At the end of the row of houses was a separate building, on top of which was a metal tower. The radio station? He'd heard about Hal's business but hadn't seen it yet.

John hopped the fence and knocked on the old man's back door. "Mr. Nelson?"

The old man had donned a threadbare checkered robe. "Did you catch the killer?"

"Uh no, just a deer I'm happy to say."

His eyebrows dipped and disappointment reigned on his face. "Shame. You could've had this all wrapped up."

"Well, I appreciate your diligence."

"Didn't help though. You haven't caught her yet."

"Her?" John wanted to cross his arms on his chest and let the guy know he was mad. But he was trying to be diplomatic. "What makes you think it was a woman?"

"Pshaw. Everyone's talking about it."

"That doesn't mean it's true."

Peter Nelson closed his mouth. "No, I don't suppose it does."

Music was playing from a radio on the counter. The low sound might have been The Eagles but John couldn't be sure. "Is that Hal's music?"

"It's just noise. But he also does public announcements." Nelson's eyes brightened. "Hey, you should have him broadcast a message for you. Can the killer please come forward, or something like that. Might help you figure out who it is."

"You're right, I could do that."

Apparently the consensus in town was John seemed to be having trouble figuring out who killed Betty. Did they think it was easy to catch a killer? The residents of Sanctuary might be eager for him to make an arrest but that didn't mean Andra had done anything. It was like they would do whatever it took to make this drama run its course so they could get back to their normal, murder-free lives.

John excused himself and drove to Hal's radio station. The building was the same design as the schoolhouse. As if whoever designed this place had absolutely no imagination whatsoever—which sounded like the government.

He knocked and let himself in. If Hal was DJ-ing he probably wouldn't hear it anyway. A buzzer rang at his entry. The hall was dark but for low yellow lights. The Eagles song had changed to Charlie Daniels, coming from the end of the hall where there was a red light above the door. He started for it when the door opened and Andra stepped out.

"What do—oh, John?"

He froze. "Uh, hey. You're here." Great. He sounded like an idiot.

"Where's Pat?"

"In bed."

She looked at the clock on the wall. "It's late. Is...there a problem?"

"You're running the radio station?"

Andra flattened her hands on the legs of her pants, ones that cut off below the knee. She looked so young. "Hal had a dinner date with his lady-friend."

John grinned. Andra's lips twitched and then she grinned too.

"And he asked you to cover?"

She shrugged. "Usually once a week."

"Oh."

She motioned to the room. "Want to see?"

John expected a computer and not much else. Wasn't that how it was done these days? Instead there was a board with a million buttons, a mic that dangled from above in front of the chair, bulky military-style headphones and what looked like an 8-track tape deck with slots for four cassettes.

"Wow. This place is ancient."

Andra laughed; a rusty sound that stopped when he turned to her. She cleared her throat, pulled over a second chair and motioned for him to sit. "That it is."

John stood. "I'm going to need you to provide the sheriff's office with a set of your fingerprints." She just looked at him. "Can you come in tomorrow?"

Andra's mouth moved back and forth. "Why now?"

"I found a possible match to the murder weapon. I'll need to take probably everyone in town's prints eventually, unless we get a match. But I'm starting with a core group."

Her eyebrows drew together. "So just because Harriett said I did it, I'm considered a suspect?"

"It's a process of elimination." And it couldn't be affected by his personal opinion. However he was starting to feel about Andra, he had to be impartial or he would be doing a poor job.

"But I am a suspect."

"Right now basically everyone is a suspect." He smiled. "Except me and Pat."

Andra slid her chair closer to the mic. Why did she have to be like that? It wasn't like he was arresting her. John was only trying to do the job he'd been hired to do. It was nothing personal.

"Wouldn't you rather I ruled you out first?"

"Fine."

"You'll come in?"

"Yes." She slid over, loaded a new 8-track tape and ejected the one above it, pressed two buttons and listened while the song changed to a new one.

"Do you think Hal would let me make an announcement? I'd like to ask anyone who has any information about Betty Collins' death to come to the sheriff's office and talk to us."

Andra pointed at the other chair. John didn't know if that meant yes or no.

He sat anyway. "So...did it take you long to learn how to do all this?"

She glanced at him with one raised eyebrow.

Guess not.

"Hal should request some new equipment. This stuff is a little...dated. They probably just do it all on computers now, don't you think?"

"You're assuming Hal has the money to pay for new equipment."

"Don't you just request it from the marshals?"

"Everything has to be ordered and paid for by the purchaser."

"Everything?"

She nodded. "It's a moot point since Hal swears up and down 8-tracks sound better than anything else. Although, I'm not sure he's actually ever listened to a CD in his life so it's hard to tell. He's been here since seventy-two. Did you know he was a tunnel rat in Vietnam?"

John shook his head. The song ended and Andra glanced at him. "Ready?"

"For what?"

"To make your announcement." She clicked two buttons, slid a dial up the board and moved the mic toward him.

He swallowed. "Good evening. This is Sheriff John Mason. If you have any information regarding the tragic death of Betty Collins, please contact the sheriff's department. Your assistance could enable us to bring the killer to justice."

Andra winced. She pressed more buttons and a song started. What was wrong with what he said?

The phone rang. Two buttons lit up on the base...three, and then a fourth. Andra hit a button on the telephone's keypad and a voice came through the speakers mounted to the wall. "Hello? Is anyone there?"

Andra folded her arms so John said, "This is Sheriff John Mason. Do you have information about the death of Betty Collins?"

"I want to know when you're going to arrest Andra Caleri," a gravel-voiced woman said. "Everyone knows she done it. Everyone. How come she isn't in jail?"

"Ms. Caleri is afforded the same rights as every citizen living in this town."

"Rights-shmights. She done it. She's the killer."

John didn't look at Andra. "Whether she is or not, evidence must be obtained before an arrest warrant can be granted. And I don't think—"

The caller hung up.

"I'm sorry."

"Don't." Andra shook her head. "I don't care what they think. I didn't kill Betty Collins."

John didn't think she had either, although he didn't know why he felt it so strongly. There just didn't seem to be any reason why she would have. Andra was nothing if not content with the life she'd made in her cabin. And apparently helping out Hal. He wondered who else in town was the recipient of her time and energy and they didn't even know it. But he couldn't say that, because it would be showing bias to her when she was as much a suspect as anyone else.

He couldn't even tell her he didn't think she was the killer.

"You want to take more calls?"

John looked at the lights beside Line 2, Line 3 and Line 4. "Not really." Andra smiled and her cheeks flushed pink. "How long are you here for?"

"Hal shuts down around two a.m. usually. I have a while left and then I'll lock up and drop the key in the hide-a-slot."

John glanced at the shelves of tapes. "Can you play whatever you want?"

"Uh, no." She lifted a paper he hadn't seen yet. A hand-written list. "Hal plays what Hal wants to play."

"Even when Hal isn't here?"

Andra nodded; her eyes bright with humor. "I don't mind. It's his radio station and it's not my thing."

"Then why do you help out?"

She shrugged but John thought there might be more, so he waited. Sure enough, she said, "There was a bunch of extra supplies left over when he built this place. I bartered for lumber and use of his tools. I figure I'll be about done paying him back in...oh, fifteen years or so."

John laughed. "Doesn't sound like it was a good deal."

"It built my house."

"You built your cabin?"

Andra shifted in her chair. "It beat the lean-to I was living in before. Especially when it snowed." She fingered the edge of her sweater. "Hal was out walking. He'd had a fight with his lady-friend and he was blowing off steam. He found me halfway passed out with the flu and carried me to town. To his house.

"It nearly scared me to death, waking up in a strange man's bed. I screamed so loud Hal dropped the tray of soup he was bringing in. We talked. He won me over but I persuaded him to take a trade for the materials and he helped me build the cabin."

She didn't look at him. John wasn't going to pass up an opportunity to study her on one of the rare occasions she was opening up.

He cleared his throat, wanting to share his story in return. If she was ever going to trust him, it was a good place to start. "I was married. Pat's mom...she's a lawyer. I'd like to say it worked in the beginning but that's probably not true. We just ignored the friction because she was having Pat. I think she was relieved when I started going undercover. The assignments got longer and longer and then home wasn't home anymore. Pat had started going to school. One of those private places that costs a whack."

He took a breath. "She wanted out. I wasn't going to fight it so long as my son knew who I was, knew I loved him."

"And now?"

"She has her life and I got the better end of the deal. Pat with me full time for the first time in...I don't even know. Years."

Andra gave him a small smile. "He's a great kid."

"He is." John glanced down. The lights on the phone were dark, but he'd probably have a crowd in the office tomorrow. Hopefully something would pan out into a lead. "How about you? Have you ever been married?"

Andra swallowed. "Once."

"Didn't last?"

"Uh...no." She hesitated. "It's complicated. And a long story."

"I've got time."

Andra's body stilled. She looked up at the corner where the wall met the ceiling. "His name was Drew."

John barked out a laugh. The guy's name was Drew? Andra's wide eyes met his. "Uh, sorry." He coughed. "Excuse me."

She didn't smile. "He was nice...ish."

What did that mean? "How long did it last?"

"A few months." She reached for the tapes, switched out two for new ones and pressed play. "I can't really talk about this. I'm sorry."

"Hey, it's okay if it's too painful."

Andra looked like she'd slapped him. "Right. It was a tough time. And it's late so you probably won't want to be away from Pat for very long."

"You're right. I don't really know what the rules are for kids and being alone."

"I'm not the person to ask."

"No worries." She was shutting him down again. After he thought they were getting somewhere. "I'll find out."

Her eyes widened. "I'm sure you will."

She wasn't talking about Pat. John waited; he couldn't just leave like this. There was more to what was between them than brief periods of sharing followed by awkwardness. He must be rusty.

Andra held his gaze. "Sooner or later you're going to figure it all out."

Chapter 13

Andra watched him leave. His footsteps echoed down the hall and the front door shut. Andra blew out a breath and twisted around in the chair. After a few seconds, the bathroom door inched open.

Nadia Marie stepped out, hands up. "Okay...okay...hold on." She laughed. "What. Was. That?"

Andra couldn't help it, she chuckled. "I have no idea."

John showing up was the last thing she'd expected tonight. The fact he stayed and chatted was even more bizarre. The man thought she might have killed Betty Collins. Probably he was getting a feel for her to see if she was the homicidal type.

Little did he know.

Nadia's head tipped back and she laughed, full out. She stumbled over and practically fell into the chair. It barely dipped, since she weighed about a hundred pounds even though she was easily five-eight. Andra had more curves, despite the fact Nadia forced her to hike around the mountains for days with only protein bars and bananas.

The woman was a nut but she made it so Andra wasn't so lonely.

"You can stop laughing now."

"No way." Nadia sucked in a breath. "That man has a crush on you. I'm not lying. He does. He might not want to be but he's totally into you."

And that was funny? Why wouldn't John want to be attracted to her? There wasn't anything wrong with that.

"So?"

Nadia's lips twitched...and then she started laughing again. "So? That's priceless." She wiped a tear away. "That's the most hilarious thing I've heard in weeks."

"He thinks I'm a murderer."

"Trust me, that man is hedging all his bets on the fact you didn't do it. Otherwise, why did he stay and tell you about his wife. And why did you talk about Drew? You like the sheriff." She ended on a sing-song voice.

Andra rolled her eyes.

"You do." She gasped. "You do like him."

"I do not."

"It's not a crime, you know."

Andra sighed. "Finally, something I'm good at that isn't."

"You're allowed to have a relationship. You can be happy. And not just all alone in your cabin. You haven't been excluded from falling in love." Nadia shoved her shoulder. She should do some strength training if that was all she had.

Andra folded her arms. "I have nothing in common with Sheriff John Mason. There's no point in even considering a relationship with a cop. A cop who has a son. There's no way it would work."

Nadia pouted. "Why do you have to be so reasonable? Thinking things through all the time. What's up with that? Dream a little for once, will you?"

"You know why it's impossible." Andra changed out the tapes and started a new track. She lifted her coffee cup but it was cold.

"Because of the job thing...or because of the other thing?"

"Honestly? Both."

"Why would John care that you had a child? It was a long time ago and you gave her up for adoption." Nadia paused. "Do you think he cares about your past enough it's going to make him turn away?"

Andra pulled at the side of her jacket, hung on the back of the chair, and got the envelope from the pocket. It was the mail she'd received just that morning. She handed it to the only person in town who knew Andra had delivered a baby girl weeks before she arrived in Sanctuary. It was one of the biggest reasons she'd wanted out of her former life. A serious wake-up call she never would have chosen for herself. But it brought her to where she needed to be, even while Helena was where she needed to be.

Nadia's face sobered. She pulled the photos from the envelope and flipped through them fast, then again much slower. When she looked up, her brown eyes were big and wide, full of all the emotion Andra was feeling but would never talk about. "She's beautiful."

Andra thought so too. That was mercy; that Helena looked like her and not like Drew. And more mercy, that the adoptive parents willingly sent pictures—not often, but enough. Andra couldn't ask for more.

Nadia tilted one picture so Andra could see it. A birthday party. "How old is she?"

"Eleven." Andra swallowed.

The crying sound came from Nadia.

Andra smiled. "You're such a softie."

"I feel like a proud auntie and I've never even met her." Nadia sucked in a breath and sobbed.

"I've never met her either."

Nadia's head came up.

"As soon as I gave birth they took her away." Nadia looked ready to explode, so Andra said, "I told them to. I knew if I held her I wouldn't be able to let her go."

"Why did you?"

Andra turned away. She didn't need recriminations, not from Nadia of all people. But that was her way. Nadia said what she was thinking. It wasn't always kind but there was no pretense, which to Andra's life of silence and lies was like fresh water.

"I'm sorry. It's just...why didn't you bring her here? You would be a great mom."

Andra took a breath. "I wasn't in a good place. I needed Helena to have a better life than the one I could give her. Petros and Anya give her that. Two parents who love her and love the Lord. I couldn't give her that. Not back then and not when I came here."

Nadia tucked the pictures back in the envelope. There was no letter. But when you received a gift that rich, there was no need for words.

Andra tucked it back in her jacket.

"He seriously likes you." Nadia was good at a lot of things. One of which was deflecting Andra from the swirling drain of her life before Sanctuary.

Andra grinned, even though she didn't feel it. "What about you? You went into the lion's lair on Battle Night. Any chance encounters with a certain someone?"

Nadia stilled, which meant trouble since the woman was pure energy. "Uh...I got the flag."

"Yeah, there's not a story there." Andra turned her chair toward her friend. "Spill, woman."

"I told you, I got the flag."

"What about Bolton Farrera? He must have been there, guarding it with his boys."

Nadia chewed her lip. "He...uh...might have caught me."

"No! Why didn't you tell me this before?"

"Because it's embarrassing. He got me in like two seconds even with the distraction you showed me. It's like he knew. He must be trained in that stuff. Maybe he's secretly some kind of superhero, but it all went wrong and he had to hide his identity here. That's probably it. Anyway, I don't want to talk about Mr. Tall, Dark and...what was your name again?"

Andra groaned. "Tell me Bolton didn't say that to you."

"So embarrassing. Ugh, whatever. I've decided it's my lot in life to be tragically attracted to men who don't even know I'm alive. And also men who steal fabulous paintings, sell reproductions and then try and blame it on *moi* so those two snooty French guys try to kill me instead."

"Sorry."

Nadia shrugged. "I'm over it. Ancient history. I like my life, cutting the same hairstyles week-in and year-out and getting crappy tips. It's the high life. Excuse me while I go drown my sorrows by listening to Kelly Clarkson and eating a giant bag of peanut butter cups."

"You'll find someone. You're gorgeous, you have a fabulous smile."

"Now I know you're lying. Next to you, I'm totally the plain one."

"No way, you look like a young Jamie Lee Curtis."

"Actually, I heard they're getting Sandra Bullock to play me in the TV movie detailing the tragic story of my life and the downfall of an international ring of art thieves. But seriously, other than making a great Princess Leia for Halloween, exactly what good does that do me?"

Andra smiled. "Maybe Bolton will dress up as Han Solo."

"I'd like to see that." Nadia's lips twitched. "I'd actually pay money to see that."

"There you go."

"I'd still kill to have your exotic, Spanish coloring."

Andra chuckled. "My mom was from Nebraska."

"Seriously, how did I not know this?"

"Maybe because I haven't told you." She hadn't told anyone. "How do you think I'm American? Anyway, I'm serious. Miss Nebraska, 1972."

"No way. How do you know that?"

How did she think Andra knew that? "The internet."

"Oh. Right. How did she meet your dad? Isn't he Spanish?"

"Yep. She became an actress and my dad was a movie producer. I figured they met through a work thing, but I never could work out how. I only found pictures of them together, in magazines. They had me and then dropped me at boarding school in Barcelona when I was five. I don't really remember them, but I remember the nanny. She smelled like lavender."

"Where are they now?"

Andra swallowed.

"You know?"

"They have a pied-a-terre in Paris and a summer home in Palm Springs. It's busy being rich. Not a lot of time to be social with your only daughter."

"Wow."

"I saw my dad once. I was twenty-one."

"No way." Nadia's mouth dropped open. "You met him?"

"No. It was a big party and I was across the room. He had on this expensive suit. His hair was slicked back and he had all these rings. Fit, you know, like he hired a personal trainer. I just saw him for a second. I was...uh...working. And I don't know what I would have said. Hi, I'm the daughter you abandoned and forgot about. How do you like how I turned out?"

Nadia closed her mouth. Probably because she knew exactly who Andra had been in those days. It wasn't something even an estranged parent was going to be proud of.

Andra didn't like the silence, not with Nadia. She looked at her friend but Nadia said, "You know, you give off this air of being all tough. But you're like an egg. Crack the shell and the middle is all goo." She smiled, like she'd had a happy epiphany.

Andra didn't move or react in any other way.

Nadia laughed. "Fine. Ignore me, what do I know? I only cut people's hair."

She waited but Andra wasn't going to give her the satisfaction of being right.

"Don't you have to change a tape?"

Dead air. "Crap." Andra loaded up the next song and got it playing. "Quit distracting me."

"Are you sure it's not Sheriff John Mason doing that?"

"I'm sure."

Nadia was quiet for a second and then she said, "What if you could have a relationship?"

"I can't."

"But—"

Andra shifted to face Nadia. "What do you think is going to happen when he reads my file? Nothing is going to be fine. And definitely not fine enough for a relationship. He's going to arrest me for Betty Collins' murder."

"But you didn't do it. You were coming to meet me with the flag."

"No one else believes that."

"I'll vouch for you."

Andra took a breath. "Do you really think when he figures out what I used to do for a living, he's even going to care about that? All he'll be concerned with is keeping the town safe and keeping me away from his son."

Nadia pressed her lips together, conceding the point. Which was good, because Andra didn't want to argue about what couldn't be.

"It's going to happen. He's going to arrest me." Andra sighed. "Can we just talk about something else while I have a night to breathe free before the inevitable happens and my whole world is gone again?"

"You don't know that."

"I'm not naïve, Nadia." Andra sighed. "I just want to enjoy what I have while it lasts. I'll deal with whatever comes later, when it happens. I'm just not looking forward to the look on his face. That's always the worst part."

Nadia Marie's voice was quiet. "Did I do that...look at you like that?"

"You were fine. That's why I told you at the diner because if I'd told you half a mile out of town on the ridge you'd have thought I brought you out there to kill you and hide the body."

Nadia's lips flickered in a smile. "I'm glad you told me."

"Me too."

"I'm sorry about everything that happened to you."

"It was a choice. A lot of it was just choices that I made. Good or bad, they're done and I can't erase any of it. But the fact you're sorry is exactly why I told you." Andra smiled. "And why I don't mind you showing up all the time and talking my ear off."

"Ha." Nadia laughed. "You're the chatty one. Can't get you to shut up half the time. Yeesh."

**

Pat sat on the steps of the school with his backpack on his feet. He should just get back on his bike and ride...somewhere. His dad had been tired and grumpy at breakfast, yelling about wearing a coat even though it wasn't cold. And telling him being on time for school meant you were late. Whatever that meant. On time was on time, right? Tardy was tardy.

He sighed. His mom had dropped him at school every morning. It was a long drive, not a walk. But still, she made sure he got there. Just not that he got to Sanctuary. Apparently she didn't care anymore. Who did that? Who just stopped loving someone all of a sudden?

What if she never loved him in the first place?

Pat didn't want to think about his mom, but not trying to think about her meant he didn't see the girl until she was blocking out the sun peaking over the mountains. She didn't say anything. She just stared at him with her beady eyes and her mean-looking mouth.

Was he supposed to talk first? "Hi, I'm Pat."

"I know who you are." She dumped her backpack at the bottom of the stairs and folded the arms of her sweater. Apparently she didn't have to wear a coat.

"Well, who are you?"

She shrugged.

She wasn't going to tell him what her name was?

"I heard your dad's protecting a killer. He won't arrest Andra because he's full-on hot for her."

Pat didn't know what that meant, but it didn't sound good. "Andra didn't kill that lady. She's nice."

"Nice? She's a weirdo. I heard she lures people up to her cabin, and murders them and buries the bodies in the woods where no one will ever find them."

Pat's cereal did a twist and swoop in his stomach like the diving guy on the Olympics. "I don't believe you."

"Yeah?" She shoved his shoulder. "Wadda you know? You only just got here. I've lived here my whole life."

Three of the teenagers walked up, two girls and a boy. "Leave him alone, Clara."

That was her name? Pat looked at her. If that was his name, he'd probably be mad at everyone too.

"His dad is protectin' a murderer."

"I heard about that," one of the girls said. "Andra Caleri killed Betty Collins."

The other girl turned to her. "So? We didn't like Betty Collins, remember?"

"Yeah but we didn't not like her enough we don't care she got stabbed. What if one of us is next?"

The boy ignored them, looking at Pat instead. "What's your dad waiting for? Why hasn't he arrested her already?"

Pat looked at each of them, standing over him. He swallowed. "Andra didn't do it."

"Yeah? How do you know?"

Clara stuck her hands on her hips. "That's what I said!"

"Yeah," the first teen girl said. "Well, no one is asking you." She zeroed in on Pat. "Are the sheriff and Andra...you know...?"

Pat swallowed. "No, I don't know."

Clara snorted. "He doesn't even know what you mean." She laughed but it wasn't nice.

"Quit being a turd, Clara." The boy shoved her aside and then looked at Pat. "Your dad's protecting her. Everyone knows she killed Betty."

"She didn't."

"She's done it before. Up at her house."

Clara shoved her way back in. "She buries the bodies in the woods!"

Pat stood up on the step so he was same height as the teenagers. "I've been to Andra's house. There aren't any bodies in the woods." At least, he didn't think so. She was a nice lady, friendly to Aaron when she didn't have to be. And she made nice lemonade.

"What's going on?"

They all froze. The teens turned and moved aside so Pat could see Mrs. Pepper. She was dressed in gray, like she was trying to be depressing on purpose. She should get her hair cut like his mom did, where they put streaks in it and made you look sunny even when it was cold outside.

"Does anyone want to tell me what this is?" She looked at the three teens and then Clara, but none of them said anything. "Pat?"

"Nothing, Mrs. Pepper."

She sighed. "All of you inside." When Pat got up to follow the other kids in Mrs. Pepper put her hand on his arm and said, "One minute, Pat."

"Yes, Ma'am?"

She smiled. "I heard you say you've been up to Ms. Andra's house, was that right?"

He nodded. "With Aaron. To deliver her mail."

"Must've been quite a walk."

"It wasn't too far. Just up the trail. Aaron said it was a mile." He smiled. "She gave us lemonade."

"That's nice. But, you know, some people want you to think they're nice even when they're trying to hide something. So you should be careful. Maybe go with your dad if you need to go up there again. Or better yet, stay clear of Ms. Andra. I don't believe what everyone's saying about her..."

"Neither do I."

"It's nice to believe the best of people. But sometimes being careful has to be more important than being nice."

"Okay." He didn't really get that. But she wasn't saying bad things about Andra so it wasn't hard to just agree. "Can I go inside now?"

"Yes, dear."

Pat worked some on his art project, making a dodecahedron out of cardboard and paper maché he was going to paint with the Dolphins colors.

After that they went to the library. Pat's computer was pointed at the front door and Mrs. Pepper was in the middle. He logged on with his ID and then onto the school website, but didn't click on his assignment. No one was looking, so he went online and logged onto his email instead.

There was nothing from his mom.

He checked the sent folder. The three messages were in there, so she must have gotten them. Why didn't she email him back?

He slumped lower in the seat. The only good part of being here was getting to spend time with his dad. And he couldn't even do that right now because his dad was busy catching who killed that lady. Even in summer, when he wouldn't have to go to school, his dad would be working all the time. Just like always.

Pat's eyes burned. It didn't feel like he'd gotten his dad back and now he'd lost his mom too.

A window popped up at the bottom corner of his email.

Pat?

He sat up and typed back. *Hi Grandma.*

How are you, pumpkin?

Okay. I guess.

That doesn't sound good. Did you get my cookies?

Cookies?

Maybe they'll be there next week. They'll still be good, I'm sure.

Grandma's cookies were the best. But that wasn't what he wanted to talk about. *Have you heard from my mom?*

Oh, honey. No. I'm sorry. She hasn't emailed you?

Pat didn't type anything. His eyes were burning again. His cheek tickled and he swiped his face. He was crying. Great. Now everyone was going to think he was a total baby. He sniffed and wiped his sleeve across his face.

I'm sure she means to. You want me to call her and tell her to email or call you?

Not if she didn't even love him anymore.

Pat typed, *It's fine.* Even though it wasn't.

His dad didn't get it and neither did his grandma. They didn't even like his mom, so what did they care she didn't love them anymore? Pat was the one she left. She'd made a show of being all sad she was going, but she just said that stuff to make herself not feel so bad.

I love you, Pat. Don't be sad, baby. I know you miss your mom but your dad loves you and he's there.

Pat typed, *K.*

He won't know you feel bad unless you tell him. So you need to tell your dad how you feel, okay?

Okay.

But he wasn't going to. Pat typed bye because he didn't want her to tell him any more stuff to do. His dad was busy working and it was important. He didn't need to know Pat was sad or he'd think Pat didn't like it here.

Chapter 14

John scanned the headlines on the three day old newspaper. Being out of touch with what was happening in the outside world didn't sit well with him. It was like being on vacation with no news show to watch, picking up a newspaper just for the sake of something to read and playing catch-up. Not a sustainable long-term plan.

Sources at the White House will neither confirm nor deny last night's events were, in fact, an assassination attempt on the President.

What?

The door swung open and Pat walked into the sheriff's office. John took one look at his face, set the newspaper down and crooked his finger. Pat ambled over, his shoulders low. He dropped his backpack on the floor and John pulled him onto his lap. "What's up, chuck?"

Pat's lips twitched but it didn't reach his eyes. "Did you just call me up-chuck?"

"How are you doing? How was school?"

"School was fine."

Dotty was typing, headphones on. There hadn't been any call-ins yet, even with his late night radio announcement. Apparently no one was coming forward. Palmer was at his desk, looking like he was working.

John looked at his son. It didn't look like things were fine. But sometimes a man didn't need his father to make a big deal about his feelings. At least, that was the way John's dad had raised him. They just went out back and threw a ball until whatever was churning in John had worked itself out.

"Feel like going for a drive?"

Pat looked up, cautious. "Where to?"

"Well, Matthias did say you could come out to the ranch and see him. I need to go over there. So...you wanna come?"

"Awesome." Pat grabbed his backpack and ran for the apartment stairs. "I'm gonna take a whiz before we go."

Palmer chuckled.

"Hold down the fort, yeah?"

The deputy smiled but it wasn't happiness there, it was something else.

"Dotty?"

The receptionist paused what she was doing and looked over. "Sheriff?"

"I'm headed out. Radio me if you need anything."

"Sure thing."

John stood and grabbed his jacket. It was probably just being somewhere new. He was going to have to get used to the people and the atmosphere and eventually it wouldn't feel weird.

Pat ran back down in shorts and a t-shirt.

"You need a coat, don't you?"

He looked at John like he doubted his sanity. "It's warm out."

John motioned to his computer. "Not according to the weather report."

Dotty piped up. "The valley Sanctuary sits in actually won't be on the weather. It's below the elevation of the surrounding area so they don't report it because no one lives here anyway. If you want accurate temperatures, listen to Hal. The mountains are almost at freezing, the snow on the tops is early. This morning Hal said fifty-eight and sunny."

"Well I'll be." John hung his jacket on the back of his chair. "Maybe I should get me a thermometer."

Dotty hissed. "Can't. That would be transporting chemicals."

"How does Hal do it?"

She grinned. "Claims he can smell the temperature."

John chuckled. "Of course he can."

Pat looked back and forth between him and Dotty, so John shook his head at his son. "Ready?"

**

The ranch consisted of a two-story house, a barn—which for some reason wasn't red—and a big cabin all across the field from the landing pad. Without helicopter rotors to blow away the odor, the whole place smelled like cows. Bolton's bright red diesel truck sat under an awning growing like an eyesore out of the side of the house.

Matthias emerged from the barn and strode to the Jeep with a coil of rope over his shoulder. He was smiling wide. John hesitated for a second. Why was everyone in this town so friendly? It wasn't natural.

"What's up, little dude?" Matthias bent to high-five Pat. "Wanna come see the horses?"

"Yeah!"

John put a hand on Pat's arm. "Uh..." The horse at Dan's farm had been taller than him. To Pat they'd be huge. Fully able to crush him.

Matthias had a knowing smile on his face. "I'll be with him at all times. Pat will be fine with the horses. I'll teach him how to be around them and be safe."

Guess the secret was out. Apparently it was too much to ask Dan not to notice John's reaction to the huge beast on Battle Night, or that Dan would keep the information to himself.

Pat did look really excited. "I guess it's okay." John glanced at Matthias. "Before you guys go, can I ask you something personal?" When Matthias shrugged, John said, "Is everything okay with Maria?"

A shadow crossed Matthias's face, darkening his eyes. "What's your concern?"

So the guy wasn't going to give anything up. He was going to get John to spill what he knew first—which in itself spoke of having to be careful when talking about the subject of Maria. Maybe for years.

"I was just wondering if there's anything about her situation I should know. She seems like she might be having a hard time."

Pat had wandered off a few feet to pick rocks from the dirt. Matthias frowned. "She had post-partum depression pretty bad after the twins were born. I thought we were past that."

"And Tom?"

"Tom is..." Matthias shrugged. "He's just Tom. He does his job at the nursery, but he lives for Maria."

"You'll let me know if there's anything I can do?"

"Sure. I'll tell Mama. She'll probably call a family meeting, which means you can expect to get an invite to dinner pretty soon. And she won't take no for an answer." Matthias grinned but it didn't reach his eyes.

John glanced at Pat, who looked to be getting bored of finding rocks. "One more thing." He trotted to his Jeep, got the file from the dash and pulled out the picture of the knife. "Do you recognize this?"

Matthias studied it like it was one of those magic-eye pictures. Put your nose to the picture and draw back slowly to see the dinosaur. "Hunting knife."

"You guys do that here?"

"It's mostly taking a few older guys out over the land, sometimes we set up targets and they'll wager on accuracy."

"But it's illegal to transport weapons into town."

Matthias shrugged. "Talk to Bolton about that."

"Any idea who this knife belongs to?"

"Can I help you?" Bolton marched across the grassy dirt straight toward them. "Sheriff." The way he said it, the position wasn't a good thing.

Bolton's clothes weren't cheap. But they were clearly working attire, and not just what he wore to look like a rancher. The guy was western through and through. John figured in another life he'd have been just as comfortable wearing an expensive suit sitting in an office—or wearing a bullet proof vest and carrying a shotgun, kicking in the target's front door.

"Farrera." John flashed the picture. Pat had perked up, looking a little awestruck at the sight of the big man. It wasn't like he was that much bigger than John.

"Recognize this knife?"

Bolton's eyes narrowed. "Hunting knife."

"Which is kind of funny when you think about it." Except not. "Since weapons can't be transported into town and there's no contact with the outside world that isn't monitored. So not only did a murder take place because of this knife. It also begs the question as to whether or not I'm now investigating a possible breach of Sanctuary security as well."

Two men strode out of the barn. One was Diego and both were dressed in what seemed to be the uniform around here—blue jeans and a western shirt with a cowboy hat and boots.

Matthias backed up toward Pat. "We're gonna go see the horses."

The three men crowded around John, so he dipped his chin to Diego and the other guy and then looked at Bolton. "Who in town has a knife like this?"

Bolton mashed his lips together. "It's actually mine. All the weapons in town are here on the ranch; three knives, a shotgun and two rifles. No one else—so far as I know and that's pretty conclusive—has a weapon. When people come here to hunt, weapons are loaned. That knife—" He motioned to the picture with his index finger. "—was lost two months ago on a hunt."

"Faux hunting?"

"I guess you could call it that, since they weren't going to kill anything."

"They weren't looking for deer?"

Diego flinched. "Deer?"

The guy beside him said, "Ain't no deer in this town. They can't get over the mountains."

John frowned. "I saw one last night."

Diego crossed himself.

Bolton rocked back on his boot heels and rolled his eyes. "The locals think seeing a deer is a sign. An omen that you're about to die right here in death valley."

"Good thing I don't put much stock in omens."

Bolton's lips twitched. "Yeah, good thing."

"Did Betty Collins see the deer?" He couldn't keep the derision from his voice.

"A week ago." The guy beside Diego looked suddenly energized, his eyes wide. "That's how long it takes."

Then John had better hurry up and solve this murder before he was offed too. He sighed. "Who went hunting with the knife?"

"The mayor and his buddies." Bolton worked his jaw back and forth. "It was a two day hunt. They were to hike the designated areas on the map we gave them, camp overnight and return in three days. They lost points for not collecting what was at each checkpoint and not coming back with everything they took, even the trash. They were trying to beat Hal's team's score from the week before."

"Seems like a lot of competitions go on around here, between this and Battle Night. Anything else I should know about?"

Bolton's eyebrow lifted and he shook his head. "They need to blow off steam, that's all. Otherwise they're cooped up. And when people get stir crazy it's never pretty."

"I can imagine."

"I'm guessing you can't." Bolton gritted his teeth. "A lot of bad stuff went on here back in the day. People not wanting to co-exist with others not of their...kind. Sam had it rough for a while, and that is an understatement."

"How long have you been here?"

"Four years." The rancher folded his arms, stretching the sleeves of his shirt in a way that made him look more like a wrestler than a rancher. "People have calmed down somewhat. Settled into the fact they're going to be here for the rest of their lives most likely."

"Death valley," the guy beside Diego muttered.

Diego nodded, solemn.

John wasn't interested in local spook stories, legends and whatever else the residents had thought up to make their lives less mundane. "I have something else I need to talk with you about."

Bolton didn't hesitate. He turned to the two guys. "Head on out, I'll catch up."

"Sure boss." They strode toward the barn where Pat and Matthias were at the fence to the corral, feeding one of the smaller horses.

"Matthias will look out for him. He's a good kid."

John turned back to him. "How old is Matthias?"

"Twenty-six. The father—Olympia's late husband—had family connections with a Venezuelan cartel, got in deep transporting smack. DEA busted him and he rolled over on the rest of the operation so the cartel came after his family."

"He was killed?"

"No, he lived long enough to come here with them and continue to screw up their lives. He had a heart attack not long after but Matthias doesn't talk about it. In fact, he won't mention his father at all."

"Then how do you know all this?"

Bolton shrugged one shoulder. "I know a lot of things."

"Which brings me to another interesting point. Why is your entire file nothing but your name and some basic physiological details?"

"If you knew what was supposed to be in it, you'd know the answer to that."

"That doesn't really help."

Bolton grinned. "Don't suppose it does. But until your brother replies to my email and I'm certain you have the appropriate security clearance, I can't tell you squat."

"Did Sheriff Chandler know?"

"Nope."

"Do I need to know?"

"Debatable. But I'll read you in if you're cleared."

"Good enough." John figured it had something to do with a federal agency. The guy looked sort of familiar, and he had that manner other agencies had. The fact it was four years ago might narrow it down. He'd have to call his brother or do a computer search when he got back to the office. There couldn't be that many guys named Bolton in law enforcement, even with the different last name. The NSA might monitor usage from the library but John had a longer leash. With a guy like Bolton it just wasn't worth flying blind, or waiting for Grant to decide.

Matthias and Pat walked over. John had one more question for Bolton. "Anything else I should know?"

The big man shrugged. "Just if you need anything you can call. I've got weapons I know how to use and sometimes extra backup doesn't hurt, especially when you're going up against a whole town."

Bolton strode away, leaving the echo of his words ringing in John's ears. He was going to face the whole town? Maybe the majority, if they persisted in telling him he should arrest Andra. But he hoped not.

Pat ran at him and John braced. "Dad, that was awesome!"

"I'm glad." He looked at Matthias. "Thanks for showing him around."

"We'll have to get both of you out for a ride next time."

John swallowed. "Uh..."

"Yeah, Dad!"

"Sure." But it didn't sound convincing, even to his ears.

John led his son to the Jeep and they drove back to town. "So you liked the horses?"

"Did you see them? They're awesome."

"So you said." John smiled. "You like it here? School, the town, the people all that?"

Pat's light dimmed. "Yeah, I like it."

"But what?"

He looked out the passenger window.

"Do you miss your mom?"

Pat didn't say anything.

"I can call her if you want. See what's happening."

Pat shrugged.

John studied his son. How was he supposed to know what was up with Pat? At his age, John had been all about baseball. His parents had been happily married. His brothers had beaten up on him relentlessly but they'd never ever let anyone else give him a hard time. He was navigating this without a map.

John puffed out his cheeks and let the breath go without any noise. Pat probably didn't want to seem ungrateful for getting to spend time with his dad. What was with kids? One minute they were wide-eyed and innocent and then a teenager with an attitude emerged. The boy was eight for crying out loud.

"It's okay if you miss your mom. I'm not going to get upset or mad."

Pat kept staring out the window.

"I was gone for a long time. It might take us a while to get into a rhythm of you and me and how this is gonna work. But I'm willing to put the time in if you are." He parked behind the office. "What do you say, Pat?"

When he turned from the window there was a sheen of tears in Pat's eyes. "She hasn't even emailed me back."

John took hold of the side of Pat's head where his neck met his shoulder. "That's her loss. If she can't see it then I feel sorry for her." What was the point sugar coating the fact if she cared, she would've kept him?

"You were gone, too."

"I was and I missed you every single day. I'm hoping I can make up for that by being here now. I'm going to be busy with this case but that doesn't mean I'm not thinking about you, trying to figure out ways we can hang out. Okay?"

Pat sniffed and finally, he nodded. "Can I ride my bike?"

"So long as you stay close to Main Street. No exploring." Pat nodded again. "Do you need money for a cupcake or something?"

Pat's face brightened. "No, Frannie doesn't take money. I can charge it to your account and then she'll settle up with you later."

"Okay then."

Old west order of things in yet another aspect. John wondered what these people would do with smart phones and YouTube. Hal would probably have a heart attack if he heard what passed for music now. "Have fun, I'll see you at dinner."

Pat tumbled out of the Jeep and two minutes later he pedaled down the alley between the sheriff's office and the laundry next door. The other side was a vacant store-front. John would have to find out if anyone lived in the apartment above. Maybe he could buy it, knock down the wall between and renovate his entire living space. It wouldn't be long before either he or Pat chafed at each not having their own space. But that smacked of long-term, which had never been John's strength. He'd have to decide whether they were going to stay here first.

John dialed Ellen's number from the sat phone and it rang through to voicemail. "Ellen, its John. Call me. Better yet, email your son."

He hung up. It was nicer than a lot of messages she'd left him over the years. Like evidently attracted like, since they both sucked at this parenting thing. Why did some people seem like they knew what they were doing? As if it was easy.

The office was quiet, which suited his frame of mind. He'd never had to worry about being personable on assignment. Criminals weren't overly accustomed to people being polite to them. They seemed to notice common courtesy faster than just about any other sign you might not be one of them.

John unlocked the file cabinet and pulled open the drawer to get Andra's file. That was one mystery he could solve quick enough. Then he'd be able to get everyone off her back and narrow down his suspect list...by one town resident.

He flipped through the paper files but it wasn't there.

Andra's file was gone.

Chapter 15

"Palmer, get back here now."

John tossed the radio on the desk and winced at the sound it made when it hit the wood surface. He didn't want the thousands it would cost to replace the thing deducted from his paycheck.

He checked the front door but it was locked. The windows were shut and there was no sign of forced entry. He'd used his key to come in the back. Who had taken Andra's file?

The door swung open and Palmer sauntered in with a smear on the front of his shirt that looked like mustard. "What is going on? I half expected the place to be on fire. It doesn't look like a disaster happened in the middle of my pastrami sandwich."

"I'm glad you had time for dinner." John held his body taut to save from pummeling the belligerence out of his deputy. "Andra Caleri's file is missing."

Palmer glanced at the cabinet, his orange brows crinkling together. "From your files?"

"Yes, Palmer. Missing from my files. It was there when I looked yesterday. And now it's gone."

"And you didn't take it with you?"

John didn't answer.

"Or leave it out?"

Seriously? These were sensitive documents.

"You're the only one with a key."

John motioned to the set attached to his belt. "They've been on my person the whole time. No one took the key, which means someone broke in here and stole the file. The question is, who?"

"And why."

John jerked his head in a shake. "I know why."

"Because she killed Betty Collins?"

"We don't know that for sure, Palmer. The evidence doesn't confirm it or rule it out at this point."

"But it's been three days. How come you haven't figured it out yet? They do it in like forty-five minutes on CSI."

"This isn't television." John examined the lock on the file cabinet. "This lock wasn't broken or picked, which means someone used a key. And if it wasn't mine then there's another key floating around that opens this file cabinet. You know anything about a spare key, Palmer?"

He gasped. A little too astounded. "No. Of course not."

"Who in town wants Andra's secrets revealed?"

The deputy removed his hat and scratched his head, like this was a surprise algebra quiz. "Whoever is trying to blame her for Betty's death?"

"Good. Now we just have to figure out who that is." John locked the back door. "Let's go."

"Where?" Palmer trotted behind him out the front door.

"To hang around and see who knows what Andra never told anyone. Whoever took the file will spread it around. But if we can catch the rumor fast enough we might have a chance of finding out where it started."

John would have to address his deputy's attitude and belligerence later.

Across Main Street a crowd had already gathered outside the Meeting House. From both ends of the street people were walking toward the building and not one of them looked happy. In fact, their faces were set to angry.

Not good.

"Excuse me." John pushed between two men. "Let us past."

The interior of the Meeting House had been recently redecorated. White pages of printed text and photo after photo were pinned on the walls around the room.

"She did it."

"For sure, it had to have been her."

"Look at this."

"Did you see that one?"

John turned in a circle. The pages covered all four walls, even the windows. Olympia pushed in the front door with Andra behind her. Andra's face was flushed like she'd sprinted all the way from her cabin. She gasped and did the same as him, turning in a circle for a three-hundred-sixty degree view of her history splashed around the room.

Groups of people gathered to read the pages, while others turned to stare at her. Palmer walked to the wall behind John, scanning as he moved along. Page after page.

Andra ran to a collection of photos and started ripping them down. The glossy prints floated to the floor.

"You can't do that," someone yelled. "We have a right to know!"

Olympia strode over to the white-haired lady—one of the sisters who'd been in the sheriff's office yesterday—and set her hands on her hips. "No one had the right to do this. You are all invading Andra's privacy. How would you like it if your past was splashed all over, in full view of everyone?"

"I've never done anything like this." The lady pointed her knobby finger to the wall. "Or that." She swung her arm aside, nearly smacking the lady beside her. "I want her gone from here. She murdered Betty."

Andra tore down sheets of paper almost in a frenzy. Could she even hear what they were saying? John hoped she wasn't listening. He needed to get her out of here before this got more out of hand.

Terrence, who John had met in the dinner line Friday night, sprinted across the room. He pulled Andra's arm back and John winced.

She whirled around. "Don't touch me!"

Terrence got right in her face. "You leave that up, murderer. Then everyone will know what kind of filth you are. We won't have to put up with someone like you in our town anymore."

Andra slapped him.

Terrence swung around and his gaze found John. "Did you see what she did? She just assaulted me. Arrest her. Arrest her for Betty's murder. She killed a sweet, innocent woman and now she's attacking me!"

"Terrence—" John moved to shut this down.

"Which one of us is she going to kill next?" Terrence's face was red.

"Take a breath, man. Okay?" John raised his voice. "Let's all calm down and take a minute. Palmer, start taking this stuff down. Whoever did this needs to come forward. Your files are confidential and I want to know who put this up."

"She killed Betty!"

"We know she did it!"

John stuck his hands on his hips. "That remains to be seen."

"We know she did it. Of course she did," an old lady in a leather jacket said. "She was an assassin. She killed Betty and she's going to kill us too."

John whipped his head around to Andra but she'd already turned away.

An assassin?

She pulled pages off the wall, apparently not satisfied with the snail-pace job Palmer was doing.

Terrence grabbed her arm again. Andra used the momentum of his pull to turn and kick his knee out from under him. Terrence landed flat on his back with a thump, choking from the wind being knocked out of him. Another guy ran at her and John moved, pushing aside two old men while Andra wrestled with the guy trying to take papers from her.

John wrapped his arms around the guy's torso, lifted him and set him away from her. "Enough!"

Andra's eyes sparked, her breath coming fast and heavy. Her gaze flicked to the man behind John. Both of them moved toward each other. John got between them again, shoving the guy back. Andra grappled with his arm.

"Calm down."

She struggled, sucking in air like she was trying to breathe. Or trying not to explode.

"Andra, calm down."

She kicked his leg. John took hold of both of her wrists and held them by her sides. Her body bucked.

"Andra."

She kept struggling.

"Andra, stop."

"They—" She choked.

"I know. Calm down." He dipped his head so he could see her face. Her eyes were on the row of photos tacked to the wall across from them. She sucked in another breath and coughed. What sounded like a moan came from her throat and she squeezed her eyes shut.

"I'm going to let go of you now." He released her and she stepped back, her body still shifting.

"You're not going to put handcuffs on her?"

John looked at Palmer, who blanched the same color as the paper in his hands.

"She's going into custody, right? You should put cuffs on her. I know she's just a woman but she's a dangerous fugitive."

"Palmer—"

He took down another paper. "Everyone's waiting for justice, Sheriff. Aren't you going to take her into custody?"

"Did she murder Betty?"

"She's a murderer. You see this, right?" He shook the papers in front of him. "An assassin. No one was expecting this. But it proves it, doesn't it? She has to be the one who killed Betty. Who else would have done it?"

"Palmer."

Did he really think they were going to have this conversation in front of a room full of people? Or that he was going to talk John into arresting her?

"What's more important right now is the breach of Ms. Caleri's confidentiality."

It didn't feel like that, though. John's chest hurt like something was tearing. An assassin? It was hardly believable the woman who'd served Aaron and Pat lemonade could be a cold blooded killer.

"I'm just sayin'."

John clenched his jaw. "I know what you're saying, Palmer."

"I need to go." Andra's voice was small and full of pain.

John turned and saw the brokenness in her eyes. He wanted to reach out, but he had to stay impartial. Professional.

"I need to go."

Hurt warred with determination on her face. Then her chin lifted, resigned to whatever was going to happen. She was going to face it with grace.

John stared at her. She'd really thought she could hide this from them all, forever? Was she hoping for more mercy? Not likely. Eventually mercy ran out and consequences stepped in.

"You can't leave." John kept his eyes on her while Palmer moved down the wall. "You have to stay here and face this. No more hiding up in your cabin."

Her eyes widened.

The door flung open and slammed against the wall. The mayor pushed through people, shoving everyone out of the way to get to John and Andra. "Where is she?" The minute he saw Andra, Samuel Collins stopped. "You killed her." His voice was a whisper. "You killed my wife."

Andra flinched like she'd been struck. "I didn't kill Betty."

"Don't you say her name," the mayor screamed. "You don't get to say her name!"

John moved to the mayor. "Samuel, let's take a minute and sit." He took hold of the mayor's bicep to lead him away.

The muscle flexed and he shook John's grip away. John reached for him again but the mayor shook him off. His elbow swung back and slammed John in the face. John blinked and the mayor had Andra.

"Samuel." John's voice boomed as he blinked away the blurry vision. His forehead was pounding. "Let her go, now."

The mayor swung her around and Andra cried out. "You should arrest her!"

"That's not how this works." John took a breath. "Let her go. This isn't a show. And you don't make the rules."

He wanted to reach out a hand and have Andra take it, to pull her away from these people and guard her from their accusations. But they were right, weren't they? An assassin. How easy it must have been for Andra to slip that knife into Betty Collins. She probably figured one more kill wouldn't matter. No one would know enough about her to accuse her and she'd be able to go back to her cabin, safe in the knowledge that she got away with it.

The door opened again and more people filed in, talking. Someone gasped.

Andra struggled to move but the mayor held onto her.

"Samuel, let her go."

"So you can arrest her, right?"

John wasn't going to lie. It was looking like she did it, but it wasn't conclusive. Everything on these walls concerned what happened more than a decade ago. Before Andra had arrived here.

"Let her go."

Palmer set down his stack of papers. One wall was clear. He strode over and stood at a right angle to John, between him and where the mayor held Andra. "Give her to me, Collins. I'll take her from here."

John didn't let it grate him too much that the man obeyed Palmer instead. The two of them might be wearing the same uniform but it was one sheriff's office. They were a team.

Until Palmer pulled out his handcuffs.

"Hold up." John took Andra, pulling her to a chair. He motioned her to sit. She didn't. He wouldn't either. It was a vulnerable position that reminded him entirely too much of being at Alphonz's mercy.

The crowd was still there. John made eye contact with as many of them as he could in a sweep. "It's time for you folks to leave."

No one moved.

John put his arm out, ushered Terrence and the other guy toward the crowd and then bodily moved all of them to the door until they funneled out. He shut the door and locked it. "Get all these papers down, Palmer. Now."

Andra stood with her fingers linked in front of her. Arms straight and tight to her sides. Her face registered only shock as she took in the contents of her file. Her gaze hit the photos again and she winced, pausing on the image of a man. Were those her victims? John didn't know what to say. His stomach churned, full of coffee and not much else.

Palmer and the mayor shared a look—what was that about?—then the deputy sauntered to the nearest paper-covered wall and resumed taking down the contents of Andra's file.

John looked at the mayor. "You should head home. I'll update you later as to the status of my investigation into your wife's murder."

"I want this woman arrested."

Sometimes we don't get what we want.

John didn't think that would go down well. He needed a statement from Andra first. And then he had to speak with Justice Simmons about the evidence. There wasn't enough for an arrest warrant, not yet. But he did need to interview her.

The door shut behind the mayor.

John motioned Andra to the door. "Let's go."

"You're really arresting me." She sounded resigned.

"We're going to talk at my office. I'm not handcuffing you and I'm not reading you your rights."

"But you think I killed Betty Collins."

"Because you did." Palmer's voice drifted over even though he was facing away from them, which meant John caught the slice of pain that flashed on Andra's face.

She held his gaze with her big brown eyes and whispered, "I didn't kill her."

Could he trust that? Maybe she knew exactly what those eyes looked like when she looked up at him. He could almost imagine falling into them so deep he didn't know what was coming until it was too late. She was mesmerizing. Why hadn't he seen that? He'd just assumed quiet little Andra Caleri wasn't capable of hurting anyone, when the reality was so far from what he'd figured it was astounding.

He turned away. "Walk with me."

**

Andra forced her gaze up to the shoulder seam of John's sheriff shirt. He opened the door of the Meeting House and stepped aside. The crowd he'd removed from inside was congregated around the door, standing in the bright sunlight. Andra squinted, hating that she was forced to show weakness even if it was only from something as innocuous as the light outside.

John's hand settled on the small of her back and she flinched. The lady closest to her squealed and jumped back. Andra glared at her and the people around the lady came to her aid, staring wide-eyed at Andra.

Like she was going to hurt any of them.

Like she'd ever killed anyone because she felt something at all for them—anger, obsession, hurt, pleasure. None of those emotions had any connection to the things she'd done.

Not after the first time.

It had only been about doing a job. One she did for the sake of owning her own life and never for the money—which hadn't been that good.

John opened the sheriff's office door. Andra looked back. All their eyes were on her still—white-hot blades of hatred she could imagine flying from their gazes to her, their poisoned arrows sinking into her flesh. She didn't blame them. Those were the choices she had made.

It wasn't lost on Andra she could have been a waitress, or a librarian or a teacher. Whatever she could have chosen, for some reason at eighteen she hadn't gone that direction. Instead she'd been pulled into a world she never imagined existed and then made the decision to stay there. For five years.

Sixteen kills.

The first had been a crime of passion done in the heat of the moment. Kill or be killed. Then Sheila became part of her life and there were eight more jobs that made her name.

Enough the CIA found her and offered her a contract. Seven more for the U.S. government took her to the finale, the pinnacle of a career which left her pregnant with a dead husband.

Flying to Washington and offering the government all the knowledge she'd amassed hadn't been hard at all. Not even with the accusations, the recriminations and the distrust they showed her until she proved her information was worth what she was asking for. Never mind that she'd already been working for them for a year. It still hadn't been hard, not compared to everything she'd already done. Killing hadn't gotten easier each time she did it. That was a lie.

Andra took one look at the open door to the jail cell and swallowed. John pulled a chair over from the other desk—Palmer's—and said, "Sit."

Andra settled. Was she supposed to talk first? What was he thinking? Was he regretting spending time with her now he knew who she really was?

John folded his arms, his mouth pressed closed like he was saying everything he needed to say just by looking at her. Was she supposed to read his mind?

He opened his mouth and then closed it again. Took a breath.

For crying out loud. "I told you I didn't kill Betty Collins. I wasn't lying."

"I need proof what you're saying is true, otherwise I'm never going to get the town to believe you didn't do it."

"Why do you think I kept the past to myself?"

Nadia Marie knew enough. She could vouch for Andra, although not enough to provide her with a solid alibi. They hadn't been together the night of Betty Collins' death, since Nadia had been caught up with Bolton at the time.

"I'm beginning to understand that."

He wasn't going to give her anything? Not even a simple, "I can see you're not that person anymore"? She'd thought it was obvious she was different now. Everything about her was different.

What was she supposed to say? The truth was, if she had killed Betty then John wouldn't have had to clean up such a big mess. But Andra didn't think saying that was going to help. Knives weren't her style, not after the first time.

She held his gaze with her own. "I haven't killed anyone in a decade."

Not since she'd given birth. It wasn't much as far as recompense for what she'd done. But it had been a turning point.

John gave her a look. Guess that didn't help, either. He would think differently if he'd been here for any length of time. There were plenty of instances she'd figured murder would be justified, given the people who lived in this town. It was like they wanted to make her angry. But Andra didn't kill because the person made her mad, otherwise she probably would have killed Harriet Fenton a long time ago.

"What am I supposed to do now?"

Andra linked her fingers on her lap, squeezing until her body quit shaking. "You mean, now that I've been tried and convicted in the court of public opinion?"

"You're going to have to give me something."

"Like a killer? Because someone needs to take the fall for Betty's murder and clearly it's going to be me. Unless I can do your job for you, that is."

John straightened in his chair. "You want me to arrest you and let you get flown off to serve a life sentence?"

"Of course not." Andra stood. "You think I'm going to let you arrest me?" She smirked. "I'd like to see you try. I'll be gone so fast you won't even know until you come looking."

"You're standing here right now."

Andra folded her arms. "You have no warrant. I might be a killer, but I'm not stupid."

Nadia Marie rushed in the door and put both hands out in front of her. "Don't say anything. I'm your lawyer."

Chapter 16

Princess Leia stood in the doorway. Just without the circles of braided hair. John sighed. "And you are?"

She narrowed her brown eyes at him. "Nadia Marie."

The alibi. Right.

Andra didn't seem surprised at the intrusion. "*Cariña*, you are not my lawyer."

"Well, you need one." She planted her hand on one hip and her short jacket flared. "You're crazy if you think I'm going to let you get thrown to the wolves."

Palmer strode in with a mish-mash pile of papers. He dumped it all on John's desk. "I'm out. Need anything?"

"Nothing I can think of." His stomach rumbled.

Palmer smirked. "I'll grab two specials for you and Pat and bring them back over."

"Thanks. That would be great."

John checked his watch. How much longer was Pat going to be out riding his bike?

John waited until Palmer left and then glanced at the two women. Why the look? It seemed something unsaid was being passed between them. Because of Palmer?

"Something you ladies want to share?"

Nadia Marie's spine snapped straight and her face flashed with guilt.

It was Andra who said, "No."

If they didn't want to share he could hardly pry it out of them. John pulled out his notepad and looked at Nadia. "Where were you at around nine-thirty, Saturday night?"

If she'd been with Andra close enough to the time of the murder, John could calculate how far from the body she was and how much time it would take to get from one place to the other. It could potentially prove Andra couldn't have had time to do it.

Nadia Marie reacted immediately. "Busy."

John waited but she didn't elaborate. "Maybe I should get your fingerprints also, since we're all here."

She rolled her eyes. "Fine. I was talking with someone."

"And this person can verify your whereabouts?"

Nadia Marie pouted. "I was with Bolton Farrera, taking their team flag. You'll have to ask him."

"You're team C as well?"

She nodded.

"Where did you go after you spoke with him?"

"To meet up with Andra. She was already at Hal's radio station when I got there around nine-fifty."

John sighed. That meant Andra had been close enough to town to have time to kill Betty between when he saw her in Dan's barn and when she met up with Nadia. It also meant she could be the woman the two young guys who found Betty had seen running away. In the right direction to make it not look good for Andra at all, if she'd been heading to Hal's in time to meet Nadia.

John stood, motioning to Dotty's chair. He pulled out a fingerprint kit and worked through both of them, getting full sets of prints. He'd have to load them onto his computer and compare the images with the latent partial he'd taken from the knife handle in order to try and confirm or disprove their involvement.

He sat back down, locking his gaze on Andra. "I take it Nadia knows about your past?"

She nodded.

"Actually, it's Nadia-Marie. As in, Nadia-Marie Carleigh."

"Okay then, Ms. Carleigh."

She smirked. "To answer your question, yes. I know about Andra's career. Not the gory details, just the highlights."

He turned back to Andra. "How do you get into that? What makes a young woman become an assassin?" She didn't speak, so John added, "If you don't mind me asking."

Only her mouth moved. She didn't react in any other way. "Maybe I do mind."

"This is a murder investigation. And right now you're the chief suspect."

"She didn't do it," Nadia Marie said. "She's innocent."

That was debatable. Andra must have seen it on his face because she turned to her friend. "He doesn't believe that. He believes what everyone else does, that I'm a stone cold killer."

Nadia Marie looked like she was about to cry. "That's not true."

"I know, *Cariña*," Andra said. "And the fact you believe that counts for everything."

The other woman shot up. "I have to go." She dashed from the sheriff's office, almost colliding with Palmer coming back.

The deputy set a cardboard take-out container on John's desk and smirked at Andra. "Killers don't get meals."

"They actually do, Palmer."

The deputy's lip curled. He sat in the waiting area and took out a burger from his own box. "Did she confess yet?" He took a huge bite. Grilled onion and mushrooms spilled out, landing in the box he was holding under his chin like a bib.

Andra sat completely still, like she was made of marble. Did nothing faze her? The only time he'd seen a reaction was with Nadia Marie. They must be close. He'd guess Nadia had simply worn down Andra's defenses. Was that the key to getting through to her? John decided to file it away for later use—if he could figure out this mess.

"Well, did she?"

"No, Palmer. We're still talking." He glanced at her and she gave him a slight nod. "Andra was about to tell me how she got into that career."

"Who cares? Once a killer, always a killer."

"It's necessary to form a complete picture, Deputy Palmer. Ms. Caleri was likely not born an assassin. So I'd like to know how she became one."

If he was going to have to convince half the town she didn't kill Betty, he might as well start with his deputy.

Andra shifted in her chair and cleared her throat. "It was my eighteenth birthday and a group of us snuck off school grounds to go clubbing in Barcelona. I met this guy. Refined. Older. After dancing and a few drinks he convinced me to go outside with him." She swallowed. "We were in the back alley when he...tried it on with me. I couldn't fight him, so I grabbed the only thing in reach and slammed him in the head with it. One second he was on me, the next he was bleeding everywhere. He just...died.

"This woman strode round the corner almost like she knew we were there. She was wearing a skirt suit and gold jewelry, and she looked like a model but older. She hauled me to my feet and told me to grab his arms. I was shaking so hard I could barely get a grip on him but we threw his body in this huge trash container. She asked me if I wanted to go to jail for the rest of my life, or if I wanted to go with her. She said the *Policia* would catch up to me eventually and my life would be over, so my only option was to run.

"We got in her car, a brand new Mercedes, and we drove to another club. She walked me inside to this back room where two men in suits were talking. She pulled out a gun and shot both of them. I remember one of them dropped his glass and I got a cut on my leg. That's how the CIA started tracking me—because my blood was at the scene.

"Sheila, that's what her name was, killed two more people that night. The last guy, she held him and gave me a knife. Told me to stab him. I was in shock. He said he was going to find both of us and kill us. She grabbed my hand and pushed the knife in. It cut my finger."

Andra's head was bowed but her face had gone pale. John wanted to go to her and do...something. He was in shock just listening to it. He could barely comprehend what she was saying.

"We took a boat to France, rented a car and drove through to Frankfurt. It was a few weeks before she got another assignment. It came in the mail, to a P.O. Box. By that time she had me convinced this was the only life for me. She'd been injured so she couldn't have kids of her own. I was going to be her "legacy". That's what she called me."

Andra took a breath. "In two years she killed fourteen people and I killed seven until one day this CIA agent approached me at the market. I didn't know who he was at first, he just chatted. Flirted with me. I was clueless. I'd never had an actual relationship with a man before. Drew and I met for coffee a few times and he eventually told me the

U.S. government knew who I was. Sheila had been on a spree, taking jobs for some guy who wanted CIA assets in Europe killed. They wanted to hire me to do their work for a specified period of time before they would give me a new life somewhere else. I'm pretty sure he mentioned Kansas." Her lips flexed into a pseudo-smile for a second.

"My first job was to kill her."

John studied her as she talked. The darkness in her eyes and the way her voice had dropped in pitch, she was someone he barely recognized as the woman he'd eaten lunch with in her cabin.

"I slipped something in her espresso and walked away." Her eyes lifted, pinning him to his chair. "Sometimes I swear I can still hear her choking."

Palmer snorted. "You expect us to believe this crap? Some kind of crazy Stockholm syndrome conveniently manufactured so it's not your fault?"

"I never said that." She turned her head toward Palmer and her jaw flexed. "I killed those people. I worked for the CIA long enough to figure out that the guy was stringing me along. There was no Kansas. But by then Drew and I had married. I bought a new identity, ready to leave. But he came home while I was packing." She pulled up her sleeve to reveal a long, jagged scar that snaked up her forearm. "I hopped a plane to Virginia and turned myself in to the FBI."

"You killed a CIA agent?"

"It was tough, proving he was acting alone and without authorization. Drew was highly connected in Washington. I had to come up with more than I'd brought with me in order to convince them everything I was saying was true. But I did it."

John studied her. "Witness protection?"

"Drew's Washington connections hired a guy who knew my face to come and kill me. He almost got to me twice. Once in the hospital after I had the baby and once after the adoptive parents took her home to Spain. I was deemed a flight risk and sent here to live out my life with no contact with the outside world except that I can receive mail from Helena's parents. I'm restricted from any internet usage and from sending anything out in the mail."

"Helena?"

"My daughter."

John's head was reeling just taking in the wealth of information she'd shared. He'd have to read her file and corroborate it all. But no one with a history like hers needed to manufacture anything. He had no doubt it was probably all true.

"I knew there was something about you." Palmer tossed his to-go container in the trash. "Something I didn't like at all."

"Palmer." What was with this guy? It was like he had something personal against her that made him hostile to everything Andra said or did. "Is there something I should know?"

The deputy shrugged. "Like what?"

Andra didn't say anything.

John turned back to the other man. "I'll take it from here. You can go home, but we're going to have a conversation in the morning. If you'd like to continue being a deputy then you need to be here at eight-thirty sharp."

Palmer's cheeks pinked. He didn't look at Andra. "Is she spending tonight in the jail?"

"That depends on Ms. Caleri. She was deemed a flight risk and earlier inferred it was possible for her to disappear in order to avoid being arrested." John didn't need Palmer thinking he was deferring to her. "I need time to compare her fingerprints with what I took from the knife." He studied Andra. "Do I need to worry that you'll take off?"

She opened her mouth but frowned and then said, "I'm not going to disappear."

What did she want him to say? Of course he had to question her intentions. He needed to know she would stick this out with him until the verdict came in, or the killer was found. She had to trust he was going to do his job regardless of what everyone in town thought. Their opinion wasn't going to sway him, no matter the pressure.

She looked concerned, but John couldn't see any worry on her face or guilt. Just a wary observation of the two law men in the room, particularly John. Was he supposed to be angry at her story?

He felt nothing but deeply sad for the child she'd been, sucked into a world she knew nothing about. The Sheila woman she'd mentioned had been little more than an abuser, twisting Andra's mind. Not only had she survived that, but she'd even fought for her future. And giving up a baby? No wonder she'd wanted solitude when she came here.

Palmer scratched the back of his red hair and stuck his hat back on his head. "I can escort Ms. Caleri back to her house."

Andra didn't react. John figured that meant she was okay with it. "Very well, Palmer." He looked at her. "I'll be by tomorrow to let you know my assessment of the fingerprints."

She stood.

"I shouldn't need to tell you to lay low." John paused a second but she didn't look at him. "Let me know if you need anything."

Palmer held the door and she strode out; chin high, not even sparing him a glance. "Uh boss?"

John frowned at him.

"She doesn't have a phone at her place. And no radio either. She's off the grid. Couldn't call for help if she wanted to."

The door shut.

John didn't like it. He didn't like any of this.

He pulled up the fingerprint from the knife on the computer screen and loaded Andra's prints, starting with the index finger. He put them side by side and zoomed in, then rotated Andra's print until the lines matched. The print on the knife was the side of the finger pad.

John blew out a breath, sat back and stared at both pictures. He moved his gaze between them like a grid search. Whatever he found would have to be confirmed by a lab, but Justice Simmons would likely grant him an arrest warrant on the grounds of a good match—even by the naked eye.

His satellite phone rang.

"Sheriff Mason."

"Nice ring to it; sounds more natural now. I take it you're settling in?"

"Yeah, Grant. Thanks." He sighed. "But I'm guessing that's not why you're calling."

"Then you guessed right, since the congressional panel requested Andra Caleri's file and they've been calling every half hour all day asking for updates."

John sat up straight. "How do they know she's a suspect?"

The back door swung open and Pat bounded in. John handed him the take out box Palmer had brought for them and motioned him to the waiting area chairs. Pat grinned at the contents and dug in to the burger.

"They won't say how they know but someone told them. What is going on there?"

John sighed. "Andra's WITSEC file was plastered all over the walls of the Meeting House. Now everyone in town knows she was an—" Pat was in the room. "They know what her job used to be."

"So you know?"

"She shared her story with me and Deputy Palmer."

"Is she in a cell?"

"The fingerprint on the knife is very possibly a match to hers. But it's a partial so I can only say inconclusive at this point. She's home for the night. I'll rouse her first thing. She needs to come back and answer more questions at least."

"Who took the file?"

John gritted his teeth. "I also need to figure that out."

"Do it fast."

"Seriously? It's been three days since Betty Collins was murdered. I'm not a miracle worker."

"Those sound like excuses to me." Grant paused. "This doesn't have anything to do with the fact she's hot, does it?"

"Excuse me?"

"No, I don't think I will. I'm asking you straight out, John. Is this woman's...physical appearance affecting your ability to be impartial? I want an honest answer and not because Congressman Thane—"

John groaned at the mention of the pompous windbag from the hearing.

"—is breathing down my neck. The man wanted a video conference so you could lay out the details of the case."

"They want me to explain myself?"

"They called it a briefing. But basically, yeah. They want you to prove you're doing a good enough job. They're pushing for an arrest. They want Andra Caleri detained and Congressman Thane wants her out of town because he thinks she's a danger to the residents."

"I'm not arresting her just because I need to provide them with results. I want the truth. And what Andra looks like—" Or how John might feel about her. "—has nothing to do with this."

"I sincerely hope not, brother."

John glanced up. Pat's ears were at attention. Great. Now he was going to have to figure out how to explain this in a way an eight-year-old would understand the gravity, would know to have a care around town and would also not be completely traumatized. "I need the fingerprint analysis, ASAP."

"Done. Anything else?"

John worked his jaw back and forth. "I need to know who I can trust, who I can call on for help."

Palmer's allegiance was up for debate as were his abilities as a deputy when he was required to do something other than provide a presence around town for the sheriff's department.

Grant didn't take any time to think about it. "You need anything, call Bolton Farrera."

"He's solid?"

"He's ex-DEA. Undercover until things got seriously hot and he blew the lid off internal corruption that was spread wide."

That explained how he got to bring his truck. Testimony like that would have given Bolton a great deal of pull with the U.S. Attorney's office.

"I offered him the sheriff's position first. He turned it down in favor of his cows. Can you believe that?"

John pressed his lips together.

"Not that I didn't want you. You were the clear choice."

"After Bolton."

"I didn't expect him to accept, anyway. It was more of a courtesy thing."

"And me being the second choice?"

Grant sighed. "Untwist your panties for a second. You were made for this job. Who else can uphold the law and be a peacemaker at the same time?" He laughed. "Do you remember that time you told Dad that Ben and I got black eyes because we both fell, when we were really fighting over who got to put the frog in Sally Fisher's lunchbox? Then you did it yourself and blamed it on that redheaded kid—I forget his name—and no one thought it was us at all. I can still remember you telling dad it was such a horrible thing, and how could he even think we were capable of something like that. Dude, you should have been a mediator or something."

John smiled. "Yeah, but then I'd have to listen to people argue all day."

"Which is different from this job how, exactly?"

Shoot. "So we're done here?"

"Actually, there was a reason I kept you on the line a while longer. I was waiting for word and I just got it."

"What's going on?"

Grant blew out a breath. "Did you read the newspaper about what happened at the White House?"

"What does that have to do with me?"

"Well, it was an assassination attempt. Just not on the President. The First Lady was nearly killed in a coordinated attack on Camp David three days ago. Their daughter was with her at the time. The whole thing was unreal. The attack on the White House was the second attempt."

"Are you serious?"

"It gets worse. The whole thing was masterminded by a Secret Service agent who it's looking like has ties to an eco-terrorist group. They're mad at the First Lady for supporting oil drilling. It's a colossal mess in Washington right now but they've kept a pretty tight lid on it so far. Everyone is scrambling and people are starting to figure out something huge is happening.

"The President has to stay and keep at his post. But they want the First Lady out of there. Somewhere no one will know, only the Secret Service. They have no idea who else might have been compromised. The only people who will know where they'll be are me, the President and the FBI pilot I hired. And now you."

Of course.

"Oh and she's bringing her daughter."

"Elizabeth Sheraton is in her thirties, right? It's not like she's a dependent. And isn't she married?"

Grant sighed. "She was there and Elizabeth is directly named in the death threats. There's just one snag."

"All this and you see only one snag?"

"You're right. Elizabeth Sheraton is apparently now Mrs. Elizabeth Myerson."

John blew out a breath. "Is the husband coming too?"

"We can't reach him. He left a week ago. He's a lieutenant with the Navy SEALs currently OUTCONUS on a mission. He could be unreachable for weeks."

John figured Outside of the Continental U.S. was a bad acronym for being in the line of fire, but there it was. "And you're sending them to—" John caught himself before he said the town name. "—here?"

"Special delivery. All goes well they should be there in about eight hours." Grant paused. "Oh and one more thing."

John winced. What now?

"I'm shutting off your internet. For the time being all communication in or out of town is restricted to your satellite phone. No other outside contact. By order of the President."

Chapter 17

Andra walked the trail up to her cabin. Deputy Palmer's light bobbed with his steps behind her. She didn't need the aid to know the way, and she didn't think he was being chivalrous. It was like he was guarding her from doing something.

Did he think she was going to kill him up here? Spur of the moment crime of passion was hard to get away with. Although whoever had killed Betty seemed to be doing fine staying anonymous.

But why pin it on Andra? It didn't make a whole lot of sense, unless there was some other motive that had nothing to do with her having this supposed grudge against Betty.

"You think you got away with it, don't you?"

Andra's abs clenched. *Don't do this, Palmer.*

"Walking up to your hideout all smug because you think you're home free. Well, you're not. It's only a matter of time before the sheriff realizes it and your butt is in jail."

Andra kept walking. It wasn't far to her house but it was far enough Palmer had a few more minutes to say whatever he wanted and she couldn't do anything about it. One wrong move and he'd be hauling her back down in handcuffs.

"Nothing to say? That's how it is when you're guilty. Now all that's left is to face the inevitable."

She didn't turn, just kept climbing the hill. "And if I didn't do it?"

"Unlikely." He was quiet for a second. "You're gonna find it hard to convince anyone otherwise. Even if you didn't do it your life here is basically over. Now everyone knows who you are. You should probably request a transfer to another city."

Leave it to Palmer to assume that was even possible. Had he listened at all to her story?

Andra turned. Palmer's eyes went wide for a second and then narrowed. He stepped right into her space and looked down at her. It was a shame she hadn't worn heels in ten years because she could use the four-inch boost right now.

He smirked. "Something to say, murderer?"

The passage Andra had read in her Bible that morning hadn't left her mind all day. As though today of all days she'd needed precisely those words.

She sighed. "No, I don't have anything to say."

Andra turned and started walking again. *El Señor peleará por ti, y deberá tener su paz.*

The Lord will fight for you and you shall hold your peace.

The flashlight jabbed her in the back. Andra held her breath, lips pressed together. Her life had been fine the last decade. Why did God seem to think things needed disrupting like this? What good could possibly come of it?

She glanced up at the stars.

I'm trusting You, Lord. You gave me all this, I don't believe You'd take it away now. But I know You're doing something big.

Palmer waited at the top of the trail while Andra crossed the clearing and went inside. She walked through the living area without switching on the light. The lack of curtains had never bothered her before.

Andra lit a fire and sat on the floor, staring while it fanned to life. She must have dozed off because she sat up straight some time later when the fire was only glowing embers. She winced at the crick in her back and her neck. She was way too old to be sleeping on the floor, her back against a ratty armchair.

A shuffling noise outside brought her head around so fast she sucked in a breath. Ouch.

The noise passed in front of her door, the sound of shoes on the front porch. Splashing, then the sharp tang of fuel permeated the air...diesel.

Andra climbed to her feet and yanked on her hiking boots. She didn't wait for the smoke or the flames. She pulled her shoe box of photos from the top of the refrigerator and stuffed it in her backpack.

With a rush of heat and flames, the entire front side of Andra's cabin was engulfed. She ran to the bedroom, tugging the backpack on her shoulders, and jimmied open the window. She hopped out onto the grass and made her way around to the front, giving the cabin a wide berth. She'd cleared a sizeable area of brush and kept it maintained in case exactly this happened. She didn't want the whole mountain to go up; therefore it was necessary to have clearance between the house and the trees.

The air was thick with smoke but she didn't see anyone hanging around. Thank God for the wet September weather. The ground was virtually saturated. Had it been autumn after a long, dry summer they'd have all been toast. Literally. The mountains would trap the smoke in the basin unless a weather system passed over that was strong enough to clear it out.

Andra didn't need a town full of people with lung problems added to her account.

The smoldering fire was so bright she had to squint but there it was. The flames had gone now, leaving only glowing embers. As though the fire had whipped up and burned out in minutes, all the accelerant consumed. The letters were clear on the grass.

MURDERER.

Andra lifted her elbow and coughed. Her throat burned. Circling out of range of the heat, she walked to the opposite side of the cabin where the outside spigot was. It was stiff but she got the water running, praying enough of it would cool the heat. The whole system ran off a hot spring, so it wasn't always all that cold.

Though there was a fire department—of sorts—they weren't likely to come up here. Not for the sake of her cabin. It was down to her to make sure it was out. Her home was gone. No one else would care about added water damage besides her.

"Hey!"

Andra spun around, nearly spraying Hal with the water. He lifted both hands.

"It's just me." He bent over, hands to his knees as he sucked in air.

Andra went back to spraying the cabin. "Did you run all the way up here?"

"Of course. I was walking home when I saw it." He straightened. "Your house is on fire."

"Did you meet anyone coming down when you were running up the trail?"

He stilled and then shook his head. "No, I didn't."

Andra scanned the clearing in all directions.

"You think they're still up here?"

"I wouldn't rule it out." She shut off the water. "We should get to town."

The porch roof collapsed.

Hal flinched. "You have everything you need?"

Andra nodded and hitched the backpack higher on her shoulders. Hal trotted along behind her so she slowed her pace while she kept her ears open. Whoever had done this was still around, unless they'd taken an alternate route back to town that went between the trees.

"You're not upset about this?" Hal panted.

"Oh, I'm mad."

"You don't look mad. You don't look like someone who's losing everything. You just look...ready to move."

"It's just a cabin."

He huffed. "That place was never just a cabin to you."

Andra pressed her lips together but kept walking. He was right. Still, if life had taught her anything it was to hold loosely to the things she thought "belonged" to her. The most valuable things did not have a price-tag.

Sure, part of her thought maybe all of this was recompense—the consequences of her actions coming due. Lives had been taken by her hand; families grieving for years now because of her. Even though her WITSEC agreement meant she hadn't been prosecuted for her crimes, the legal ramifications still hung over her head. Her sin might have been washed away when she became a believer in Jesus. But that didn't mean people hadn't been destroyed.

If someone in town wanted to blame her for Betty Collins' death that was one thing. It was a lie. But how could she be mad at being called a murderer? That was true and she'd come to terms with it. At least as much as anyone could come to terms with the realization they were the thing people feared. The monster in the dark.

Poison had been her preferred method. It meant she didn't have to be present, or even have physical contact with her victims. But that didn't make her any less of a killer.

Andra kept walking, even though her lungs were burning. Even though her throat felt like knives every time she swallowed. She reached Main Street with Hal at her side and shot him a glance. The older man was frowning, his beard jumping up every time his lips pressed together. What exactly was he confused about?

No faint glow on the mountain said the fire hadn't re-ignited. Good.

The nascent day's sun was on the horizon. Andra had no clue what time it was. She pounded on the front door of the Sheriff's office. When there was no answer, she kept banging with her fist. Whatever it took to wake the man from his beauty sleep.

"I can go back to my place and call it in," Hal said.

Andra shook her head.

The whomp of helicopter rotors crested the mountains. She watched as it flew overhead, toward the ranch. Not the normal transport of mail, or supplies, or the chopper that took the trash they couldn't compost or re-use. Air pollution from burning waste would give them as much of a problem as a forest fire. This looked like someone was arriving. Before daybreak? Way to wake the town.

Andra pounded on the door again.

It opened but there was no one there...until she looked down. Pat Mason squinted and then focused on her face and smiled. "Oh, hey Andra."

She tried to swallow but couldn't.

Hal nudged her aside. "Your dad around, son?"

"Uh, no. He had a thing this morning." Pat hesitated, as though he didn't know what to say. Or he'd been told not to share. "He'll be back soon."

Andra backed up. "That's okay—"

Hal grabbed her elbow and dragged her inside, moving Pat back along with the door. "We'll wait."

**

John stood by his Jeep while the helicopter settled. Unlike his arrival, this time the pilot shut off the engine and got out. He opened the back and helped the first of two women down. Sure enough, it was the First Lady and her daughter—albeit slightly more rumpled than they appeared on television.

Bolton and his guys were crowded on the porch, watching and drinking from travel mugs. John wouldn't mind some coffee. He'd have to make it himself when he got the ladies back to the office.

Sorry, there's no welcome committee. She was murdered last weekend.

John strode to meet them and the pilot shoved two roll-on suitcases into his hands. Guess that made him the bag boy. He set them down and tried to look welcoming. "I'm Sheriff John Mason."

The First Lady looked like Jane Fonda, but with naturally aged beauty instead of making use of the merits of plastic surgery. Her back was straight, her posture perfect. She gave him a pleasant smile. "I'm Susan Sheraton."

He chuckled and shook her hand, making sure to be gentle. "Yes, ma'am, I'm aware." Aware, too, she was a lot more than that. "And this is Elizabeth?"

"Beth." The younger woman shook his hand with her tiny one, the sleeve of her thin sweater pulled down over her long fingers. Her other arm was wrapped around her stomach and she looked distinctly off-color around the edges.

"Welcome to Sanctuary."

The First Lady was still smiling. "You're hoping we have a pleasant stay?"

"That's the plan." If not, he'd probably get fired.

John motioned to the Jeep, since Beth didn't look like she was doing so well with standing. "Let's get you both settled."

He stowed the bags while they climbed in and then used his radio to call Dotty. This was a rough situation. John didn't do well with "delicate" and Dotty's warmth would go a long way in soothing the recently displaced.

He waved to Bolton, whose cowboy hat dipped. Beth was in the rear seat with her head back and her eyes closed. He glanced at Susan Sheraton, sat in the front passenger seat. "Is she doing okay?"

Susan's smile dimmed, but she remained the refined lady he'd been expecting. "The last few days have been...difficult. For both of us."

He nodded.

"I have no idea how long we'll be here. But I'm hoping we can settle in quickly and this will be the break both of us need."

He pulled up out front of the sheriff's office.

"So quaint."

"Yes, ma'am."

"Please, call me Susan."

"Yes, ma'am."

She chuckled. John grabbed the bags and Mrs. Sheraton roused her daughter, who climbed out with a groan. Both of them looked more than a little shell-shocked.

John's attention landed on a plume of smoke in trees on the mountainside in the vicinity of Andra's cabin.

He dashed inside. Andra looked up from the waiting area. Hal was slumped next to her, his chin to his chest as he snored.

Pat paused mid-bite, his feet up on John's desk. "Hey, Dad. You want a sandwich?"

He shook his head and looked at Andra. "There was a fire?"

All she did was nod. Hal snorted and blinked. "Hey, oh. Right."

"Are you okay?"

Hal frowned. "Guess that's what's important, even if her cabin has probably burned to a cinder by now."

"Why didn't you call me?"

Andra sighed. "Pat seemed to think you were doing something important."

Movement behind him preceded the First Lady and her daughter making their way in.

Hal stood up, chest out. Pat's jaw dropped—his mouth full of peanut butter sandwich. Andra stood, though it appeared reluctant.

John smiled, though he didn't feel like it. Who was he supposed to deal with first? He made introductions. That was a start.

Hal looked like he was about to burst out of his skin with excitement. "Welcome. Wonderful to meet you, Ma'am."

She smiled, but didn't offer for him to call her Susan. Still, it looked like Hal might actually be blushing.

Beth pressed her fist to her mouth. "Bathroom."

John pointed to the hall that led to the back door, where there was a single bathroom. "On the left."

Beth Sheraton—Myerson—rushed to the bathroom and seconds later, John winced. The sound of puking always churned his stomach. He couldn't help it, he was a sympathy puker.

He crossed to the fridge and drew out two waters, sipping from his until Beth emerged. Her color was better but she looked relieved when he offered her the other bottle.

John blew out a breath. "Right. Hal, think you could put on some water and make these ladies tea while we figure out housing?"

Hal nodded, so John turned to the First Lady. "If you'd like to take a seat, I'll be with you shortly." He turned back to where Pat was still eating. "Can you run and get Olympia, bud? She might know what houses are available."

"I'll ride my bike over." Pat hugged John around the hips and then tore upstairs.

John turned again. "Andra, let's talk outside." He didn't wait for her acknowledgement, just stepped out and held the door for her. When she joined him on the sidewalk he didn't hang around for her to start. "What happened?"

He needed the lowdown, even though technically he should be questioning her about why her fingerprints might be on the murder weapon.

"Someone lit my cabin on fire."

He'd figured, what with the smoke. But still... "Did you see who it was?"

"They used diesel." Her eyes darkened. "There's only one person in town I can think of who uses diesel for their vehicle."

John squeezed the bridge of his nose. Given what Grant had told him about Farrera's history with the DEA, did that really make sense? "You think Bolton did this?"

"Either he did, or one of his guys. I don't figure anyone else would have the guts to steal his fuel."

"No, I don't guess they would." Unless someone was still trying to deflect attention and now Bolton had been pulled into their web.

Andra glanced at the sheriff's office for a second. "Was that really the First Lady?"

"In the flesh."

"Wow."

"I know." He smiled, suddenly nervous. "Why do I feel like the nerd in school and a cheerleader just deigned to say hi to me?"

She smiled. "Sort of feels like that, doesn't it."

John almost smiled. Then he remembered the partial fingerprint.

Andra sighed. "That smile was nice. But now it doesn't look so good. And my morning was going so well. You know, except my house burning down and all. What gives?"

John held her gaze. Where was she going to stay? Hal or Nadia Marie would probably offer Andra a place to crash. Would she accept it? "You need to stay in the office a while."

"Why?"

"I just want you close-by."

"Do you think they'll try again, maybe try to kill me for real next time?"

That wasn't why he needed her where he could find her. "Look, there was a partial fingerprint on the murder weapon. The test I conducted was plausible. But it needs to be verified by a lab computer. That's going to take some time. I want to talk with you some more about how that could be."

Andra's face hardened. "I know I told you my story. I just thought maybe you would be different than almost every person in this town. I've killed people. Maybe you could even say I've killed a lot of people. But I didn't do that to Betty."

She paused a second. "Not that you care about the truth, but it would violate my Memorandum of Understanding to murder someone. Why don't you just arrest me now and get it over with? Why bother waiting for the test results when you and everyone else already think I'm guilty. Why not hold a trial in the Meeting House and you can all decide my fate here and now?"

"Andra—"

"No."

He reached for her but she backed away, her eyes full of pain. No one would think her a killer. It wasn't a wonder she'd managed to get close enough to her victims. "You can't leave."

"You're going to do it aren't you? You're going to arrest me."

"Will you disappear so I have to search all over town for you? The other option is you stay here where I can find you. Just until I have a moment to think." He sighed. "But if you're not willing to work with me on this then we're going to have a problem."

"Work with you?" She laughed but there was no humor in the sound.

"You want to get arrested?"

"No, I've just accepted the fact I might've had it good for a while, but the consequences finally caught up with me. Honestly, it's a miracle it's lasted this long. But I've been thankful every single day because I've been allowed to live quietly on my mountain and feel like maybe I could have a good life."

"And the clock ran out, is that it?"

"It was bound to eventually." She folded her arms. "It's okay. I learned a long time ago not to expect people to react well, even though I feel like that's not me anymore. That's why I only told Nadia Marie. Hal knows some of it, but not all. He doesn't know about Drew, but how do you tell people that? Oh, hey, let's go out for pizza. And did you know, I killed my husband?"

"Andra—"

"Forget it."

"I'm not going to do that." John wanted to kick the wall. "Whoever killed Betty may be framing you for it. They may've tried to kill you. Let's face it, you make a good scapegoat. And if you're dead then you're not going to argue, are you?"

Andra looked like she was going to be sick. "I can't fight it. I have to let what will be, be. That's the whole point of this."

"You're just going to lie down and take it?"

"What pull do I have? None. And I know it's not your thing, but I believe God is doing something. This is just how it's going to happen. It's not the finale. So I have to wait it out and when we get to the end that will be what He has planned for me."

"You'd give up control like that?"

She tipped her head to the side. "Look at what He's given me. Friends, a life, a healthy and happy daughter. What more is there to ask for, when I don't deserve even one iota of what I've already been given?"

"Mercy."

She smiled bright and brilliant. "Exactly."

"Then you'll need to wait this out inside."

"What?"

John took hold of her arm. "I'm not arresting you. But if you're in here then we can minimize the damage and maybe you can get through this unscathed."

Andra struggled. She saw the first lady and tried to make herself look dignified, choosing instead to growl under her breath.

John walked her into the cell and shut the door.

Chapter 18

John stood in the clearing looking at what was left of Andra's cabin. Smoke laced the air, the deep tang of fire left to smolder for hours. The front half of her home was a blackened mess of charred wood, the front porch had collapsed into the living room/dining area and the rest of what she owned was likely hot and steaming.

He'd be surprised if she'd be able to get the smoke smell out of anything. It looked like a giant with tar on his shoes had stepped on the front of the cabin and crushed it.

The three guys who made up Sanctuary's fire department milled around. They'd trudged up the hill to "the assassin's lair" as they'd called it, an hour after he notified them. Two of the guys had only agreed to come after John explained about the danger of a wildfire taking out the whole town. Reluctant didn't quite cover how they felt about coming to the aid of Andra's worldly belongings.

Tom trudged with a limp over to where John stood. Maria's husband was the de-facto fire chief. He'd turned out to be a decent guy. And the only one who didn't balk when John mentioned it was Andra's cabin. Apparently not everyone had written her off as a killer.

"Fire's out."

John nodded.

The other two guys were out of earshot. Older men with stubble-covered jaws and bellies that might have come from too many beers if this wasn't a dry town. One poked at what used to be the porch with

Andra's shovel, while the other cleared charred wood and wet pine needles from around the house. The guy clearing wandered over to the other and they chatted like they were on a golf course, before they made their way to where John and Tom stood.

"So are we done?"

John tore his eyes from the charred grass. "I guess."

Tom sighed. "I doubt Ms. Caleri's going to be able to salvage much of anything. Not considering how long the place was smoldering before we got here."

"Yeah," the brush guy said. "The damage to her cabin was considerable. Shame."

Right. His face said he couldn't care any less about the work Andra would have to do now. John figured Andra's stubbornness had a lot to do with that. Why else would she just walk into town and implicate Bolton? She didn't seem so concerned about the fact she could have died, just that someone had set fire to her cabin. Nor was she apparently concerned about the word MURDERER he could see in charred spots across her lawn. She hadn't cared enough to even mention it.

What made a person accept the complete destruction of the life they'd been building for the past ten years? She'd said God was in control and she was at peace with that. John couldn't fathom what made a person trust someone to that extent. She'd given God control of her whole life. Who just surrendered like that?

Tom said, "I'm gonna take the guys and head back down now, since the danger has passed."

"I'll walk with you." John trailed behind them with Tom.

The first guy muttered, "I figure she deserved it, considering who she was."

The other guy nodded. "I heard about that. An assassin? Not hard to believe, the way she keeps to herself."

John gritted his teeth. Tom glanced at him but John didn't look at Nadia's husband. He didn't need sympathy. Nor did he need to know if the man was checking to see how John would react. He wanted to defend Andra, but not to these guys. Maybe her tactic of lying down and taking it had some merit. He wouldn't lose his job, not because of them.

"You guys have any idea who might have done this?" John didn't believe it was Bolton who set fire to the cabin.

He got a "duh" look from the first guy. "She probably did it herself. You think of that?"

"Not my first thought, no."

The guy smirked at his friend, his face smeared with soot like he'd rubbed his cheek. "I heard about that, too. You and Ms. Calcri, all tight and stuff." His diatribe dropped off into a mumbled interpretation of what John and Andra had supposedly been up to.

"You realize I only arrived in town on Friday. Most of what you just said is impossible given the time frame." John stopped. They were only halfway down the trail and his insides were a mess. He was hungry, but if he ate anything it wasn't going to end well. "Andra Caleri and I are not having an affair."

"Not yet." The two guys smirked at each other.

John wasn't going to argue. Part of him still hoped to find the murderer and convince everyone she wasn't guilty. Then he'd finally be able to ask her out—which seemed so lame given all they'd shared of their lives. And what they'd been through in such a short space of time. He wanted a future with her; that was the gist of it. The outcome of the murder investigation was down to him. He was the one who was going to clear her name and make it so she could have that future.

What if he couldn't do it? Andra would go to jail—or worse. Sanctuary would be the first assignment that he'd failed at. She might be a phenomenal actress who killed Betty and then feigned innocence. But that would mean he'd made a colossal mess-up of reading her in the first place. Sort of like his ex-wife.

What kind of mercy took away everything Andra wanted after she had finally found it? He couldn't muster up a whole lot of respect for a God, a Heavenly Father, who gave a gift only to take it away again. Andra seemed to think it was fine. Was it really?

John trotted to catch up with the three men. Tom gave him a commiserating smile.

"You guys can't think of anyone in this town who would retaliate like that? Burn MURDERER on the lawn of someone they're convinced killed Betty Collins?"

Given Andra's past, he couldn't see how the rest of them were so squeaky clean as to have the right to be this judgmental.

Tom said, "I guess a lot of people could have done it."

"And given that the accelerant was diesel?"

Surprise widened his eyes. "There's no way Bolton did that."

John couldn't figure out the rancher. His brother's first choice for sheriff was another mystery this town held. "Why not. It could've been any of us, right? Or one of Bolton's guys. Heck, it could even have been me." He shrugged. "Think about it. What better way to take attention from Andra's possible guilt than to make it look like a war started up against her? Make her look like the victim in all this."

"So you are sticking up for the assassin." More smirks from the two guys. "I heard she was fifteen the first time she killed a guy."

They'd had her file and still misinformation got out? John blew out a breath. "Anyways, I appreciate y'all coming up to help. Wouldn't be good if a full blown fire broke out now, would it?"

Tom cleared his throat. "That would pose a problem, not that it's happened before. Since you're the only point of contact with the military, you'd have to be the one to get ahold of them and request a water dump."

"Like with wildfires?"

Tom nodded. "That's basically the only way to put out a fully engulfed fire. The irrigation system in town is very...basic. It's geo-thermal, off the hot spring. It's difficult to get the volume of water to combat a sizable blaze."

"You've been a firefighter long?"

"Four years, FDNY. I was working my way out of the rookie spot when I landed in the middle of a buddy of mine, another firefighter, making a deal with some guys for a night with an underage girl." He blew out a breath. "Not exactly the hot dog and ball game I'd been expecting. Voila. Here I am."

"Wow."

"Yeah, you ain't wrong."

John shared a sympathetic smile with him, glanced at the two guys in front and saw their attention was on Tom. What was that about?

**

Andra sat on the cot in the jail cell, simmering. John really thought keeping her here was the best idea? Of course he was going to be gone long enough her steaming frustration had boiled its way down to low and she had to sit here being glared at by Palmer.

There was no way locking her up was going to solve this. But no, she hadn't been arrested. The difference—just a technicality—

apparently meant something to him, while to her it felt exactly the same as every other time she'd been detained.

Palmer got up from his chair and strode in front of the cell. It was barely big enough for a bed and a toilet hidden behind a half-wall—like she was actually going to go in there. Yeah, right. Heaven forbid there were two people in town who committed a crime on the same day. Wherever would John put them both?

"You know—"

Andra didn't even want to know. She wasn't even slightly curious. "Don't start, Palmer."

His eyebrows rose. So she'd surprised him. Big deal.

"I'm sure between the two of us we can manage to be civil. Jo—Sheriff Mason will be here soon and then you won't have to deal with me at all."

"You think I can't take care of this on my own?"

Andra bit the inside of her lip.

"You think I'm not sheriff enough to be the sheriff? High-and-mighty Director Mason has to bring in his brother to police us, like we don't know that's why Johnny-boy got the job."

The question Andra wanted to know was how Palmer had managed to keep his job all these years. He cared more about his agenda with the ladies he'd befriended across town than about his duties as a deputy sheriff. Andra couldn't even imagine what they saw in him, though there was reportedly more than three.

Especially considering that incident two years ago, where Palmer had skated out from under responsibility for Elma Sanders' death. Sheriff Chandler had let way too many things slide over the years.

"For all we know, Mr. Sheriff killed Betty Collins because he and his brother have something going on we don't even know about."

Andra feigned interest with a lift of her chin. "Oh yeah?"

She needed him to think she might believe him, while not looking too interested. Then he'd just think she wanted to frame anyone who made sense and get herself out from under suspicion of Betty's death.

"If that's true, maybe he didn't send John here for just that one murder. Maybe he's going to try and kill someone else, too."

Palmer's gaze settled on her. The black ice in his eyes chilled her to her core, but she didn't react to it. He would notice. "Maybe he's going to kill you next. Did you think about that?"

Andra didn't move.

"Maybe it's why he wants you here, so he can fake an accident and blame you for the first murder."

The door swung open and Pat strolled in. "The internet's off. No school today."

Andra grinned at him, though she suspected she didn't look exactly happy. "That's awesome."

"Yeah." He dumped his backpack by his dad's desk. Then he skirted around Palmer, who moved to sit at his. "I mean, it sucks for Susan and Beth and all. But..." His eyes flashed and he grinned. "Having them here is good for me."

Andra couldn't help smiling. The kid's enthusiasm was infectious, breaking the spell of Palmer's assertions about John. Thank God she didn't have to sit here and listen to him anymore. John didn't need a suspected murderer to defend him.

Pat was still talking, something about exploring and cupcakes with sprinkles.

She smiled. "Big plans for the day, huh?"

"Yeah, but I have to check in with my dad first." He jerked, like he'd realized something. "Hey, you wanna play Go Fish?"

Palmer looked up, mouth open and ready to object. Andra ignored him. "So long as you teach me how to play it."

His jaw dropped. "You don't know how to play Go Fish?"

Andra grinned. "I bet you're a good teacher."

"I'll go get my cards."

**

The clock on the dash said 9:04 a.m. He'd been up practically a whole shift already and the day had barely started. Before going up to Andra's cabin, he'd settled the First Lady and her daughter into an available house and given charge of them to Olympia, who rushed over with Pat and graciously welcomed them to town. They were in good hands.

Main Street was dotted with people. John threaded the Jeep—which now smelled like smoke—at a crawl until someone waved him to stop. He pulled forward until he was outside the sheriff's office and walked back to speak with the drab looking woman—the school teacher.

"Mrs. Pepper." He was pretty sure that was her name. When she didn't correct him, he said, "Did you need something?"

She rocked back and forth on the balls of her feet. He couldn't help thinking maybe this was the extent of what she was capable of showing when she was overly agitated.

"The children cannot do their work without a connection to the internet. It's been shut off and we'll be disconnected for an indeterminate period of time." Like John didn't know that. "We cannot complete the required assignments without it. Neither can I contact their assigned teacher to explain the problem in order to make other arrangements."

"I'm sorry for that, Mrs. Pepper. The decision was not mine. Our new guests require the extra level of security."

"The First Family is really here? It's true?"

John nodded and kept doing it, as though he fully understood the problem it posed for her and was genuinely working through a viable solution in his head. In reality, he got to tell Pat that today was the Sanctuary equivalent of a snow day and it would continue until the teacher figured something out.

John swallowed to hide the grin that wanted out. "As soon as it's turned back on, you'll be the first to know."

Mrs. Pepper lifted the papers she held to clutch them against her chest. "I should think so."

John wasn't even going to touch on that comment. "What's that you've got there?"

"This?" She lowered it. "Oh, it's the Sanctuary newspaper. More like a newsletter really. Wilson used to be a big-time Dallas editor. So he thinks his paper still ranks with the nationals." She smirked. "Hardly worth reading. But there's something to be said for the first murder ever to occur in this town, it does make for good entertainment."

John snatched the paper from her and strode inside, shutting the door on her sputtering.

He opened his mouth, the words dissipated and he couldn't remember what he'd been about to say. Andra was sitting on the floor on one side of the cell bars with Pat on the other side. They appeared to be playing a particularly vigorous game of Go Fish.

"I win!"

Andra smirked, her eyes full of humor like when Pat did something cute and John's mom saw it. Her eyes moved to him. The affection dissolved as she pressed her lips together and set her cards down. "You saw the paper."

Pat twisted around. "I get the day off school!"

Palmer shifted in his chair and huffed, apparently not looking forward to Pat being underfoot all day.

Andra's attention was still on him, so he said, "I didn't read it yet."

Betty Collins had mentioned something about a newspaper in her welcome speech. Where had this Dallas former editor been hiding the past four days? Sure, John hadn't met every single town resident. But shouldn't a reporter be more interested in a new arrival? Especially when it was their new sheriff.

"Care to give me the highlights?" He crossed the room and poured himself some coffee.

"Depends." Andra stood. "Can I get some of that?"

He glanced at Palmer who was concentrating exceptionally well on his computer screen. "Did you eat, Andra?"

She stared, apparently not wanting to stir something up. "Coffee is fine."

He nodded. "Pat, you want to run upstairs and get Andra a granola bar, or some cereal?"

Pat jumped up, holding all the cards in a bundle. "Do you like Fruit Loops?"

"Just a granola bar is good. Or a banana. Something like that?"

He nodded and ran on his little kid feet upstairs. John took a second just to soak up the sound of it, his eyes on the door where Pat had gone. Then he looked back at Andra...in time to see the same look she'd been giving his son was now directed at him. What was that about? She blinked and turned to sit on the cot. John poured her coffee and not just because it meant she had to take it from him.

When she grasped the cup, he waited a second before letting go and lowered his voice, "Everything okay?"

Something flickered in her eyes but she said, "Mm-hmm."

That was supposed to convince him everything was fine? John slumped into his chair and downed half his coffee. The newspaper really did look more like a newsletter. Regular printer paper. Heaven only knew how much ink the man went through producing enough copies for the whole town.

The headline read, *Assassin Kills Again.*

John wanted to bang his head on the desk, but he kept reading. There was enough to bring the man up on charges of libel. He turned and saw Andra's attention was on him as she ate the apple Pat had given her. She shrugged, like, "What are you gonna do?"

John wanted to yell. She should be angry, more furious than she'd been about the fire even. The woman was just going to sit there and let people say this trash about her?

She swallowed a bite of apple. "The mayor called a town meeting."

Sure enough it was listed on the front page. Noon that day at the Meeting House, all residents expected to attend. He lifted his eyebrows to her. "Are you planning to go?" They were going to eat her alive.

"It seems my schedule is open."

"Andra—"

"I don't know how my print could have gotten on the knife when I didn't touch it. I didn't kill Betty." She shot a glance at Palmer and then back at him. "They deserve an explanation."

"The print was inconclusive. It could easily not be yours, just as it could easily prove to be a match. But what exactly are you going to say to them?"

"Whatever I need to."

"To convince them you didn't do this?" He blew out a breath. "What, you're going to produce the real killer out of nowhere? Do you know who did it?"

Andra sank onto the cot. "Reasonable doubt, isn't that what I need?"

Palmer snorted.

John shot him a glare and turned back to Andra. "Maybe you do need a lawyer."

"Do me a favor, don't call Nadia Marie. She'd make a crappy lawyer." The ghost of a smile crossed her lips as she stretched out and closed her eyes. "This is all I've got, John. I have to face it."

John lifted his hands and let them fall, slapping the legs of his pants. She wanted to do this? Fine. The town was going to crucify her because of what she'd done in the past and there wasn't anything he could do about it.

John pulled up the file on his computer. If she was going to stand up to them, he was going to have to scour every inch of this case for a possible suspect that wasn't Andra Caleri. Because she might be fine accepting whatever fate was dished out, but that wasn't the way he did things. No matter what Grant asked of him, an innocent woman wasn't going to go to jail. Not if he could help it.

Chapter 19

Coffee was being handed out to all. Someone had rustled up a table of sandwiches, chips and cake. Nearly everyone in the already crowded room had a loaded paper plate, standing around staring at their eats to avoid awkward conversation. John walked across the Meeting House, escorting Andra. The hum in the room stopped as everyone turned to look.

"I'm calling this meeting to order!" Justice Simmons banged a hardback book bigger than his head on the podium until everyone settled.

Chairs had been set out in rows enough to fill the room. Still, maybe only half the town had turned out. The other half evidently either didn't read the newsletter, or they didn't care all that much about Betty Collins' death. Or Andra's life.

Simmons surveyed the crowd with his tiny eyes. "This is not a court of law. Whatever decision is made here has no legal standing. All we are attempting to do is find the truth of the murder of Betty Collins."

John strode to the front and leaned down so only Simmons could hear him. "This isn't for you to do. The investigation is still underway, evidence is being tested and you're going to have to wait for my findings. This meeting isn't only absolutely not legal, it's also not right."

He pushed the podium microphone to the side, just in case. "You're one of the few people here who actually understand how this works. I would trust your judgment, but this is not what you're supposed to use it for. This is not about you reliving the glory days of your career. You want to issue an arrest warrant, fine. But that's the only assistance I require from you."

Muttering filled the room. The disgruntled sound rose in volume until John pulled the mic back over and spoke into it. "Enough."

Mouths shut.

"This isn't happening." John straightened and faced the crowd. "A member of this community was murdered and I'm not going to allow anyone to turn it into a source of entertainment. Not any more than it already has been. Whoever stole Andra's file was way out of line."

He might never figure out who it was took the file. But that didn't mean John wasn't going to let them know exactly how bad it was it'd been stolen.

Halfway back in the seats, Terrence shot to his feet. "Andra Caleri needs to answer for what she did. I, for one, am done waiting for you to decide what we all already know to be true."

A rumble of agreement swirled around the room.

Terrence jabbed his index finger in Andra's direction. "She needs to be arrested. But if you're not willing to do what is necessary, maybe someone else should."

John unlocked his tablet screen and swiped through to the copies he'd made of Betty Collins' files. It was a long shot, but he prayed to whoever was listening that it would work.

He scanned Terrence's page and shook his head. "Yes, I can see how you would be concerned about finding Betty's killer. The question remains, though. Do you simply seek justice, or do you want to make sure whoever killed her doesn't spread around what they learned Betty knew...about you."

The notation not only confirmed Betty's knowledge of Terrence having an illicit relationship but that it was with Harriet Fenton, the doctor's wife, of all people. John couldn't even picture that, nor did he want to.

Terrence shifted, standing his ground. "I'm sure I don't know what you're talking about."

"Do you know Betty Collins kept files on everyone in town? She added a note to her file on you four months ago. Apparently she witnessed a disagreement between you and a woman she names. You threatened to kill the woman if she ended the affair between the two of you. Now, you tell me, who is more likely to kill Betty Collins? Someone with a secret they might be willing to murder to protect and threatened murder only months ago. Or a woman who has by all accounts changed her life and lived a peaceable existence for the past decade?"

"Once a killer always a killer."

John didn't look at Andra. "That's not going to cut it, Terrence. Your personal opinion is not evidence and Justice Simmons knows it. Which is why, even with the revelation of Ms. Caleri's file, he still has not issued an arrest warrant."

"He's right." Justice Simmons bounced on the balls of his feet. The old man was enjoying this? "Even better than strong physical evidence is a witness."

John ground his jaw. Did Simmons think a bunch of people enrolled in the witness protection program didn't already know that?

Many of them had testified, securing the case for the U.S. attorney. They ought to know the difference a witness statement made when the witness could identify the perpetrator without a flicker of doubt.

Which begged the question, if someone was trying to frame Andra why hadn't they contrived to seal her fate with witness testimony? Either they figured that was too obvious, or couldn't get one for some reason. It could have been they didn't have time or enough planning in place.

The door burst open. "We're here!" The two guys who'd discovered Betty's body—Sam and Bill—strode in. Bill's smile dissipated. "You guys started without us?"

Justice Simmons elbowed John aside from the mic. "Boys, we're going to need a statement from the two of you—"

John said, "Let's go over to the sheriff's office."

They both blanched. "What?"

Bill said, "Why?"

Simmons breathed into the mic. "Are you able to confirm the identity of the woman you saw the night of Betty Collins' murder?"

John pulled the mic over and said, "Don't answer that. Not here. Come back to the sheriff's office." He turned to Simmons. "That's not how this is done and you know it."

"I'm just getting the answers you need. I'll issue you a warrant and you can arrest the suspect. Case closed."

"It was her!" Sam jabbed his finger in the air. "Everyone knows she did it!"

Andra folded her arms, her eyes on him. Her lips were pressed into a thin line like she was biting them to keep from saying anything.

Simmons said, "You can confirm this was the woman you saw that night?"

John whipped his head around to pin the older man with a stare. "Justice—"

"Answer the question, boys."

"Sure."

"Yes," the other one said.

John shook his head. "Your testimony is no good. Not like this."

The crowd surged into a new round of shouting, calling Andra every name John had ever heard. He wanted to whisk her out and shield her from the force of their accusations. But while she didn't look especially happy, she also didn't look like she needed help.

Simmons pounded the book on the podium. "I'm granting a warrant for the arrest of Andra Caleri."

The crowd cheered.

John shook his head. "This is out of control and you know it. There isn't sufficient evidence. Plenty of people in this town had motive, given what Betty knew about them."

Simmons shrugged. "Got you a result, didn't it?"

"Not one I'll accept."

Simmons pulled out a piece of paper and unfolded it. *Arrest Warrant.* "How about now?"

John shook his head. He'd prepared it before the meeting?

The old man flashed his teeth. "I'll have Deputy Palmer arrest her. And I'm going to be contacting your brother to let him know you weren't willing to do what was required. Murder is nothing to mess around with."

"Then why create this farce?"

Simmons didn't back down. He just peered at John above the rim of his spectacles. "I spent my whole life trying to shake up the establishment. Now I finally got a result for all the effort I've put in. And if that means a murderer was captured, then good. Because it's plain to see Ms. Caleri is guilty. Why else would she just stand there through this whole thing and say nothing?"

The man was right, she hadn't said anything. "You don't have the authority to decide her guilt or innocence."

Simmons sneered. "Perhaps you're not fit for this job, Mason. Someone else might be better. Someone more decisive."

Ire rose in him. "This isn't right."

Palmer had his handcuffs out. He yanked Andra's arms behind her back, but she didn't react. "Nothing to say?"

This incident would be added to her file and Andra would never get out from under the cloud of doubt over being arrested for murder—whether or not she committed it. She would likely get kicked out of the witness protection program. It wasn't worth it to Grant to take the risk she might have actually done it. Not when the security of an entire town was at stake.

"What is going on?" Olympia stood at the door, her eyes were wide and rimming with moisture as she bounded over to John. "She didn't do this."

"At this point the evidence neither confirms it, nor puts it in doubt." John gritted his teeth. "My hands are tied."

"You're going to let her be arrested while you just stand there?"

"What else can I do?" He took her elbow and led her away from listening ears. "I can't show favoritism. Even if I think she'd never have done this, I can't prove it."

Tears spilled onto Olympia's cheeks and she swiped them away with a sausage finger. "But she didn't do it."

"That isn't enough. I need to figure out who did. Only then will Andra be truly in the clear." He swiped a hand at the crowd in the room. "All of this isn't helping. I'm not going to be swayed by the force of their opinion."

"Because you believe yours is the one that's right."

John nodded. "I do."

Olympia got close to his face. "So prove it."

"What if I can't?" John didn't realize the depth of his fear until he voiced the question. "What if I do everything I can and it's not enough?"

"Then you have to call on something deeper than yourself."

"You mean like God?"

Olympia shrugged. "That's up to you."

And here he'd thought she would give him something useful. "I have to go. Palmer's going to be all over this thing. I think he's been itching to book her into custody since the murder."

"Yes, well. A man's wounded pride will do that."

John stilled. "She turned him down or something?"

Olympia lifted her chin. "Or something."

**

Pat could see Deputy Palmer and Andra through the crack in the bathroom door. He couldn't make out what they were saying, except for a few words. And none of them were nice. Had Andra really killed someone? Maybe the kids at school were right about her. Maybe she did bury people in her backyard.

No, that was gross. And weird.

"—finally." Palmer slammed the jail cell door. "...serve you right."

"Because I said no, or because I gave you a black eye?"

Palmer's body went all stiff.

"Maybe you shouldn't have broken into my house in the middle of the night."

The deputy was the one who'd burned her house down? Pat listened.

"What else did you think was going to happen?"

Palmer stepped forward, where Pat couldn't see him anymore. He said something low that sounded almost dark.

Andra laughed, but not like she was having a good time. "That was never going to happen."

"You ungrateful—"

Pat ducked out the bathroom and ran for the rear door. He turned the handle and looked back in time to see Palmer peer around the corner.

"Hey!"

Pat ran outside, tore across his dad's parking space and went left down the street. Where was he going to go? Palmer was going to tell his dad he'd been listening and then Pat would get into trouble. Never mind that Palmer was being mean. His dad wasn't going to do anything about an adult's behavior. His mom always said Pat was her only responsibility, not what anyone else did.

Pat ran so far it burned when he tried to breathe. He stopped and leaned forward, trying to suck in air. Palmer hadn't followed. He was probably busy doing all the stuff sheriffs had to do when they arrested someone for murder.

"Pat?"

He flipped up straight. "Mrs. Pepper."

"Is everything okay, dear?"

"Uh..." Should he tell her about Palmer being mean? "I guess."

She squinted like she didn't believe him. "Are you sure?"

Pat didn't want Palmer to have said those mean things to Andra. But what if she did kill all those people like everyone said? And what if she killed the welcome lady? Andra was nice to him, but what if she'd only been playing Go Fish with him so she could look like someone who was nice to kids? Maybe she'd spent the whole game trying to decide how to kill him.

Mrs. Pepper smiled. "Whatever it is, you can tell me."

Pat toed the ground with his sneaker. "Did Andra really kill that lady?"

"I'm afraid so, dear." She made a noise like she had bad news. "Some people are simply evil creatures. They may look nice and act nice, but inside they're rotten. A bad seed. Those are the people you have to watch out for because they can seem good when they really aren't."

Pat didn't want to believe that about Andra. But what did he know? No one ever gave kids the whole story.

"Will you be careful around her, Pat? I wouldn't want anything bad to happen to you."

Pat nodded. Andra was in jail, so what was she going to do to him anyway? Still, Mrs. Pepper's words gave him a chill enough that he excused himself and started walking.

It was bright and sunny, but Pat wasn't warm. He liked Andra. Why did everyone think she'd done so many bad things? Was Mrs. Pepper right, did he need to be careful in case she did something to him?

Before long, he got to the park. Aaron was on one of the swings, moving back and forth. But not like he was trying to swing. "Hi, Aaron."

Pat sat on the swing next to him. Aaron's eyes were weird. Maybe he was one of those people too, pretending to be nice when they were...what did Mrs. Pepper call it? A bad seed?

"Registration number..." his voice disappeared into mumbling Pat couldn't understand.

"You okay?"

Aaron flinched, shifting the swing to move more. "Too much blood."

Pat froze. "Where?"

"On the bricks. On her shirt."

Pat had seen the stain on the wall where Betty Collins' body had been found. He didn't need anyone to explain what it was. "You saw Betty?"

"Checks and balances."

"All Aaron."

"Knives and blood. Clothes and bricks."

"Betty Collins."

"Leave it alone, Aaron. It's nothing to do with you." Aaron's voice was different, higher sounding, like a lady. "Don't touch. Don't tell."

Pat's stomach twisted. "Did you see something, Aaron?"

Aaron's mouth moved, but no sound came out. Then he said, "Checks and balances. All Aaron."

Did he even want to know? Maybe he should run and tell his dad Aaron might have seen something. He would, if he thought Aaron would tell his dad what he knew.

"Aaron." Pat tugged at the hem of his t-shirt. "Did you see Betty?"

His voice was a whisper. "Don't touch. Don't tell."

**

With Palmer gone, John saw a difference in Andra. She'd relaxed but she still wasn't talking. "What happened between you two?"

Andra lay on the cot, staring at the ceiling.

"Fine, don't tell me. Don't give me anything at all that might help you, since you're so all-fired to take the wrap for a murder you didn't commit." He slumped into his chair.

"How do you know I didn't do it?"

John opened his mouth to say, "Because I know you." But realized he didn't, not really. He didn't know any of these people.

"What do I care if you go to jail for the rest of your life?" The words made him sick. "I'll still be here, living in Sanctuary. Raising Pat and doing this job. You're the one who is going to be carted off to spend the rest of your life in a cell."

And why did it feel like he would be the one in prison? It should be enough being here living his life. It should be enough having Pat. He looked at her and saw her eyes were on him. She would be gone. John and Pat would have to survive in this town of people who had taken one look at Andra's file and deemed her little more than an animal.

"Why did you have to be an assassin?" He shook his head. "You could have been anything. Why this?"

She didn't say a word. John stood watching her. It took a minute, then she finally sighed. "Whining isn't going to make your life easier. Things are what they are. I can't change them any more than you can."

John was a grown man and grown men did not pout. "I'm not allowed to ask?"

"They're not always like this."

"They're ready to crucify you and you're defending them?"

Andra looked at the ceiling. John didn't care who she was beseeching, not if it might work for her.

"Olympia told me I should look to God to help me fix this colossal mess-up."

Andra's eyes settled on him, her gaze cautious; guarded but full of something that looked an awful lot like hope. It was a good look on her. "Maybe she's right."

"Is it going to help?"

"You're the only one who can find the answer to that, John."

Gees, he liked the way she said his name.

John ran his hands down his face. The reality was, for the first time his judgment could be called into question. Andra's future rested on his ability to do this job impartially. But more than that, he needed to find the real killer. Because if something happened to her when he could have prevented it, the one who wasn't going to survive this was him.

Andra started humming, a warm sound that was partly the song and partly the cadence of her voice. John picked up his coffee cup and took a sip, finding a second to just breathe in the middle of all this.

The back door slammed open.

John jerked. The coffee sloshed and spilled on the leg of his pants. He shot to his feet. "Pat!"

The kid didn't falter. "I think Aaron knows who killed Betty."

Chapter 20

"He was right here."

John turned, scanning the park while his son did the same thing beside him. "He's not here now. Tell me what he said."

Pat's brow wrinkled. His face was red with concern for his friend. "It wasn't like he just said it. It was like Aaron-speak, you know. Something about blood and bricks and clothes. Don't tell. Like that."

"Okay." John put a hand on his son's shoulder. "Let's find him." He reached for his radio. It wasn't on his belt. He must have left it on the desk. "Come on."

They went back to the office, where Andra was deep breathing. She was asleep, now? John's full cup of coffee was probably cold, and his radio wasn't there. He snapped up the phone and found Dotty's home number in the list in his binder.

"Yes?"

"It's Sheriff Mason. I need an address on Aaron...I don't know his last name."

"No one does, dear. Try number thirty-two, A Street. The house is on the north side, halfway down. It's been converted into one room apartments and his is in the loft, I believe."

"Thank you, Dotty."

"When we get some time, I'll show you how to look up addresses on the computer." John hung up and turned to Pat. "Maybe you should stay here and keep Andra company."

Pat glanced at her and back at John, a look on his face. Okay, so she was asleep and she didn't need company. Parents weren't always logical.

The boy lifted his chin. "I'm coming with you."

John didn't waste time arguing. Who knew what had happened? They drove to Aaron's while John tried to figure out where his radio was. He'd had it earlier at the sheriff's office. Before Palmer left, John set it on the desk. He needed to find it, and soon, since it was the only point of contact between Sanctuary and the outside world. Had somebody taken it? Was that why?

The yard at Aaron's was a mess of weeds. The flowerbed was just dirt and some grass that'd migrated toward the house. John pounded on the door and then realized he probably didn't need to do that now he was a Sheriff and not a marshal. At least he hadn't yelled, "U.S. Marshals! Open up!" That would have been embarrassing.

He relaxed his hand and tried to knock politely.

The door swung open. Bill's t-shirt was dirty with Cheetos finger swipes. A distinctly sweet, earthy odor wafted from inside and his eyes widened.

John shook his head at the smell. "Dude, seriously?" If the kid's testimony hadn't already been questionable, it definitely was now.

Bill sputtered. "What? I've been stressed out."

"I'm not here for that right now. I'm looking for Aaron."

"You and the little deputy came to the right place." His smile faltered. "Uh...I'll...go get him for you." He glanced back over his shoulder. "Aaron!"

"I'd like to come in."

"That might not be a good idea." Bill swallowed. "Sheriff."

"Yeah, I'll bet."

Bill frowned and looked back at stairs covered with seventies-style floral carpet. "Aaron, get down here!"

Pat ducked under Bill's elbow and sprinted up the stairs. Bill yelled, "Little deputy!" and ran after him.

John followed them up, making a point not to look into the living room. He didn't want to know what he'd see on the coffee table. He'd deal with the fact someone was growing weed they'd smuggled into Sanctuary. Later, when he wasn't trying to solve a murder. It wasn't like any of them were going anywhere.

"Dad!"

The two of them crowded on the stairs. Aaron was at the top, lying face down, with blood on the back of his head.

"Who has been here?"

Bill jerked his head side-to-side. "No one, man."

"Pat, run for the doctor."

Bill turned to him. "Be quicker if you took him yourself."

John checked Aaron's pupils and took a look at the wound. He gathered the young man up in his arms. When he saw the smudge of blood inside on the frame of the front door, he paused and looked at Bill. "Where did this come from?"

It looked like someone with bloody fingers had touched the door on their way inside.

"I have no idea, man. That wasn't me."

John stepped outside and strode to the Jeep. Aaron had been attacked and made it home to the place he felt safe. Why had he tried to hide it? Who had done this?

**

Andra shifted on the bed but couldn't seem to open her eyes. Her head was a fog. This wasn't her bed. The thought was enough to pry her eyes open.

Bars.

She was still in the Sanctuary holding cell.

Booted feet crossed the floor tiles, the muted steps belonging to a dark figure Andra could barely make out through the cloud obscuring her vision.

What was wrong with her? It was like her brain was awake but her body wouldn't cooperate with what she was telling it to do. She couldn't even lift her arms. Her head would only turn a fraction. She tried to sit up. No, that didn't work either.

What was...what was going on?

The figure moved to John's desk, then away to the door and it clicked shut.

Andra tried to rise but she couldn't.

Where was John?

**

John started his evidence search at the park. He walked from there to Aaron's residence, using the most direct route. He found nothing, so he pounded on the door again.

No answer.

As John walked back to the park, he scanned everything from the other direction. In case he'd missed something on the first walk-through.

A Sanctuary resident had attacked Aaron. Likely they were warning him in a more compelling way not to tell anyone what he knew, but the plan had backfired. If Aaron could tell him what he knew, this might be John's chance to get the information he needed and close the case.

Could Aaron really have witnessed the murder? He could simply be remembering some other traumatic experience. This could be nothing but PTSD and a nasty accident. Aaron could've thought it wasn't too bad and made it to his place before he collapsed on the stairs.

Until Aaron woke up, John wouldn't know for sure.

He was almost to the park when something in a shrub caught his attention. A rusty pipe had been tossed into the bush. John pulled on a pair of latex gloves and picked it up. Blood and hair was stuck to the end. He was going to have to take prints from this, too. It was attempted murder. At least until Aaron woke up...or didn't.

John took pictures, stowed the metal pipe in a brown evidence sack from his trunk and got it all noted down. This wasn't looking like Aaron had an accident of his own accord. Whoever hit him had tossed the pipe in the bush to hide their actions. But who? Aaron was lean, but he could still be strong enough if he needed to defend himself.

Aaron had no problem showing his back. He'd done it in the sheriff's office plenty of times when his mind was on the intricacies of his mail delivery. That could have happened this time, if he was preoccupied with everything that had gone down.

Whoever hit him must have rushed up on him from behind and took him by surprise. Was it someone he was comfortable enough with to feel safe...until he was struck?

John didn't like any of it, least of all the fact his son was caught up in this. Pat and the murder investigation were supposed to have remained two separate things. Did whoever attacked Aaron know the young man shared something with John's son? If they tried again, would they try to silence Pat?

John parked outside the medical center. The reception desk was empty although two people waited to see the doctor.

John strode straight to the hall, where Pat was sitting. "Hey, any word?" His son shook his head, so John crouched in front of him. "Doctor Fenton is with him?"

"He didn't wake up."

"I'm sure Doctor Fenton will patch him up."

At least, John hoped so. He sat, using an arm around his son's shoulder to pull Pat into his side. The clock ticked, the only sound in the hall until Fenton emerged from Aaron's room, typing onto a tablet with one finger. The fact the doctor had computerized records when so much of Sanctuary was woefully outdated was surprising. How long would it take John to get a handle on everything going on in this town?

Pat jumped up from his chair.

John said to the doctor, "How is Aaron?"

"Stable. I patched up his head. We won't know how he is until he wakes up and I can check his mental status."

John didn't envy the man that job. Aaron struggled with straight answers at the best of times.

"Can I sit with him?"

Doctor Fenton looked at John, who nodded. He glanced back at Pat. "So long as you're quiet and you let Aaron rest."

Pat let himself in the room.

John waited until he shut the door. "I found a pipe."

Fenton nodded. "It was a good, solid blow. He has cranial swelling, so we'll have to wait until that goes down before he's likely to be coherent. He could be asleep for hours."

"I want someone protecting him."

Fenton lifted his arms and let them fall. "I'm working solo. That's not something I can provide."

"I'll make a call."

"You can use the front desk phone." The doctor strode away. He reached the end of the hall and looked down at his tablet. "Mrs. Culler?"

It didn't take long for Bolton to pull up outside the medical center. John met the rancher on the sidewalk. Both doors of the truck opened and Matthias climbed out also. He lifted his chin to John and went inside.

Bolton came around to where John stood on the sidewalk. "He wanted to make sure Pat was okay."

What was John supposed to make of that? He didn't want to be suspicious, but what twenty-six year old man made friends with an eight year old? Given everything that'd happened, John had to be cautious. It could be perfectly innocent, a kid who clearly needed friends. And a man who could relate, and was willing to give Pat time out of his day.

"Diego is off on one of his benders. Matthias doesn't want to sit around at home wondering what his brother is up to, so he's distracting himself."

"Diego gets up to trouble?"

Bolton nodded, clearly disturbed about something. "And I can't figure out who or where, but someone is making moonshine. Probably up in the mountains."

"Seriously?" First weed, and now moonshine. Couldn't these people just live within the boundaries that had been set for them? "Why does it feel as if this job is going to be like trying to babysit a bunch of rebellious teenagers?"

Bolton laughed. "Why do you think I prefer my cattle?"

John figured the man had a solid point. He'd known there was a reason Bolton turned down the job. If this was it, John didn't blame him even if he had been Grant's first choice. Still, John was the one getting stuck with the crappy end of the stick.

"So how's Aaron?"

"Still unconscious. He was hit on the back of the head with something hard but not sharp. I found a pipe. Once he wakes up, Doctor Fenton will run some tests. We won't know anything until then."

The big man blew out a breath. "That's rough. He's a good kid."

"Yeah? I mean, Aaron seemed nice and Pat likes him. But I wasn't sure."

Bolton folded his arms. "Watched his dad kill his mom and then agreed to testify against his dad, who was this big time preacher. TV shows and all that, thousands of people in his congregation. Turns out on the side he has millions in gambling debts and owes most of it to the mob. Your brother pulled some strings and had him brought here. I think it's been good for him."

"Wow." Given Aaron's aptitude for coordinating the mail delivery, John was inclined to agree. Grant had done a good thing. "Thanks for coming. I appreciate your help."

"I'll be here. Matthias will stay until Aaron wakes up. After that we can switch off."

"Matthias can protect them both if you're not here?"

Bolton nodded. "I trained all my guys. Matthias will call when Aaron wakes up and I'll bring them back to the ranch."

"Think you can get Aaron to tell you what he knows?"

Bolton nodded. "If we give him time and make him feel safe enough, I think he will. And I have a secret weapon."

"Truth serum?" John didn't have much time. He needed to get to the bottom of this. If it was days before Aaron said anything...Andra was going to be taken from town on Monday, when the transport came. John couldn't help thinking that if she went, she would never be able to come back.

He had four days to solve this case before Andra was done in Sanctuary.

"Not truth serum. Horses." Bolton smirked. "Some people like them."

John narrowed his eyes.

"Aaron loves them. We'll take care of him, and the horses will settle him. Pat being there will help and with Diego gone we have an even better chance. I'll let you know."

John led the big man inside. Doctor Fenton was at his front desk with one person now in the waiting area.

Bolton rested his elbows on the counter. "Harriett's out today?"

The doctor's mouth betrayed how he felt about that, but he didn't glance up from the computer. "Turns out I can do both jobs, since hers requires almost no brainpower and only a minimal amount of computer skills."

John got down to business. "Bolton and Matthias will switch-off staying with Pat and Aaron. No one else gets in the room except you."

The doctor looked taken aback for a moment. He nodded.

"I need to get back to the office. I don't like leaving Andra alone." Plus it was getting dark. She would need something to eat pretty soon. "You'll send someone and let me know? My radio is AWOL right now."

Bolton nodded and they shook hands. "If this stretches into tomorrow, Pat can bunk with the boys for a couple days."

John smiled. "He would probably love that."

"Yeah, the four a.m. wake up call for chores before breakfast will be fun for the first day at least."

John chuckled and went in to tell Pat goodbye. His son was laughing at something Matthias had said. "Hey, I appreciate this."

"No worries." Matthias shrugged. "Gets me out of evening chores. But don't tell the boss I said that."

"Bye, Pat." John squeezed his son's shoulder. "Let me know when Aaron wakes up, okay?"

Pat nodded and gave him a small smile. John drove back to the sheriff's office. The back door was still locked, not that it had stopped someone stealing Andra's file. She was in the holding cell, sitting and rubbing her head.

"You okay?"

She looked up, her eyes glassy. John unlocked the cell and crouched in front of her. "What's wrong?"

"I...something..."

He touched her cheeks, scanning her face before he held her gaze to get her to focus on him. "Go slow. Tell me what happened."

"I feel weird." She paused a moment as though measuring her words. "Slow, like I've been drugged."

"You haven't had anything except coffee."

John didn't want to register how soft her cheeks were, or how big her eyes were up close. The hardness he'd seen over the last couple of days as her past was revealed and Palmer had arrested her, was now gone. John took a moment to study her when she wasn't trying to keep him at a distance.

"That must be it." She nodded. "I just haven't had anything to eat, so the coffee went to my head."

John wasn't convinced. "I'll get you something to eat, but I want Doctor Fenton to come and look at you."

She shook her head before he'd even finished talking. "No. I'm okay, really. I just need water and something to eat. It'll pass."

John left her sitting on the cot and shut her in. If he called the diner, could he have Sam send someone over with two meals? He snapped up the phone—

His radio was on the desk.

John set the phone back down and turned to Andra. "How long has this been here?"

She blinked and glanced at it. "I have no idea. You didn't have it?"

"It wasn't here before. Then I was busy getting Aaron medical attention." He saw the question on her face and said, "He's okay for now. We'll know for sure when he wakes up."

Her gaze darkened; her eyes much clearer now. "And you didn't have it?"

"No."

It had been gone and then reappeared? John was surer now someone could have taken it. Could they have drugged Andra so she didn't know?

He rubbed his eyes, then stared at the cold coffee on his desk. At the half-full pot. Could whoever killed Betty have drugged his coffee, attacked Aaron and then come to the sheriff's office to use his phone?

"Was anyone in here when I was gone?"

She glanced to the side. "I can't really remember."

John sat back in his chair. What would have happened if he'd drunk his coffee? Would he have been passed out on the floor like Andra while Aaron bled to death? Pat would have found him unconscious, unable to help. John would have been here while someone was in the office, helpless to defend Andra if they'd tried anything. And if Pat had been there, too...

John squeezed the bridge of his nose. This was getting out of control. Spiking the coffee in his office? He didn't have the equipment to test it; he couldn't even get it sent off to whatever lab Grant was using until Monday. Which meant Andra would be on the same helicopter out of town, cuffed to the floor like she was a danger to the airmen transporting her.

There was no way he was going to let that happen to her.

John turned to Andra. "Tell me about Palmer."

Her gaze shifted to him.

"You know something. I need to know if I can trust him."

"I don't know that he's a bad cop." She shifted. "Where was he Saturday night?"

John thought back to Battle Night. "Not in the Meeting House like he said he'd be. When he showed up at the scene, his buttons were off like he'd put his shirt on in a hurry."

"I'd guess he didn't kill Betty because he was with a woman. And being as it was Battle Night, I'd guess it was the wife of someone involved in the game."

John sat back in his chair. "Does he do that often?"

Andra shrugged. "How should I know? I barely come into town unless I need to. This is the most I've been off my mountain in years."

"Palmer has a history with women?" John caught the look she tried to hide. "Tell me."

She sighed. "He came up to my cabin once, acting all weird. Riled up. Maybe drunk, I don't know. He did smell odd and he was slurring, talking about how it was time."

When she didn't say anything more, John said, "And?"

"That...situation." She looked at the ceiling. "It was like history repeating itself. A man up-close about to do something horrible. It was dark and I was scared. I didn't react well."

"Understandable."

"He threatened to tell Sheriff Chandler I'd attacked him. But since he was the one at my cabin in the middle of the night it wouldn't have been easy to explain away."

"You think he has it in for you?"

"I know he has it in for me."

John thought for a minute. "Your cabin?"

"I don't think he set the fire. It's more his attitude. He's way too gung-ho over me being taken away. I think I dinged his pride by not wanting him."

"That's not okay, Andra. That's not a reason for you to be convicted of murder. Palmer should know that." He blew out a breath. "I'll talk to him."

"No." She shook her head, then winced and lay down.

"Are you okay?"

"Don't say anything to Palmer, okay? It's not worth stirring it all up again."

John shook his head. He was absolutely going to say something to Palmer. He couldn't have a deputy who let his personal agenda cloud his judgment. That wasn't going to work.

The satellite phone rang.

"Sheriff John Mason."

"Please hold for the President."

Chapter 21

The line clicked and a voice John had heard, but only on TV, came on the line. "Sheriff?"

"Yes, sir." John sat up. Not that the President could see him but he couldn't exactly slouch, even if he wasn't face-to-face with the man. "Your wife and daughter are all settled in, sir. I've made sure they're going to be taken care of."

"I'm sure you have, Sheriff. But that's not why I'm calling."

"Excuse me, sir. What can I help you with?"

President Sheraton chuckled. "Under the circumstances, you can probably just call me Thomas." He paused for a beat. "I understand there's a murder investigation going on there."

John had a brief flash of panic thinking Sheraton might say the name Sanctuary over the phone. Grant should've briefed him. "That's right."

"And the suspect is in custody?"

"I have an arrest warrant." John glanced at Andra. She was lying down still, but her eyes were open and her attention was on his end of the phone conversation.

"To be honest, sir, the warrant was provided because of information relating to the suspect's past, which all occurred over a decade ago. Yes, it's incriminating. The people of the town are convinced she did it. At this point I don't have any good evidence to confirm the suspect is guilty."

Who knew if the President even wanted all this information. Didn't he have better things to worry about? Although, if it was John's wife and daughter then he would probably be taking a close interest in the town they'd been sent to.

"So you buckled and arrested her?"

"Her cabin, which sits in a remote area, was torched. It's unlivable now. Honestly, I'm concerned for her safety. Another resident who may also have a connection to the case was attacked this afternoon. The suspect is now in my custody."

"I see." The President paused. "And do you have any idea who might be behind it all?"

"Whoever it is, I think they're in contact with someone outside town. This phone, the only method of communication in and out right now, may have been compromised earlier tonight."

"I want this wrapped up, Sheriff."

"Yes, sir."

"I want the killer on Monday's transport."

John blew out a silent breath. Grant had briefed the president on how Sanctuary worked. Likely in trying to convince him why sending his family there was the only safe option. "I promise you that your wife and daughter are safe. But if you're worried, I can have someone permanently assigned to watch out for them."

"I'm sure you'll do everything you're able to, Sheriff. I'm worried, but I can't say I'm not feeling pressure from this end also. The congressional committee wants this wrapped up. In fact, they assure me the woman you have in custody is the person responsible."

"Given the evidence and the way the case has progressed, I can only say the entire town appears to be prejudiced against this woman."

It would take a psychologist to figure out why they'd turned their ire against Andra. What made them think they were so much better than her?

The president said, "Congressman Thane was adamant the woman is guilty. He assured me the case you have is solid."

The pompous windbag was stirring things up again? John gritted his teeth. "I'm not sure how he could know that, sir."

"I'm pretty sure the oaf is planning to run in the next election. What he really called about was to complain nothing was going his way. Like your town is his responsibility. And he inferred he intends to knock me off the top spot. Like people would be fool enough to vote for him. But I suppose stranger things have happened."

"I see." Not that John did, but it was like the president wanted to vent to someone. What better way to do it than over probably the most secure phone in the country? Which begged the question of whether John's phone was being traced. Maybe he could find out if whoever had accessed it had made a call and who they'd contacted.

He liked the idea this was "his" town but still, "Congressman Thane wants the town shut down, Mr. President."

Behind him, Andra made a noise. John turned to her, but said, "I'm not sure what his problem is with Ms. Caleri, specifically—"

"Andra Caleri?"

She was looking at him, her eyes wide.

"Yes, sir."

"That explains a few things." The President sighed. "I hadn't heard her name. But I'm familiar enough with her reputation and the decision made by a predecessor of mine. I should have realized she'd have been sent to...there."

John's attention was still on Andra. He mouthed, *What?*

She just stared.

"I expect this to be wrapped up, Sheriff. For both our sakes, get the killer on Monday's transport and you'd better be sure it's the right person."

"Yes, sir."

"And if you could arrange for my wife to call me tomorrow, I would appreciate it."

"Of course." Because clearly part of John's job was to play secretary between the President and the First Lady.

They said goodbye and John was polite and thankful, even though he felt like he'd been reprimanded by the principal. As soon as he could, he ended the call.

"What?"

Andra shook herself from whatever had her in a daze. "Congressman Thane?"

"He's on the committee overseeing Sanctuary. You want to tell me what it is about this man has you all twisted up?"

"It might be nothing."

"I'm guessing it's not."

"I've heard the name before." Andra touched her hair. A nervous gesture? "Drew talked about Doug Thane, a pseudo Godfather of his, in every sense of the word."

"Your husband knew Congressman Thane?"

Andra flinched. "The husband whose Washington connections nearly resulted in my untimely death. Several times."

"And now he's on Sanctuary's congressional committee?" John frowned. "How does that happen? He must have been screened."

"They played it close. Drew may not have told anyone else about the connection. Thane probably kept quiet too, biding his time until he could get to me." Tears filled her eyes. "Maybe he didn't even know I was here until he got on the committee and I fell into his lap."

"That's why he wants you detained and on the transport out of town."

"He wants to get me back for what I did to Drew."

John pointed at her. "Drew was a rogue CIA agent who tried to kill you and your unborn baby."

"And I'm a better person? I killed a lot of people, John. I have their blood on my hands like anyone who takes a life. I'm the worst kind of human being."

"Not anymore."

"It doesn't just go away."

John knew that was only the fear talking. "What about mercy?"

"Doesn't mean I won't end up dead or in jail for the rest of my life. It only extends to the spiritual things, like freedom from my sin and the eternal consequences."

"Well, what good does that do you right now?"

Andra laughed. "A lot of good actually. It's the knowledge of that freedom. And it's not deferred, I feel it now. But I still have to face the consequences here if they come."

"I'm not going to let that happen."

"Why?" She shook her head. "Why do you even care what happens to me?"

John studied her allowing his gaze to roam her features. "Because you're important."

"I'm really not."

"You are to me." He looked down at his lap for a second. "I'm not sure if I can even explain it, but since we met there's been something about you."

She was quiet for a moment. Then she said, "I get it."

She felt it too?

Andra lifted her chin. "It doesn't mean anything."

John frowned. How could it not mean anything?

"This can't happen, John. I'm a killer and you're a cop. That doesn't work."

"You're not a killer anymore."

"You're telling me you won't ever worry for Pat's safety if I'm around him all the time? That it won't cross your mind I might get mad and snap. Wake up from a nightmare and do something before I have a chance to catch myself? That's what happened with Palmer and he ended up with a black eye. What kind of damage could I do to Pat?"

John worked his mouth back and forth. It sounded an awful lot like PTSD to him. Didn't people learn how to deal?

"Don't tell me we can make it work. I'm not willing to try because there's no point." She lay back down.

"You really believe you're a danger to Pat?"

Andra scowled, apparently not liking the fact he would ask. "Let's just drop it, okay? There's no point in having this conversation because it's not going anywhere. We're not going anywhere."

John gave her a pointed stare. "You're right. We're not going anywhere."

Andra flinched. John didn't want to cause her pain. She was going to think he agreed with her, which he most certainly did not. But she had to understand; neither of them was leaving Sanctuary until he figured this out. It was true, she had done terrible things in the past. But so had he.

He'd also seen too many innocents destroyed by other people's selfish actions.

Andra might have been an assassin once, but that wasn't the woman he'd come to know. Not because she'd been forced into it or because she hadn't had a choice. He wasn't going to explain it away and he didn't think Andra would do that either. People made their own decisions, even if there were sometimes only bad options available. Despite how the town felt, when he looked at her that wasn't what he saw. What he saw was a woman with a truck-load of regret trying to live a better life than the one she'd lived in Europe.

John grabbed his phone and went upstairs to make his call, not looking forward to telling Grant the phone might have been breached.

But Congressman Thane had just become a bigger issue, piled on top of the stack of issues John already had.

**

Andra winced as she listened to John's half of the conversation. How had Thane managed to wheedle his way onto the congressional committee overseeing Sanctuary? When John had said the name it was like a knife to her gut. Everything Drew ever said about his godfather rushed back to hit her with the full force of the realization her hiding place had been exposed.

Suddenly being transported out of town to a jail cell was so much more than she'd considered. If Thane knew her every movement once she left town, a guilty verdict wouldn't mean anything. She would be dead before she ever set foot in the courtroom.

"That's not good enough!"

Andra grimaced; glad Pat wasn't here to overhear his father's outburst.

"I want to know how on earth this could happen!"

Andra knew exactly how it could have. If someone killed a member of her family, she would hunt them for the rest of their lives and then after she was done, she would ask God for forgiveness. That was the one exception to her rule to live as a pacifist—if harm were to come to Helena. And, in a way, she could say the same now for Pat. Vowing not to kill anyone was one thing. In order to avoid even approaching the person she'd been, Andra had to steer clear of violence altogether.

She had to consider what happened to Palmer. Four years later and he still hated her. Well, she didn't think too highly of him either. She knew peace in her heart despite what was going on around her. She had joy, not the laughing at something funny kind, but the rejoicing that came from knowing how wide, how long, how high and how deep God's love was.

After all, if He could save someone like her, then who could possibly be exempt?

She was still hungry, since John had forgotten to order the food. Was he going to come back down? Only silence could be heard from upstairs. Maybe he was sleeping, since it'd been almost midnight according to the screensaver on his computer and that was a while ago.

Her feet tapped the rhythm of a song she'd heard on Nadia Marie's iPod. Calm descended over her and Andra smiled to the dark room.

For You, I sing...

In a holding cell of all places. Even though she was guilty of many things, there was something poignant about singing praise in jail which struck her enough she laughed out loud and sang the next line.

How else could she describe it? She'd only known God in a vicarious way as a child, understanding faith through the framework of the Catholic Church. But something had happened here, with a new start and wide open spaces.

God's country. She knew why they called it that now. This truly was the place He'd spoken to her, drawing her gently to Himself. Maybe she even knew how Adam had felt when God breathed life into him.

Sometime later Andra awoke.

She wasn't alone, she knew that even before tape was slapped over her mouth. Several sets of hands grabbed her, lifting her up. She kicked and struggled, but all she could produce as she was carried outside was a muffled moan.

**

John snapped awake. It took him a moment, lying on his couch in the low light of dawn that hadn't yet peaked over the mountains, but his brain eventually caught up. He took a quick shower, changed into his only clean uniform and then took the coffee pot from his kitchen downstairs. He had no intention of drinking from one that might have been drugged.

The cell door was open. As was the front door.

Andra was gone.

John set the coffee pot down. He strode outside like she would be standing there, and then cursed his brain for thinking something that idiotic.

Main Street was empty. John jogged one way and then the other, before circling around to the street behind the north side of Main. He should radio Palmer, get a search party organized. Just as soon as he—

John approached the spot where Betty Collins' body had been.

"Andra!"

She was propped up, her back to the wall while her head dipped forward. Blood dripped from her chin onto her lap. For long enough now that her jeans were stained. John dropped to his knees and lifted her chin. He sucked in a breath.

Andra's face was a mass of bruises. One eye was swollen shut and blood was coming from her nose and mouth. There was a cut on her cheek, like a ring had sliced through the skin.

He was going to have to go get his car.

"Andra."

She didn't move. But she had a pulse.

"Andra, honey." He grimaced. "I'll be right back. Sit tight, okay?"

John found an alley and ran between buildings across Main to the back, where his Jeep was parked. It felt like five minutes but was likely not that long. Thankfully, it was early enough there wasn't anyone on the road so John could get back to her in half the time. He'd give himself a speeding ticket later.

John crouched again, hardly able to breathe. "Andra."

Her eyelids flickered.

"I have to lift you. I have to get you to the medical center." He slid one arm under her knees and the other behind her back. "Please don't have internal bleeding."

The noise that birthed from her throat when he lifted her was low and feral. John winced and laid her on the backseat of his vehicle. The drive to the medical center was slow for her sake. When he banged on the door, Matthias emerged in the waiting area.

"It's Andra. Get me a gurney and go get Dr. Fenton."

Matthias didn't argue, he just got the bed and together they placed Andra on it. John wheeled her in and Dr. Fenton's first words were, "You moved her?"

"I didn't have a choice."

The doctor's eyes were hard. "There is always a choice." He tugged the gurney through a set of swinging doors with Matthias helping. "Wait out here. And pray you didn't do further damage."

The door swung closed.

John wheeled around and kicked the wall, his boot going straight through the drywall. He gripped the sides of his head.

"Dad?"

John lowered his hands and spun around.

"What's going on?" Pat was still in yesterday's clothes, now rumpled like they'd been left in the dryer.

John crouched and Pat moved into his arms. "Andra was hurt. The doctor is going to help her." John prayed this was true, that her injuries weren't so extensive she needed what doctor Fenton couldn't provide. "How is Aaron?"

Pat shrugged. "He didn't wake up yet."

"Did you sleep okay?"

"Yeah. Matthias brought a bed in from another room so I could sleep on it and he slept on the chair. So we were all in the same room."

"Want to run to the diner and get everyone breakfast?" Hopefully it would be open.

"I could do that." Pat nodded. "For all of us, Matthias and doctor Fenton and you and Andra, and Aaron?"

"If you can carry all that. We'll have to find out what Aaron and Andra are allowed to eat."

"Can I get Aaron's golf cart? I think I can reach the peddles."

"How about, no."

Pat pouted, but bounced back fast like kids do. He wrapped his arm around John's neck.

John stood, holding his son in a hug for a moment while Pat's legs dangled. Probably he needed the embrace more than Pat did. "Love you, buddy."

"Love you too, Dad."

"Sheriff?"

John turned to the doctor and set Pat down. "How is she?"

"Not good."

John followed him into the examination room, where Matthias had his sleeves rolled up. He snapped off a pair of bloody gloves and said to Pat, "Did I hear something about breakfast?"

John mouthed, *Thank you.*

Pat was trying to glance around him, to see Andra. John waited until Matthias reached him and then moved aside to let the younger man out. Just before he shut the door, John heard Matthias and Pat start talking about pancakes versus waffles.

Andra's cheek was bandaged and she had been dressed in a gown. Her eyes were open.

"Hey." He touched her cheek, keeping it light and to the areas not so bruised. She'd been worked over and good.

He turned to the doctor, praying she hadn't seen what he felt on his face. "She'll recover?"

Doctor Fenton nodded. "Multiple bruises. Cracked, possibly broken ribs. We'll do an x-ray and I've already called our ultrasound tech in to check the abdomen for internal bleeding. Ms. Caleri needs to stay and be monitored for her pain until I'm satisfied she's stable enough to get up."

John blew out a breath and looked back at her. Andra's lips moved, but no sound came out. "What is it, honey?"

"John..."

"Who did this to you?"

Fear sparked in her open eye. Who had taken her from the holding cell and beaten the tar out of her?

Andra reached up and touched his jaw. Her fingers were chilled. John realized he was clenching his teeth.

"Tell me who did this to you." He didn't care if it sounded like he was pleading. John should have heard her being taken. He should have come back down after he'd called Grant instead of falling asleep on his couch.

He'd known how the town felt about Andra, so why hadn't he seen this coming? Now she was barely hanging on, breathing shallow like it hurt. Even cleaned up and bandaged there was still blood everywhere.

Her gaze flickered back and forth across his face. "Don't."

"Too late." He took a breath. "Tell me who did this."

She shut her good eye and shook her head. A tiny motion he wouldn't have seen if he hadn't been looking right at her.

"You don't know, or you won't tell me?"

She stared at him, imparting something with her gaze that he didn't want to know and wasn't going to listen to anyway.

"At some point your principles are going to have to give out. Especially if I'm going to find whoever did this to you." John backed away from the bed and turned to doctor Fenton. "Keep me posted."

Matthias met him in the hall with breakfast. "What's your plan?"

John looked at him. He didn't look tired. Apparently the guy was young enough that sleeping on a hospital chair wasn't a problem. "Can you call Bolton? Tell him I want him here since now there are two people to protect."

"Sure."

"Oh, and tell him to find Nadia Marie. Andra's going to need her friend with her."

Matthias grinned. "Definitely."

Chapter 22

Andra's whole body hurt. But the ache would likely be excruciating without whatever was dripping into her from the IV. The dull murmur of humanity broke the silence of her room in the medical center, while she stared at the ceiling tiles. The light fixture. The sprinkler heads. The corner of the wall...was that a spider web? Gross.

She couldn't close her eyes. If she did, she'd be back in the dark, surrounded by black figures. Being punched, hit with something hard. Kicked in the face, the stomach. The boot print on her abdomen hadn't come out of nowhere.

At least doctor Fenton agreed to not tell John. The law man would insist on seeing her stomach, which would lead to photos and a written report. Not to mention the look in John's eyes that she wasn't ever in her whole life going to forget. If he found out who had abducted and attacked her, he was liable to put his job in jeopardy.

Nothing about this needed to be documented. Her file was full enough already. She didn't need more to make her look like the sad victim of a bunch of thugs, even if she could identify the instigator. She'd seen him with her good eye after he grabbed her chin and turned her face to his.

An eye for an eye.

Hardly, since if they wanted to repay her for Betty's death she should be dead now. Or maybe they figured her lying here suffering the damage they'd inflicted was worse. As for the mayor, he must have been sure she killed Betty if he was willing to incriminate himself by making such a statement. Or did he know she wouldn't press charges? Maybe she should, although it was in poor taste since the man was grieving.

Andra snorted, which hurt a lot.

She turned her head and felt her eyes widen. Pat stood in the open doorway, holding a cup with a lid and a straw.

He didn't move. "Hi."

She let her gaze drift away from him. "You shouldn't be in here."

Not because here wasn't safe, it just wasn't fine with her heart. Pat was John's son and there would never be a relationship between Andra and the kid's father that would make Pat anything to her. He'd said it himself, "We're not going anywhere". It wasn't worth knowing Pat better and seeing what she'd be missing. Andra didn't need any more regrets.

"I brought you some breakfast. Doctor Fenton said you could have a smoothie and Sam at the diner said you like mango. But he didn't have any so it's strawberry." His voice was small, like he wasn't sure if she might leap from the bed any moment and attack him.

"Thank you." Andra held out her hand, the one with the plastic bracelet. She felt the bandage on her face when she smiled. It was hard to hold the expression and breathe around her tightly wrapped ribs. Thank you, God, they were only cracked in two places and nothing was broken—or sticking into her lungs. That would've been a lot worse.

Pat gingerly stepped over and set the cup in her hand. She took a sip and put it down, even though twisting hurt. Pat hadn't moved. "Did you really used to kill people?"

He was a kid, sure. But Andra didn't like lying.

She nodded.

His eyes flared wide for a second. "Did you ever kill a kid?"

Was he worried what she would do to him? "No, never."

"Maybe they deserved it, like when Batman kills people because they're bad."

Andra didn't say anything. The world was an ugly place, brutal and somehow beautiful at the same time. But the beauty was only there if she looked hard enough—like into the eyes of a child who wanted to believe the best in her. How was that even possible? She had no right to accept that much faith from another human being after everything she'd done. Maybe it was just Pat and his need to see the good, even where he'd been tossed aside by both his parents at one time.

Andra couldn't receive it, even if Pat wanted to give her his trust and believe she could be good until she proved otherwise. She couldn't let herself melt at the feeling, because then what held her together now would crumble. Pat didn't need to see her crying. Still, Andra felt her eyes burn. The swollen one hurt a lot. She looked away.

"Oh my gosh!" Nadia Marie's clippy footsteps entered the room. "I heard what happened. Are you okay?"

Andra opened her eyes to answer her friend.

Nadia Marie was crouched in front of Pat, her hands on his shoulders. "That must have been just awful, finding Aaron like that!"

Andra felt the humor bubble up from her stomach. Even so, the feeling emerged from her mouth as full-on laughter. Ouch. Her stomach hurt and the sound was corroded from disuse, but she could still do it. Who knew? The realization made her laugh even louder. They must have hit her in the head pretty hard if she found anything funny about this. But what else was she going to do? There were too many people in the room for her to cry.

Nadia Marie looked over, her brow furrowed like she was concerned for her friend's sanity. Beyond her, Bolton Farrera stood in at the door. His mouth twitched. Andra swallowed her laughter and groaned. "That hurt."

Pat smiled. Nadia Marie straightened and folded her arms, nothing but sass on her face. "Glad you're feeling okay. You look like someone ran you over."

"Actually, they left that part out."

"They?"

Andra shot a pointed look in Pat's direction and shook her head.

Bolton motioned Pat over with a wave. "Why don't you go see if Matthias needs anything?"

Pat straightened, but Andra couldn't see his face. "So you can talk about adult stuff I'm not supposed to know about?"

Bolton didn't react. "Yes."

Pat sighed and padded out of the room.

Nadia Marie whipped around and flounced to Andra's bedside. "That is one stinkin' cute kid."

"You're not wrong."

She settled on the bed, the humor gone from her eyes. "How are you?"

Andra wanted to shrug and brush it off, but that wasn't how their friendship worked. "It'll take a few weeks. I'll be okay." She paused. "For right now, it hurts like my body is more bruises than not."

Bolton was still at the door, looking at Nadia Marie like she was an anomaly he couldn't figure out. Served him right. It was too late to notice her now.

Andra glanced at Nadia Marie. Her friend's eyes went wide, like, "What is he still doing here?"

Andra smiled. "Did you need something, Bolton?"

"What—uh, yeah." He strode further in the room. Suddenly all business, folding his arms. "You think you can ID who did this to you?"

Andra shifted on the bed, which was a good idea but painful in execution.

Nadia gasped. "You know."

She glanced at her friend. "Nadia—"

"No." Nadia Marie jumped up from the bed. "If you know who did this to you then you have to tell. You want them to get away with it?"

"Most of them I couldn't tell you who they are."

Bolton said, "But..."

"Everyone in town believes I killed Betty. They're going to think I'm only saying it out of spite. No one is going to take my word for it except John and it won't help him. I'm not going to be responsible for his downfall."

Nadia Marie touched her arm. "You don't think he'll do the right thing?"

"He'll think it's the right thing." She shifted her arm to draw it away from Nadia's attempt to connect with her. She wasn't going to budge on this. "If he believes me, then it's going to undermine his standing with the town."

Bolton said, "So it was the mayor."

Andra squeezed her eyes shut.

"He shouldn't have done that to you." Nadia's voice was quiet. "It doesn't matter what you've done or what he thinks you did, it wasn't okay for him to hurt you like this."

She knew that. In theory.

"But you're going to keep quiet because of John?"

Andra looked at her friend.

"You are," Nadia said. "You think you're saving him."

"It's noble." Bolton tucked his thumbs in his pockets. "But you're still going to have to live in the same town as the people who did this to you." He motioned to her face.

"Except not, if I'm leaving town on Monday's transport to be put on trial for Betty's murder."

Nadia Marie straightened. "We need to find a way you can stay, and the mayor can pay for what he did."

Bolton's attention was on Andra. "Do you think he killed Betty?"

She thought about it. "I honestly don't know."

"They weren't exactly friendly." Nadia nodded. "I say it's definitely possible."

"Either way, someone is going to end up leaving town." Andra shrugged one shoulder. "What does it matter if it's me?"

Now she'd had time to think on it, why wouldn't she come to the conclusion being away from John was best? What was the good of seeing him every day and knowing what couldn't be? Surely a clean break, and the separation of miles and a murder sentence, would be preferable. It wasn't like the conviction would be untrue; she just hadn't murdered this particular victim.

Whether she ended up in a jail cell or she was free to live on her mountain, she was still the same sinner saved by grace through faith.

Nadia's eyes flashed wide and full of hurt. "You're going to let them do this to you?"

"You mean, am I going to do this to you?"

"I'm not being selfish."

Andra bit her lip. "But you don't want to lose your friend."

Tears filled Nadia's eyes. "How am I going to live here without you?"

Andra swallowed.

She hadn't thought of that.

**

Dotty twisted around in her chair. "Susan seems content enough. I met the First Lady and her daughter last night for dinner. Sam treated them like they were royalty."

John smiled. "Good."

"Beth is harder to read, but I'm guessing she has a lot on her mind at the moment. With her husband being gone."

She probably did, given the attempts on both of their lives and her husband being out of contact. Having no idea when he was going to be home. The Navy SEAL didn't even know what was happening to her.

John looked at the flip calendar on his desk. He turned three pages until it was on the right month and tracked down to the day he and Pat had arrived in town. Tomorrow it would be a full week since they set down in the helicopter and were driven into town by Matthias. How had so much happened in just a handful of days?

But the upheaval was likely to continue. There were only three more full days before Monday's transport took Andra away. And no way he could stop it. Not when the town, Justice Simmons, Grant, Congressman Thane and the President were all pressuring John to get a result.

Given Andra's silence, it would be the wrong one.

And yet, why was there this niggle of doubt that maybe Andra had done it? That would at least explain why everyone seemed to think she had, more than just out of spite for the one person in town who refused to be one of them. What if he took a page from Andra's book and refused to bow to their dictates? The sheriff didn't answer to the town, although Grant's authority was clear even if he wasn't here. Congressman Thane was a gray area.

John didn't have to send her on Monday's transport. He didn't have to send anyone, even if they demanded it of him. If he wasn't certain who the killer was, then he shouldn't do it.

"Is Andra talking?"

John pushed aside his thoughts and looked over at Dotty. "Bolton spoke with her."

"Did she say who attacked her?"

He shook his head. "She wouldn't admit it, so all Bolton could get from her was a statement as to the details. A blow-by-blow." That had been fun to read.

"Do you think it was Betty's killer?"

"I think it was simple revenge by people who believe she killed Betty. But unless she can identify them or we can nail down who in town has bloody knuckles this morning, there isn't much we can do about it."

Dotty shifted in her chair. "So we just have to go on as if everything is fine? As if we're not living in town with a person who will stab a woman in the stomach multiple times, and gangs who are little better than lynch mobs spreading their hatred and hurting a possibly innocent woman."

"Basically, yes."

She shook her white hair. "I don't like it."

John felt the smile on his lips. "Me either."

"You know, your desk phone has this function where you can dial all the phones in town at once, sort of like an intercom thing. You could make an announcement. Call a town meeting and get everyone together where you can check their hands for cuts and bruises like they've been in a fight. Or see who is missing."

"Like roll call?"

"Worth a try, don't you think?"

She had a point. "I want to talk to Andra first. See if she can remember more. I'm also waiting for Aaron to wake up and tell us what he knows."

"So you're just going to sit here until something falls in your lap?" She shook her head and tsked. "Sheriff Chandler used to do that. And here I thought you'd be different."

"I have no idea what kind of a sheriff Chandler was, but I can tell you I'm nothing like him. Investigations take time."

"That's your story, huh?"

John couldn't believe this. "It's not a story."

"Why not just go rouse some suspects? Kick some doors in. Toss a few people's houses and get the lead you need, instead of sitting around waiting for it to come to you." She shot him a look. "Isn't that what you marshals do?"

"We catch criminals."

"So go catch one."

John folded his arms. "Is this your weird version of a pep-talk, with a little reverse psychology thrown in?"

Dotty grinned. "It's definitely something."

John shook his head. Why did she think she needed to do that? It was like no one believed in him enough to give him the space and time to figure this out on his own. What a great vote of confidence. *I want an arrest. She killed Betty. Keep my wife and daughter safe.*

John ran his hands down his face. The responsibility of this job didn't just mean protecting Andra and keeping her from being taken away from him and the life they could have. It was about taking care of all of them, at the same time as fielding the concerns of everyone else who knew about Sanctuary.

Maybe they were right, maybe he wasn't cut out for this job. Someone who knew more about regular day-to-day police work would be able to take all this in stride. But Grant chose John to be sheriff—even if he wasn't the first choice—which counted for something, surely. Things should have been simple enough, safeguarding these people's lives. And now he was faced with a mob that refused to have faith he could do his job.

Pat was the only person in town who trusted him and even that was on shaky ground. Andra—who he wanted to believe in him, in them, more than anything—wasn't even willing to trust him to help her.

Palmer finally showed up. John looked at his watch. "Nice of you to join us in time for lunch."

The deputy ignored John's comment.

"Rough night last night?"

Palmer slumped into his chair and set his hands on the desk in front, ready to work. Was that supposed to count for something?

John glanced at the skin on Palmer's knuckles. He was in the clear, for now. If he'd been there he hadn't used his fists on Andra, at least.

The thought of what happened to her made John's fingers curl into fists. He wanted to pound on something. Some*one*. Why not Palmer? The man had a serious beef against Andra and he hadn't bothered to hide it. It would make sense if he had been involved in her abduction.

"Nothing to say?"

Palmer shrugged. "I'm here aren't I?"

"You were supposed to start work at eight. It's almost noon." John gave him a minute. It seemed the deputy's cognitive abilities were a little slow. "Where were you all morning, Palmer?"

His face morphed into belligerence. He lifted both hands like he couldn't see what the problem was. "Who cares? It's not like there's much for me to do around here anyway. Chandler never had a problem with me making my own hours. What's the big deal?"

"The big deal is Betty Collins was murdered."

"And I arrested Andra Caleri."

John leaned back in his chair and folded his arms. "So where's your evidence proving it was her, or even pointing in her direction?"

"Bill and Sam said they saw her."

"Coercion, which would be inadmissible. Given the circumstances it barely qualifies as hearsay."

"Look at her history! She used to be an assassin, for crying out loud."

"I suppose no-one ever changes, and people can't turn their lives around?" John walked over and put his palms on the deputy's desk. "If you can't take an objective eye and search out some other possibility than the first suspect who falls into your lap, then maybe Chandler was wrong. Maybe you're not cut out for this job."

Palmer stood. "Says the guy who won't even consider the fact she's as guilty as sin."

"Why are you pushing this, why do you want Andra out of town so badly?"

"Why do you want her to stay?" Palmer's face went red. "You think you're gonna get anywhere with a woman like that when—"

"When she turned you down?"

"That lying piece of—"

"Palmer." John's voice boomed in the tiny office. "That's enough. I would read the report for myself, only there isn't one. So you tell me. A resident of this town assaults you, and you don't file a report or press charges? Why is that?"

Palmer sputtered. "It wasn't worth it."

"You didn't want her out of town then, but you want her gone now. Why is that?" John hadn't even thought it through before he said it, but it made sense. Something had changed for Palmer since what happened between them. Whatever it was made him adamant Andra should be gone now.

The idea his deputy could be behind all of this was next to the last thing John would have imagined. Looking at the man now, he could almost believe it. The question was what did he do with the theory? He could fire Palmer, but then the man would be home and—if it was true—back to scheming. John should keep him here, where he could see what Palmer was up to. He might not have been involved in the attack on Andra, but he could be the one who used John's phone.

All Grant had found in the satellite phone's history was a three minute call placed to an unregistered cell. He'd run a trace last night while John had been on the phone with him, but come up with nothing. Which meant the phone had been used and switched off. That smacked of a pre-arranged time.

What if John left the phone unattended again, but this time where he could see who used it?

That idea was definitely worth considering.

John's desk phone rang. The display said *Medical Center*. "Sheriff Mason."

"Dad." Pat sucked in a breath, winded. "Aaron woke up."

Chapter 23

"Checks and balances." Aaron shifted on the bed, his eyes glassy. "All Aaron."

John turned to the doctor. "We're getting nowhere."

Fenton lifted one shoulder, motioning for John to step with him away from the bed. "The tests are as normal as they can be. The rest is down to Aaron. He either can't say or he won't. And to be honest, both of those choices might be best for him. He has to find a way through this. If it means falling back on what is familiar to him, so be it."

John couldn't argue. "We don't even know if he was talking about Betty Collins. For all we know he could have brought up what he witnessed years ago and mixed it up in his head, flashed back to his trauma."

"I doubt we'll ever know."

"What would happen if he saw the person he talked to? How is he likely to react?"

Fenton glanced at Aaron for a moment. "It wouldn't be good. I doubt Aaron could control an extreme reaction. His ability to handle stress is even more limited, given he's in the hospital."

"What will you do when he's well enough to be released? I'm assuming he'll need to be monitored."

"Olympia has already been by this morning. She said when he's ready she intends to make sure Aaron has everything he needs to get better."

Of course she would. John smiled. The town needed a new welcoming committee and he couldn't think of a better person to take the position. Hopefully Olympia would overlook the demise of the last woman who held it.

John strode out, leaving the doctor to his examination. Aaron had been his best shot so far at clearing Andra's name. The kid's own defenses would make it so whatever he might have seen had been lost in his mind.

"I got it!" Pat's sneakers squeaked on the floor all the way down the hall. He stopped in front of John to hold up Aaron's mail ledger.

"Great." He squeezed his son's shoulder. "You okay, you need anything?"

"I'm fine." Pat looked like he was enjoying all this.

"What about school, do you need to take a break here and give that some of your time today?"

Pat screwed up his nose. "Mrs. Pepper said we couldn't do school work because the internet is down, but one of the teenagers said we can do other stuff and she's just faking it so she doesn't have to work."

"Huh."

"So...do I have to go in?"

"I'll find out and let you know." John grinned and sank into a crouch. "If you spend much more time helping out, I might have to deputize you...or enroll you in medical school."

Pat puffed out his chest. "I could be a deputy."

"Junior deputy."

"Would I get a badge?"

John grinned. "I might be able to work that out."

"What about a gun?"

"Water gun."

Pat's eyes narrowed. "BB gun."

Oh, so he wanted to bargain, did he?

"Nerf gun."

"Deal." Pat grinned. At least John knew what to get him for Christmas now.

"Listen, if you get bored or you need a break, let me know, okay?"

Pat nodded. Beyond him, Bolton strode down the hall with Dan Walden, the farmer with the over-compensating horse. Thinking about it that way at least distracted John from remembering how huge the beast had been.

He squeezed Pat's shoulder. His boy with a soft heart that had been forgotten too many times, took the ledger to a young man he barely knew. Content to stay with him until he was better.

"You okay?"

John waited until his son closed the door to Aaron's room and then glanced at Bolton. "Thanks for coming." He included Dan in his statement.

Dan, who stood almost hat-brim to hat-brim with Bolton, shrugged with a sideways tilt of his head. "Farrera filled me in on what's been going on with Aaron and Ms. Caleri." Dan hesitated. "Farrera said it was revenge. Did she kill Betty Collins?"

John shook his head. "I don't think she did. I just can't prove it."

"I'd be more surprised if she had."

"Why's that?"

"Got a request in for one-on-one discipleship a number of years back."

Bolton said, "Discipleship?"

"Loosely, you could call it counseling. But more with a view to encouraging someone in their faith—usually a new Christian—and teaching them how to walk the walk they're learning."

Dan paused for a second. "I pair the request with the person who fits, but who the heck matches up with an assassin? Although in this town, that's not such a stretch as it normally would be. So I pulled in Nadia Marie and put it to her. She jumped at it herself, wanted to get to know Andra. I get regular updates, but they're really non-specific because we want to respect a person's privacy. As far as I know Andra's been doing well for a long time. And I'm talking years."

John digested all that. "She's been doing the discipleship thing all this time?"

"At some point it turned into a solid friendship. It happens. It's a good thing."

"So is it like a sponsor, like with Alcoholics Anonymous?"

"After a fashion."

Bolton shifted. "With Nadia Marie?"

Dan glanced at the other man with look in his eye and a slight smile. "What's it to you?"

The rancher's eyes went wide. "No reason."

"Sure, man. Whatever you gotta say to convince yourself Nadia Marie is just another resident you'll be forced to spend the best years of your life living alongside." Dan grinned. "The minute you want to step things up, come see me. I'll let you in on a few things you're gonna want to know."

Bolton folded his arms. "Is that right?"

"Yeah, it is."

"Gentlemen." John cleared his throat about ready to start laughing at their antics. Evidently there was a little friendly rivalry going on, that had nothing to do with Battle Night. He glanced between them. "Any of your men around Main Street Saturday night maybe saw Aaron, or a woman?"

Dan was shaking his head before John even finished the question. "They wouldn't have seen Aaron."

"Because he wasn't out that night? Your team guys live in the same house as he does."

"That doesn't make him any less invisible. I've already spoken with Bill and Sam."

John snorted, remembering the smell of their house and the affect that would no doubt have on their memories.

Dan frowned. "They didn't see him. And they say he wasn't even out that night."

"He could have snuck out." Bolton didn't look happy. "And the kid is far from invisible."

"Bill and Sam told me they barely ever see him coming and going, and they live in the same house."

John said, "That's likely due more to the weed than Aaron."

Bolton's head whipped around. "They have weed as well?"

"We'll worry about that next week. Right now there's a murderer loose and a woman—" John glanced at Dan. "—a member of your congregation, was abducted from jail and attacked."

"Weren't you watching her?"

John shot Dan a look. "I was within earshot."

"Don't you have a security system?"

"This isn't the Federal Reserve. We're a hick town, with barely any resources."

"Duh," Dan said. "I've lived here my whole life. I know that."

"That's right. How'd that work?"

He nodded. "My dad was sent here in the seventies, couple of years before I was born."

"I'll have to meet him sometime."

"He passed when I was fifteen."

John pressed his lips together, then said, "I'm sorry for your—"

Bolton clapped Dan on the shoulder. "Probably saw the deer. Am I right?"

Dan chuckled, shrugging off Bolton's grip. "Likely that's where the story came from, if you actually believe in all that. Which I don't."

John nodded and moved his face to look gravely serious. "Good, because if it is true then I'm next."

Dan hissed out a breath between his teeth. "Sucks to be you, man."

Given everything which had landed in John's lap since he arrived, even though he'd met Andra, even though Pat seemed happy, he couldn't really disagree. "Brother, you are not wrong."

Dan smiled, though the sadness in his eyes was unmistakable. "So what now?"

John said, "I find the killer or Andra gets shipped off to a life sentence on Monday."

"Not a problem, since she's clearly the killer." Bolton's eyebrows rose, like a challenge.

"What is that supposed to mean?"

Bolton didn't react. "Calm down, *brother*. I'm just saying what everyone in town is thinking. Seems to me like the only person who doesn't expect Andra on that plane Monday morning is you."

"If they're so sure she'll be out of here, then why the attack?"

"A warning," Bolton said.

Dan shot John another "duh" look.

Bolton continued. "To her. To you. You name it. Either way, statement's been made. Only one left to fall in line is...you."

Right. "You're telling me you think she did it?"

"Does it matter what I think?" Bolton shrugged. "I barely know the woman and I can't say I liked Betty Collins much either. Life is life, doesn't matter whose. But I gave up the fire of following leads, collecting evidence and seeing the result come in when I left the life. It's not in me anymore."

"Just like that, you quit?" John didn't think he'd ever stop being a marshal, not even after he retired. It was part of who he was. "Suddenly you're all about your cows...oh, but with a little looking into whoever's making moonshine and where the weed came from."

It was Dan who spoke, "People see what they want to see. But that's never the whole story."

Bolton shot Dan a look. "When did you become a sage?"

But John couldn't stop thinking about everyone's being so sure Andra was responsible for Betty's death. They expected her on the plane on Monday. A plan like that wouldn't have originated in Sanctuary. Whoever wanted Andra would need to communicate with the person at this end. When the internet was turned off, their only method of communication in or out of town was John's satellite phone.

The attack on her aside, it fit. John was inclined to think it was revenge for what she'd supposedly done; meaning whoever did it really thought she'd killed Betty. The mayor? John would have to pay the bereaved husband a visit.

"Where in the blue blazes have you been?"

All three men turned to see doctor Fenton looking like a cherry sucker, given the color of his face versus the white lab coat.

Harriet Fenton shrugged off her jacket. "What do you care?" The scrubs underneath were pink and somehow she managed to make them look good.

John's gaze moved straight to the doctor's arm as it snaked out and he grabbed her, pulling her attention back to him.

"I said, where were you."

"And I said, What. Do. You. Care? Suddenly you want to play the doting husband, the fabulous doctor saving the day. All because two hopeless cases got themselves hurt?" She slammed her hands down on her hips. "Big fat whoop."

Harriet grabbed a file off the front desk and flounced down the hall. When she saw the three men staring, she faltered and pasted on a smile, sashaying past them. "Fellas."

She stepped into Aaron's room and John caught Bolton's look. Within a few seconds there was a commotion. Someone yelled and then there was a louder yell that broke into a scream made by a lower pitch voice. Aaron.

John flung the door open.

The kid was flailing, eyes wide as his unfocused stare darted around the room. Andra was in a wheelchair. She pulled Pat back until he was behind her. Harriet was on the opposite side of the bed, facing away from John. She held her hands out, trying to placate Aaron with senseless words. She touched his shoulder.

Aaron screeched and almost jumped from the bed.

Doctor Fenton pushed in behind John. "Harriet, that's enough. Andra, you too. Everyone back up. I want you all out of this room."

The way Fenton said it made John think he saw both women as equally responsible, like he didn't know who Aaron was reacting to. John had assumed Harriet was the culprit, but could Aaron feel threatened by Andra? Either way, John needed answers. So having a word with doctor Fenton about man-handling his wife was going to have to wait.

"Harriet." John waited until she looked at him. "If you'd like to come with me, I have a few questions to ask you."

The first of which probably shouldn't be, "Did you murder Betty Collins?" Still, it was tempting to get straight to the point.

John wasn't familiar with the layout of the medical center, so he let Harriet lead him to a break-room with a vending machine and a fridge. A tiny TV was up on the wall in the corner, tuned to a national news program with the volume low and subtitles on. John sat facing it, so Harriet wouldn't be distracted.

She settled in the plastic chair across from him. "I can't imagine what this might be about. I thought Andra Caleri was in custody, and there she was in Aaron's room like a free woman."

No mention of the state of her face, or the fact Andra had been holding Pat back with one arm while the other was wrapped around her waist.

"How are you, Mrs. Fenton?" Maybe that wasn't the best lead-in, given there was apparently trouble in medical center paradise, but the formality was ingrained in him. "Are you doing okay since your friend's death?"

She sighed and her gaze dropped to the table between them. "It's been a hard few days."

He would give her that, being as her hair was rumpled and her husband seemed to feel she was being distant. But other explanations fit too. Betty Collins had reported her as having a relationship with Terrence.

Palmer had shown up Saturday night with his shirt all disheveled. And he'd been absent a lot. Were they in a relationship—in this— together? She could easily be the woman Bill and Sam had seen in town, running away from Betty's dead body. Harriet could also be the cause of Aaron's reaction, the one who told him not to tell. He couldn't be sure she'd hit the young man over the head, but Palmer sure could have. Just as he could have drugged Andra and used John's satellite phone.

"So what just happened with Aaron?"

Harriet's eyes saddened a little too quickly. "He just doesn't like me." She wasn't going to blame the reaction on Andra? "Aaron is...sensitive. It's something we all have to deal with."

John hadn't found him to be the least bit sensitive. He didn't believe in placating people and making them feel like a burden, he'd rather give them the tools to handle themselves. And yet, Aaron seemed to be doing that himself.

Still studying Harriet, he sat forward in the chair and tried to look like he cared. "Why do you think Betty was killed?"

"I have no idea."

"You were friends, would you have known if someone hated her?"

Her face screwed up. "Like Andra?"

John shrugged.

"Maybe she was just in the wrong place at the wrong time."

"You really think that?"

Harriet considered it for a moment and then said, "Betty said someone had called her, told her to meet them where she was...killed. I bet it was Andra."

"She doesn't have a phone."

"Still, it must have been her since she was the one who stabbed Betty all those times in her stomach."

John digested that. Word got around, but were the details of the murder common knowledge?

"She probably borrowed someone's phone." Harriet sneered. "It isn't that hard to do."

Did he really believe any of that was the truth?

**

Andra released the grip on her waist and took a breath before she glanced back at Pat, who had pushed the wheelchair down the hall for her. She should go back to her room now. The alternative was to waltz right in—or as much as you could waltz in a wheelchair—and get the soda, like it was no big deal Harriet was framing her for murder.

"Outside of her former occupation and your personal feelings toward Ms. Caleri, what makes you think she killed Betty?" John's voice was even, like the question was about whether or not she thought ironing was worth the work.

Pat didn't say anything; he just gripped the handles of the wheelchair. It was plain on his face he knew what was happening. His faith in her was tentative and this was going to destroy it.

"You said so yourself and everyone knows. She's a killer. She totally stabbed Betty."

Andra looked at the ceiling. Of course, it made total sense someone with a career of poisoning people would break a decade-long drought by falling off the wagon and stabbing a woman just for being annoying.

Harriet went on, "I heard Betty was going to get her evicted from her cabin. You know it's not legal she lives up there. It might even violate the terms of her Memorandum of Understanding."

Andra could see the look on the woman's face. Tight smile. Smarmy, just like when she'd declared Andra's arm wasn't broken and told her to sit in the waiting area for hours. At least Andra wasn't the one who had to clean up the mess after the pain got so bad. Her stomach did a backflip just remembering it. The meds were wearing off. Pretty soon the doctor would want to give her more, but she couldn't weather this if she wasn't thinking straight.

"What's the big deal about where Andra lives? She's still in town."

Harriet sputtered. "It's the principle of the thing. Living up there like she's lording it over us. Better than everyone else, too good to live in town. And then showing up at church on Sundays, all holier-than-thou."

This was the best the woman could come up with? If anyone had been lording it over anyone else, it was the mayor and his wife for sure. But that wasn't Andra's purview. Evidently, in trying to live a quiet life she'd become a source of speculation because she didn't fit in with the rest of the town. Go figure. She'd never fit in anywhere, even without the assassin thing over her head.

John spoke next. "Maybe she does need taking down a peg or two."

Andra held her breath.

"I'm sure a murder conviction will take care of that." He chuckled. "It'll certainly get her out of town, which seems to be fine with everyone."

"You're not going to defend her?"

"What's the point?" Andra heard his hands slap down. "Everyone knows she did it. For all I know, she probably is the murderer."

Andra tasted blood, so she relaxed the bite on her lip. He really thought that? Please, please, please, let him just be playing devil's advocate and not starting to wonder if she was the killer. Or...this killer, at least. She didn't need that, not from one of the few people who didn't look at her like she was some kind of abomination who did the unthinkable for money.

John's faith in her had been part of what kept her going all this time. His face across from her at her table was what she'd thought about in the middle of getting punched and kicked. He'd brought her through that and he didn't even know it.

She knew he had to stay impartial, and she knew he couldn't tell her even if he didn't think she was guilty. Still, John was the first man in a position of authority over her who didn't make her afraid.

"I knew she killed Betty." Like Harriet hadn't been the one to implicate Andra in the first place and she was just now finding out.

"Guess I can stop looking for the killer, since she's down the hall." John chuckled and the sound sliced through Andra just like the killer's knife had sliced through Betty.

"I'm so glad you've realized, Sheriff."

She could imagine Harriet leaning forward to touch his thigh and give it a gentle squeeze. Andra was going to throw up. She reached down and gripped the wheels. She was ready to go, even though Pat was behind her still holding the handles.

"I'm so glad you see her for what she really is."

We're not going anywhere.

The look on his face said anything but, and she'd hung onto that. Now she knew what he really thought.

They had no future. Instead of hanging on to hope, Andra had to face the fact he'd given up on her. John wasn't going to fight the battle she couldn't fight herself. She had to let go of the hope he might be how God resolved things for her, if He planned to at all.

Andra had to face the fact she was going to prison for life.

"Ms. Caleri will be out of town on Monday and then all of us will get what we want."

Chapter 24

John stood, not willing to spend another moment in the presence of someone so quick to believe Andra would kill Betty. He strode out, squeezing the back of his neck. This was getting entirely too personal. He just couldn't bring himself to care.

Down the hall, Pat wheeled Andra back into her room. John's steps faltered. Had she heard what he said?

He still couldn't believe how convinced the town was as to her guilt. He'd joined in for a moment—albeit sarcastically, though that might not have been obvious. Despite the sick feeling it gave him, John had considered things might be easier with this over and done. It didn't mean he wanted Andra on the transport, especially not when she would be convicted of murder and sentenced to life in prison. And especially not when the move brought her directly into the path of whoever wanted her out of town.

But what if sending her away meant he found out who framed her? He could clear her name and discover the truth. Not just who the killer was, but find out who was behind this entire conspiracy.

"Thanks for helping me, Pat. I appreciate it." Andra's voice was tight. John looked into the room as she lay back on the bed, her lips pressed into a white line.

"I bet my Uncle Nate has nurses helping him." Andra frowned at him, so Pat said, "He's the quarterback for the Dolphins, but he sprained his ankle again on Sunday."

"I'm sure he has lots of help."

"Plus my Grandma went to Miami to help him out, too."

John leaned against the doorway. "Of course Nate has help. But he's home now. He has enough money he can hire whoever he wants to cook and clean and do anything he needs." By the time he'd finished talking John knew it wasn't the right thing to say. He sighed. "Pat—"

His son turned to Andra. "I'm going to see if Doctor Fenton needs me to do anything else."

Pat squeezed past John without speaking or looking at him.

John gripped the back of his neck and looked at the floor.

"You think maybe Pat would rather he was there, than your brother fork out some of his vast amounts of cash to hire people to help him?" Andra tipped her head to the side. "I'm guessing."

John folded his arms and rested his hip on the end of Andra's bed. "We can't leave. Pat knows that's the deal. Not until the end of the month and we make the decision to stay forever, or go for good."

Her eyes flickered. Apparently she hadn't known. "You're leaving?"

"Maybe. We haven't decided. This is a probationary thing."

"So it really wouldn't bother you if I was carted off to prison, then. You'll just leave anyway and the town will continue on with Palmer as the sheriff, unless your brother brings in someone else." She paused. "Is there someone else?"

"I have no idea."

"So you just go back to your life and pretend this unfortunate episode never happened?"

"No, that's not what this is about." John blew out a breath. "I haven't decided yet. There are a lot of factors involved, not the least of which is Pat."

The focus of her good eye moved over his face, but she didn't give a thing away. Why did some women do that? What was so bad about letting him know what she was thinking?

Finally she said, "I don't blame you, you know." But it wasn't absolution, not when she looked sad.

"You think I'm giving up?"

"I heard you tell Harriet you've decided I really did kill Betty." She picked at a loose thread on the blanket. "I'm not worried about going to prison, John. I've been through worse and I'm no innocent."

He knew that, logically. Only, was he really supposed to let her go? He could plan for every eventuality and stake all his bets on this conspiracy idea. But in the end, sending Andra off as the arrested suspect might only end in a guilty sentence. It was a long-shot, so there wasn't much point in getting her hopes up. She was resigned to her fate, whether he tried to help her or not. Whoever was behind the murder and intent on framing Andra needed to believe she was left with no one to help her, which meant they also had to believe John had turned his back on her.

"I just wish you could have believed in me. Apparently that was a lie, too."

John's chest tightened. She was going to make this easy for him. But if that was the case, why did it hurt so bad? He sucked in a breath. "I guess it was."

"You talk a good game, John Mason. But at the end of the day you're no different than Drew, hiding your agenda behind your skewed idea of duty." She brushed at the blanket on her lap, never looking at him. "Good thing I'm being arrested for murder, given the track record of my last marriage. It's been a while, but how do I know history won't repeat itself and I'll be forced to do the worst to someone else I care about?"

John didn't think she would get into a relationship and end up killing the person. He would be more inclined to believe Andra intended to avoid relationships altogether, and thereby eliminate the risk of betrayal. If he stayed in Sanctuary with Pat and all this worked out so Andra could come home, would he have to see her week-in and week-out and pretend he didn't want her in his life? All the while she would be battling fears he figured were unfounded anyway.

John lifted his chin. "Looks like it's all going to work out." At least he hoped so, maybe enough he'd have to say a prayer about the whole thing just to be sure. Too much could go wrong for him to relax.

"One more thing." He reached to his belt for his handcuffs. "You're a murder suspect, so no more leaving this room." He cuffed her left wrist, and then cuffed the other end to the bed rail so she had some movement. "I'll be in the hall. If I need to leave, someone else will be guarding the room."

"Because I'm such a danger to everyone?" She rolled her eyes. "I can't even walk."

"It's procedure."

"Of course it is. Now get out." She shifted on the bed to face away from him, but John caught the flash of pain on her face that came with moving.

✶✶

Andra sniffed away tears. They never did any good anyway. What was it with men? They always said one thing and then did completely the opposite. She'd honestly believed John might be different. That maybe he would be the one person who never lost faith in her, even when she was forced to lay down her faith in herself.

Everyone was guilty of something and still innocent in many ways, at the same time.

Andra had trusted for a long time now that God had brought her here for a reason. If He wanted to take her away from Sanctuary, it wouldn't be because John decided she was guilty. Only because God had allowed it.

Now John had written her off. Pat wasn't hers to take care of. Helena didn't need her. There was only Nadia Marie and Hal, both of whom had other people to support them. Andra had a feeling Nadia Marie might find comfort in the arms of a certain rancher, given how he'd been looking at her in the hospital room. Although if he did like her, Bolton needed to wake up and do something about it or Nadia was going to move on.

A tear slipped from her eye. Andra swiped away the moisture even though it hurt to touch her cheek.

If she was ever going to fight for a long life, there had to be a pretty compelling reason to want to stay.

And right now, she just couldn't see one.

✶✶

John sat in the hall until the sun went down and Pat's occupying the chair beside him turned into his son's weight slumped against his side. Aaron still hadn't told the doctor anything to help identify the person who killed Betty, and neither Matthias nor Bolton had been able to get anything useful out of him.

Boots echoed in the dim hallway and Bolton strode toward them with to-go boxes from the diner stacked in his hands.

"You brought us dinner," John said quietly when Bolton stopped in front of him. "How kind."

"Yeah, right." The rancher grinned. "These are for me. Shift change."

"Are you sure?"

"Don't got nothin' better to do with my evening than sit on a prisoner for you."

John cracked a smile. "Sure you don't. But I appreciate it anyway."

Pat roused enough John didn't have to carry him, and they took the Jeep back to the sheriff's office. It was Friday night, which meant there were two days before Andra would be flown out of town. Two days in which to figure out the real perpetrator and make it so she didn't have to leave at all. But that would mean the murderer not only confessed, but also told him the identity of the co-conspirator on the outside of Sanctuary who wanted Andra within their grasp.

Pat walked up the stairs to the apartment ahead of John. He glanced back. "What's for dinner?"

John shrugged. "Let's see what's in the cupboard."

He found a box of macaroni and cheese and tossed some cut-up hot dogs in with it as it cooked, while Pat settled on the couch with the TV on. All normal things, but John still couldn't get rid of the unsettled feeling in his stomach. He didn't want to be responsible for an innocent person being sent to jail, or for the real killer going free. But it was more than that. The reality was it had everything to do with Andra—who thought he had given up on her.

John grabbed his satellite phone, ready to dial Grant's number. Instead he looked at the unit for a moment. If this really was a conspiracy, he needed proof. Whoever "borrowed" his phone before might need to use it again.

After their late dinner, John tucked his son into bed. They really did need two bedrooms, especially if John was going to get rid of the twinge in his back from being kicked in the middle of the night.

He sat on the side of the bed and smoothed down the blanket. "I'm going to be downstairs doing some work. But I'll leave the door open, okay?" Pat nodded. He wasn't going to pull John down for a hug, like normal? "Everything okay?" Maybe he was just tired.

"I'm fine, Dad." He burrowed down into the blanket, his eyelids drooping.

"Goodnight, Pat."

His son's eyes drifted shut. "Night, Dad. Love you."

John smiled even though Pat said it out of habit. So they had a ways to go. That was fine, especially with everything that'd happened between them and the stress of the last week.

Downstairs, John grabbed his tablet but left the satellite phone on his desk like last time. He flipped Dotty's light on and then sat sideways on the steps up to the second floor apartment. Having his back to the wall wasn't the most comfortable, but he was going to have to deal with being old. He'd been on worse stake-outs than this. An inch-wide vertical strip of dim light was his only view into the sheriff's office.

For more than three hours John studied the case notes. The autopsy had confirmed the cause of death was multiple stab wounds. The only other thing of note that the medical examiner Grant had found to do the procedure had recorded, was a high level of anti-depressants in Betty Collins' blood. Tomorrow John was going to have to talk to the doctor about that.

John hit stand-by on his tablet and set it on the stair above him. Muted steps in the sheriff's office passed the crack in the door, casting John into full darkness for a second as the person walked by.

Palmer.

He stopped by John's desk, presumably going straight for the phone. But John couldn't see anything except the deputy's back. He swiped his tablet back on and found the app to record sound, praying Palmer wouldn't turn and see the screen light of the tablet on the apartment steps. Even with the brightness turned down, the deputy would still see the glow.

"It's me."

This was it. Proof Palmer had sold out Sanctuary's security for whatever he was being paid. What good was it? Palmer couldn't leave to spend it, and he couldn't live large here in the middle of nowhere. What deal had he made?

"It's all coming together." Palmer chuckled. "The mayor even had his cronies pull her out of jail to beat the tar out of her. I caught the end of it and it was a statement, let me tell you. He's convinced she did it."

There was a break of silence and then he said, "The sheriff should have her on the chopper Monday and I'll make sure I'm escorting her to the marshals at the other end." He paused. "The sheriff has to stay and protect the town. I'm the only other option."

John gritted his teeth. It figured Palmer hadn't worked out Bolton was more than just a rancher. He would pick the former DEA agent in a heartbeat over Palmer, if it wasn't a risk to Bolton's identity.

"Got it. I'll make sure we're there."

Palmer wanted out of Sanctuary bad enough to manufacture a murder investigation. Was he the killer? Was his need to escape the town he'd grown up in enough for him to kill Betty Collins, or had he gotten someone else to do it? It could have been coercion or a partnership, since witnesses claimed the killer was a woman.

"You'll get what you want and I'll get the rest of my payment, right?" Palmer's head bobbed. "Good. Because you don't get the woman until I get my money. I can hand her into marshal custody easily enough and I'll never have to explain anything. I can still disappear."

John wanted to jump out and arrest the man right then. But he would never get the partner or the murderer that way. The number Palmer had called was likely the same burner phone, which would be switched off again by the time the trace was run. Whoever was the money behind this would be in the wind, leaving Palmer to swing for conspiracy and a murder he may or may not have committed.

"Be that as it may, I'm the one who holds all the cards here and don't you forget it." Palmer's voice betrayed him and the threat didn't hold the weight it could have. "I'll see you Monday." He set down the phone and left.

John ended the recording. The internet was off, so he'd have to call Grant and get it reconnected long enough to send the recording of Palmer's end of the conversation to his brother. This evidence didn't absolve Andra of the murder charges. It was, however, further proof something more was going on than a simple stabbing.

John let a couple of minutes pass and then grabbed his phone. Grant answered on the second ring, his voice thick with sleep. "This better be good."

"My deputy sold out Andra Caleri to someone who wants her out of town and I think its Congressman Thane."

"Okay, wait a second." Muffled movement was the only thing he heard, then a whispered, "I'll only be a minute. It's John."

A door shut.

"Okay, tell me what you've got."

John laughed. He couldn't help it. "So...how's Genevieve?"

"She's fine, thanks for asking."

Apparently. John swallowed the chuckle and got down to business, catching Grant up on what had just happened.

"So you're going to do, what? Stop the plane?"

John went back upstairs and slumped onto the couch. "Actually I want him to think he got away with it. Can we trace his bank accounts, see if he has the first half of a payment stashed somewhere?"

"I'll get someone to go back over his email, too. See if they can find any communications with an account which might be Thane."

"Good." John squeezed the bridge of his nose. "Andra's in recovery but she should be able to walk by Monday. That will help things along. Palmer will be the one to transport her."

It goaded him though, since the deputy wasn't going to aid her. If it came down to it, her injuries would make defending herself very difficult.

"I'll assemble a team to follow him when he arrives, see who he meets to hand her off to. Or have the marshals take her into custody and sit on her. Assuming someone's going to try and abduct or kill her after she's delivered."

"That's all good."

"But—"

John squeezed his free hand into a fist. "I want to be there. I need Palmer to think he got away with it, and then I'm going to follow them."

"I can't get another chopper to town. The military is never going to go for two in and out of Sanctuary in one day. Not unless it's a serious medical emergency."

"So get a private chopper."

"From where? I'm not made of money, you know."

John rolled his eyes, but then it came to him. "You and I might not be. But we know someone who is, and he's currently in a period of downtime."

Grant sighed. "Mom's going to hit the roof."

Chapter 25

Hal set the backpack on the end of Andra's bed. "You're really gonna do this?"

She looked up at his bearded face but didn't say anything. He had the look of an aging biker, a veteran. A man who somehow managed to freeze time within his world, keeping everything the way he liked—the way he was comfortable with it being. Andra had tried her best to do the same thing with her cabin and keep her life the way she wanted it, but a town full of people hadn't let her do that.

He pressed his lips together, making his long beard rise and fall. "You really are going to do this." He sighed. "You're like the soldier in this book I was reading. He got an edict from his king to stand down."

In a way, he was exactly right. This was the next part of her story, and the place God was leading her to. Maybe He had something for her to do in prison.

"Why do you look happy?"

Andra smiled. "Just the idea of you reading a book."

"You're not foolin' anyone, girlie."

She sobered. "I'm going to miss you."

"Now why would you go and say a fool thing like that?" Sure enough, his eyes got wet. Andra reached for his hand. Hal had to move his closer so she could squeeze his fingers. "Fine, I'm going to miss you too."

"Miss helping me out?"

"I'll miss my nights off from the radio, that's for sure."

"Nadia Marie can take over from me." Andra let go of his hand. "She's looking for something new."

"Won't be the same."

"I know that—" Andra shifted and then cleared her throat when pain ripped through her middle.

"All right, calm down."

She fought to settle, but it was the cool touch of Hal's palm on her forehead which calmed her. It was something he'd done when Andra was sick at his house. Something about the sensation let her take her first full breath in days.

"You're really not going to fight this?" His voice was gruff.

"I can't."

"Because you think prison is what you deserve?"

Maybe a little. But that wasn't the whole of it. "It's not for me to fight this."

"I've never understood that about being a Christian. I've followed orders before, even when I didn't want to. But how do you even know for sure it's what you're being told to do? You can't even see God, or hear Him."

"What if I could?"

Hal closed his mouth. He was silent for a moment, while his gaze flickered over her face. "What does it even sound like?"

"Spanish." She felt the smile curl her lips up. "But then so is my Bible and that's my frame of reference. So..."

Hal gave her a half-smile. "I don't think I've ever understood you."

"I'm not sure you're supposed to."

"Ain't that the truth?"

Andra chuckled, but low and soft since it hurt. "I meant it when I said I'd miss you."

"I know, darlin'." He leaned down and laid a scratchy kiss on her forehead. "Doesn't mean I have to like it."

Hal left and Bolton glanced in the door, looked around the room. He pulled it to behind him, but didn't shut it. Hal's visit was the only break from the monotony of lying in bed she'd had all night and all day.

Only one more day and she'd be able to get on with whatever this was because she wasn't entirely certain it was going to be a life sentence.

At least, not one that meant years in prison.

**

"First time out of Sanctuary, isn't it?" John looked over at Palmer in the passenger seat.

The deputy nodded, downplaying what John knew was excitement. Palmer had packed a bag, given he was supposed to be gone a few days. Only John knew the man wasn't planning on coming back at all. Who knew what he'd told his family.

John drove up to the house where Olympia had settled the First Lady and her daughter. Pat climbed out of the backseat and John walked with him. Susan opened the door even before they got to it.

"Good morning."

John set his hand on Pat's shoulder. "I really appreciate you doing this."

Pat shuffled his feet. They'd already had the conversation about not burdening Olympia or Matthias more than they had. John felt a lot more comfortable leaving Pat with the first family, especially after the president had explained to his wife what was going on.

He turned to Pat. "Dotty is going to bring your bag after Palmer leaves, in case I'm gone overnight."

Pat nodded. John knew most of his reluctance was not being able to help Aaron with the mail. Aaron couldn't leave the medical center yet, so Matthias was going to do the hauling and sorting and Aaron would enter the information in his ledger from his bed at the medical center. Pat badly wanted to help.

"Have a good day."

Susan smiled. "I'm sure we will. I heard Sweet Times has some great cupcakes, but I'm going to need help choosing which one to have. We might have to sample a few of them."

Pat perked up, and John caught Susan's smile. The first lady was a smart woman.

"I should head out."

Pat wrapped his arms around John's hips. "Bye, Dad."

Susan shot John a smile, which he returned before he walked back to the Jeep.

Palmer didn't say anything on the drive to the medical center, and John didn't feel the need to chat just for the sake of keeping up the farce. Andra was in bed, on top of the covers, fully dressed with her shoes on. Her bag was the same brand as Palmer's, making John wonder if the government ordered from one company, or if they were standard issue for witness protection.

"Ready?"

She sat up and grabbed the bag, her handcuffs clinking.

Doctor Fenton sighed, clutching his tablet to his chest.

John shot him a look. "Doc?"

"I don't like this at all."

That was fair enough, but they had to go today or the whole plan would be screwed up. Still, Palmer didn't need to know. "She's not okay to travel?"

"I'd say barely. She can't walk far. She shouldn't be carrying anything and no sudden movements. It's just not worth making her injuries worse. Ms. Caleri has refused strong painkillers, which means she'll be in considerable pain if the ride is bumpy."

John figured Palmer intended on making the ride as bumpy as possible. He wanted Andra to know he was sorry, but couldn't do that with the doctor and Palmer looking on.

"We could wait until next week." John saw his deputy tense in the edge of his vision.

The doctor scratched his chin. Palmer strode over and took hold of Andra's elbow. "She'll be fine. Where Andra's going there'll be plenty of medical attention when she needs it."

The deputy had his gun on his hip. He was wearing a vest only because John told him he needed it. The man knew next to nothing about prisoner transfer, at least not until John explained that to him too. John guessed he was supposed to chalk most of what was about to happen up to Palmer's inexperience. Did Palmer really think he was stupid?

John grabbed her bag and they walked her to the Jeep. Just as they pulled up at the ranch, the helicopter landed. Palmer hauled Andra out of the car, but John stopped their forward progress while he grabbed two things from the trunk. John shut the rear door so Palmer couldn't see what else was in there.

He put a vest and a helmet on her, while she stared up at him with those dark eyes.

"Is that necessary?"

John didn't look at Palmer, he wanted this moment of Andra's focus on him to communicate, without words, he intended to do everything to make sure she got through this in one piece.

Her dark eyes were wary. John tightened the chin strap. "We wouldn't want anything to happen to Ms. Caleri, would we Palmer?"

"But she's guilty of murder." Palmer's voice betrayed him, like he didn't quite believe his own lie.

"It's still our responsibility to safeguard her until she goes to trial."

He tightened the chin strap. Andra's brown eyes looked more gold in the morning light. It was almost eleven, but the sun was starting to peak over the eastern mountains. Why hadn't he noticed their color before?

"Once you're on the chopper she'll be your responsibility, Palmer." He glanced at the man. "Got all the paperwork?"

"Yup." He swung his backpack over his shoulder.

Having one hand holding the strap wasn't going to help him much. In a fight, Palmer would be dead before he dropped the bag and had the chance to draw his weapon.

John stepped back. "Looks like you're all set."

Over at the aircraft, Matthias was helping unload the mail. John waited while Palmer assisted Andra into the chopper and the door was shut. Within minutes, they were in the air and over the mountains.

Seconds after they disappeared, a small plane glinted white in the sunlight as it peaked the mountains. John watched as it banked an arc in the sky above Sanctuary and the Cessna landed on the road.

While it taxied around to face the other way, John opened the trunk of his Jeep. He took off his uniform shirt and pulled a vest over his white undershirt, then topped that with his blue shell jacket with US MARSHALS stenciled on the back.

After glancing around to check no one was in viewing range, he sat on the edge of the trunk, shucked his shoes and pulled off the awful uniform pants, changing them for blue jeans before he put his boots back on. He buckled his belt and transferred his weapon to the holster at his waist. He pulled out his shotgun, too, just for good measure. And topped it all with the ball cap Grant had given him for Christmas two years ago, which he'd only just broken in.

The airplane steps popped open and lowered to the ground. Two men climbed out, one with a considerable limp.

John shook his head. "You guys cannot be here. This is a massive breach of security."

Nate grinned his touchdown smile. "You wanted a plane." He waved at the Cessna behind him. "Voila, Nate to the rescue."

"And him?" John waved in the direction of his brother, Ben.

Nate said, "I needed a pilot."

Ben, who tended to be as quiet as their other brother was effusive, frowned at Nate. "I can speak for myself."

"You were supposed to send anonymous personnel. Retired military, or someone else Grant could approve. Pat is going to be ticked off you guys were here and he didn't see you." John sighed. "They just left. We have to get going."

Nate raised one hand, palm out. "I vote to stay here and hang with Pat."

"You can't. This town is the federal government's best kept secret."

"I swear, I won't say a thing."

John wanted to groan, but there was no time. "You know what? No. I love that you want to see my son. But the people who live here, their lives count the security remaining intact. Now get on the plane. We have to go."

Nate cracked a smile. "Man, you're testy when your woman's in danger."

A ghost of a smile crossed Ben's lips, but he sprinted up the steps. John followed them and Ben pulled the door shut.

John stopped beside his brother. "You really know how to fly this thing?"

Ben lifted his dark blue eyes. "Their chopper is bigger and heavier. It won't take long to catch up. They have to radio in regularly, so if we can find their signal we'll know where they are."

John nodded.

"You haven't put on weight, have you?" Ben tipped his head to the side. "Because these things have a limit."

John shoved him toward the front of the plane. "Just get us in the air."

Nate had settled on the rear seats, four on either side facing in from the walls. He set his bandaged foot on the opposite seat and buckled the belt, donning bulky headphones.

"Ready!"

The ceiling didn't allow John to straighten all the way, so he bent and walked to sit with his brother up front.

John glanced at Ben and they grinned. Nate's exuberance reminded him of Pat. His brother and his son definitely needed to spend time together before Nate went back to Florida.

Ben got them moving, smoothly lifting the plane off the ground. They flew over Main Street on their way over town before banking right toward the mountains. Beyond the peaks stretched miles and miles of terrain which dipped and swelled. Snow dotted the whole area as they flew low, following the southerly route the military aircraft would likely take back to Mountain Home Air Force Base.

The radio crackled and Ben reached low on the console to flip through channels of static. John glanced at his brother, who kept his attention out the window while he searched for the channel the military was using. None of them knew what Ben did for a living and it didn't help to ask either, because he'd say they didn't have the clearance to know. When questioned, their stoic brother simply withdrew further, barely speaking at all.

The crackle smoothed out. "...Delta-Tango-Seven-Six. I've got a light on signaling low coolant. It's dipping pretty fast. I might have to set her down, over."

Ben glanced in John's direction for a second. "He's downplaying it. He could very well have to make an emergency landing."

A voice on the radio replied, "Roger that, Delta-Tango-Six-Seven. Keep us apprised. Out."

John looked out the window. "Where's he going to set down out here?"

"Not sure." Ben waved to the far side of John's lap. "Get the map out. See if there are any flat spots, or a stretch of highway. He won't need much to be able to set down. We'll need more. A quarter mile is plenty if we're going to stop without hitting a mountain and exploding into a ball of fire."

"Good to know." John pulled out the map, but it was all mountains.

Ben pointed to the center of the page. "This is where we are. We're going south-east."

"There's nothing but mountains. A river..." John looked further out. "There's a highway to the south." He tipped the map so Ben could see it. "You think they're down there already?"

"Count on it. Those things might be bulky, but they can move."

John folded the map so the highway was on top. It snaked across the county. There was a straight stretch just under a mile long.

"Base, this is Delta-Tango-Six-Seven, we're setting her down." He rattled off a series of numbers.

Ben glanced at the map and then pointed. "That's where they're headed."

"Requesting emergency assistance. Over."

John's already tense stomach tightened further. "This can't be a coincidence."

The other person on the radio confirmed help was on its way. Ben said, "It's a leak. It could happen at any time."

John shook his head. "Do you really believe that?"

"Given what Grant told us when he briefed us what's going on... No, I don't think it's a coincidence."

"Someone sabotaged the military aircraft."

Ben nodded, his eyes focused on the window and his jaw was tight. "Likely, yes. They want your girl, so they're probably going to intercept the chopper on its way and extract her."

John pulled off his headphones and called Grant to fill him in.

"I agree with Ben's assessment."

John squeezed his free hand into a fist. "Can we get some help? We have no idea how many there will be."

"No can do, sorry. There's no personnel anywhere near you except who the military sends out. They can help. And Ben is armed."

John glanced at his other brother. "Why is Ben armed?"

"Let's just say he's worth at least three Marines, and that is no slight to the Navy."

"That's not exactly helpful, either."

"It's the best you're going to get. And I only know because the President read me in. I have higher security clearance than God now."

"Anything else I need to know?"

Grant said, "The connection to Sanctuary is back up. We're hoping someone will make a move so we know who the murderer is, assuming it was a woman and not Palmer."

"And Pat?"

"The First Lady sent me an email saying they had cupcakes and both she and Pat had chocolate on their faces. So he's doing okay."

Some of the knot in John's middle unraveled. "Thank you."

"You'll get this done. You always do." Grant paused. "And Ben will help."

"Later." John hung up.

Grant had faith in him. Maybe it didn't matter if John wasn't convinced he could pull this off. Was he enough? Andra's life was at stake, and there was no way he was prepared to have this end with any of their deaths.

"Base, this is Delta-Tango-Six-Seven. We've set down and shut down. Over."

"Help is on its way."

Ben banked the plane to the right and they topped a ridge. Empty highway stretched out in front of them.

"Where are they?"

Ben said, "South. Mile and a half."

The radio clicked on. "Base, we're being approached by a black SUV. We may be able to catch a ride, over."

"Understood, Delta-Tango-Six-Seven. Help is ten minutes out."

John didn't like the sound of this. Unless the SUV was a federal car, it might not spell anything good. "How long?"

Ben pointed at the hill where the highway disappeared. "Over that hill."

John set the phone in his lap but didn't put the headphones back on. Instead, he closed his eyes.

Okay, this is weird. It was like being a kid again, saying nightly prayers. Why didn't he do that with Pat?

God, Andra loves You. She needs Your help right now. She won't fight what's going to happen, but I can't lose her.

He figured giving God an ultimatum wasn't really the thing to do, so he said, *Help me save her. Please.*

Strong fingers and a calloused palm touched the back of John's neck. He looked up at his brother and Ben squeezed.

John stuck the headset back on. "For what it's worth, I'm glad you're here."

Ben nodded. "It's worth a lot."

The chopper had landed on the highway, a ways down from where the road leveled out. He checked his watch. Seven minutes until more Air Force personnel showed up to help.

Ben hit some levers and dipped the rudder forward to lower the nose. They slowed, descending onto the highway beyond the chopper.

Ben flew to the end, circled around and then landed the Cessna on the road facing the military aircraft. There was no one else in sight.

A wrong feeling settled in John's stomach.

Ben shut down the plane and John didn't wait. He flipped the stairs down and drew his weapon as he ran to the chopper.

The front window was smashed, a small circular hole in the center of both sides where bullets had taken out the pilot and co-pilot. He sprinted around to the side. Ben caught up to him as John approached the open door. One airman lay with his torso out of the chopper, blood on his chest. Dead.

Three down.

And it was empty.

"She's not here. She's gone." John sucked in a choppy breath. "We were too late."

Chapter 26

Andra unclipped the helmet and slipped it off, even though she was still handcuffed. She tossed it on the floor by her feet.

Death hadn't changed, not in all the years since she'd seen it up close the last time. It was still cold and ugly, and there was nothing honorable about it. That was a lie people told to make themselves feel better. In reality, the only people who benefited from the farce were those left behind, and it didn't do them much good either.

Three men, shot like nothing at all. Bang. Gone.

Andra crossed herself and then realized what she'd done. Slipping back into old ways of doing things and old methods of thinking wasn't going to help.

To these people, she was the assassin who flew all over Europe, and once to Japan, for contracts—the one who lit a candle for each victim.

The SUV which ambushed them had held four guys. Two were sitting up front now, one driving and two behind. They flanked Palmer and Andra in the middle row.

The deputy had seemed as surprised as she was when four Hispanic guys jumped out. Likely he'd never met drug runners or mercenaries or hit men in Sanctuary. Not Venezuelan ones, anyway. Apparently Palmer had been expecting someone else—Congressman Thane probably—and not four guys who shot the three airmen in cold blood. He'd puked on the road.

Way to show them you're a tough guy.

Now he was sitting beside her, looking smug. Probably figured these were just hirelings and he was on his way to get paid.

Little did he know.

The front passenger glanced at the driver and Andra got a full look at the scar running from the corner of his eye to his chin. "Highway goes another thirty miles before we hit town."

Palmer glanced between the two men with just his eyes. Andra knew he didn't understand a word of the Spanish they were speaking. She was having trouble enough, given their accents and the slang terms they used. European Spanish had some differences to it, much like the variations in phrasing used by Americans and Brits.

The driver said, "He'll be there with the plane?"

"Si. He's on route now."

"And the government man?"

"Already waiting for us."

"Good," the driver chuckled. "I'm ready to get paid and have him do the dirty work. Getting this moron to come along so he can take the blame for it all was a great idea."

Andra stared out the window at low grass and shrubs whizzing by as the SUV roared down the highway. So they were going to kill Palmer and double-cross Thane?

"The boss doesn't care about any of that. All he wants is the other fed."

Her stomach did a backflip. John? She probably would have thrown up thinking about John being killed by these guys but there wasn't anything in her stomach. They didn't want her, or Palmer or Thane. Just the money.

And their boss wanted John.

Her head swam. John would be blown apart like the airmen, giving her a courteous smile one moment and then dead the next. Tossed aside like trash.

"What about the girl?"

She stiffened. They weren't going to kill her?

"What do you think I'm going to do with her?" The driver chuckled a low laugh. "After, if the boss isn't going to keep her for himself, we can sell her."

The guy in the passenger seat turned to her. She could feel his stare. "Once she's fixed up a bit, we should be able to get a good price."

Andra shifted. Her ribs hurt, but not as bad as they would had John not tightened the vest so much. She closed her eyes, trying not to let her mind run through the implications of what they were talking about.

You're really going to push me this far, God?

Asking her to hold her peace and go to jail for life was one thing. Doing nothing while *that* happened was entirely another.

She squeezed her eyes so hard the swollen one hurt. *Don't make me do this.*

If it came down to it, Andra might not be able to stop herself from trying to kill them before she let that happen. She couldn't even defend herself? She'd made a promise when she became a Christian she wouldn't kill. Period. Was she wrong to have made that promise? She couldn't have known something like this was going to happen. Would she have to take back her word?

And yet, this wasn't just about her. They wanted John, probably dead or eventually they'd kill him. God must have brought her here so she could get John clear of the threat hanging over his head. If she could do the same for herself or if John managed it, then they might be even. Free to go their separate ways. She wouldn't always feel like she owed him for saving her from Palmer and Thane.

She could quit WITSEC, but she needed to be able to do so with a clean slate. If the threat was eliminated then she would be released from the program. That was the only way she would be able to see Helena; to live her life as a free woman for the first time in...forever.

But John was in Sanctuary. He didn't even know any of this was happening. Her stomach sank. John was going to try and rescue her.

He must have figured Palmer would lead him to whoever was behind this. He was determined to set everything right so she could come back. But what was the point, unless he thought it meant they would be together.

"No."

The two guys in front chuckled. "I guess she understands."

Palmer laughed too, though not because he knew what they thought was funny. He leaned over and grabbed her chin, forcing her to look at him. "Won't be long now."

He was right. It wouldn't be long.

John was on his way and these guys knew he was coming. The trap would spring shut, and he would be dead.

And there was nothing Andra could do about it.

**

John got between Ben and the Air Force lieutenant. "This isn't helping. We know who did this."

The lieutenant snarled. "So do we."

"It wasn't us, it was whoever took my deputy and the prisoner. If we stand here all day, they're going to get away. Do you want that to happen?" John didn't wait for an answer. "No. And neither do we. So call more of your guys in to take care of your people and let us go after them."

The officer glanced from John to Ben.

Ben said, "Or we can just leave. Since we have the right to do so."

John wasn't sure it was exactly accurate, not that he knew what the jurisdiction of an air force officer was when their people had been killed on American soil.

The lieutenant geared up to yell some more.

"Enough!" Nate emerged from the plane, hopping down the steps and over to them on his boot.

The airmen who'd flown the lieutenant in, both gaped. One turned to the other. "Dude, it's the Dolphin's quarterback."

"Nate Mason, nice to meet you." He flashed his million dollar smile—okay, it might be good for something—and lifted his hands, placating everyone. "Let's all take a second. Something tragic has happened, but my brothers and I—"

The two airmen and the lieutenant all glanced between the three of them, like they were trying to see the similarities. One whispered, "This is so cool. Look, one's a marshal."

Like John hadn't already introduced himself.

Nate said, "We really need to go after these guys. We want to get them as much as you do. The woman my brother loves is in that car, along with a man trying to frame her for a murder she didn't commit. You see, she used to be an—"

John swung around. "They don't need all the details."

"Okay." The lieutenant sighed. "I'm not leaving. You can go, but I want to be briefed." His dark eyes focused on John. "And you better get these guys."

John nodded.

They sprinted back to the plane. Ben shut the door and said, "Nate, did you have to almost tell them Andra was an assassin?"

He lifted his hands. "What? I was on a roll."

"Can we just go?" John went to the front and regained his seat. Ben turned them around, and John called Grant while they took off.

"Hey brother." Grant blew out a breath. "I'm on my way to you. I heard word through official channels about what happened. Although there was some question as to whether you guys were the killers. I explained the situation to the General and he's mobilizing personnel, so you'll have help. The FBI got on the line and they have two teams, including SWAT, coming up from their satellite office in Boise."

"I appreciate that." Then again, it might not be a help. John prayed they wouldn't get there until after the danger was over. He didn't particularly want to go up against four guys, plus Palmer. Not when it was just him and Ben. Extra people meant the operation got a whole lot more complicated, and he wasn't going to wait for anyone else's go-ahead. "So where are we headed?"

"Satellite image shows the men in the SUV loaded up Palmer and Ms. Caleri, and went south. There's a mountain town a sixty-five miles away."

"Why would they head there? You think they're going to stop or keep driving through?"

"I'm thinking they're going to try and use the airstrip just outside of town. The Kicking Corral ranch is there, and they have a small aircraft. The runway is a little short but Ben might be able to land."

John stared out the window. More mountains. "Will we get there ahead of them?"

"Maybe."

"So they could see the plane and make a run for it. We'll scare them off."

"It's possible. But those are your choices."

"Got it." John hung up. Guess he was going to have to pray again.

**

Andra winced, but she didn't want the guy pulling her along to know she had cracked ribs. The driver pulled the SUV inside a barn. The farmhouse had cracked windows and a boarded up front door with a sign saying, "No Entry".

He tugged her into the barn and shoved her toward the back corner. "Boss should be here in fifteen."

Hadn't he said the "government man" would be waiting? She glanced around. Palmer looked like he was watching for something to happen.

The guy nearest the door pulled it open and Congressman Thane strode in, the bulk of his girth hanging over his belt. His face was red, as though he'd run a 5K before he came here.

He pulled a handkerchief from his pocket and wiped his shiny forehead. "Gentlemen."

Thane's eyes settled on Andra and all the hatred the town of Sanctuary had shown toward her was there, times a thousand.

The Venezuelan with the scar strode forward, holding out a tablet. "Enter your account number and we can begin the transfer."

Thane tore his gaze from her and pecked the numbers on the screen with his meaty index finger. "There."

He strode past the man, dismissing him, and walked until his face was an inch from Andra's. "I've waited a long time for this." His breath smelled like spicy chips. "Years, where all I've dreamed of is killing you with my bare hands the way you killed Andrew."

Andra didn't give him the satisfaction of trembling; though her stomach hurt from how tight she held it. She sucked in a breath half the depth of her normal lung capacity. Likely pretty soon she would pass out. Which should make this easier, even if there were some things she'd like to do before then.

She said, "Drew spoke of his godfather often. I figured if anyone could find me it would be that man. So...bravo."

He flinched, eyes wide. "You're congratulating me?"

She shrugged one shoulder. "Just a little sentiment, one killer to another."

That appealed to his pride. When he took her elbow, he was smirking. They got two steps before the Venezuelan closest to him pulled his gun up and shot the Congressman in the chest.

Andra jerked to a stop.

The Venezuelan shifted and shot Palmer, who was fumbling for his weapon. The bullet hit him low on his torso. Blood soaked his shirt and the vest he was wearing. Palmer glanced from the gun to the open front of his jacket, wide eyed.

He collapsed.

"Pitiful, really." The Spanish words were full of disgust. The Venezuelan strode to the door and cracked it an inch so he could look out. "How long?"

His associate, who had just watched two murders with no reaction, said, "Two minutes."

Sure enough, the sound of engines preceded a small aircraft landing behind the barn. The Venezuelan with the scar pulled the doors open and a man stepped into the room. His suit was Italian and extremely well cut, and he had rings on at least four fingers. His gaze flitted over the two dead guys and settled on her. "Excellent." He glanced at scar guy. "When is Mr. Mason expected?"

Scar guy pulled out a phone. "I'll make the call now and confirm." He ducked out and the guy in the Italian suit followed.

The other two stepped closer to Andra. One on each side of her, both held automatic weapons. One glanced over to the other. "I don't know why we can't do him the same way we did Alphonz."

Andra waited for more.

"Rats deserve it, but undercover feds get more. The boss doesn't like being played for a fool."

"True."

They both nodded, making "mm-hm" noises in their throats.

One motioned back toward her with a tilt of his head. "You think we have time to..."

"Probably not."

"Yeah, probably not."

Andra looked down at where Congressman Thane lay beside her. His suit jacket had flapped open onto the straw on the floor. An expensive-looking gold pen was tucked in his inside breast pocket. A piece of wood lay on the other side of her, long enough and thick enough to do some damage.

She hefted it up in a swing toward the guy on the right, ignoring the screaming pain in her ribs. The wood cracked across the back of his head and he went down. The other guy turned with his gun. She side-swiped the weapon with her palm, whipping it across her body. It cleared her torso before it let rip, the noise like fireworks. She punched and kicked, trying to get his legs out from under him, but the guy weighed probably twice what she did.

His punch came out of nowhere. It slammed into her swollen eye like a thousand flare guns lit off inside her head. Andra collapsed back and his weight slammed into her. She grasped for his face, but her fingers were slick with sweat.

He grabbed her head and slammed it down onto the floor.

**

John and Ben had seen the plane land at the farm, so they circled around toward a neighboring piece of land. Ben gripped the rudder. "Hold on!"

The plane lowered. It juddered along the dirt, tearing the underside of the Cessna apart, but they made it down in one piece. Nate yelled from the back, while John just sat sucking in breaths. He looked at Ben. The guy was smiling.

John would've thought they'd all perished in a ball of flames, given the way Nate was carrying on about how terrible it was.

John unbuckled and got up, shooting his brother a look. "I'll spot you the security deposit."

Ben actually laughed as he and John trotted down the steps onto the rutted ground of furrowed dirt. Nate hobbled after them as they sprinted to the farm they'd seen from the air. It was at least a mile of rough terrain. And the longer it took the longer Andra was in danger.

The satellite phone rang.

Ben hissed. "Turn that thing off."

"It's Grant." John reached the edge of the field, crouched and answered it. "What's up?"

"We found out who took Thane's offer of money for Andra. Took some digging, but it's the same guys who blew up Alphonz outside the courthouse in Kansas. They're not after Andra so Thane can get revenge. They're using Thane's money to get to you."

John froze. "Alphonz's boss has Andra?"

"Give the phone to Ben."

John didn't have words. He lowered the phone and Ben snatched it out of his hand without him having to say anything.

"Yeah?" Ben's gaze moved to John and his eyes went dark. "For sure."

He hung up.

"Grant's suggestion is I knock you out and leave you here, then go get your girl on my own."

John straightened and backed away. Ben would totally do that. The fact Grant had been the one to suggest it cut through him with a depth of pain he'd rarely received from family. Nate stood to the side, same distance from both of them, cautious enough not to visibly take sides. For once, his usual smile was absent.

Ben's jaw worked back and forth. "I'm not going to. All I want to know is, if it comes down to you or Andra will you give up your life to save hers?"

"Of course."

Ben's expression didn't change, remaining a steady focus that gave no indication he was in a high-stress situation. "You need to understand I'm not going to let that happen."

"I won't let her die, and I won't let them take her."

"And I'm done arguing. I'm not going to let you die." Ben turned and strode away.

John followed, trotting after his brother's long strides. They climbed a wire fence and jumped down onto a dirt road. Why did he suddenly feel like a little kid? What made Ben more trained at this than him?

"You do know I'm a marshal, right? You might have the super-secret job but it doesn't give you superiority."

Ben kept walking. "The simple fact this is personal for you means I take the lead."

"Doesn't work for me, Ben. My town, my charge."

"So this has nothing to do with your personal feelings?"

"My personal feelings are moot if they kill her." John took the lead. "Until I know for sure that didn't happen, I'm holding them in reserve."

"Gees, you're such a romantic."

"Like you would know anything about being romantic."

A flash of something which looked a lot like pain crossed Ben's face.

But there wasn't time. John put out his arm to stop Nate's forward motion.

Ben stopped too. "I see it."

They crouched beside a gate, a turn-off leading to a farmhouse. In front of the barn was a dirty white Lexus, two rough-looking Hispanic men with automatic weapons who were guarding the door and a bigger guy in a suit. Sticking out from behind the barn was the tail of a small silver plane.

John squinted under the bill of his ball cap. "How do we approach?"

Ben opened his mouth to reply. A loud voice boomed across the expanse between the road and the farmhouse. "U.S. Marshal John Mason!" It was low in tone and had a Spanish lilt which sounded nothing like Andra's. "I know you're out there. I've got your girl and if you want her back then we make a trade."

Ben snorted.

"You for her!"

"Of course." Ben shook his head. "Because it takes too much effort not to be completely cliché."

John moved. "I'm going in."

Ben held him back. "Give me the jacket. We look enough alike I can stall him while you get to the barn. Nate, you disable their plane while John gets Andra."

Either way it meant John would get to Andra first. "Okay."

Nate nodded.

Ben circled the open gate and started walking down the dirt lane to the farmhouse. His stride made him look like he was going for a leisurely stroll. Did anything faze him?

John stayed low, climbed between the fence rails and army-crawled down the field to the plane.

He was alongside the front of the barn when he heard, "Well, well, well. If it isn't the man of the hour. Nice of you to join us."

Nate gave him a quick nod and continued, giving the barn a wide arc.

Ben planted his boots, still a distance away from Alphonz's boss. "Where is she?"

"Oh, you'll get your little killer. All in good time."

"You think I give a crap about her?" Ben shrugged. "The woman's a murder suspect. I'll be in more trouble if she goes AWOL. I gotta make my quota of arrests, you know?"

John crawled forward, praying the two sentries out front didn't see him approaching. A back way into the barn would be nice.

The suited man laughed. "Figures cops are more about the numbers than letting a businessman make some money. No respect for the little guy, you know?"

"So let her go. She can wait for the FBI. You and I will be long gone."

"A man of action. I like it." The suit sniffed. "Too bad your girl is not of this earth anymore."

John's hand slipped and his face smashed the dirt.

"Say again?"

The suit's eyes had narrowed. "Your girl is dead." He pulled out a gun and pointed it at Ben. "Why would we take off when I can kill you right here?"

He fired.

Chapter 27

John watched his brother fall, thrown down by the force of the bullet which slammed into him, point-blank in the torso. Ben hit the dirt and dust poofed up around his body. John tried to suck in a breath around the lump in his throat.

Both of them, dead.

John squeezed the grip on his gun and stood. He fired four shots before they reacted, dropping the two guards at the barn door before they could return fire. One of the guards must have pulled his trigger because bullets spurted out.

John crouched and ran, firing in Alphonz's boss's direction. The man fired back. Round after round chased John as he raced for his brother's prone body.

Fire cut through his calf.

John stumbled and hit the deck, sucking in a breath of dust and dirt. He coughed and rolled over, squinting against the bright blue sky. His hat had come off.

Footsteps on dirt closed in on his position. "Not so fast, Mr. Mason. You and I have some unfinished business."

His face came into view, shadowed by the sunlight so John couldn't see his features clear enough to make out his intentions.

"The resemblance is significant but you can't have thought sending your brother to fool me would work." He glanced a second to where Ben lay. "Not the director of the marshals, surely. No. Another brother."

John gritted his teeth.

"You've cost me a great deal of money, deceived my men and disrupted my business." He moved the gun until it was all John could see. The end. "I should put a bullet in you right here and right now. But I hardly feel it would be satisfying. Besides, you probably want to know the name of the man who is going to kill you."

John took a breath and coughed, his lungs full of Idaho dirt. "You think I care?" He twisted to look, but couldn't see where Ben lay. Was he really dead?

"You're still going to walk to the plane. There are many who want a piece of the marshal who brought low Carmen Santerra."

The name was familiar, the boss of an organization with its fingers in some seriously deep dishes. A South American mobster.

John lifted his chin. "How'd you know I'd be here?"

The man smiled. "A man with a high-profile family is easy enough to keep tabs on. Especially when he calls his brother the quarterback to ask about renting a plane."

Great. John didn't think he could walk fast. If the guy kept talking long enough the cavalry would arrive. Air Force. FBI. Other U.S. Marshals. Probably local police and sheriff's department, too.

He flicked the gun. "So get up."

John groaned like he was in serious pain. The reality was adrenaline had his entire body humming. The pain in his leg was little more than an irritation, but he could feel the sticky wetness on the back of his jeans. He could play this up a little, act hurt and distraught. "Give me a second." He put his hand to his head and willed tears to form in his eyes. It didn't take much. Ben still hadn't got up.

John thought back on Christmases. On Thanksgiving afternoons where they'd worked off the turkey dinner with full contact football. No pads, no bandages. Nights when they'd stayed up late to play pranks on Grant's girls, laughing so hard tears slid down their faces.

Sure enough, moisture gathered and ran from his eyes to the hair above his ears. He rolled over, using a push-up to lift himself so he could get his good knee under him.

"Move it. I've got a schedule to keep."

John looked at Ben, curled on his side facing the other way. John stared at the back of his brother's jacket. Was he bleeding out? He couldn't see any movement which could be breathing.

The suited guy took a step back, likely getting out of range of John if he decided to attack. As if that was going to work.

John stood, holding his injured leg bent as if he was planning to hobble to the plane.

The guy's eyes narrowed and he flicked the gun again. "Start walking."

John bent his good knee, ready to pounce. He'd have to push off on his injured leg. This was going to hurt. He glanced once more at Ben and the suit guy did the same. John launched at him, by-passing the gun to slam into the gunman. He wrapped his arms around the man's girth and used the momentum of his tackle to throw him down on his back. The gun was tossed aside. The man's legs came up and John was flipped, tossed over to land on his back again.

That went well.

He jumped up and spun around in time to receive a punch to his cheek. John whipped his head straight and followed through with his own hit. They traded blows. The suit man battered John until he had no breath, but John still fought back. *Come on, Grant.* Where was their backup?

His assailant shifted. John moved with him. The sun hit his eyes and he missed another blow. His whole body ached and his leg stung, but the brunt of it was on his face. They wrestled. John glanced around for the gun, saw the suited man move toward it and jumped. He wrapped his arms around the man's legs and they both hit the ground. The suited man scrambled forward, kicked John and snapped up the gun. His torso twisted and he swung the gun around. Arms straight, lying on his back, he pointed the gun in John's face.

Again.

His finger flexed. John flinched, squeezing his eyes shut.

Click.

John slammed his palm into the suited man's face hard enough his nose crunched. This man wasn't going to get him on a plane. John wasn't going to let the guy get revenge just because he did the job Grant asked him to do. That was ancient history now. His life was in Sanctuary, even if Andra wasn't going to be there—even if he had to live without her.

John flipped them so he was on top and slammed both palms into the guy's ears. Then he lifted the guy's head, thumping it against the ground. Andra was dead because John had decided letting her go was the best course of action. Ben could be dead, or dying, because John hadn't been able to do this by himself. He had to keep something from happening to Nate, too. And John had to stay alive, because Pat needed his father.

His thoughts whirled like a tornado, out of control, until they dissipated into nothing but the sensation of the suited man's neck in his hands. Squeezing the payback out of him.

For Andra. For Ben. For all of them.

For all the times John failed.

For not being there for Pat when he should've been.

**

First, she heard shuffling. Then further away, gunshots. Drifting in and out, Andra tried to take account. Was she still in one piece? The fire in her chest indicated otherwise. This was not a good time to puncture a lung with one of her cracked ribs. That was not something she needed.

Shallow breaths. Low and slow, Andra took in enough air to build up a store, so when she opened her eyes she could see. The room had stopped spinning but her head was hammering like a carpenter at work. The SUV was still by the door and the guards were gone. Thane was dead.

Where was—

Across the far side of the barn, Palmer bent over the tablet. Blood stained the side of his shirt, below the bottom edge of where the wet outlined his vest. A bullet-proof vest. They didn't know that when the guy shot him.

What was he doing?

The transfer—the money. He was probably trying to get it all for himself. It was what he came for after all; to sell Andra to the one person with the most desire of anyone in the world to see her dead. But Thane was the one who was dead now.

Who was still here? They couldn't have just left.

Andra braced her foot on the straw-covered floor and rolled her hips to the side, careful not to twist her torso. The wood she'd hit the guard with was gone. She hadn't killed him. That counted for something, right? She could have turned back in to the assassin she used to be and it would have been self-defense. But she knew far too much about how to dispatch a person for the argument to be accepted.

It was way too easy to kill someone—especially when emotions were ablaze.

Palmer kneeled, tapping away at the tablet. Had he waited for the moment the guards left to get the money? And why hadn't they taken the device? Either it wasn't worth it for him to try and transfer the money to himself, because it wasn't going to work. Or the guards had been more concerned with getting out of there. Had something gone wrong?

Why had they left her?

Hirelings, probably. Men who didn't have a stake in Andra's well-being, so they split to save themselves...from whatever was coming.

Andra got her feet under her, careful to move silently. She lifted the wood to hip height because she couldn't get it higher. She should be able to at least incapacitate Palmer for good this time. Then when he came around he would know what it felt like to be arrested. John could find out who killed Betty and she could keep her life. Such as it was, or would be, with the stain of being a murder suspect.

She swung, but the pain in her ribs tugged the wood down and Palmer caught the force of the blow on the back of his shoulder. He fell to the side, rolled and came back up to grab the wood swing it at her. Andra slammed into the SUV. Stars exploded behind her eyes and she had to brace her hands on the car to keep from falling.

Palmer tackled her and they went down, right by where Thane had fallen dead.

She pushed against his torso but felt only vest. He wouldn't move and she was rapidly losing strength.

The familiar noise of helicopter rotors brought Palmer's head up. Andra looked around. Thane's suit jacket was open. Inside was the gold-plated pen. She grasped for it, stretching her fingers until they felt like the joints would separate. It wasn't far enough. She stretched more, crying out.

Palmer's head whipped back to her.

Finally, she pulled the pen free of the pocket.

"No you don't." Palmer slammed his arm onto hers.

Andra cried out, but didn't let go of the pen. He was going to kill her. Could she accept this, if it was God's will? Would He accept her need to fight until her last breath to preserve her life?

John's face flashed through her mind and something in her surged to life, remembering the familiar comfort of his presence. Eating together. Playing cards with Pat. They would be a family, but he wasn't here. He hadn't come after her. John had let her go to meet whatever fate God decreed she accept, like that was fine with him.

Well, it wasn't fine with her.

Now she knew the two of them, Andra didn't want to lose John or Pat. She wanted them in her life. She wanted to know what could be between them all of them. Could they be happy as a family?

Peace washed over her, but underneath the familiar zing of adrenaline still fueled her muscles.

Andra rolled them both. Over and over they tumbled across the room until Palmer's head slammed into the rim on the tire.

Without missing a beat, Andra clambered up and raced for the door. She squeezed through the opening into the blinding sunlight, searching around even as her eyes adjusted to the brightness.

John was grappling with the boss. He'd come? But not for her, for the men who were going to take her, the ones who'd been working with Palmer and Thane. Doing his job.

His gaze hit her and he yelled, "Andra!"

Palmer slammed into her back. They tumbled to the ground, and Andra twisted and came up with the pen in her hand. He grabbed her. She screamed and slammed the pen into the side of Palmer's neck. He collapsed on her, choking for breath while Andra lay under the crushing weight of him, forced to listen as he died.

She'd done it.

She had killed someone again.

A fist hit flesh, the sound of John fighting with his attacker. Andra pushed Palmer off, wincing at the sight of his dead face. She should apologize. Beg God for forgiveness. But there were no words in her brain.

She stood, fell to her knee, struggled and finally managed to get up. Her chest was on fire. White spots tingled in the edges of her vision. It wouldn't be long before she was out for good.

The noise of rotors got louder. A helicopter circled low and dipped down as the chopper flew closer. Come to aid John. To arrest her, now she really was guilty of murder—and of a cop, no less. There was no way they were going to believe Palmer was the one who set this whole thing up.

The door to the helicopter slid open and it circled around again. Whoever was in the door lifted a bullhorn. "This is the FBI. Stand down. Drop your weapons and put your hands on your heads."

There was nowhere to go.

She was hemmed in. John had come, but not because he cared for her.

"Hands on your head."

Andra lifted her arms. Pain tore through her chest and she hit the ground.

**

John saw her fall. The helicopter landed and booted men ran over and dragged the suit guy off him, pinning the gunman's arms behind his back as he raged and screamed.

John rolled, crawling to where she lay. Ben was up, too. "What...?"

Ben hauled him to his feet. "He hit my vest."

They stumbled, even with Ben holding the bulk of John's weight. "So you just lie there. You don't help me?"

"I wanted you to feel like you did it yourself, like you won under your own steam." Ben lowered him by Andra's side.

John touched her shoulder, but said to his brother, "He winded you, didn't he?"

"Of course he did. It hurts getting shot, even if you do have a vest on."

"I wouldn't know." His fingers searched Andra for signs of injury. "I only got punched and hit."

Ben squeezed his shoulder. "I'll find out if they brought a medic."

John stroked the side of her face. "I'd like to see you open your eyes, but you look like you've had a rough day."

His gaze drifted down, searching her for signs of injury. Her shirt had pulled up to reveal an inch of skin at her waist. Was that...John lifted it higher. Sure enough, there was the imprint of a boot on her stomach.

He pulled her shirt back down. "When you do wake up, I'm going to want to know who did that. Because I'm going to arrest them."

Hot tears burned his eyes. He wasn't crying, he was just exhausted and that guy had packed some serious weight behind his punches.

"My brothers are here. I'd like you to meet them, but don't get too enamored. They're nothing special."

He touched his fingers to her hairline and brushed back a few strands of jet-black hair. The sensation was both familiar and new at the same time. "I'd like to do that more too, if you'll let me. And maybe kiss you." He stroked her jaw with his thumb. "I'd also like to—"

Her lips parted and breath pushed out. "You talk a lot."

Behind him, someone chuckled. John didn't take his focus from her until her eyes flickered open and she smiled with the side of her mouth.

"Hi."

She inhaled and winced. "Hi."

"Don't try to talk, okay?" He looked back at Ben

His brother nodded. "Life Flight is on its way. They said to keep her still. Her broken ribs might have punctured a lung."

John felt the tension evaporate from his body and he slumped lower by her side.

"Is that her?" Nate hobbled up.

John watched Andra take in the two Mason brothers standing by their huddle on the ground. She lifted her hand and wiggled her fingers in a wave.

Nate grinned. "What's up?" He looked at Ben and then John. "Is it over now? Because I don't think my contract allows for gunfights."

John looked back at Andra. Ben said, "It's done." There was a chill in his words, as though if it weren't over he'd have ended it himself.

"Honey—" Her gaze moved back to him. "There's a helicopter coming. I'm going to go with you, okay?"

She blinked, enough of a nod for him. Her breath was coming in pants now.

"I'll be with you the whole time. I'm not leaving."

She breathed. "—kay."

John took her hand. "Good."

Palmer lay beyond her, a gold pen sticking out of his neck. John looked back at the fingers he'd threaded his through, fingers with blood on them. "You killed him?"

Her eyes darkened and she licked her lips like she was parched...and nervous. "It's not something you forget how to do."

Ben laughed. "I thought I recognized her."

John turned. Ben's eyes widened like he realized what he'd said. His eyes locked with John's and Ben shook his head. "Forget I said that."

Right. John sighed. "Andra..."

This was going to be their future. John was going to get familiar with the woman who had built a new life, then she—or someone else—would do or say something and it would hit him all over again who she'd been. *Assassin.* That word was going to get thrown around unless he could make peace with it.

She'd shut her eyes again.

"Honey, will you look at me?"

Her lips compressed and her face screwed up. She sucked in a breath and tears pricked in her eyes.

"Honey—"

"I wasn't supposed to. It just happened and now they're going to kick me out of Sanctuary." She sucked in air. "I won't be able to come back."

"Listen—"

"I killed him, John. And now I'll have to leave. They won't let me live there. I won't be able to see anyone." Her whole body jerked with the sob. "I won't be able to...see you."

"Andra."

She hiccupped a breath.

John said, "I need you to know, I—"

Her face scrunched even more and she moaned low in her throat like she was in serious pain.

"Honey, what is it?"

Andra pressed a hand against her side.

"Make some room." Two medics dumped their bags and John was pushed out of the way. Andra wasn't moving. Or breathing.

"Something's wrong." John gasped. "You have to help her!"

The paramedic leaned down and listened to her chest. His eyes lifted and met his partner's. "Pneumothorax."

Nate said, "What's that?"

The EMT didn't look up. "Lung collapsed."

Ben helped John to his feet and he watched, helpless as they stuck a needle in her chest. Nate grabbed his hand and squeezed. Andra's whole body jerked and she sucked in the first full breath since he crouched beside her. John exhaled too. They wasted no time loading her on a backboard and John walked alongside her as they carried her to the helicopter.

He moved to climb on, but Grant put his hand on John's chest. He looked at his brother. "I'm going."

"Let them work."

"I said I'd go with her." What was wrong with Grant? "I told her I'd be there the whole time."

Grant didn't let him go. Nate and Ben closed around him, and Ben took his other arm. John waited for one of his brothers to explain why he couldn't go with Andra. "What?"

The door on the helicopter slammed shut.

"What is going on, guys?"

"Walk with me." Grant didn't wait for an answer because it wasn't a question. Ben led John behind Grant, while Nate hobbled after them all the way to the helicopter Grant must have arrived in.

"I didn't think you were coming. You didn't say you were on your way."

Grant climbed aboard the helicopter. "The president called me."

John shook his head. "Why am I with you and not Andra when...What does the president have to do with this?"

"Where is Pat?"

"Pat? He's with..."

"The first lady."

They climbed in and Ben pressed a hand against John's chest, holding him in the helicopter seat while Nate buckled the safety harness. They sat either side of him and buckled up while John stared at his brother until his eyes burned. "Grant. Tell me what's going on."

"The first lady emailed the president and he called me straight away. The school teacher—"

"Mrs. Pepper."

"She came to the house, told them Pat needed to catch up on some missed work. Mrs. Sheraton let him go, but that was hours ago. Mrs. Pepper said it wouldn't take long, and the first lady was worried when he didn't make it back in time for dinner." Grant took a breath. "Susan called around and no one has seen either of them all day. Not anywhere in town. She called the sheriff's office and Dotty got Bolton on it."

"Grant..."

"Elma Pepper took your son. Bolton searched her house. He found bloody clothes he thinks she was wearing when she killed Betty Collins."

John tipped his head forward and tried to breathe, suddenly acutely aware of all the bruises in his chest. Someone squeezed the back of his neck.

"Bolton has no idea where she took Pat."

Chapter 28

The helicopter landed and John jumped out. Bolton's truck barreled toward them and pulled to a stop in front of them. Ben flung the door open and Matthias looked back from the front passenger seat. "Load up."

John and Grant slid in, while Nate and Ben climbed in the bed.

John saw the worry on Matthias' face and nodded. The man had spent a good amount of time with Pat; no doubt he was feeling the loss too. John's butt hit the seat and he didn't waste any time before he said, "Mrs. Pepper?"

Matthias' face was dark, his hand gripping the handle as Bolton sped into town. "I never would've guessed it."

"What about Aaron. How's he doing?"

"Better. Doctor Fenton is talking about releasing him, but we're not sure where he's going to live. He can't go back with those two losers for roommates."

Bolton gripped the wheel and turned them in a tight circle before he slammed his foot down and didn't waste any time, saying, "It's been six hours. No one's seen them anywhere since Pepper took him from the first lady and she has no method of transportation. No known hang outs other than her house and the school, both of which have been cleared.

"We've done a house-to-house search and every single person in town is accounted for except the teacher and your son. Dan and I have checked all our respective outbuildings, and Matthias got a shirt of Pat's from your apartment. Our next course of action is to have Dan's hound sniff the shirt and see if he can get a scent."

John's gut churned. Bolton drove so fast he had to swallow down the urge to throw up. First Andra and now Pat. When would he finally have them both together healthy and happy? Andra needed to fight to get better. Wherever he was, Pat had to hang on until John could get to him. And Mrs. Pepper had to not hurt him, or touch him at all. Hopefully she just wanted John's attention and she only needed Pat for a bargaining tool. That meant she'd have to keep him well so John didn't refuse whatever she was looking to get out of this.

"That's good." Grant nodded. "We should get on that."

John blinked and then remembered. Right. Dan's tracking dog.

Bolton said, "It's where we're headed now."

Grant glanced aside at John. "What about the woods? That's the only other place she could be hiding him. Any buildings you know of, or cabins?"

Matthias turned back from the front seat. "Andra's?"

John agreed. "Maybe."

Grant frowned. "We can check her place, but who in town knows those trees?"

Bolton motioned to Matthias with a wave of his hand. "The boys and I know the area around the ranch, and Dan would say the same about his end. The General has everyone at the Meeting House and they're going to put together a search party, but its rough terrain up there so not everyone will be able to navigate it."

Grant said, "Anyone you can think of who might know if there are any other cabins, or blinds, or anywhere she could be holding him?"

Matthias shook his head, "Not that I can—"

John remembered. "Nadia Marie."

Bolton jerked. "Nadia?"

"Andra said she's all about hiking the woods around town. She might know hiding places."

"Then we'll go to Nadia's house first." Bolton swung the truck left and they all braced.

Two minutes later they pulled up in front of a house with a mishmash of flowers of different heights and sizes that seemed to have been crowded in the flowerbed for no other reason than they were all pink.

"There's a note on the door." Matthias jumped out and retrieved it. The front said, *John*. Matthias unfolded it a page-sized copy of the same map of Sanctuary tacked to the wall in John's office.

In the top right corner, at the end of a long trail, was a big X.

"She already left." John didn't know whether to be mad or relieved. It would be a long trek up the mountain, past Andra's burned out cabin, to the place Nadia Marie had indicated. How much of a head start did she have, and exactly what did she think she was going to accomplish on her own? They had to get there fast before there were more casualties.

"Why would she be certain this was the place?"

John turned to his brother. "No idea. It could easily be a ruse."

As they drove, John called the hospital Andra had been taken to. When he hung up, he told Grant, "Her lung collapsed two more times so they've taken her into surgery. The nurse is going to call me when she's out." He paused a second. "What I want to know is why they told me anything at all without questioning who I was?"

"That's because Ms. Caleri is your fiancée. I made sure they knew. You didn't know?" Grant smirked. "Plus, it probably helps that your mother is there to be with Andra in your absence."

"Of course she is." John rolled his eyes, but he was glad. His mom was probably beside herself if she knew anything about what had gone on today. She'd need to feel like she was doing something to help. "Does she know about Pat?"

Grant's eyes darkened. "I'll let you make the call when we get him back."

"Okay." John was trying to convince himself as much as his brother and the other two men in the truck. He couldn't lose Pat. Not now he'd finally reached a place where they had a shot at a great relationship.

Bolton pulled up beside the mayor's house, where the trail started. They piled out.

Grant gaped. "Who lives here?"

"The mayor."

Grant shook his head and the confusion on his face dissipated by force. "Let's get to work."

Matthias handed Bolton the map. He studied it for a few seconds and shoved it in his back pocket.

John turned to his brother. "Stick with Matthias." When Grant started to argue, John said, "Nate, stay here. Ben?"

Their other brother was gone, which wasn't bad. The more people involved, the more complicated the operation became.

John tipped his head to the trail and looked at Bolton. "Ready?"

The big man nodded. "Two miles."

John figured he could handle that without passing out.

"Half a mile after Andra's cabin there's a fork. Head left."

John looked at Grant. "See you guys up there." He looked at Bolton and saw the man was ready. "Okay. Let's go."

Side-by-side they sprinted up the trail.

**

Nadia Marie brushed sweat from her forehead. With her back against the structure's splintered siding she twisted around and up to peer in the window. It was little more than a shack, mostly used by guys when they did their ridiculous hunting games which were more like orienteering. Anyone could follow a map.

Lately she'd had the impression someone else was using the structure for more than just a stopping point. Though, why they would need to come all the way up here just to do the horizontal tango was anyone's guess. Not like there weren't enough beds in town. It wasn't that hard to sneak around unnoticed. Elma Pepper had done it well enough when she killed Betty.

The cabin was dim. Nadia couldn't see much and couldn't hear anyone inside. Was she wrong? She bit her lip. What if she'd led Pat's father on a wild goose chase up the mountain, and the kid was still safely in town? No. Someone would have found him. But she'd been gone an hour already and Pat could be home, unharmed. The thought was enough to make her want to get down on her knees and fold her hands like a little kid in dire need of a new bike.

Elma walked past the window, eyes down and wringing her hands in front of her. She turned away and Nadia lifted up more. Pat's head jerked and his eyes widened. Nadia ducked back down.

The clearing was quiet.

Who knew how long it would take the rest of them to get up here. Now she knew where Pat was, and he wasn't in need of emergency medical attention, so she could stay outside and wait for help. Go in only if it was necessary—like to get between Pat and the blade that killed Betty Collins.

Who are you kidding? You're a stylist, not a hero.

But facing the fact Bolton wasn't ever going to see her as anything other than...well, nobody, Nadia Marie had come to the realization life wasn't going to get better unless she made it that way. Pat had seen her. If she didn't go in, he'd think she had abandoned him. She didn't want that for John's son. Especially not after Andra told her they'd played Go Fish while she was in jail. The poor kid was probably scared out of his mind.

Nadia Marie glanced inside one more time. Pat sat on the edge of the bare mattress while Elma paced back and forth like the nut-job she apparently was.

Nadia Marie crept around the structure and eased the door handle around slowly, hoping she could get inside before Elma even noticed the door was open. She ducked her head in first and then opened the door all the way. Elma swung around, mid-rant. The words were a mumble and Pat didn't look especially terrified. Just relieved.

Elma screamed and ran at Nadia Marie with her arm raised. The huge knife glinted.

Nadia waited until the last moment, side-stepped her and ran for Pat. He wrapped his arms around her and they moved to the far corner of the cabin. Elma was breathing hard, still brandishing the knife. Nadia Marie shoved Pat behind her. "Put the knife down, Elma. You won't get what you want if you kill us."

"I could kill you. I'll still have him." She waived the knife at Pat. "The sheriff won't care about someone who only cuts hair."

"Hey," Nadia huffed. "You said you liked the way I cut your hair."

"Guess what? I lied."

Nadia swallowed. "Why are you doing this, Elma? What's this going to achieve, other than getting you sent out of Sanctuary to jail?" It dawned on her. "Is that what you want? To leave?"

"You'd think killing Betty would've got me arrested. But he had to blame it all on Andra, didn't he. Harriet is such a liar. She hates Andra almost as much as Arnold does."

Palmer. Nadia Marie couldn't even think his name without her lip curling in disgust. "So you killed Betty, and Palmer got Harriet to frame Andra."

"He thinks he can escape. Like I'll stay here and it'll be for nothing?" She waved the knife around, froze and went to the door. "Someone's coming."

Nadia Marie pulled Pat to the far corner of the structure.

He looked up at her. "You're Andra's friend."

She nodded, hearing the note of anxiety in his voice. "I am."

"She killed people."

Nadia crouched and pulled him down beside her. "When I was in third grade there was this boy who used to pick on me. Called me names, pushed me around, that kind of thing. You know what I did?"

Pat shook his head.

Nadia glanced fast at Elma, who was squinting out the window at nothing, and then looked back at Pat. "I went and found the biggest girl in school and made friends with her. You think he came after me when she was around?" Nadia shook her head. "Now I'm in Sanctuary and there are plenty of people it's worth staying away from. She's not one of them. Andra isn't bad, but she is dangerous. You think anyone's going to mess with me if she's my best friend?"

The corners of Pat's mouth curled up, but it didn't reach his eyes. "Cool."

"I know." She smiled. "Now I need you to do something for me."

Pat nodded.

Nadia leaned even closer. "When I tell you to, you're going to run. As fast as you can out the door and down the hill. Okay?"

His lips pressed into a white line and he nodded again, standing straighter now.

"Good man."

Nadia eyed the chair, wondering if she should grab it and run at Elma. She took one step and the door slammed open. "Hal."

Elma swung around aiming the knife. Hal didn't side-step like she had. He grabbed the wrist holding the weapon, ducked his shoulder and flipped Elma onto her back. Pat's hand folded into Nadia's and he gripped her fingers.

Elma came up with the knife. Hal intercepted the swing and took hold of her wrist, this time with both hands. He glanced at them. "Go!"

Elma scrabbled around, grasping at Hal's hands with her free one. Nadia tightened her grip on Pat and tugged him outside.

Bolton and John were running toward them both sweating as they sprinted up the trail. John didn't look good, his face covered in red marks and bruises.

"Dad!"

"Pat." John hugged his son. "Where's Elma?"

Nadia said, "She's in there. Hal's with her, he needs help."

Bolton gave her a dark look and ran to the cabin.

John crouched. "Stay with Nadia just one more minute." He ran inside.

Nadia tugged Pat to the side of the trail and they waited. A minute later Bolton came out, hauling Elma by the arm. His grip on her made the muscles in his arm and shoulder flex. He shot her a look. "We're gonna talk about what just happened."

Nadia felt her eyes bug out.

Bolton strode down the path with the crazy teacher as if that one sentence didn't make it sound like there was something between them. How could there be? Since when did Bolton see the need to share his opinion on anything with her? He barely knew her name.

John, who walked with Hal, looked more battered than the older man. Pat hugged his dad again and Nadia stepped away to give them a moment. She touched Hal's arm. "You okay?"

"Sure, darlin'. Haven't felt that alive in forty years."

She chuckled. "You know, I could have done that. I was about to hit her over the head and send Pat out." Nadia set her hands on her hips. "I was taking care of it and you jumped the gun."

Hal grinned. "You snooze you lose, darlin'."

**

Andra stared at the older woman beside her hospital bed. Expensive haircut, but she wore it like it was no big deal. Pastel purple knit sweater and white jeans, earrings and a thin gold bracelet.

"I'm Brenda Mason." She smiled. "John's mother."

Of course she was.

Andra swallowed. Her whole body was weighed down by bandages and layers of hospital blankets. The room smelled like a chemical she was sure they'd smeared all over before they cut her chest open. Yes, *cut her chest open.* Because that was what doctors did when someone wasn't breathing. They said they fixed it all, but it didn't exactly feel like it. The doctor had said something about...pneumonia and a thorax, whatever that was. She couldn't piece it all together. If she was better, why did it hurt this much?

She blinked. The woman was still there, reading a magazine now.

Brenda Mason looked up. She set the magazine down and came over. She seemed nice enough when she smiled. "Hi, honey."

John had called her that.

Where was John?

Andra couldn't keep her eyes open.

"You're drifting in and out." Soft fingers squeezed Andra's hand. "But you're safe. Everything is fine."

Andra tried to breathe, but her chest felt like some creeper from a bad horror movie had done a number on her. She tried to speak, but all that came out was, "John."

"He went back to Sanctuary."

He wasn't here?

"I'm sorry, honey."

Andra squeezed her eyes shut and something warm tickled her face. Softness—a tissue—wiped it away. John hadn't come? He said he would, but he'd left her here and sent his mother. It made no sense at all.

He'd said he wanted to stay with her and make sure she was okay. Andra wanted him there with her so she could cry and scream and yell at him for letting her down when she'd actually trusted his words. Her head swam. Maybe there was some other explanation. Some other reason he'd been called away.

Or maybe she was just kidding herself.

Andra was supposed to be above that. She'd kept her heart separated from any kind of romantic attachment for so long, she couldn't believe how massively she had failed. Had she learned anything? Love wasn't for her. Relationships, other than her friendships with Hal and Nadia Marie, weren't for her either and she needed to remember that.

Especially when it hurt this much to be wrong.

**

John watched Pat, who sat on Nate's lap on a bench both of them laughing.

John said, "We need to find a way they can see each other. Pat needs his uncles."

Grant shifted beside him. "Clearly you need us, too."

John folded his arms. "I had it handled."

"Seems to me like Hal subdued Elma and Nadia Marie rescued Pat before you even got there. Good people."

The reality was they were friends of Andra's who would risk their lives for his son. Those were the best kind of people. That they loved Andra said a great deal about her, too. Namely, she was the kind of woman who inspired loyalty in others. She had friends who cared about the safety of a child enough to intervene.

Warmth swelled in his chest. "I really think we'll be okay here."

Grant rubbed the back of his neck. "Maybe I should deputize Bolton, just to be on the safe side."

John glared. He didn't need Grant interfering, at least not more than just being his boss. He looked around. "Where did Ben disappear to?"

"No idea." Grant looked down Main Street. "Nice place, isn't it?"

"Right." John remembered. "You've never been here."

"Could use some fixing up, though."

"You said that at the hearing." John chuckled. "Good luck getting approval to turn into actual money."

"I don't know." Grant grinned. "You could probably ask the president to work that out. I hear you have his number."

"And his wife and daughter."

Grant's eyes went wide.

John sputtered, "That didn't come out right."

"I should hope not." Grant clapped him on the back.

John blew out a breath. Matthias had driven Hal and Nadia Marie over to the medical center to get checked out and to check on Aaron. They'd given Bolton and Elma a ride to the sheriff's office first, where she was being detained until the marshals' chopper arrived. All in a day's work. Or a week, whatever.

"So you're coming with?"

John looked at his brother. "Yeah, I need to get to Andra. Nate is going to stay with Pat. I don't want him on the helicopter with Elma, anyway."

"I'll get the report written up and convince the U.S. Attorney's office to drop the charges against Andra for Betty Collins' murder. I'll need a report from you before I can completely clear her. There will be a lot of mess to sort through, but she'll be back with you before you know it."

"Good." John looked around, exhaling a big breath. His chest had been constricted for a long time. Longer than the last week, for sure. In fact, it might have been the first full breath he'd taken in years. It felt good.

"So you're staying?"

"I have to talk it over with Pat, but yeah." He looked his brother. "We're staying."

**

The mayor slumped in the chair, blood dripping from his chin.

Ben had seen Andra's face, the days old bruises and her swollen eye. The boot print she'd had on her abdomen. The mayor coughed, expelling more blood onto his white dress shirt.

Ben Mason grabbed the mayor's hair and pulled his face up so he could look into the man's eyes. "You don't mess with my family."

Then he took the rag and wiped off his hands.

Now they were even.

Chapter 29

When Andra awoke, Brenda was gone. The man who had replaced her sat in the same chair, wearing a crumpled suit and loosened tie. The U.S. attorney looked frazzled from being overworked and underappreciated. But the addition of two marshals with their jackets and guns providing an armed guard made the impression a whole lot more formidable. They both stood either side of the door, feet planted and arms crossed.

Andra told them all about the helicopter ride, the men who'd killed the pilots, the barn and how she'd killed Palmer with a pen.

The U.S. attorney looked up from his laptop, eyes wide. One of the marshals snorted. Andra looked over but he'd squashed the humor from his face.

Here it was.

She'd killed a man. Now it was time to accept the consequences. They would probably cuff her and then leave a guard at the door. The nurses would have to be escorted in and out. The care she had received so far would turn to fear and detached professionalism. As soon as the doctor cleared Andra to leave, she would be escorted straight to jail—detained for violating the most important part of her WITSEC agreement. She'd been given a page-long list of stipulations specific to her case. Not murdering anyone else was at the top of the list.

And now she'd gone and done it.

That was why John wasn't here. She'd seen the warmth in his eyes as she lay on the dirt and cried for her future. He'd obviously realized the significance of what she'd said. Grant probably filled him in, and he'd decided not to come with her but to go back to Sanctuary instead. The one place Andra would never be allowed to go.

The man's pale eyes assessed her, like Andra was a difficult math problem he was trying to solve. "You understand you've damned yourself with your statement?"

Andra nodded. It was about all the movement she could do, even though the bulk of her injuries were in her torso and the rest of her was relatively unscathed. "I'm not going to lie to you. I didn't kill Betty Collins—"

"One—" He glanced down at his screen. "—Elma Pepper has already confessed."

"The teacher?"

The U.S. attorney nodded. "Mrs. Pepper kidnapped Patrick Garrett Mason and held him hostage until—"

"What!" Andra shut her eyes and breathed through the pain sparking behind her eyes. When it dissipated, she looked at him. "Is Pat okay?"

"Safe and sound. Rescued by a—" He looked at his laptop screen. "—Nadia Marie Carleigh and Hal Gorge."

"He was?" Except it actually made perfect sense. "Of course he was." After all, Nadia and Hal had both successfully rescued Andra in their own way. She smiled. Of course they would do the same for a kid.

The U.S. attorney's brow crinkled. "This is amusing to you?"

Andra cleared her throat. "Sort of. Not that Pat was in danger. I'm glad he's okay because Nadia was right. That is one stinkin' cute kid."

The marshals glanced at each other.

"I was laughing because that's precisely the kind of thing Nadia and Hal would do. Despite the fact most people in...where I live, hate me for being a stone cold killer and they'd sooner see me gone than accept the fact they aren't much better than I was. I still liked living there." She paused for a beat. "Being arrested for murder, notwithstanding."

The marshal to the right side of the door cracked a smile.

The U.S. attorney's face lost whatever pleasantness he'd tried to bring with him. "It's a shame you won't be going back home."

The marshal left of the door reached behind his back and drew out a pair of handcuffs.

Here it was: the end.

"Deputy Marshal John Mason seems to feel you should be cleared of the charges. But the fact remains your WITSEC contract, the Memorandum of Understanding you signed, clearly states murder revokes all concessions you've been given. For you to kill someone violates the contract and voids the immunity agreement offered to you by my office. Even if the director of the marshals also wants to dismiss the charges. As though I'm going to be swayed by the simple fact he and the sheriff in charge of the case are brothers. Their opinion of the situation is one thing. But it doesn't excuse the fact a law enforcement officer is dead."

His statement made her wonder if he knew anything about Sanctuary at all.

He looked at her for a long moment. "Despite your statement, self-defense does not excuse you in this instance."

Andra swallowed. "I—"

"These marshals will remain here." He shut the lid of his laptop and stood. "You will be issued a new identity and go to trial for the crimes you committed prior to being accepted into witness protection."

He should have added, "Have a nice life" but he didn't. Which was a shame, since he was essentially giving her the kiss of death. Life in prison was what she had to look forward to, if not the death penalty. It was a good thing John wasn't here, especially since he would try to stick up for her. The last thing she wanted was to see his face when she was taken away.

Someone's cell rang. The marshal on the right of the door pulled out his phone and looked at the screen. He ducked out the door and shut it behind him.

The other marshal smiled, more of a sneer than anything that could be construed as amusement.

The U.S. attorney wrapped his coat over his arm and picked up his briefcase in which he'd stowed his laptop. "Thank you for your time, Ms. Caleri."

The marshal snorted.

Despite what had happened, Andra managed to smile. "I'm sure the pleasure was all yours."

He gave her his back and walked out.

The marshal clipped one bracelet of the handcuffs to the bed rail and attached the other to Andra's wrist, just below the hospital ID bracelet.

He shut the door and Andra closed her eyes. She'd told the truth, and in doing so had incriminated herself. In this case, the truth wasn't going to set her free. The real truth—Jesus—had already done that. Still, in this life Andra would only know incarceration.

The U.S. attorney had chosen not to take Grant and John's word for it and release her to return to Sanctuary. She'd had it good and been blessed with a facsimile of freedom for ten years. Now it was time to go back to the real world. Mercy had been granted to her, liberty from the price of her sin. But the crimes she'd committed still had to be paid for.

Andra was going to have to live the rest of her life knowing the taste of what could have been. The dream of a family with John and Pat, and spending time with Nadia and Hal, was gone now. And that taste was going to have to sustain her in the desert of the rest of her natural life.

**

John strode into the hospital lobby with Grant just after eight in the evening.

One of the marshals on Andra's detail was waiting. When John approached, the guy stuck out his hand. "Mason."

John nodded, waiting while the man shook hands with Grant.

"Director."

But John didn't want to wait through more pleasantries, so he cut to the chase. "What happened?"

The marshal rubbed the side of his head, wincing in sympathy at John's injuries. "She's cuffed, in protective custody pending trial. He isn't backing down even though it was self-defense."

"How is she?"

"Quiet."

John nodded. He didn't expect much besides stoic acceptance of her fate. But that wasn't going to stop him from doing everything he could. "I need to speak with Ms. Caleri."

The marshal nodded. John moved to follow him down the hall, but Grant grabbed his arm. His brother's face was hard. "I have a couple of calls to make."

As they walked to her room, John tried not to think about what she was going to say. He said a prayer that she would actually admit she felt the same way he did, that she would fight for her own life for once.

The marshal on the door looked John up and down. "Nice of you to join us."

The one who'd met John in the lobby sighed. "Sanders."

He'd met them both before on different jobs that never required him to make friends with them.

Sanders motioned to the door he was guarding. "You need something, Mr. Director's brother?"

"Yeah. A minute with Ms. Caleri."

John didn't know what they knew past Andra's basic details. Probably nothing about Sanctuary or the fact John Mason was now both a small town sheriff and a U.S. marshal. Neither would be allowed to write up what had happened in any report, and the likelihood was he wasn't going to see either of them beyond this.

He turned to the marshal beside him. "It was good to see you, man."

He grinned. "You too, Mason. Take care."

John let himself in the room. Andra's face didn't look much better than the last time he saw her, though she had color in her cheeks. Her eyelashes were fanned out on her cheeks, dark against her pale skin.

He took her hand, cradling her fingers in his. "I should just wheel you out of here right now. Have Grant create a diversion. Bust you out of the hospital and get someone to fly us back to Sanctuary." He smiled to her sleeping form. "I could do it. I'm getting pretty good at rushing around on airplanes. And no one would be allowed to come to Sanctuary and look for us. Grant wouldn't give them the clearance."

She sucked in a breath and John watched her push it out through the tube in her nose. He closed his eyes and thanked God she was still alive. Andra had a long way to go before she would be up and running again, but she had time enough to get there.

John pulled up a chair and sat with his forearms on his knees and his fingers linked. He wanted her to wake up. He wanted her to cry and say she didn't want to go to jail, that she needed his help to escape her fate. They'd have to pick up Pat on the way, but John had absolutely no problem running with her.

He'd miss the rest of his family, but they could make a new life together. A home and babies of their own. Little girls with Andra's dark hair and eyes, pleading with him to watch them twirl and dance—girls who would have Pat as their big brother. His son would make a great big brother.

Now he just had to convince Andra how good it could be.

**

U.S. Attorney Thomas Rutherford the third set his belongings down on the hotel room desk and slumped into the chair. He'd never liked plane flights and today's tiny prop combined with high winds had left his stomach unsettled all through the interview.

Tomorrow he was going to have to take the same journey home.

He flipped open his laptop and stared at the statement. Although perfectly reasonable, his decision had left him uncomfortable in an area inside of him that he rarely bothered with. Long ago he'd have let emotion sway his decision. That was then.

His life wasn't going to follow the course he'd mapped out, if he didn't endeavor to lead it that way himself.

His phone rang.

Thomas nearly dismissed the blocked number, but tonight he was in the mood to give a telemarketer a few choice words. "What do you want?"

"Thomas Rutherford, U.S. Attorney?"

"Yes."

"Please hold for the President."

**

Andra shut her eyes and tried to think of what to say. "Tired."

"You're right, I'm sorry." He looked so disappointed. "You're not well enough for this."

"John."

He turned back, already twisting the door handle. "What?"

"Sit down, John."

His eyes sparked with something dangerously like hope and he settled back into the chair. Andra tried to untangle her thoughts long enough to figure out what she wanted to say.

"You didn't leave because you wanted to." She spoke slowly, trying to match her words with the speed her thoughts were able to generate them. The hospital room was dark, except for the light above the tiny sink in the corner. "Pat was in danger and you had to go save him. So you sent your mother to sit with me."

He didn't say anything.

"She seems nice."

John laughed. "She likes to feel needed and we like having her around so we try to include her when something is happening."

Andra blinked her nod. Her eyes drifted closed and she sighed.

"Does it hurt?"

She shrugged by crinkling her nose. "Fuzzy. Tired."

"Sorry."

She reached out her hand, her eyes still closed; her thoughts like wisps of smoke. "Don't go."

"Honey, I need you to speak English. I only know a couple of cuss words in Spanish, and how to ask where the bathroom is." John's warm fingers interlaced with hers.

Andra wanted to laugh with him, but she had to concentrate real hard. "Don't go."

"I don't want to."

His fingers twitched. She heard him shift and then felt his breath on her face. His lips touched her forehead, lingering. "John."

She heard him chuckle a slight expelling of breath. "I like the way that sounds. I'd like to hear more." He paused. "You're out of it on whatever medication they gave you and half asleep, but this might be my only opportunity to get an honest answer out of you so I'm going to say it anyway."

She was still smiling. "—kay."

John laughed again. "Andra, do you want to come back to Sanctuary with me?"

"Yes."

"Do you want to go out to dinner with me?"

Dinner? Andra felt her eyebrows draw together. How about get married and give Pat some little brothers who adored him and had the same coloring, John's coloring.

"No?"

Andra opened her eyes. The look on his face wasn't good, but she still shook her head. The promise of dinner wasn't going to cut it. "I'm going to prison."

"What if you don't?"

"Then no, I don't want dinner." She took a breath. "I want...the rest of...all of it."

He cracked a smile. "Is that supposed to make sense?"

"¿Quieres casarte conmigo?"

"What—"

She had to stop and think it through, so he would know what she was saying. She wanted him and she wanted the question. The one said on one knee. "Marriage. I want to get married. I want Pat."

"What about kids...our own baby?"

She didn't hesitate. She wanted that more than anything. "Yes."

His smile got wider. "What if our house had a room for Aaron?"

"Good."

He laughed.

It was a nice idea, but was it going to be possible?

"No, don't do that." He shook his head. "I can see it on your face. Don't think about it. I only want you to worry about getting better. The rest of it I'll figure out." He scratched the side of his head. "Somehow."

Andra shut her eyes and took a long breath. "Te amo."

**

John watched the clock tick around. He watched the rise and fall of Andra's breathing. His "minute" with her had turned into hours as he sat waiting for her to wake up and remember their conversation. He'd borrowed a smart phone and completely mangled the spelling, but the internet had told him what she said. *Quieres casarte conmigo.*

Marry me.

They'd both made a mess of their first marriages. There was no guarantee things would be perfect this time. But the promise of what they had swelled in him until he didn't even care about statistics and rationality. He was in love with her and he wanted to build a life with her in Sanctuary while he worked as the sheriff and Andra did whatever she wanted to do that made her happy.

He sat back and rested his arms on the chair. The last week felt more like a year so he had no problem talking to Andra about marriage.

It didn't mean they had to get married tomorrow. These things took time to plan, but at least they'd be heading in that direction.

The door cracked open and Grant walked toward him.

John stood up from the chair and took the paper his brother handed over before he ducked back outside.

John unfolded it a faxed paper from the president. *Pardoned of all crimes.*

He scanned the printed text and sank back onto the chair.

However, since the witness has resided in the WITSEC community of Sanctuary, it is the decision of this Office that she be allowed to return to her home instead of being released from the program. If she chooses to be released from the witness protection program, Ms. Caleri will be required to sign a new agreement prohibiting her from returning.

She needed to choose: return to Sanctuary or leave forever.

John had chased her halfway across Idaho, determined to get her free of Palmer, Thanes and the murder charges. He'd done that. Pat was safe, Elma had confessed. Palmer and Thanes were both dead. John's threat had been eliminated, too. It was up to Andra now if she wanted to come back to Sanctuary when she was released from the hospital. Likely that day would be weeks from now when she could walk under her own strength. When her ribs were healed and the chance of infection or any other lingering complications had passed. He'd gone over it with the doctor while she slept, but when did they ever give you a definitive answer?

John was a package deal, a built-in family and a life in Sanctuary that meant she'd never be able to visit her child. Not to mention more extended family than she'd probably know what to do with, given how she reacted to his mother. John allowed himself a small smile. Life would never be dull, and there could be a considerable amount of kickback from the town now they knew her past.

Could he convince them all she was in the clear, given it was down to Elma Pepper and Deputy Palmer? John would have to earn their trust, to show them all that life could be good. There was a drug problem and Bolton had mentioned someone making moonshine. He didn't think the sheriff's job would be dull, given the amount of trouble people who got stir-crazy could think up.

John stepped to the side of the bed. He pushed back a strand of her hair and let his fingertips linger on her face. When she woke up, she'd have to decide. And that was all her. In the meantime there was plenty he could do—especially if he was going to make his and Pat's living space actually livable. Nate and Ben were still in Sanctuary and there were plenty of other guys who could lend a hand. Perhaps the town would warm up to John and Andra if they saw him building a permanent life there. He should rebuild her cabin, too. See if any of that was salvageable.

He held her cheek in his hand, traced the bruise around her swollen eye with his thumb and said the other words he'd looked up.

"Te amo también."

Epilogue

Four weeks later

John stood over the body of Harriet Fenton. Her living room was trashed and an end table had been knocked over. The lamp now lay in a mess of broken glass. Harriet was stretched out on the couch haphazardly as though she fell and landed that way.

John picked up the needle and deposited it in its evidence container.

"Hey."

Bolton stood in the doorway, his face resigned like this was a scene he'd witnessed many times.

"Hey." John's eyes were hot and gritty, his jaw rough since he hadn't bothered to shave in days. He'd discarded the Sheriff's uniform almost a month before in favor of jeans and a button down shirt with his marshal's star clipped to his belt.

When his vision tunneled, he stepped back and looked again at the room at large.

"Overdose?"

John worked his jaw back and forth. "Likely the oxycodone that went missing from the medical center yesterday morning. We won't know until the autopsy for sure."

"You're thinking suicide?"

"Disgraced, marriage disintegrating. Accusing Andra of murder and then finding out it was Mrs. Pepper." John sighed. "Suicide would be my guess."

"How is Doctor Fenton?"

"I told him there was nothing he could do to help. He went back to work."

Bolton made a noise, deep in his throat. "Right."

John's radio buzzed the noise that preceded Pat's voice, "Dad!" John pulled it from his belt. "Dad, are you there!"

John smiled and pressed the button. "Yeah, Pat. I'm here."

"Dad a helicopter is coming, just like Uncle Grant said."

John's stomach looped itself into a knot and he glanced at Bolton who tilted his head to the side, indicating John should go. John hit the button again. "I'll pick you up on the way."

He raced out to his Jeep and sped down Main Street, pulling up outside the sheriff's office. Pat ran out, followed by Aaron. The young man had recovered from the assault and was back to his normal self—although now considerably happier since he'd moved into a spare room at John's house.

John set off toward the ranch.

His son's face was bright, the same way it had been every time he walked back from the library after Skyping Andra over the last month, while she recovered in the hospital and then at John's mom's house under marshal guard.

John had spoken to her over the phone a couple of times but she'd been cautious with her words and he'd been scared to ask what she decided.

Still, he'd gone ahead with the remodel of the apartment. The neighbors hadn't been using their upstairs space, so he'd had Grant sign it over to him and immediately knocked down the wall between, making the living room and kitchen area twice the size.

With the help of Bolton and Matthias, Hal and a handful of others, they'd stripped out everything and completely redone the two apartments. Now John had a home with room for Aaron, Pat and himself. Hopefully someday, Andra too.

As an added bonus the bathroom was no longer green.

That wasn't all he'd been working on. John's faith still felt new, but the past four weeks had been a crash-course in walking the truth of what God had done for him.

John took a second to glance at his son. "Is that paint?"

Pat scratched at his temple, where the white stuff was crusted on his skin and hair. "Ouch. I guess." He rubbed at it.

"Did you get the dining room finished?"

He nodded, his eyes sparking again.

In the rearview mirror, Aaron smiled. "All Aaron and Pat."

As they got closer to the ranch the helicopter hovered and then set down. John parked and the three of them climbed out of the Jeep. Behind the vehicle, two golf carts and a truck with its bed full of people all parked and the residents made their way over.

The helicopter sat there, door closed, while they waited. The crowd of people who had come from town caught up and assembled around John, Pat and Aaron.

Then the door opened.

Andra's eyes were bright with tears as the wind whipped her hair. She stepped out slowly, like she didn't want to jar anything not all the way healed yet. She touched her hand to her front, just below her throat.

Tears tracked down her face.

Pat ran full speed before John could stop him. He barreled into Andra and the tackle sent them both flying back until Andra was sitting on the ground.

John rushed over, praying his son hadn't sent her straight back to the hospital. Before he reached them, Andra tipped her head back and she burst out laughing.

She grinned at John, her arms tight around his son. John hauled first Pat and then Andra to their feet. She looked past him, taking in the crowd standing behind him. "Hi, everyone."

She shifted her gaze to him. "Hi, John."

John pulled her into his arms. He bent his head and whispered in her ear.

"Welcome home."

Lisa Phillips is a British ex-pat who grew up an hour outside of London. Lisa attended Calvary Chapel Bible College where she met her husband. He's from California but nobody's perfect. It wasn't until her Bible College graduation that she figured out she was a writer (someone told her). Since then she's taken the Apprentice and Journeyman writing courses with the Christian Writers Guild and discovered a penchant for high-stakes stories of mayhem and disaster where you can find made-for-each-other love that always ends in happily ever after.

Lisa can be found in Idaho wearing either flip-flops or cowgirl boots, depending on the season. She leads worship with her husband at their local church. Together they have two children—a sparkly Little Princess and a Mini Daddy—but there's only one bunny rabbit now (sad face).

To find out more about Lisa Phillips, visit:

www.authorlisaphillips.com

Where you can sign up for a Newsletter and receive email notifications of new books. You can also follow Lisa on Twitter @lisaphillipsbks

Printed in Great Britain
by Amazon